WHO ASKED YOU?

TERRY McMILLAN

WHO ASKED YOU?

VIKING

VIKING
Published by the Penguin Group
Penguin Group (USA), 375 Hudson Street,
New York, New York 10014, USA

USA | Canada | UK | Ireland | Australia | New Zealand | India | South Africa | China

Penguin Books Ltd, Registered Offices: 80 Strand, London WC2R 0RL, England
For more information about the Penguin Group visit penguin.com

LIBRARY OF CONGRESS CATALOGING-IN-PUBLICATION DATA
McMillan, Terry.
Who asked you? / Terry McMillan.
pages cm
ISBN 978-0-670-78569-8
Export edition ISBN 978-0-670-01586-3
1. African American women—Fiction.   2. Dysfunctional families—fiction.
3. Domestic fiction.   I. Title.
PS3563.C3868W46 2013
813'.54—dc23   2013016963

Printed in the United States of America
1   3   5   7   9   10   8   6   4   2

This is a work of fiction. Names, characters, places, and incidents either are the product of
the author's imagination or are used fictitiously, and any resemblance to actual persons, living
or dead, businesses, companies, events, or locales is entirely coincidental.

For mothers, who do the best they can.

There ain't nothin' I can do, nor nothin' I can say,
That folks don't criticize me.
But I'm gonna do just as I want to anyway
And don't care if they all despise me.

If I should take a notion, to jump into the ocean,
Ain't nobody's business if I do.
Rather than persecute me, I choose that you would shoot me,
Ain't nobody's business if I do.

If I should get the feelin', to dance on the ceilin',
Ain't nobody's business if I do.
If I get me best companion, drive me right into the canyon,
Ain't nobody's business if I do.

If I dislike my lover, and leave him for another,
Ain't nobody's business if I do.
If I go to church on Sunday, then cabaret on Monday,
Ain't nobody's business if I do.

If my friend ain't got no money, and I say "Take all mine, honey,"
Ain't nobody's business if I do.
If I give him my last nickel, and it leaves me in a pickle,
Ain't nobody's business if I do.

After all, the way to do is do just as you please,
Regardless of their talkin'.
Often times ones that talk will get down on their knees
And beg your pardon for their squawkin'.

—"T'ain't Nobody's Bizness If I Do,"
Porter Grainger and Everett Robbins, 1922

The Folks

Arlene

Betty Jean

Dante

Dexter

Lee David

Luther

Nurse Kim

Omar

Principal Daniels

Quentin

Ricky

Social Worker

Tammy

Trinetta

Venetia

I

YOU GO FIRST

Betty Jean

It's my day off and I'm in the kitchen getting ready to fry some chicken. When the phone rings and I see my daughter's name on the caller ID, I'm tempted to let it go straight to voice mail; the only reason I decide to go on and answer it is because I'm worried it might have something to do with my grandsons. Plus, I don't trust her. Trinetta is not in the habit of calling just to chitchat or to check on her daddy. She always wants something. Her life is one continuous emergency. Since I've got flour all over my hands, I wipe them on my red apron, pick up the portable, and tiptoe into the living room because the last thing I want to do is wake up Lee David.

"Ma, I need to borrow a hundred forty dollars today and I swear as soon as I get my check I'll pay you back, but the good news is I might have a job and I was wondering if I could bring the boys over for a couple of days so I can study for the test? Please say yes, Ma. Please."

"Did I miss hello?"

"Hello, Ma."

"Is something over there getting cut off?"

"No. But it's important. I swear to God, I'll give you my check

3

when it comes, Ma. I owe Twinkle and her rent is past due and if I don't give it to her by six o'clock she's gonna get evicted."

"That girl who lives down the hall from you?"

"Yeah. Her."

"Isn't she a drug addict?"

"Twinkle? No. She's got three kids."

"You and Twinkle seem to have a whole lot in common, then, don't you?"

"I ain't no drug addict, Ma. I might dip and dab every now and then, but I'm a long way from being strung out."

"I know I didn't just hear you say 'ain't' on this phone talking to me."

"My bad. 'I'm not a drug addict.' Better?"

I rest the phone on my shoulder and brush my hands again on my apron. "Why can't you get it from what's-his-name?"

"His name is Dante. He moved out."

"Why?"

"'Cause the Section Eight people was gonna raise my rent."

"What a pity, and he was so helpful."

"Ma . . . please?"

I hate it when she begs. And I know there's more to this story than what she's saying, but since getting the truth out of her is damn near impossible, I just say, "I'll write you a check when you bring the boys over."

"I can't do nothing with no check, Ma."

"Since when? You've managed to cash all the other ones."

"I had to close my checking account. And please, don't ask."

"I swear to God, Trinetta. You just go from bad to worse."

"Yeah, well, I had a good teacher."

"What did you just say?"

"I said I shoulda had better teachers."

4

"That is not what you said."

"Can we not go there today? Please? I'm trying to fix a problem over here and I just need your help."

"About what time should I look for you and the boys?"

"Between three and four. We gotta take the bus 'cause I had to let Dante use the car."

"I thought you just said he moved out."

"He did. But the only way he could move his stuff back out to his parents' house was he needed a car."

"Has he ever heard of U-Haul?"

"He didn't have that much stu—"

"Forget I asked. When is he bringing it back?"

"In about a week or two, 'cause he might have a job opportunity, too."

"Well, wouldn't that just make you both lucky? Don't answer that. But tell me this. And don't lie, Trinetta. Did you pay the insurance like you said you would?"

"I paid half of it."

"So, if you or Dante got in half of an accident do you realize who could get sued for their whole damn house?"

"We are both very careful drivers, Ma."

"You sound like a damn fool, Trinetta. You know that?"

"I'll see you in a few hours."

I just shake my head and head on back to the kitchen. I can hear these boards creaking under the carpet but I pretend I don't hear it. I didn't dare ask what kind of job she might be applying for that required her to study for a test, but I'll just cross my fingers I won't have to add it to the long list of things she didn't end up doing.

Oh Lord. Did I just hear him move? Please don't let this be a Commercial Break Nap. He only watched four episodes of *Dora the Explorer* and he's got six more to go. Plus, I am not in the mood for entertaining him while I stand in this hot-ass kitchen in front of this electric stove in the middle of the afternoon with no air conditioner. It's broken. Just like he is. And I'm right behind him. I can live without fried chicken. I'm just doing this to make Lee David happy. He doesn't ask for much these days but he did manage to say, "I want some soul food," and then flapped his bony little arms and made a clucking noise, which is why I'm in here suffering. It's amazing what you'll do for your husband, even if you never loved him but he convinced you he loved you so you went on and married him and had his babies. Hell, I could be ironing my uniforms or writing Dexter a long-overdue letter or reading a good paperback instead of struggling to fix enough food to last two or three days, since I can't be Julia Child every day.

Even though I propped that fan on top of four old encyclopedias and a phone book, it's still not cutting it, so I go to Plan B. I open the door and slide a chair in front of it, then set everything on top of it, turn that oscillator on, but all it's doing is pushing warm air on my behind, which is big enough to generate its own heat. I stick my head inside the freezer for a minute; inhale the cold, hoping it'll spread inside my body, which of course doesn't work.

I think I hear him stirring in there again, so I lean my left ear toward the bedroom, but just to be on the safe side, I say, "Anything I can get you, Mister?" (Which is what I call him when I'm talking directly to him.) While I wait for the response I hope not to get, I tighten the strings on this apron, cup my chin in my palms, and press my elbows on the damp counter. I look out the window at the orange trees at the side of the driveway. Not a single leaf on any of them is moving. This feels too much like earthquake weather. I don't appreciate this kind of stillness. We hadn't been

6

here two days back in '71 when that 6.6 sucker hit at the crack of dawn. We had come from New Orleans and I thought what a fucked-up welcome to California this was. But like fools, here we are thirty years later. You kind of get used to your house shaking, and you almost feel grateful if nothing breaks or the walls don't crack.

He clears his throat. So I carry on, making sure the oil is hot as I flick a few drops of water into a giant skillet and jump back. When a geyser shoots up from it, I know it's ready. I wish I could get rid of this big old electric stove and get a gas one. And a Kenmore. Stainless. It took years, but our Sears card has a zero balance and I'm afraid to charge anything until I can be more certain about our future.

I pick up the Ziploc bag full of flour and sprinkle some seasoning salt, garlic powder, white pepper, and paprika inside it. Chicken breasts and thighs are piled up on a floral platter. These are the only pieces Lee David likes. After thirty-seven years of marriage, I've forgotten how much I used to love wings. I dip a few pieces in a bowl of whisked eggs, drop them inside the bag, shake them back and forth, and then place them in the skillet. I wash my hands in warm water, stand in front of the sink even though I should sit down, and start snapping string beans.

"Mrs. Butler? You got a big brown one from Dexter today. Want me to set it inside the screen door for you or leave it out here on the top step?"

"Inside is fine. Thanks, Mr. Jones. And you have a nice day."

"Is that fried chicken I smell?"

I just chuckle. Mr. Jones has been our mailman since we moved into this house, and it doesn't seem like he's ever going to retire. He's been a widower going on five years now. I don't know how he manages to do so much walking, especially in those thick black special shoes he has to wear. "Stop back by when you get to Tammy's and I'll wrap you up a couple of pieces."

"You are so very kind," he says.

I walk through the dining room and living room and down one step onto the sunporch and pick up the mail. I recognize the bills by the color of the envelopes and set them on the buffet. I put Dexter's big envelope inside the magazine pouch on the left side of my La-Z-Boy with a ton of his letters I have not read. I get one every week, sometimes two. I can't read them like I used to.

I'll be the first to admit that I probably could've been a better mother, and I've got three grown children to prove it. It goes without saying that I do love them. I'm just disappointed in how they turned out. Trinetta is the baby, and at twenty-seven she seems to have a hard time saying no to drugs and low-life men, which has made her allergic to working more than a few months at a time. Sometimes, it's hard for me to believe she's the same daughter who lived on the honor roll all during junior high school. But then between ninth grade and junior college she fell in love too many times to count and lost her mind. She also loved beautiful teeth and was on her way to becoming a dental technician when she got pregnant. Over the years, Trinetta tiptoed back and forth, and the last I heard, she's only twelve units shy of being employable. I used to remind her of this small fact but she would just get defensive. She has given birth to three children. The last one was Noxema. Her daddy went to court and got custody after she drank some shampoo and had to be rushed to emergency. I wish he would've claimed those other two. Who they belong to is a mystery that may never get solved. In all honesty, I'm one step away from calling Child Protective Services on her if she doesn't clean up her act soon.

My oldest, Quentin, likes cracking necks and backs, getting married, and getting divorced. He's a chiropractor and lives up in Oregon, where hardly any black people live, which has made it very easy for him to forget he's black. He enjoys being the token and hates the ghetto. He even calls me "Mother," which gets on my nerves because it sounds so official, and he says it using the same tone as telemarketers when they ask for Mrs. Butler. I've told him about a thousand times I don't like being called Mother, but he just ignores me. He was the same way when he was little. He doesn't bend. Does everything his way, which is what has made him so difficult to like. Somehow, someway, he has made himself believe he's superior to most folks. I don't know how he got this way, and why he feels more like a stranger I just happened to give birth to. The only time I seem to hear from him is when he's getting married or divorced. He's on his fourth or fifth wife. I can't keep up. One thing they all have in common is that they're white. Not that I care. But why they all have to be blonde is what baffles me. On top of everything, Quentin has the nerve to act like he's religious. He does not go to any church that I know of but claims to read the Bible every single morning. He must be a slow reader.

Then there's Dexter. He's in the middle. Another smart one who fell in love with stupidity. He's doing nine to twelve years for carjacking a Filipino woman in a Costco parking lot in broad daylight using a deadly weapon (which to this day he claims was just a flashlight and not a gun). He and his high school buddy, Buddy, thought this would be a fun thing to do since the bus was taking too long and they were both high on that marijuana and Bud Lights. Dexter said they were just trying to get out to Valencia so Buddy could go see his girlfriend in the hospital who had just had his baby, and Buddy didn't want to miss visiting hours. Dexter swore up and down this was all Buddy's idea even though

Dexter was also supposed to meet his girlfriend, Skittles, at Great America, that amusement park right down the street from the hospital. Unfortunately, that marijuana must've caused a temporary memory loss, because Dexter forgot that even stolen cars run on gas, which is why the highway patrolman didn't believe him when Dexter told him the bright yellow Jetta with DIVINA on the custom plates was his.

If I had it to do over, I probably wouldn't have had any kids. It's too much responsibility trying to steer somebody else's life when you're still trying to navigate your own. Back then kids didn't come with instructions, so you had to wing it. And based on all these modern books full of recipes on how to be a deluxe parent and raise damn near flawless children, I guess I'd have to give myself a C or a C– because apparently I did a whole lot of things wrong.

For starters, I didn't always put my kids first. I mean I had needs, too. Back then, between them and Lee David, I felt just like a pie. Everybody wanted a piece of me and barely left me with a little crust. Plus, I had to work. I did not talk to them in what they now call an inside voice. I talked to them like they were hard of hearing. It was the only way I could get their attention and let them know I meant business. Plus, I didn't like being a repeater. Saying the same damn thing over and over and over again and still not getting the results I was after. They were hardheaded. I'm proud to say I did not swear at them, but every once in a while they did hear me say *shit* and *damn* and *oh hell no,* and five or six or ten times the "F" word. Apparently this was supposed to ruin them but I don't think that was what did it. I also said no a lot because many of the things they asked for were unreasonable. Or ridiculous. Time-outs hadn't been invented yet, which is why if they disobeyed me, I sometimes popped their little behinds. I didn't beat them, mind you, and never used any hand-held items. Again, my kids were hardheaded, so I doubt if sitting on a little stool in a corner would've worked on them anyway.

Lee David might as well have been one of the kids, because he was just as needy and actually competed against them for my attention. I think he won. But my clock was slow: It took about twenty years to admit to myself how bored I was being his wife. He was pleasant enough and a reliable father and all but sometimes he felt more like a good friend who wouldn't go home. I guess it would be fair to say that I was just too lazy to divorce him. I also discovered that you can get used to a man, much like you do a household pet.

My mama raised four of us and she made it look easy. (I shouldn't count Monroe, who was almost thirteen when she took him in after her sister died, and he was trouble from the start.) But I'm here to testify: Raising kids is not easy. It's work. Hard work. And work you don't get paid for. The worst part is when the little suckers grow up and don't appreciate the time and energy you put into them. Mine seem to have major lapses in memory. What they remember most is how much I got on their nerves. What I didn't give them. Not what I did. And they blame me for the things they didn't bother listening to. As if I never taught them anything. Or, that it was useless.

As a mother, you can't help but wonder where you went wrong and how much of your kids' confusion is your fault. I probably should've read them more fairy tales and more often instead of just on my days off, their birthdays, and Christmas. (Trinetta could already read by the time she was three and refused to let me hold the book.) It wouldn't have killed me to hug them every day instead of only when they did something that made me proud— which I'm sad to say was not all that often. And maybe I could've got down on my knees and said their prayers with them instead of standing in the doorway listening. Then tucked them in like they do in fairy tales. Wished them sweet dreams. And kissed them on their foreheads. But I didn't.

I won't lie. I wish Lee David and I could have been a little more like the Cosbys. That both of us had graduated from college and become professionals. That we lived in an upscale house in an upscale neighborhood. That our home was full of modern furniture, real art, and real plants, with a guest room we used for guests. That we went on cruises and needed passports in order to go to some of the places we traveled to, and went out to dinner where they had valet parking. That we had a car worth being valet parked. What I really wish was that we never had to suffer from any incurable diseases, we laughed all the time, and cried mostly at funerals. It would've been nice to have enough money left over to donate some. That our children would grow up and make us proud and we would die old and happy.

Things don't always go as planned, especially if you didn't really have any plans, which is probably why Lee David spent thirty-nine of his sixty-five years lifting boxes at UPS and I've spent twenty-nine pressing a little button on thousands of doors and saying "Room Service!" It doesn't matter anymore that it was (once) a five-star hotel in Hollywood, because in six more years I get to turn in my size-sixteen uniform and call it quits. And even though both of our pension checks and Lee David's Social Security will keep us going, it won't be the same. I live for those tips.

Unfortunately, I'm the only one in my family who didn't get a college degree. But I do believe there's more than one way to get an education. I'm far from dumb. I watch CNN and listen to NPR and I watch the National Geographic Channel and nature programs. I read every chance I get. Mostly novels because they take me away from all the bullshit that might be going on around me and it's a good way to escape my world and move in with folks I don't know. I don't like murder mysteries or whodunits because I don't need to read about death when I can go right down the street and see it. I don't like romance novels because you always know how they're going to turn out and I am not interested in grown-up fairy tales because I know for a fact that life is hard and there is no guarantee you're going to have a happy ending. But I do believe that even if you make a left when you should've made a right, there's still time to make a U-turn and go in the right direction. Fifty-six might be old to some folks but I think I still have time to improve myself. I just want to have something besides kids and a husband to show for my life.

I've been entertaining the idea of taking early retirement, depending on whether I can afford to live on it, and if I do, I might take some kind of college course or courses, depending. I have no idea what they might be, because I don't exactly know what I like, or hell, what I might be good at. One thing I've learned is that I can change my mind and the world won't come to an end. I have never had a vacation unless I count twelve years ago when we went to see our families in New Orleans, but that trip ended up costing us about as much as it probably would've to take a trip around the damn world. Begging, broke relatives mostly on Lee David's side of the family came out of the woodwork thinking that just because we lived in California we must be rich. Anyway, I'm so sick of sunshine and palm trees I don't know what to do. I want to go somewhere cold. I have never seen snow up close. Standing on Vermont Avenue looking up at those snow-capped mountains doesn't count. They look like they belong in Hollywood. I don't want to see anybody on skis, either. Don't ask me why, but I have always wanted to make an angel and throw a snowball. Of course, all Lee David always talked about was buying a condominium in Palm Springs, but I told him I did not want to spend the rest of my life in a desert, burning up around old white people. But then ten years ago, when he was just fifty-five, he started forgetting little things and then things he shouldn't have had to remember. It scared me and it scared him, so we had him tested and the doctor said he was in the early stages of Alzheimer's. I thought he was too young, so we got a second opinion, and the diagnosis was the same. Lee David was pretty calm about it. "When it gets so that I can't do for myself, BJ, put me somewhere comfortable. I don't want to be your burden." Then he started laughing. "And if it's before you turn sixty, get yourself a boyfriend."

I remember thinking: *A boyfriend?* I started laughing too. Of course he's been slipping downhill these past five or six years and my older sister, Arlene, has been trying to convince me to go ahead and put him in a facility. I just ignore her. I don't like anybody telling me what I should do, especially her. He's not a burden. Plus, he's my husband. I can't just abandon him because I'm tired.

As things stand, Nurse Kim looks after him when I'm at work. She used to take him on short walks but his arthritis got really bad and then he lost interest in nature. She sponge bathes him (thank God, because my sciatic nerve can't handle too much bending over). Nurse Kim is as sweet as she can be. Thirty years old and pretty enough to be on the cover of *Essence* magazine, not that Lee David even notices, but as soon as she walks in this house it's like having a Christmas tree all lit up in here. Plus, she always smells like some kind of tropical fruit.

On weekends, when I need to run errands, Tammy, who lives across the street, comes over and "Lee-sits" as she calls it. The truth be told, some days I feel sorry for Lee David and other days I get sick just looking at him. This is when I wish he would just hurry up and die so I could hurry up and grieve and then live out what's left of the rest of my life. It's a horrible thought, but one I've had on more than one occasion, which is why I keep it to myself.

"Mister, you still in there sleeping?"

"Yep," he says.

After snapping all these doggone string beans, I put most of them into plastic bags and freeze them. I don't know why I'm going to all this trouble for two people. Wait! I forgot about the boys just that fast! I get a can of chicken broth out of the cabinet and pour a little into a boiler, drop a few strips of bacon in it and a few slices of white onion, and once it boils, I'll put the beans I left out on the counter right on top of it. Sometimes I cheat and buy things I used to make from scratch and just doctor them up. Like I'm about to do to this potato salad I bought from Ralph's. I pop the lid on the plastic container and dump it into my yellow mixing bowl, and right after I sprinkle a few drops of vinegar, a pinch of salt, sugar, and paprika and start stirring, the phone rings.

I can't see who it is from over here but I pray it's a telemarketer and not either of my sisters: Venetia, who can talk all day about nothing ever since I warned her that if she started going on about the Lord I'd hang up, or Arlene, who likes to get you to talk about all the messed-up things going on in your life but won't give you a clue about what's going on in hers. She would've made a good talk show host. I move closer to the phone, since I don't have my glasses on. It's Clair Huxtable, a.k.a. Venetia. I stick the wooden spoon deep inside the potato salad so it stands up, and I answer against my better judgment. "Hey, sis," I say, as upbeat as is humanly possible. "How've you been?"

"I'm good. Just checking in."

"And how are the kids?"

"Oh, they're fine. How's Lee David?"

"The same. And Rodney?"

"In the clouds as we speak. Headed to Tokyo."

I pull the spoon out, do a quick taste test, and then start stirring again.

"Betty Bean, you still there?" (She's called me this since she was two years old. I like it.)

"I'm here, but I hear Lee David calling me, so can I call you back a little later on?"

"Absolutely. I'll be here. Love you."

Talk about raising kids by the book? Venetia gets an A+. She's thirteen months younger than I am but people often think she's the older one when we're together. Her husband was rich when she met him, and I think that had something to do with his appeal because he's still a long drive away from being cute. They live in Encino, not far from the Jacksons. Venetia wasted six years going to college and getting an MBA because she chose to be a stay-at-home mom. She spends Rodney's money for a living, which is unfortunate because she doesn't have great taste and she's cheap, which is why she has a giant house full of corny stuff that doesn't go together. It's not too late to hire a decorator, but I have not figured out how to drop the hint.

She has been a slave to two spoiled-rotten brats who grew up and turned out to be as nice as they can be: Lauren and Zachary. They both played soccer. Both play the frigging piano. Lauren speaks French. Zach chose Mandarin. I guess that's like Chinese. It goes without saying, they're both honor students. Three million carpooling miles later, Zach and Lauren will be graduating in less than two years but Venetia still drops them off and picks them up. I cannot imagine what she's going to do when those kids go off to college and their elderly dog, Pepper, dies. And what does she do with so much free time on her hands, since her husband lives on airplanes and in hotel rooms? Cleans all day. Every day. Things that aren't even dirty. I think she has orgasms doing laundry. She folds and irons everything. Even sheets. With spray starch! Of course she can afford a housekeeper, but claims she doesn't trust them.

No sooner do I cover the potato salad with a plastic lid and put it in the fridge than here comes Arlene calling. But I'm not falling for this. I wouldn't be surprised if Venetia had called Arlene and told her to call me just to see if I would pick up the phone and have a long-drawn-out conversation with her so then Arlene would call Venetia back and tell her and Venetia would know that I was just blowing her off. So I don't answer it.

Sometimes I think they both think they know more about me than I know about myself. Arlene is my least favorite out of the whole clan but I tolerate her because she's my sister. She is the one person who can get on all of my nerves at once. Why? Because she thinks she's smarter than everybody since she got a master's in psychology from Pepperdine. Venetia went to a state college and Arlene thinks Venetia's credentials are inferior, but of course Arlene has only shared her true sentiments with me and not Venetia because she is two-faced. Arlene also loves to tell people how to live their lives based on her standards, which is why I try to keep as much of my personal life as is humanly possible from her. I do share some things with Venetia because she's been saved and doesn't believe in gossip. It's too bad Arlene hasn't used any of the stuff she learned at Pepperdine on herself, which is probably why she now sells real estate. She was a therapist for years but in the black community you can go broke giving bad advice. Thanks to Arlene and Venetia, it has become obvious to me that getting a college degree doesn't necessarily mean you're smart. Or stable.

I'm not one to hold grudges, but some people who are mean-spirited as children grow up to be mean-spirited adults. Arlene is one of them. Forty-five years ago she looked at me and said, "That hairstyle was not meant for you, Betty Jean. I think you'd look much better with short hair," and that little bitch took a pair of pinking shears and cut off seven inches of my hair. "Maybe not," she said after looking at her handiwork.

I love her. But she has other qualities that have made it hard to like her. She thinks she's better than us folks who live down here in the "hood," as they now call it. She bought a split-level house thirteen minutes away, up there in Baldwin Hills, where black folks with two-car garages, palm trees in their front and back yards, gold credit cards, and money in the bank live. She has never been married, but that didn't stop her from screwing other women's husbands (I wonder what page this was on in her psychology books) and it didn't stop her from having a baby either. That *baby* is almost six feet tall, twenty-eight years old, still lives with her, and has never paid rent, but that's because it's hard when you can't seem to keep a job longer than a few months. Arlene always thinks the employer discriminates against Omar because he's fat. She talks to him like he's still fourteen, but I would never say anything to her about what I really think.

I tell Tammy. She's my best friend. She's ten years younger and happens to be white but she feels more like a sister to me than Arlene does. She's a good listener and we can share our thoughts and feelings about things without judging each other.

Personally, I try to avoid friction at all costs and don't like to argue or fight with Arlene or anyone else because it takes too much out of you. And what exactly do you win? Sometimes, I will clear my throat at the post office if somebody is taking all day to pick out what stamps they like, and even though I get to church only two or three times a year, I start humming "Just a Closer Walk with Thee" while standing in that long return line at Wal-mart when the person ahead can't find their receipt, or I squeeze my toes together when I take my grandkids to the playground and Trinetta acts like she's forgotten what Clorox and lotion are for.

Arlene and Tammy have never gotten along because Tammy married a black man. The whole interracial thing has never really bothered me. Who you love is your business. Plus, I never knew love was a color. My biggest concern was always their kids. I felt sorry for them having to explain what they were year after year after year. And now that they're out of college, they still don't know what box to check. I used to like her husband, Howard, but he broke Tammy's heart.

"Thelma?" he yells from the bedroom, which is pretty much where he lives these days. Thelma is my name today. She was the girl Lee David was going to marry back in New Orleans but then Thelma—apparently attracted to the family genes—ran off to Shreveport with his brother. That's when Lee David turned to me. And at nineteen I decided to skip college in exchange for a chipped diamond ring and a chance to live in California.

"What you need, Mister?" Lord knows I wished I could've called him *baby* but the opportunity never presented itself. I wanted my knees to buckle when he touched me, but they always stayed stiff and strong. I wanted my heart to light up and maybe sizzle, but it was a no-show, too. I wanted to feel like I couldn't live without him. But I knew I could. Even still, I have enjoyed his company.

"I could use another beer," he says, pointing to his plastic glass, which means he wants a refill for his tea.

"Be right there." I open the white cabinet, the one with the loose brackets, and pull a straw out of the mayonnaise jar I keep them in. I get the pitcher of tea out of the refrigerator, pour it into the light blue plastic glass he likes, and drop the straw inside.

"Here you go," I say, and hold it up to his mouth. It looks like midnight in this room but I can still see the bags under his eyes and they look three times bigger behind those bifocals.

"Thank you," he says, without taking his eyes off the TV screen. Of course he's watching *Dora the Explorer,* like he does every day, all day. I had to go out and buy the DVD because he would get upset when it went off. All he has to do now is press the remote to start it over. "I'm learning how to speak Spanish," he said rather proudly when he was still able to speak in long sentences. *"Perry como usta senora?"*

"Can I get you anything else?"

He flips the blanket up as his way of asking me to slide on under.

"You really do think I'm Thelma, don't you?" I say, and walk on out of the room. Dementia affects him only from the neck up. Sometimes I have come into the bedroom, like now, in broad daylight, and he'll be lying there with a small tent in his lap and the stupidest grin on his face, which makes me want to gag. Sometimes I do it just to make that thing go down. But right now, I've got six or seven more pieces of chicken left to fry.

I wrap a breast and thigh in aluminum foil for Mr. Jones and put them in a small lunch bag I keep for the boys' snacks and set it on the table. I finally sit down, since I've been on my feet now for way too long. My right knee is throbbing but I don't feel like taking a pill. I'm still sweating like a pig and I think I might have to break down and use that Sears card. Sometimes, like now, when it's quiet, I like to sneak and take a few minutes to think about my life. What I've done wrong. What I've done right. And where I am now.

Truth be told, I think I can rightly blame some of my kids' problems on this neighborhood. Years ago it was nice here. White and black folks lived side by side, and just like it was on *Leave It to Beaver* and *Father Knows Best,* we borrowed a cup of sugar or a teaspoon of coffee from one another; our kids played together without ever hearing the words *nigger* or *honky* or *peckerwood.* We were all working-class families, proud of our small homes. And it showed. We had smooth driveways. Even some two-car garages. We had velvet grass in our front yards. Sprinkler and drip systems. Every color flower imaginable. Our hedges were all sculpted. The screens dirt-free. Windows vinegar-clean. Our front doors never had to be locked. But then in the early nineties, the drugs moved in. And the gangs. Which is when most of our homes started limping. The majority of white families started leaving. Kids had to play in the backyard unless a grown-up was sitting outside watching them. Lowriders drove slow and blasted rap music and dared you to complain. Folks began to look like they were always hesitating. We swept and hosed our sidewalks, picked up trash on the curb, and people prayed longer and harder but it didn't seem to help. For most of their childhood, I couldn't let my kids wear blue or red because our neighborhood didn't belong to us anymore.

"Where you at, Ma?"

"I'm coming," I say, and get up. I must've fallen asleep back here when I fell across the bed in Quentin's old room because

Lord knows I didn't want to chance being seduced by Denzel Washington. I hear the boys running over that shag carpet and I walk out to greet them. Luther will be eight this year. Trinetta claimed she named him after Luther Vandross because she always had a crush on him. I don't know who she named Ricky after, but since I doubt she ever slept with Rick James, I don't think she had him in mind. He should be six. He was born with slight drug-baby issues and he takes medication that's supposed to help him be able to do more of some things and less of others. He acts all right to me. He can be a little hyper sometimes, and quiet at others. I don't trust those pills, and only time will tell how long they keep him on them. Trinetta never put much thought into how she was going to take care of her kids. She just had them. She has treated them like they were mistakes. Which is one of the reasons they're over here so much.

"Well, hello there, my little chocolate kisses," I say, even though they're two different shades of brown. Fudge and maple syrup. Both of them are cute in a peculiar way. Luther's forehead is big and his head on the square side, but I can tell he's going to grow into those looks one day. Ricky's features all coincide with one another but he always looks like he's thinking about something.

"Hi, Grandma," Luther says, and he almost makes me lose my balance when he gives me a long hug. His arms don't fit around my hips. Ricky just waves, sits down on the couch, and starts looking for the remote between the cushions. He keeps busy.

"Hey, Ma," Trinetta says, and gives me a phony kiss on the cheek. "So, you got what we discussed?" She sounds just like a drug addict. She doesn't sit, which means she's either high or in a hurry or both. That's why I decide to make her ass wait. I wish she would cut those damn dreadlocks off. They look like they need to be shampooed. I used to think people wore them because they had a sense of pride, being black and all, but for some, like my daughter, it's obvious that it's just another hairstyle. Trinetta is also disappearing. I can see her collarbone, and even though she's brown like me, her skin is so thin I can see green veins running up and down her arms like branches on a winter tree.

"Tell me, what kind of job is it this time?"

"It's a sales position."

She can lie on a dime. But I am not in the mood for watching her act antsy so I go ahead and reach inside my purse and hand her some folded bills I keep hidden for emergencies.

"Thanks," she says, and stuffs them in her bra. "And that's all I can tell you right now. I've already started studying for the test."

"Tell me a lie I can believe, Trinetta."

"I ain't—I'm not—lying this time, Ma. Cut me a little slack, would you?"

"Where's Ricky's medication?"

"Luther, you got Ricky's meds in your backpack like you supposed to have?"

"Yep!" he yells from the bathroom.

"Why didn't you bring some clean clothes for them?"

"I can drop some off later."

"And should I hold my breath?"

"I thought they had enough stuff over here."

"Is your cell phone working?"

"It'll be back on tomorrow."

"I would really like to ask you a lot of things, but I'm not even going to bother."

"Good," Trinetta says. "'Cause I'm really not in the mood for a lecture. Is he in his usual spot?"

"*He* is."

I don't know why she has such a hard time calling him Daddy and I'm sick of asking. She walks over and sticks her head inside the doorway. "Hey there, Mr. Butler," she says, but he doesn't answer.

"I'll be glad when you put him in one of those places," she says, then walks into the kitchen, looks at the chicken, and comes back empty-handed. "You wasting perfectly good money on that *nurse* who look more like a ho if you ask me, and you already said the doctor is only giving him two years at most, so what's the point?"

"You need to mind your own business," I say as she goes into the bathroom. It's no wonder these kids talk the way they do. I turn my attention to them. Luther is now sitting next to Ricky on the sofa like they're little strangers waiting for a train. I look above their heads. That sofa is still ugly. It's a shade of gold I've never seen anywhere else. Except for Gulden's mustard. The glass coffee table has been cracked about six years and even has a broken leg. The beige shag carpet is almost insulting to walk on these days. And those burgundy brocade drapes with the sheer nylon curtains behind them aren't fooling anybody. This is no castle. I don't know why the fake artwork I bought at the swap meet suddenly looks fake. Now my grandsons look like they're sitting inside an old photograph because everything in this living room feels wrong. Except them. I wish there was a way I could save them from their mama.

But I can't. She may have some bad habits, but she doesn't hit them. They're well fed. And always clean. But that's about it. Which is precisely why I go get them every chance I get. It's my way of keeping tabs on what my daughter is and isn't giving them. The least I can do is help them see that the world is bigger than their neighborhood. And so they don't have to watch it on television. It does take a lot of energy to handle two little boys. Believe me, I already know this. I make sure to take my vitamins before we go anywhere. And go we do: to the park, the zoo, the Tar Pits, and every museum in Los Angeles. They love Shamu. Said they want to live in Disneyland. I don't know how many of those kiddie movies I've slept through, because Trinetta makes them watch them all on video.

And that Ricky is a fish. I have to make him get out of the tub and the pool. I'm too scared to let them go into the ocean, because I never learned how to swim, but I take them over to Tammy's. Her pool is small, but to them it's Olympic size. Luther is a bookworm. He loves going to the library. Ricky's too loud and likes to run up and down the stacks. We've been asked to leave on too many occasions. They wear me out, but it's the least I can do, since they didn't ask for the life they got.

I don't hear the toilet flush, but out she comes. Looking a little frazzled.

"Say goodbye to your mama, boys."

They wave. I can tell they're anxious for her to leave. And before I can say another word, Trinetta is out the front door.

"Hello, Miss Trinetta," I hear Mr. Jones say. But I don't hear her say hello back. I pick up the lunch bag and take it to him.

"May God continue to bless you," he says.

I look at my grandsons. Their hands are clasped together in their laps. They already look bored. I'm too tired to entertain them. But thank God I always go to Target and buy puzzles, crayons, and coloring books and keep them in my big drawer.

"So, what would you young men like to do?"

"I would like to eat some of your food," Ricky says.

"Me, too," Luther says. "I love your fried chicken."

"How do you know that's chicken you smell?" I ask.

"Everybody knows what fried chicken smell like."

"Come on back to the dining room, and I'll fix you both a plate. And then would you like to color or do a puzzle?"

Ricky nods.

"I wanna play video games," Luther says. "Please?"

"How about first thing in the morning when your grandpa's sound asleep?"

"Okey-dokey. Then can we put on our new pajamas now?" he asks.

I just look at him.

"Please?"

"Let's wait until it gets dark and after you have your baths."

"Okey-dokey," Ricky says.

"He copied that off me. How many days we staying over here again, Grandma?" Luther asks.

"Excuse me?"

He thinks about what he's just said.

"How many days *are* we staying over here, Grandma?"

"Two or three."

"We wish it could be forever, don't we, Ricky?"

Ricky nods his head.

I don't even want to think about how long forever might be. I make them wash their hands. They sit at the table. They put their napkins in their laps. They bless their food. Eat every bit of it. They take their baths. Put on their brand-new pajamas. They pile onto the bed next to their grandpa but do not like watching *Dora the Explorer*, so as soon as he is fast asleep they grab the remote and turn to a western. Lee David wakes up, looks at the screen, then turns and looks at them and says, "Ride 'em, cowboy!"

On day three I don't hear a peep from Trinetta and her phone is still off.

On day four, I wake up knowing the kids have to go to school and I have to go to work, so I call her again, hoping her phone is back on. When it rings, I'm all set to cuss her out when a man answers. "Who is this?" I ask.

"Who is this?" he asks.

"This is Betty Jean. Trinetta's mother. Where is she and why are you answering her phone?"

"She busy."

"Put her on the phone. Please."

"I said she busy. I can relay a message when she finished."

"Ask her when she's coming to pick up her kids."

"What kids? Hey, hole up now. You ain't done here."

I hear what sounds like tussling and then Trinetta gets on the phone. "Hey, Ma, this Tri, and—"

"Where are you and what in the world are you doing?"

"I'm at . . . a friend's house. I'm still . . . studying. So. Would you mind? Keeping. The kids. A few. More days?"

Of course I'm worried about my daughter, but she's grown. And knows exactly what she's doing. I'm more relieved that my grandsons aren't anywhere near her, so I say nice and slow like: "Pay extra-close attention, Trinetta. Do not even think about picking these kids up until you can show me a few pay stubs and a clean drug test. Now. Suck. On. That."

Tammy

When I hear a succession of quick knocks on the front door, I know it can't be anybody but BJ, especially at this time of morning. I crack the door a few inches. "I'm standing in here dripping wet with just a towel wrapped around me, BJ, so you better not be here to tell me something neither of us can handle."

"It's Trinetta . . ."

I pick up my heart. "Please don't tell me she OD'd."

"Do I sound petrified or pissed off?"

"What'd she do this time? Wait. Don't tell me. What is it you need me to do, BJ?"

"She didn't show up to get the boys and they're on the sunporch waiting for me to take them to school and you must not've heard the phone when you were in the shower. Anyway, would you mind sitting with Lee David for about a half hour or so, until Nurse Kim gets there? But you and I both know she always runs a little late."

"Of course I don't mind. I'm not due at the attorney's office until eleven. Why didn't you call in sick or take a vacation day and just keep them at home today?"

"Because Lorinda's relatives are visiting from Norfolk and

28

she's taking them to Disneyland and Magic Mountain, so I at least have to go in for a few hours. These kids have missed enough school as it is. I'll be back in time to pick them up."

I peek over her shoulder and see the screen door opening and closing and then I see a cute little brown face poke out. That's Ricky. He's looking for his grandma. Bless his cute little heart!

"Whose car is that in the driveway?" BJ asks.

"Trevor's."

"You mean you let that boy spend the night over here?"

"She's twenty-three, BJ. What difference does it make if it's here or in his dirty bungalow?"

"Just a minute," she says, and turns around since Ricky is apparently now banging the door shut and open. "Luther! Make Ricky stop doing that. Please. I'll be right there!" She turns back to face me. "A sleepover, huh? So is this a sign she's serious about this one?"

I roll my eyes. "And counting."

"Anyway, how long will it take you to put something on?"

"Two minutes. So go! If you weren't so doggone nosy I could've been over there by now."

"Thanks, Tammy."

"Pay me later." I throw the towel over a chair and run down the hall to my bedroom to get my terry-cloth robe. Lord knows Lee David isn't exactly Jack the Ripper, so if one of these droopy girls were to plop out, I doubt if he'd even notice.

I know the lovebirds are upstairs sound asleep, but I grab my keys and lock the front door out of sheer habit. Something we didn't have to do back in the good old days. The neighbors on my left are Korean, and they don't like anybody who's not Korean. They refuse to hire a gardener, which is why their yard looks more like a desert. I planted purple and white hydrangeas all along the fence just to give them a clue of what beauty can do. They have refused to take the hint. On the right are two black racists who have not spoken to me in the six years since they moved in. A dynamic duo: like father, like son. They let their avocados, olives, and lemons fall into our yard, hoping I'll complain. But all we do is eat them. I am not intimidated by black people anymore, and I refuse to apologize for being white. Here it is the new millennium, when it shouldn't matter what color you are. But it does. Even here in liberal frigging California. For years, I've wanted to say: "Hey, I never had any slaves, so stop holding me responsible for what happened two hundred years ago!"

There are twenty-two homes on our street. None of them is worth a dime and only a handful are worth fixing up, and quite a few folks have done just that. Too bad money doesn't grow on trees, because that's one thing we've got plenty of on this block. Trees help block roofs that need to be replaced. Lee David had a new one put on right before he got sick. I'm guesstimating it's been about nine or ten years now. He painted the trim cocoa brown, which I didn't particularly care for but I pretended to love it. My own house is stucco, the color of cashews. The trim matches. It's ugly, too. I don't know how long roofs are supposed to last but it seems like mine didn't start leaking until I kicked my husband out a little over three years ago, after twenty-six years of marriage. Good thing I'm not violent or he'd be in a plot in a cemetery. For years, Howard had an on-again, off-again love affair with the crap tables, but the last straw was when I found out the hard way he had lost half of the kids' college tuition. I walk on into BJ's house and back toward their bedroom. Lee David is lying there with his hands clasped, smiling about something. The television isn't on, which is unusual.

"Good morning, Lee!" I say loudly, even though he's not hard of hearing.

He turns to look at me and frowns. "You ain't Nurse Kim," he says.

"Sorry. I'm still Tammy," I say. "She'll be here soon."

"Good. I want my snack. Then my lunch."

It would do no good, of course, to tell him it's morning and he'll probably be having breakfast. I walk over and turn on the vitamin D light I talked BJ into buying because Lee David hardly ever goes outside anymore. When he squeals and holds his hands in front of his face like he's a vampire and I just held up a cross, this tells me to turn it off. Which I do. "Sorry, Lee." I walk back out to the living room and sit in BJ's La-Z-Boy, grab the remote, and the *Today* show is on. I never watch morning TV, but I am also not in the mood to sit here and listen to that Katie Couric. I can't stand the nasally way she talks, like people from Wisconsin and both of the Dakotas. I turn it off, lean back in the recliner, and pull out an *Ebony* magazine from the right pocket. But I've read this one. I reach over on the left and my hand hits a big brown envelope that slides out and falls onto the carpet.

I already know it's yet another essay pretending to be a letter from Dexter. I used to read them while sitting here with Lee David. At first they just broke my heart. That's because I watched him grow up. I remember when he used to help out anyone in the neighborhood who needed their grass cut, their driveway hosed down, or something from the corner store. He volunteered and most of the time wouldn't take any money. BJ didn't put him up to it, either, because I asked her.

But like a lot of youngsters, he started sneaking and hanging out with the wrong crowd, and that was when he started changing. He stopped being available and it got so that BJ and Lee David couldn't manage him. It's hard to compete with the lure of the streets, and I believe in my heart this is how they lost Dexter.

Dexter gave himself permission to become a criminal, which is why I can't read his letters anymore. Now he reminds me of my two brothers. They're full of shit, too, and don't apologize for anything they do wrong either. They live on our ranch in Billings. Our parents knew they were screw-ups when they were teenagers, always getting expelled, and then in their twenties, they thought the local jail was a hotel. Their thirties were nothing but a miniseries of the previous ten years, which is probably why our parents made me executor of the whole estate years before they both passed. All hundred and sixty acres. My brothers weren't happy about this even though they got enough cash for anybody to live on for years. Just to be fair, I turned around and deeded them twenty acres each, including the house (which wasn't worth half as much as the land), since they wanted to live in it for what they claim were sentimental reasons. But a funny thing happened while they partied the years away: They blew their inheritance and are now flat broke, which is why they've decided to sue me for what they call "our fair share." Mine has been earning 3 percent interest.

It's unfortunate that Jackson, the oldest, has yet to find steady employment even at the tender age of forty-eight. He claims to be handicapped but has yet to reveal what his disability is. Clay, a year younger, a high school dropout, never quite got the hang of working and has never demonstrated any marketable skills unless you count rounding up cattle. They've always resented me for marrying a black man and have never met him or the kids, which hurts even though I understand. Regardless, they're still kin, so once I get this ordeal all straightened out, I'll most likely give them some more acreage to do with as they please, sell off the rest, give them just enough money so they won't kill themselves, and then maybe I'll move to a more pleasant neighborhood out in the Valley, and definitely get my boobs lifted.

My moving to Los Angeles was not an accident. I dropped out of college to escape my family, boredom, and the brutal Montana winters with hopes of becoming an actress or a dancer—whichever happened first. (I was also a gymnast, but a broken tibia prevented me from going to the Olympics in Mexico City.) I managed to become a professional cheerleader instead. Which is how I met my husband. Howard was a rookie point guard for the Lakers but got cut after sitting on the bench for three years. From there he followed in his dad's boots and started putting out fires. Last I heard, he retired the dice and worked his way up to captain. Instead of dancing, for the last twenty years, five days a week I have sat in a courtroom and typed into my steno machine some of the most horrific crimes imaginable when it comes to what folks do and don't do under the influence of drugs and alcohol. Some things they don't even remember. My daddy was a drunk. My mama was his memory. Everybody I knew played with guns. Especially my brothers when they were stoned out of their minds. Once, Jackson accidentally shot Clay in the foot. He didn't even feel it. Guns have always frightened me. All this stuff has added up to why I've never tasted alcohol or smoked marijuana. I didn't want any of them to play a role in my life. After all I've seen and heard, I don't think everybody who drinks a little too much on occasion is an alcoholic or that people who smoke marijuana on an occasional basis are potheads. I take that back. They are potheads. If you smoke only three cigarettes a day instead of the whole pack, you're still a smoker. It just always seemed easier and saner to deal with life with a clear head instead of one that's overcast.

Lee David and BJ were the first people on the block to treat us like our mixed marriage was no big deal. Howard and I didn't really have that hard a time. We got an occasional stare when we went out. But black women have been the worst. Whenever we were in public, when his back was turned, they'd look me up and down quickly, then again slowly, as if they were trying to figure out what I had that they didn't—nothing—and they'd cut their eyes at me or give me the finger or twitch their nose and lips to one side or mouth the word *bitch*, all while leaning back on one leg, either with their arms crossed or with their hands on their hips. Sometimes all of the above at once.

I had never even thought about dating a black guy until I met Howard. It was his smile and the silk in his voice that caught my attention more than his skin color. He was also polite and warm and extremely sexy and didn't even seem to know it. No one was more surprised than I was how much I found myself being attracted to him. I fell in love with him and his blackness was just an added bonus.

When the twins were still babies and I proudly pushed them around in their double stroller, some folks would do double takes. We got used to the stares, and white and black alike would ooh and aah and smile at the children, but most looked at me like they weren't sure if they were mine. Sadly, it was mostly white people who would say, "Aren't they just adorable!" Their problems didn't start until elementary school but lasted through middle school. They were called niggers and half-breeds and nerds and got hit because a lot of the black children picked on them. On top of this, too many kids didn't believe they were real twins, because Montana looked like me, blonde and blue eyes, and Max (short for Max) looked just like his dad: a beautiful root beer, with curly black hair. On too many occasions I had to leave work and go to their school, and there one or both of them would be sitting in the principal's office in tears, sometimes with a busted lip or a bruise or some token of the hatred or anger they faced for being mixed. This is when we took them out of one and then another school and finally into what was called a charter school. It was full of every ethnicity we could possibly imagine, including so many varieties of mixed-race children we felt comfortable. The kids thrived there. And we slept good at night.

I put the envelope back and look around this living room like I've done hundreds of times. I love how the walls are covered with family photographs but then there's me and Howard and the twins, too. The Rainbow Coalition.

When the doorbell rings, I'm thinking Nurse Kim has finally realized that this is a real job and is not only on time, but early. "It's open!" I yell.

"Mom, it's me! Tanna!"

What in the world is she doing here, and up so early?

Lately, she's been working as a fitting model for wedding dresses because she's a perfect size six, but they don't usually get started until ten or eleven. "What in the world are you doing up so early? Is something wrong?"

"Not for me. But maybe yes, in your eyes."

I study her face to see if I can detect whether this is going to be something my heart needs to be prepared for. Her cheeks are rosy. She's a dirty blonde. I'm a bleached one. Her eyes are almost cobalt blue.

"I'm pregnant and I've decided to have it. I know you've been hoping I'd become a model or an actress like you wanted to be but it's not in my cards. Motherhood apparently is. Please be happy for me. And good morning."

And she just stands there. Smiling. She's too damn young to have a baby. She's too damn smart to have a baby. She's too damn stupid to have a baby. After graduating from Loyola two years ago in history, she's been trying to "find herself" since she decided "history was not helping me grow." She sounded just like a little Valley Girl, when we've always lived in the hood. What about the fucking Peace Corps? She even has an interview coming up! And what about that amazing voice, which she got from her father's side of the family? I push the lever on this La-Z-Boy and spring up to a standing position. I tighten the sash on the robe. I'm forty-six years old. Too young to be anybody's grandmother. Especially a baby's. I clear my throat. "Are you kidding me?"

She lifts her T-shirt to show me her belly. It's flat. "It's in there. Growing."

"And how pregnant might you be?"

"Six weeks. Be happy for us, Mom."

"Who is 'us'?"

"Me and Trevor."

I want to say, "Fuck Trevor. He can take his Italian ass back to New Jersey where he came from." But I wouldn't dare.

I take a deep breath. Then another one. I want to try to say this nicely. "What in the hell are you going to do with a baby when neither you nor Trevor have a major source of income unless you count being a barista at Starbucks! What's it going to drink: lattes?"

I see her mouth quivering. Then, "I thought you liked Trevor? He's a great guy. And I love him. We'll manage this."

"I do like him, Tanna, but that has nothing to do with it. Where in the world are you two or three going to live?"

She brushes the front of her T-shirt with the palm of her hand a few times and leans against the wall, bumping up against BJ's wall mirror that you can't even see a clear image of yourself in anymore. "We were wondering if maybe you would let us stay in our house until we get on our feet. Trevor's acting classes are really helping and he goes to auditions at least two or three times a week. He's going to land something, soon, Mom. We both feel it in our gut. And don't worry, unless I have terrible morning sickness, which I'm starting to feel already, I can find something to bring home a few dollars, too."

"Like what?"

"I'm still weighing my options."

I'm speechless. Weighing her options? Why is it young girls get pregnant and decide to have a baby because it's romantic when they don't have any idea how they're going to take care of it let alone pay for it? Kids have like an eighteen- to twenty-three-year running tab. They are not a novelty. They are human beings. They live with you. You love them but they are guaranteed to get on your nerves and on some days you wish you could send them back. I look at my beautiful daughter standing there and, since it's obvious that not having this baby is not even up for discussion, I just look at her and say, "I'm warning you right now. This is not going to be the Ritz-Carlton. There will be terms and conditions. I just need a day or so to process all of this."

She runs over and hugs me so tight I'm thinking that if she squeezed me hard enough maybe the little walnut would just pop right out through her navel and things would be back to normal.

"I can still consider a singing career after the baby's born, but the Peace Corps is out of the question."

It's pretty obvious to me that a college degree doesn't have much of an impact on your heart. But just to make sure, I pose another question. "Are you sure about this? A baby? They grow up, you know, and walk across the street to your best friend's house in the early morning hours to tell you they're pregnant, expecting you to be excited for them, which you are but you're also very, very scared."

"I'm sure, Mom. Positively. And I love you, too. You won't even know we're there."

"Wait a second here. How soon does Trevor want to move in?"

"Would today be too soon?"

"You mean as in today, today?"

She nods and nods and nods.

I hold my hand up and wave it like a white flag, and she runs over, kisses and hugs me again, and then dashes out to go give the baby daddy the good news. I flop down in the La-Z-Boy and pull the lever until it stops and lean all the way back. Up until a few minutes ago, I have always been proud of both of my children. Max was definitely the more focused of the two, though I tried not to compare them just because they were twins. When Max told me he wanted to study viticulture and enology at UC Davis, we were sitting by the pool with our feet in, and I started kicking (stalling).

"What in God's name is this the study of?" He started laughing and dove in like he always did when we used to sit out there. When he came to the surface he swam over and said, "For the record, viticulture is all about the science and cultivation of growing grapes and enology is the study of winemaking. They go together. How cool is that?" He ended up getting a bachelor of science in this and then moved to France to study with some masters or heavy-duty vineyards or something. Miss Montana, on the other hand, flits. She changed her major five or six times before settling on history and would've changed it again but she had to declare or else. I don't know, sometimes these pretty girls in Los Angeles don't take themselves seriously enough.

I almost jump out of this recliner when I hear the doorbell again. I'm sick of doorbells. It had better be Nurse Kim and not Trevor. He should be on his knees telling me "Thank you."

"It's open!" I yell, and in walks my favorite person, BJ's evil sister, Arlene. She despises me because twenty-six years ago I stole a black man from a nonexistent black woman.

"What are you doing here half-naked and where's my sister?"

"She took the little ones to school and then she's going on to the hotel for part of the day, and for your information this is called a robe and I came here to sit with Lee David until Nurse Kim gets here, and if I'm not being too forward: Wouldn't it have been more considerate to have called first?"

She cuts those eyes at me as if to say, "Bitch, who do you think you're talking to?"

I am not moved. So I cut my eyes back at her as if to say, "Bitch, you." I would put my hands on my hips for special effect but I've already had one major surprise this morning. I wouldn't want to provoke my best friend's sister into doing something stupid. Plus, she doesn't know I'm a black belt.

During this one-minute standoff, the screen door opens and in comes Nurse Kim in a denim miniskirt and a tight pink T-shirt with cleavage I would kill for and pink wedge sandals. She struts right past Arlene. Nurse Kim is one sexy nurse. Her legs are long and smooth. She's a pretty reddish brown, the color I'd want to be if I were black. "Good morning, everybody," she says. "I hope nothing's wrong, is it?"

I shake my head no and head toward the screen door to get out of what could potentially become an inferno. But Arlene beats me to the punch and lets the door slam in my face. Nurse Kim winks at me and then yells: "Miss Arlene, hold up a minute!"

Arlene turns around like she's ready to jump into the ring. "What?"

"Please tell Omar I said hey!" and she makes a soft fist and holds it next to her ear like it's a telephone. I love her.

Arlene

L ast night between her spin class and Bible study, Venetia called and told me that Betty Jean called her and told her that Trinetta had almost OD'd while she was on the phone with her! That Trinetta had the audacity to leave those kids over there with Betty Jean for almost a week and now Betty Jean is planning on keeping them until Trinetta can prove to her that she's clean. "Which could very well mean never," I said.

"I pray for our niece every single night, Arlene."

"Well, maybe Trinetta's not picking up on God's radar."

"I'm worried about Betty Bean too, Arlene. At this rate she could end up like all those grandmothers you read about in magazines and see in newspapers around Christmas or on *Oprah* or after the Super Bowl when the players on the winning team send shout-outs to their grandmas: not their mothers or fathers and not their wives and not their girlfriends. They're just waving away and yelling at the top of their lungs: 'I want to send my love to my grandma, who if it wasn't for her I wouldn't be here: Love you, Grandma!' These women almost all get stuck raising their grandchildren out of guilt, and who can blame them? How in the world does she think she can possibly manage it all? This happened to Ernesta, the woman who goes to my church and ended up having a heart attack herself—may she rest in peace—not that I'm thinking something like this could happen to BB but it would sure help if she let Christ into her life to help steer her in the right direction. And if she lost thirty or forty pounds and stopped complaining about her knees bothering her and she got on over to the gym, wouldn't you agree, Arlene?"

Just to shut her up I said, "Yes, I do." I have to be very careful what I say to Venetia and how I say it. Swearing is out. In my opinion, she prays far too much, and you'd think she'd also have some faith in self-actualization, self-determination, and common sense. She also has a big mouth, and even though gossip is supposed to be a sin because it's usually done with a tinge of malice, Venetia likes to repeat things. But she puts her own little spiritual spin on it, to justify it, I suppose, and as a result, she can turn your original comment into something you didn't necessarily intend. Sometimes I wonder how she managed to graduate from college, but then again, it was a state college.

I abhor getting this kind of emotional information second-hand but Betty Jean wouldn't dream of telling me, because she knows that unlike our baby sister whose spark plugs don't always fire, I don't bite my tongue, which is precisely why as soon as I get Omar up and give him his breakfast, I'm driving over there to give her a piece of my mind before she heads off to work.

I cannot for the life of me understand why Betty Jean continues to act like she's so surprised that Trinetta is a legitimate drug addict when the child has been high off and on for years. Mostly on. Which is precisely why I called Child Protective Services on her that time I stopped over to her tiny ghetto apartment to take those kids some toys for Christmas so Betty Jean wouldn't have to spend all of her little paycheck on them like she is known to do, and there they were sitting on that ugly plaid sofa eating Pringles and drinking Diet Pepsi all by themselves.

"Where's your mama?" I asked Luther. He was five or six.

"Her went to the store."

Her? I pray that one day these kids learn how to speak English. If my niece had walked through that door at that very moment I probably would've slapped her trifling ass down that hallway and back. Some people should not have children. Period. "Who's watching you boys?"

"Me. 'Cause I'm a big boy. What you got in them bags?"

I walked over to that stingy silver Christmas tree sitting on top of a fruit crate and put some packages on the bare tile underneath it. "These are from Santa," I said.

"Where you see him at?" the little one, Ricky, asked.

This is the most I think I've ever heard him say at one time. "I saw him today. He's at the mall."

"I don't believe you," Luther said, matter-of-factly.

"I wouldn't lie to you boys. Don't you believe in Santa Claus?" Right after I asked, I wished I hadn't. I didn't want them to say no. I wanted them to believe in something.

"Yeah, but the ones at the mall is not real," Luther said.

That little one just shook his head in agreement. He needs to be tested. "Look, how long has your mama been at the store?"

They both hunched their shoulders.

Just then I heard the door open and in she walked with a cigarette hanging out of her mouth. Not a single bag. A thin, milky film had formed a circle around her mouth. She looked just like Betty Jean thirty years ago, except for those disgusting dreadlocks.

"What're you doing here?" she asked.

I rolled my eyes at her. "I just stopped by to bring some gifts for the boys."

"Don't you know how to call first?"

"Who do you think you're talking to?"

"No disrespect intended. Sorry, Aunt Arlene. I just got a lot of things on my mind."

"Don't we all," I said, but I was not about to let her off the hook. "Why would you leave these kids in here for one minute by themselves, Trinetta?"

"I just ran downstairs for a minute. Look. Thanks for the gifts and for stopping by but I need to fix them something to eat."

"And what might that be?"

"That might not concern you, Aunt Arlene, but thank you so much for asking." And she walked over to the door, opened it, and put all of her weight on one flip-flopped foot.

As I waved to the kids, she yelled out behind me. "Tell Omar I said hey. He is still living at home, right?"

I nodded yes.

She nodded too. "He lost any weight?"

"As a matter of fact he has. But don't let it concern you. Merry Christmas."

"Jingle bell rock to you too."

Trinetta has not spoken to me since. To this day I don't know if CPS ever showed up or not. Probably not. They get too many of these types of calls. Especially from neighborhoods like this. But this is the reason so many of these kids end up on the six o'clock news.

Why people take drugs baffles me to no end. Especially when they can't afford them. And why can't they do them *before* they have children? If you're that dissatisfied with the quality of your life, change it! I'm no saint. I experimented with a number of popular drugs in college. And I enjoyed them. Enough to understand why some people get addicted. If I hadn't had specific life goals, I probably could've taken the low road. But I didn't like feeling that good. I enjoyed being depressed, disappointed, and miserable when it was necessary, because it built character and it was how I evolved and came to be the woman I am now.

Betty Jean has come to Trinetta's rescue too many times to count. Some people think they're helping their kids when they do so much for them, but it's not true. I'm sick of hearing about that girl's trials and tribulations. She could've been cleaning teeth all these years but has yet to graduate. And she was such a smart child. But then again, Betty Jean's parenting skills cannot be found in any how-to book.

Deep down inside, I think the reason Betty Jean doesn't confide in me is because she has never really forgiven me for trimming her hair when she was little. Was it my fault she didn't care for the pixie? She also blames me for introducing her to Lee David, knowing he was almost old enough to be her uncle. But I didn't twist her arm. I could say a lot of things about her that she has no idea I have stored in my memory bank, but I don't like throwing things in her face just for spite. She has done and continues to do a lot of stupid things, and had she gone to college, where you can learn to think critically, it might have helped her make more intelligent decisions.

For instance, Venetia told me she borrowed against her little raggedy house to get help for Trinetta, because the bank called Venetia for a reference. Look how well that's going. Then she went and bought the girl a car and is paying the insurance; she uses Venetia's address to get lower premiums. And I know for a fact she has paid Trinetta's rent, but she lives in a Section 8 apartment, so how high could her rent possibly be? Ninety-six dollars, that's how much. And how many men have those boys called Daddy? Trinetta's had enough hoodlums living with her, you would think it might occur to her to get one that could help her with those kids or the rent. But apparently that has never crossed her mind. Which is the main reason why it just gets on my nerves to see how much money Betty Jean has spent on her and her kids. She has bought enough school clothes for an orphanage and she practically lives at Costco. Not to mention being Mrs. Claus year after year.

I try not to compare. Even though Omar was born with a few health issues that I've tried helping him learn to cope with as well as overcome, he's still the best thing that's ever happened to me, and I don't know what I'd do without him. Of course college is not for everybody and he's had a hard time figuring out what interests him. He's still young, and I'm patient and confident that one day soon he's going to walk through the right door.

I knock four times on Omar's door. I don't know why that boy won't get up even after his alarm goes off. "Get up, Omar, or you're going to be late for work!"

"I'm up," he groans.

I don't believe him. "I should hear water running, and I don't."

"I think I'm getting a sore throat, Mom."

"Open the door, Omar."

"It's not locked."

He's sitting on the side of the bed in striped pajamas I got him a few weeks ago. They were tight then, but they look a little loose now. I walk over and feel his forehead. It's warm. The last time he had a sore throat it turned out to be strep. "You think you need to stay home today?"

"I think I'll be all right once I take a hot shower."

"Are you sure? I can call your job if you really aren't up to it, Omar. We've got Theraflu in the kitchen and I can make some chicken noodle soup if you want me to."

He stands up. "I'm fine, Mom. I think it was just a tickle. Please don't go calling my job."

"You want me to take your temperature? Just to be on the safe side?"

He heads toward his bathroom.

"Omar, have you lost a few pounds?"

He yells through the bathroom door. "Six to be exact. Glad you noticed."

His weight isn't an issue for me. He's still handsome. He's the spitting image of his trifling daddy, who chose not to be in his life because he claimed I tricked him by getting pregnant so he would leave his wife, which was pretty much true. I needed leverage. The last I heard, they're still together. Omar has never met him, because I told him I didn't know where his father was. I thought that was best, and we've done just fine without him in our lives. It's for this reason that I've probably gone a little overboard parenting him. I know my sisters think I baby him, but I don't really care what they think. He's my only child, and as his mother and father I have done and continue to do all that I can do to help him feel more confident. I've told him year after year that everybody wasn't meant to be lean and lanky. "But I'm tired of being fat," he said when we flew to Vegas for his twenty-first birthday. He needed a buckle extension but I reminded him that even pregnant women need them, too. That may not have been the most tactful analogy, but I couldn't take it back. Omar's been on every diet under the sun and he just gets so frustrated, it breaks my heart, which is why he pleaded with me to stop baking.

I walk down the hall to my bedroom and close the windows because the forecast is calling for rain, which is a rarity in Los Angeles. Groups of gray clouds are clustering above us. I head downstairs to look for the thermometer and make him some hot oatmeal. Before I get a chance to put it in the microwave he's in the kitchen, dressed.

"Mom. I'm fine. Oh, and after work I'm meeting some of my buddies for happy hour." He gives me a quick kiss on my forehead and heads for the garage. "Don't make dinner for me tonight, either, Mom. And have a great day."

Happy hour? Since when did he start going to happy hour? I don't feel like calling him because I know sometimes I get on his nerves. But something is different about him. The past few months he's changed. I don't know what it is, but I'm going to find out. I put my empty coffee cup in the dishwasher, feed the fish, and water the last two living plants. I go stand in front of Omar's door and turn the handle. It doesn't open! Since when did he start locking it? I reach above the doorframe and get the metal key he obviously doesn't know I know is there, and I open the door and just stand there for a minute. His bed is made. That's from years of going to camp and being a Cub Scout. I look around. He's got a poster of Beyoncé on one wall and Janet Jackson on another and the rest are rappers. His computer is off and I know it's password-protected, because I learned that over a year ago. You just want to make sure your child isn't doing some freaky stuff or anything illegal.

Wait a minute now. His metal trash can is full of paper. I sit down at his desk and just pick up a handful to see what he printed. Every single page is about the benefits of getting a Lap Band to lose weight. Is he crazy? I read some of the information but find it disgusting, and even though I'm tempted to ball up the paper, I stop myself, so he won't know I've been in his room.

I walk into my bedroom and look out the window. No rain yet. Western Los Angeles is down below. But I can't see it. There are 747s flying overhead, about to land at LAX. Living on a hill has its advantages and disadvantages. When there's no smog, you can see for miles. Or when the Santa Ana winds come in late autumn or early winter. I wish Betty Jean would consider moving just a little closer in this direction. I could get her a good deal on a foreclosed property, but I haven't bothered to mention this. It might be better to wait until Lee David passes, which unfortunately shouldn't be that much longer. Poor fella.

I put on one of my favorite cocoa-brown linen suits because I have four open houses starting later this morning. Right after I stop by Betty Jean's I'll head over to my office and pick up all the docs. I take a ribeye out of the freezer for Omar later. He loves ribeyes. He's always hungry when he gets home, no matter what he says.

When I back out of my driveway, I see rush-hour traffic, which I've already factored in. As I inch my way to the bottom of the hill, I'm wondering how long those kids are going to be staying at Betty Jean's this time around and I pray she's not thinking about keeping them. After all, Trinetta's not dead. And this is why foster care was created. I don't know if I'll bring this topic up. It's probably too soon.

I hope like hell Tammy's not over there. She loves to show

Betty Jean sympathy when she doesn't need it. I cannot stand that little white wench. And if Lee David is blasting *Dora the Explorer* I'm going to close his door. He should've been in assisted care two years ago, but Betty Jean has never taken my advice, which is why I've tried to stop giving it. And what did she do? Went out and hired the trampiest young attendant she could find to care for him. I don't trust Nurse Kim. First of all, she's too pretty to be doing such a creepy job. Why on earth would somebody who's sexy as hell in a turtleneck want to spend all day with an old man in a dark and dreary bedroom? And in a house that creaks when you walk from the front to the back, one that needed remodeling about twenty years ago? She's probably stealing. Something. Not that there's anything of value in there, but some folks just like to take advantage.

I pull into her driveway. It's got big round oil stains on it. And her sidewalk is cracked and raised from too many tremors and earthquakes. I wish she would paint this house. Beige is such a drab color on a block with nothing but beige houses. At least the Koreans had enough sense to paint theirs mint green and the shutters white. They could stand to plant some grass and a few flowers wouldn't kill them. But I really don't care.

I knock once or twice like I always do and walk on in. And who is standing there to greet me? Tammy Wynette! Even though I usually look right through her, this morning I decide to be polite. "Good morning, Tammy," I say. "Is my sister not here?"

"She took the little ones to school and then she's going on to the hotel for part of the day. Forgive me for being half-naked but I had to rush over so BJ wouldn't be late."

"That's a beautiful robe," I say. "Bullock's?"

"J.C. Penney. But thank you," she says. "Why didn't you bother to call first instead of just dropping by?"

"Because I forgot my cell phone. At any rate, I'll try to catch her at work."

This must be my lucky morning.

"Good morning, everybody. Is something going on?"

Before I have a chance to respond, Beyoncé brushes right past me, dressed like she's on her way to a nightclub. If that Victoria's Secret push-up bra were one size bigger it would still be too small. But I'm polite. "Good morning, Nurse Kim. Everything's fine. You look lovely as ever."

"Why, thanks so much for noticing," she says, and I just wave as I head on out to the car, which is when that skank yells out, "And tell Omar I said hey!"

I take my cell phone out of my purse and don't care if they see it. I call Betty Jean at work. "I just stopped by your house to give you a hug because I heard you've taken on even more responsibility than you need to at this time in your life. What time do you go to lunch?"

"Venetia's got a big mouth, you know that?"

"She was simply sharing important information and you know the only reason she told me is because you were probably too embarrassed to and she and I are both worried about you and the boys and Trinetta, which is why I wanted to see you in person. What time?"

"I'm not in the mood for a lecture, Arlene."

"I don't lecture. I simply offer a different point of view. Sometimes we do agree on things, Betty Jean, so please don't go getting defensive. What time?"

"I'm leaving at two, but meet me around the corner at Denny's in a half hour. I've got twenty minutes and that's it."

"Not Denny's. Please. It's not real food and they're racist. Pick somewhere else, please. Besides, aren't you the supervisor?"

"Okay. IHOP. And no, I am not the supervisor."

And she hangs up.

The place smells like bacon, link sausage, pancake batter, and syrup. It looks the same now as it did twenty years ago. I wouldn't eat this mess if it were free. I see Betty Jean sitting in a booth. She's drinking coffee. She already looks tired.

"You look tired," I say even though I didn't mean to say that. I sit across from her.

"I am tired. So what does that make me besides tired?"

"So how long do you plan on keeping them?"

"They're not pets, Arlene. As long as I have to," she says.

"Do you really expect Trinetta to stop doing what she's been doing anytime soon?"

"I can't speak for my daughter."

"Well, have you spoken to her since whatever she did or didn't do happened?"

"She left me a message on the home phone this morning, when she knew I'd be driving the boys to school."

"And what did she have to say?"

"The same thing she's said before, Arlene. When she's cleaned up her act, she'll be back to get the boys."

"Which means they could be in college."

"In my heart of hearts I really don't believe she wants to lose her kids, Arlene."

"As long as she can count on you to take care of them every time she falls off the wagon, she doesn't have to worry about losing them, now does she?"

"Sometimes you have to have a little faith in your kids, Arlene. You more than anybody should know that."

"What's that supposed to mean?"

"Well, you've only got one, and look at how you dote on him."

"I don't *dote* on Omar."

"Do you make him breakfast and dinner every day?"

"So what? We live in the same house."

"And that's the other thing. When is he ever going to move out and get his own apartment?"

"When he can afford to. Is that all right with you?"

"I love Omar, and he's got a good heart. I just always thought he'd be some hotshot businessman or something."

"What are you trying to say, Betty Jean? Just say it."

"You might want to stop giving him so much advice and monitoring every move he makes. Let him make his own decisions and whatever choices he wants to make, even if you don't like them."

"You don't know what you're talking about, Betty Jean! Can I help it if he always asks me what I think?"

"He needs to learn to think for himself."

"You know what, I can say this about my son. At least he's never caused me any problems and he's certainly never been in trouble or done any drugs, if that's what you're getting at."

"I wasn't trying to *get* at anything, Arlene. Omar just seems bored and not sure of himself. Anyway, I have to get back to work."

"You should go talk to somebody in Social Services so you can get some kind of financial assistance while they're there."

"It's only temporary, Arlene. And I'm their grandmother. If I need help, I know how to ask for it. And I don't need their help."

I just shake my head, stand up, and give her the hug I promised. I don't mean to be such a bitch. I really don't. I think it's just because I want the very best for the people I love, and I get impatient when they don't see some of the tragic mistakes they're making. If I didn't care I wouldn't say anything and just keep my thoughts to myself. But I do care. Unfortunately, some folks can't handle the truth, which is why they get defensive instead of just looking at another point of view. I don't think I have all the answers. But some folks don't seem to know what questions to ask.

Nurse Kim

Good morning, Mr. Lee," I say, shaking him. "Wake up!"
He opens his eyes and smiles. He may not recognize his wife some days but he sure as hell don't have no problem recognizing me.

"You ready for your shower or you want your breakfast first?"

He shakes his head no, then points to his mouth.

Men. They're all so fucking predictable. Even the old ones. I reach between the mattress on his side of the bed and grab his bottle of blue pills. I take one out and push it into his mouth. I pick up his glass of lukewarm water and put the straw up to his mouth. He sucks and swallows. I lift the covers and toss 'em to the side. He got his morning hard-on, and oh what a hard-on it is. It's easy to understand why Miss Betty would have a hard time letting all of this fall by the wayside, and the funny thing is Mr. Lee don't look no sixty-five, none whatsoever. I been lathering him up and down close to a year now and I can't lie, I get a lot of pleasure out of touching him.

I unbuckle my sandals and kick 'em off. I pull my T-shirt over my head and lay it flat at the foot of the bed, on Miss Betty's side. I watch Mr. Lee's eyes get bigger. Glassier. Almost like they're breathing as much as he's starting to. I unhook my bra and drop it on the floor. Then I climb on the bed so I'm standing over him. I unzip my skirt and step out of it. Then throw it on the floor, too. Mr. Lee starts to moan. I wiggle out of my thong and drop it next to his face. I can see him trying to inhale me. He moans again, louder this time, and then opens his mouth. This is when I grab the headboard and drop to my knees. I feel his warm lips against my lips and that little muscle gets firm and fiery and I move like I'm rowing a boat and I ain't in no hurry to get there, but when I can't stand it no more I grab the headboard and press hard against his lips until I hear myself yell, "Shit!" But I'm greedy, so I do the exact same thing until I explode again and again and then I lean back and pull off his pajama bottoms and that thing is jumping around like it's looking for something, so I grab it in my hands and make it be still by sliding all the way down on it. It only takes three or four minutes to make him yell out, "Oh, Kimmie! Oh, Kimmie!"

Which is when I get up. I love being his breakfast. I have to admit, out of all the old farts I've tended to, Mr. Lee is the best, except for maybe Mr. Jackson. He had dentures. I made him take those suckers out because his gums were so warm and smooth I hardly had to move at all.

He falls on back to sleep and I lie next to him, turn on the TV, and watch the rest of the *Today* show. I don't know why I like that Katie Couric. She looks like a little girl and got a little-girl voice and a little body and she even got little-girl teeth. When Mr. Lee wakes up, I take his pajama top off and walk him into the bathroom. I put on Miss Betty's shower cap 'cause it takes me a whole hour to blow-dry my hair, which of course everybody in L.A. thinks is a weave just because it's long. As if black women's hair don't grow long. I take him by the arm and get in the shower with him. He acts just like a little kid when I put a million bubbles on that washcloth and rub it up and down and all over his whole body. He really don't look all that bad naked. You'd think since he's so old his skin would be all shriveled up and wrinkly, including his dick, but that thing is just as long and thick and solid as some of these young dudes I been with. What I like about this kind of situation is ain't no strings attached. Which is why a young woman like myself is grateful to have access to it. Mr. Lee has shrunk some. Standing up, it's easy to tell. He was almost six feet but now he feels closer to my height: I'm five nine and a half.

I dry him off with a fluffy towel and then put a fresh pair of pajamas on him and take him out to the dining room and sit him down at the table. He's still smiling. Poor thing. I really think it's time Miss Betty think about getting him ready for a facility, but I'm keeping my mouth shut. Hell, I'm looking at my income here. I ain't never stayed long enough for one of my patients to die on me, but pretty damn close. I can usually tell. They smell different. Well, they don't have no smell at all, really. And they get this tired look, like they know what's coming. It's creepy as hell, and this is when I usually give my notice because I don't like walking in on death.

"Hot damn!" Mr. Lee yells out, and then starts laughing.

He does this a lot. Sometimes I think he's probably remembering when somebody made a three-pointer or a touchdown or hell, I don't know. All I know is he's laughing and it makes me feel good to know that whatever's going on inside of him is lifting his spirits.

I feed him some microwave oatmeal and give him some juice in a sippy cup, and then he says, "Well, well, well," and I walk him back into the bedroom and turn on the Western Channel. It cracks me up to hear Mr. Lee say, "Giddy-up!" except when he says it like five or ten times in a row. I don't know which is worse, listening to him trying to speak Spanish with Dora or pretending like he's riding a goddamn horse. Plus, Dora is not cute and I wish they could give her a makeover, because that hairstyle is played out. Even though I'm not crazy about kids, it's a lot livelier around the crib since those boys been here. Not to be mean, but they're both a little weird-looking. That oldest one reminds me of Chucky without the freckles and his eyes look too close together. The younger one looks like he didn't bake long enough. It's obvious they got different daddies. But what else is new? Watch. They'll probably grow up to be fine as hell. My brothers were homely, too, but now women and men drool over them. (One of my brothers is gay but ask me if I care?)

There's a reason why there's not that many pictures of me in my granny's scrapbook. I wasn't no cute baby. In fact, a lot of my relatives told me people just used to bend down, look at me, and say, "She's sure got a lot of hair, doesn't she?" Since nobody had any money for braces back then, I had horse teeth all through middle school. I didn't think my ass was ever going to stop growing but years later it's turned out to be my best asset. And then there were the zits. There wasn't enough Clearasil in Thrifty's that could make those fuckers disappear. It wasn't until after I finally got my period that I realized all those years I was nothing but a human crossword puzzle with missing pieces. And then it seemed like all at once, something happened and everything on me fit in all the right places.

But being pretty don't guarantee you gon' find a good man to appreciate all you have to offer. Which is why I'm by myself. A lot of them just want a trophy. I ain't hanging on nobody's arm like I'm a tennis bracelet. There's some stuff inside me that deserves to be checked out too. I ain't no black Barbie. Besides, I'm only thirty. So I think I've still got a few good years left to catch. Ain't no doubt about it, I was wild as hell in my twenties, but I'm all about cruising now. My granny's been bugging me for years about when I'm gon' have a baby, since where I come from a husband is just a bonus. She's got high blood pressure and her cholesterol is off the chart, and I thought she might have a heart attack when I said, all proper, "I am not having any kids, because I don't want any." She looked at me like I was joking and then realized I wasn't. She couldn't think of a good comeback so she just said, "Thank God I got grandsons," and walked away. She didn't speak to me for almost a whole month, and then finally outta the blue she said: "Everythang ain't for everybody," and we went to see *The Mummy Returns,* since we both like scary movies 'cause they don't scare us, but we sat through it and ate popcorn out the same bag. She fell asleep on my shoulder.

I'm also a snooper. I like to go through the people I work for's shit so I know who I'm really working for. People act like they're one thing and then you find out they're somebody else. Everything in their house, especially the stuff in drawers and under the mattresses, tells you who they really are and what they might be hiding. And everybody's hiding something. Sometimes it's just bullshit and I can't figure out why they even bothered. I have never stolen a thing, 'cause that would make me a thief. When I first started working here, I started under Miss Betty's side of the mattress and I found some very interesting shit:

> A book called *The Prophet* by Kahlil Gibran. (It was too deep for me.)
> A juicy love letter from some dude named Parnell "C" dated all the way back to 1974. (Wasn't Miss Betty married to Mr. Lee already? I will forget I saw this.)
> A .22 with two bullets in it. (But everybody got at least one of these.)

A box cutter. (In case you ain't got time to get the gun.)
A Gladys Knight and the Pips cassette: *About Love*.
    (What's that about?)
A dried rose (pressed inside some wax paper).
A black shoestring.
A man's blue-and-white pinstriped tie.
A pair of black stockings. (What happened to that
    garter?)
A letter from Louisiana State University telling her she
    got accepted!

On Mr. Lee's side I only found four things: porn videos, Vaseline, a picture of Dorothy Dandridge, and a picture of some old lady who looked like a slave.

All of this stuff was tame compared with some of the other weird, stupid shit I have come across under other mattresses at other sick folks' homes that made me scratch my head:

Easy-Off Oven Cleaner.
Two sets of dentures.
Speeding tickets (paid and unpaid).
A bag of Gummy Bears.
A bottle of Louisiana Hot Sauce.
FDS feminine hygiene spray can (empty).
A New York Knicks jersey.
A gram of cocaine. (I did borrow a little of this but
    never got a chance to pay it back, 'cause I got let go.)

Sometimes, when I'm bored, I try on Miss Betty's jewelry and walk around in it all day. She's got very good taste in jewelry. I don't know what's real and what ain't, but since I have yet to stumble on a safe, it's probably fake. Who gives a shit? If it looks good, what difference does it make if it ain't real? I dig all the artwork in here. It livens up this old-ass house. She could stand to update all this beige and gold décor, though. It reminds me of my granny's crib. The one my older brother just bought her out in Palmdale.

If I was Miss Betty, when Mr. Lee passes, I would get the hell out of this dump with that insurance money. She'll be good for a hundred thousand green ones. That policy's in a dresser drawer. I been through all their papers and I know all about her family down there in New Orleans—it's too many of 'em to count, that's for damn sure.

I have also sat in that old people's chair in the living room and read almost all Dexter's letters that Miss Betty opened, but there's a shitload of 'em she ain't read. I don't blame her. Some of 'em almost longer than the Bible. At least Dexter can spell and sounds like he went to a junior college for a hot minute. My granny gets some from my cousins that just make you crack up. You know they looking at a dictionary or a thesaurus while they writing and some of the shit don't make no kinda sense. It's not like they gon' get on *Jeopardy* when they get out. But Dexter is intelligent and I like some of the stuff he writes about. You can be smart and stupid at the same time, but stupid is the one that weigh a whole lot more and the one that got their stupid asses locked up. Dexter got the same sob story a whole bunch of 'em got. Everybody innocent. I was set up. My own lawyer didn't believe me. The justice system is racist and want all brothers behind bars. That last one I do buy.

Since I don't make much money doing this kind of work, I had to get a roommate. A roommate I can't tolerate much longer 'cause I didn't know she was a real alcoholic until after I saw how much she could put away. Not to mention being country as all hell. She's from some wooded area in Alabama. A three-hour drive from Birmingham. She drinks whiskey like a man. I met her in nursing school. But she dropped out and became a flight attendant and just got fired 'cause she got written up for being late or hungover too many times. She's been blowing up my phone since I got here and I been blowing her off 'cause last night we had it out all because her latest boyfriend got to the apartment before she did and we was just sitting on the couch having a civilized conversation while she ran to change clothes.

"So, what kind of nurse are you?" he asked. He sounded like he'd been to college, so I decided to use my college voice.

"I'm an LVN."

"Interesting. Have you ever considered becoming an RN?"

Have I ever considered becoming an RN? I couldn't believe he was even asking me that, but I heard myself say, "I've thought about it, but I'm thinking about applying for a position as a traveling nurse. Fortunately, I've got six years' experience, so I'll see."

"Very interesting," he said. "And how's that work?" He crossed his legs and was just about to lean back and, I suppose, get comfortable when Tierra came charging outta her bedroom and stood there like she was ready to take off her earrings and put Vaseline on her face and said, "Let's go," like she was giving him a direct order or something. He didn't act like a punk until that very minute.

"I just need to go to the bathroom first."

She didn't buy it. Me neither.

"I'll meet you downstairs," she said, and he changed his mind and kind of ran after her but not before he turned to me and said,

"Nice talking to you, Kim, and good luck in your nursing career. Maybe I'll see you again."

As soon as he was out of range, Tierra shut that door and locked him out, then looked at me with those cheap-ass Betty Boop eyelashes and put all her weight on one of those cheap-ass Payless pumps and put her hands on her hips in that tacky-ass Hervé Léger knockoff and said, "I knew you couldn't be trusted."

"What did I do?"

"You ain't have no business talking to my man about yo' personal shit when I was not in the room."

"I was trying to be polite since you're the one who got here late."

"For somebody you just met, you was awful chummy chummy. What the hell was y'all talking about?"

"He asked me about being a nurse and I just answered his questions."

"Yeah, and what if I had got here a half hour later? You'd probably be fucking him. You L.A. hoes all alike. My sister warned me but I didn't listen. I want your ass out of here by the first."

"You can't put me out, Tierra. Both of our names happen to be on the lease in case you forgot, so you need to get the fuck over yourself." And I crossed my arms. Dared the bitch to say another word. She stormed her insecure ass on outta there and slammed the door.

I decide to listen to her voice message: "Kim, this Tierra calling and I just want you to know that you can stay here. All my shit'll be gone by the time you get home. Sneaky bitch."

What?

I replay it just to make sure I heard right. It says the same exact thing loud and clear. This means she's breaking the lease and I can't afford this apartment by myself and I ain't about to look for no roommate on craigslist.

I need a nap. I don't like having too much on my mind, especially when I can't do a whole lot right then and there to fix it. But if I fall asleep and Mr. Lee wakes up and I don't hear him and he fall out the damn bed and hurt hisself then this would probably be Endsville for me. And I've been on top of things here. That's funny. But I am not laughing. What I need to do is finish filling out this application for the traveling nurse program because it takes a month for them to let you know if you've been accepted. I might be homeless in a few weeks so I decide this might also be a good time to pray. But God can't pay my rent.

So I watch *The Price Is Right* and don't win, not even so much as a kitchen appliance, some boring furniture, or a trip to Hawaii. I watch two soap operas and laugh all the way through 'em. I give Mr. Lee his lunch and then decide to just leave the real world altogether, so I dig in my gym bag and pull out my Harry Potter *Sorcerer's Stone* book. I love all this wizard shit. I wish I could fly. Sometimes I wish I could disappear and reappear and come back as a giraffe. They can see everything, they can eat the highest leaves, they can run fast, and even though they ain't the cutest of jungle animals, they ain't violent. I was just thinking about something. If I get into this traveling nurse's program, I need to stop talking like I'm ghetto, because I know how. And I cuss like a fucking sailor, but mostly in my head when I'm thinking, like now. So I'm going to try to think and talk like I went to nursing school and I paid attention in English class. I can turn off the ghetto talk on a dime, especially when I'm around professional white folks. Black ones, too. Like my employer, Miss Betty.

I'm not feeling too Hogwarty. But happy birthday, Harry. Back at you soon. Right now, I have to figure out the most intelligent manner in which to solve my housing dilemma. See how many extra words that took? What I'm worried about is my credit rating. I am never late with my bills and it took me a while to get it up to 720 but that's because back in my twenties when I was depressed and didn't know why, instead of getting high like everybody else I went shopping. Fucked up all my credit cards, and then after I got diagnosed and put on meds I started paying 'em off and now I'm back on track. I might see if I can find me a homosexual. They make good roommates. They for damn sure neat and clean and most of 'em can decorate and you ain't gotta worry about fucking 'em. I'ma give this some serious thought. I know a lot of homosexuals thanks to my brother being gay, so maybe I should ask him if he knows anybody who wants to live with a quiet, sweet, clean, responsible girl. If necessary, I'll pretend to be a lesbian if it helps. Hell, this problem might already be solved.

I decide to check on Mr. Lee when I hear those little critters slamming the car door and galloping like Secretariat toward the front door. Would it just kill them to walk? I mean, what's the big fucking hurry? This is just one more reason why I don't care for kids. They annoy me. I just pretend to like them in front of their mamas or, in this case, their grandma. I'm wondering how long it's gon' take for Miss Betty to go on and get legal custody of 'em, 'cause I've heard her daughter be turning it down off Rosecrans and Adams but I always assumed Miss Betty knew her daughter was a crackhead and word on the street is she'll suck anybody's dick for a ten-dollar bag. The reason I know this is 'cause I got a couple of relatives down there competing with her and sometimes my granny made my brothers drive down there to look for 'em. They learned the hard way that you can't save nobody who ain't interested in being saved.

I can relate to what Miss Betty is going through, 'cause my granny raised me and my two brothers 'cause our mama died of breast cancer when we were little. Our daddy didn't know what to do with three kids so he left us with our granny, our mama's mama, moved to Kansas City, got married again, and I heard he had two or three more kids. That's all we know. That's all we want to know. Our granny was strict as hell and her middle name was "No!" but we did what she told us to do and things worked in our favor. One of my brothers is an airline mechanic. The other one work for Microsoft.

It should be obvious that I wasn't no honor roll student in high school. My favorite class was boys. I graduated with a C+ average, and my granny made me look through the catalog at the junior college near our house and told me to pick something out that looked interesting. I picked nursing. So I went through the LVN program only to find out that hospitals and me don't get along, just like dead people. So here I am. Just your average, everyday care-taker. I like taking care of people who can't take care of themselves. Sometimes I go a little overboard, but men like Mr. Lee don't have a whole lot of time left in this world and I feel good sexing them up and I get a little sumthin'-sumthin' out of the deal myself. It's a win-win situation and no harm done.

"Hi there, you little cuties!" I say with as much niceness as I can. That older one, Luther (what a horrible name to give to a baby), look like he's staring at my breasts when he waves but I know I'm not seeing right, 'cause he can't be no more than seven or eight now. But then when that other one runs on back to his room, and Luther sits on the couch and starts smiling at me, I feel a little uncomfortable because that little son of a bitch is looking right through my top.

"Hi there, Nurse Kim," Miss Betty says as she walks in with three Mickey D bags in her hand and sets them on the cocktail table.

What I wouldn't pay for a Filet-O-Fish and some fries about now.

"How're you doing today? And how's Lee David?"

Because I like Miss Betty, and she is nice to me, I always try to use my junior college voice with her too, because it's important to sound like you went to college in front of the people you work for. "I'm good. Mr. Lee is fair to middling. He didn't have too much to eat today and they might need to step up his meds. But I'm not a doctor. How about you? I see you've got the grandkids today."

"Yes, Lordy," she says.

She collapses in that La-Z-Boy like it's her life support. But it's cheap and the back is lumpy and the noise the massager makes can get on your last nerve. She woulda been better off sitting on the couch if Young Mac Daddy here would beat it, but Luther looks like he's waiting for the right moment to ask for my hand in marriage. He grabs a pillow and props it behind his short little neck, like he ain't going nowhere no time soon. Miss Betty leans all the way back in her La-Z-Boy and turns on the massager, but then she jerks like something scared her and sits straight up.

"Lord, it sounds like drums beating, doesn't it?"

"Yep. Lots of drums," Luther says.

She presses the lever so the chair is upright and walks over to sit down at the opposite end of the couch from Luther. "Forgive me, Nurse Kim. Luther, you know what Grandma does when she gets home from work and she's tired and her knees and feet hurt," she says, not like she's waiting for him to answer, 'cause no sooner has she said "hurt" than she yanks that sad 1985 pageboy wig off and drops it on the end table. She's got a fishnet on, and even though I only see a few gray strands around her edges, it looks like Miss Betty got a head full of hair. She needs to throw that damn wig in the trash and go to the beauty shop and let somebody bring her look up to 2001, or just buy a new wig or think about trying a weave. Old people wear weaves, too. Now that I can see her face, Miss Betty ain't a bad-looking woman for somebody about to be a senior citizen. If she lost about twenty or thirty pounds, she could probably be attractive again. A nice foundation and the right lipstick and maybe get those bushy eyebrows waxed, and she could lose about eight or nine years right there.

She looks over at Luther, who still sitting there looking at me. It's a little fucking creepy.

"Luther, why don't you take your and Ricky's bags and go on in the back to the kitchen and eat it before it gets cold."

"I ain't hungry, Grandma."

Miss Betty cuts her eyes at him and I'm just watching.

"I mean, I'm not hungry, Grandma," he says.

"You were starving a half hour ago."

"I have homework, Grandma. I can write, Nurse Kim. You wanna see?"

"I do, but not today, sugar. Nurse Kim needs to finish talking to your grandma and try to beat that rush-hour traffic."

"I can write fast," the little fucker says.

"Luther. Say goodbye to Nurse Kim and please do what I just asked you to do." She picks up those Mickey D bags and hands 'em to him. No drinks?

He still act like it's killing him to stand up.

"I would love to see how well you can write, Luther, just not today, sweetie. Now, perhaps you should do what your grandma asked like a good little boy."

He finally jumps up and dashes out of the living room like I pissed him off or something. He'll get over it. I'm glad Miss Betty told him to beat it, 'cause Lord knows I did not feel like talking to him in my elementary school teacher's voice another second. I wish I could appreciate what children have to offer but I just don't see it. I mean, they can be cute and adorable and all that, but some of that sweetness is just a act they put on to pimp their parents so they can get what they want. And it works. All they do is beg. For everything. All the time. They take up too much energy. Your best energy. And they ain't stupid. They know when you worn out, but they will wake you up from your nap to ask you for a glass of fucking milk. This mess goes on for at least eighteen years. To be fair, I do know that sometimes they can make you proud, but look how long you have to wait to see if you're going to get a return on your investment. I don't like the odds.

"Do you eat McDonald's, Nurse Kim?"

"Every now and then," I say.

"I have an extra Filet-O-Fish and some fries in there I am not in the mood for. You're welcome to them, if you're hungry."

"Are you sure? You might want to warm it up a little later."

"Have you ever reheated anything from McDonald's, honey?"

I shake my head no and reach for the bag and try not to act like my dream came true. "Thank you, Miss Betty."

She leans over to make sure the boys are doing what they supposed to be doing even though I hear video games and laughing, which mean Luther ain't doing no homework. Miss Betty look like she got something on her mind and she about to tell me what it is.

"Trinetta's into some things she shouldn't be into so I'm

keeping the boys here with me until she gets back on her feet. You understand what I'm saying?"

"I do. But if you don't mind me asking, Miss Betty: Hasn't she been off her feet for some time now?"

"Yes, she has. I know you're not blind, Nurse Kim. I'm just trying to do right by my grandsons because I can't save my daughter."

"No, you cannot."

"Anyway, I'm going to have my hands full around here and I know you're applying for that traveling nurse position and it sounds like a wonderful opportunity, but I was wondering if you do get accepted, would you be willing to stay on a little longer, just until I get things figured out around here? Is that too iffy for you?"

"Not at all, Miss Betty. Anything I can do to help you and Mr. Lee," I say.

Luther

Here come Grandma, Ricky!" I point at all them cars in a line that look just like a funeral but we just happy we getting picked up from school. I'm holding Ricky's hand. I hold his hand everywhere we at and everywhere we go. He a runt. Big kids like to pick on him.

Ricky in first grade. He in special ed. But he way smarter than the other special ed kids. He told me. And Ricky don't lie to me. I'm in second grade. I wait for him outside his room. I like being his big brother. I'm tall for my age: seven and a half. Everybody always saying it: "Luther, you tall for your age, son."

We standing with a whole lotta other kids but we can't move till Grandma's car is right in front of us. I hope she take us to McDonald's drive-up window so we can get some McNuggets and I hope we get to spend more nights at her house, 'cause me and Ricky don't wanna go home today or tomorrow, 'cause we don't like where we live and we don't gotta sleep together on the let-out couch and Grandma is nice to us and she don't call us names or say get out of my face can't you see I'm busy and don't no strange men knock on the front door and walk past us without saying hi and just go in our mama's room and close the door. And don't nobody bam on the door and wake us up and say: "Yo mama at home? She owe me

71

some goddamn money." And I ain't gotta lie through the door and say, "She ain't home and I don't know where she at," even though she be down the hall hiding in Twinkle's apartment.

I wave to Grandma since she getting closer. Ricky start waving too. He a copycat. Try to do everything I do but he can't do everything I do. He can't spell and he can't add or subtract and he can't make a basket. He a runt. He have to take medicine 'cause our mama had drugs inside her body when he was born. I don't.

One thang I do know, when I grow up, I ain't doing no kinda drugs. None. I don't care if they free. And I will kick Ricky's ass if he ever try any. We don't wanna be drug addicts. We don't wanna live in the projects, either. I'm going to college so I can be somebody when I grow up, even though I know I'm somebody now. That's what our grandma always be telling us, which is why she always be trying to stop us from talking like we do. She be making us repeat stuff over and over even though she know what we saying. "It'll all pay off, boys," is what she always be saying whenever she take us places. I don't know what she mean by that, but I just know it's good.

Anyway, don't nobody hardly believe me and Ricky is brothers, 'cause we don't look nothing like each other. I think it's cool. We don't know who our daddy is and I really don't care. Plus half the kids in this school and in the building where we live don't know who they daddy is either. Whoever he is, I think he got a lotta nerve not showing up for our birthday and Christmas. If I ever meet him, I'm gonna tell him he can kiss our ass.

We used to have a little sister but her daddy came and got her to live with him when she only had six teeth. She should have a mouthful now. I wonder where she at. I wonder who her new mama is. I wonder if she remember me and Ricky. I wonder if she got her own bed. I don't know if I really care or if I'm just wondering. I think she still our sister. And I think she probably always be our sister. But you never know.

Grandma need a new ride. I think it might be old as her. Like seventy or eighty. I don't know what kind it is but it's a color that almost ain't got no color. It look like my milk after I eat all the Cheerios out the bowl. I ain't about to complain, 'cause at least me and Ricky ain't gotta walk home today. Sometimes we run. So nobody won't mess with us.

"I hope Grandma take us to McDonald's, don't you, Luther?"

"Yeah," I say, and pull his Spider-Man backpack up on his shoulders. Ain't much in it but his stupid meds that sometime I forget to give him, some coloring, and a whole buncha sideways papers with the same alphabet letters he write over and over and some not even on the line. I remember when I had to do the same thing. Kindergarten got on my nerves. I looked out the window a lot 'cause Miss Prince just said the same thing over and over and over. I wanted to say, "You must think we all dumb or something!" Plus she talked to us like we was retarded. Some days she was real nice and talked like white people on TV but then sometimes she would yell at us when didn't nobody even do nothing and she would pinch our ears or make us hum a song or stick our tongues out for like a lot of minutes or make us sit there and not move for like a year and then she would laugh and give us all hugs. She didn't teach me nothing except how to sit up straight and how to pay attention and not to point. I wish I coulda skipped kindergarten and went straight to first grade. I'm glad Ricky didn't get her and I ain't even seen her in the hallway no times, so maybe she went to another school.

I like second grade. I get to write real words. A lot of words. Writing is easy. And so is math. But math is funner. I like adding and subtracting. Borrowing and carrying. I don't gotta sit there writing so hard the lead on my pencil break or till my desk look like orange sand from erasing so much. And I don't gotta guess either. I see the answers in my head. Which is why I get A's in everything. I'm smart. And I can't help it. Sometimes I wish I wasn't, 'cause a lot of kids tease me. "Smart-ass!" My mama told me to kick they ass but if I do that I get in trouble and I don't wanna get in trouble and plus they got big brothers and sisters and some of them is Crips and Bloods so I just act like I don't hear 'em or like it don't bother me. It don't. I rather be smart than dumb any day. Ricky ain't dumb either. It just take him longer to learn.

Now that Grandma is closer she look weird. She got on that brown wig I don't like and I can see her gray hair going from one ear to the other like the headbands our mama wear. Grandma look like somebody whispering in her left ear. Something she don't wanna hear. Maybe when I tell her the question I got to ask my teacher today it a cheer her up.

"Hi, Grandma!" I say real loud so everybody can hear me. I bend down and open the back door and push Ricky in. We put on our seat belts.

"Hi there, my sweet boys," she say and then, "You two want to go to McDonald's?"

Me and Ricky just look at each other, then give each other high fives. We can't believe our grandma know what we be thinking. We like her. Then, at the same time, we scream, "Yeah!"

"What did you boys just say?"

"We mean 'yes,' Grandma," I say for me and Ricky. He just nod about ten times.

"That's much better. Thank you."

Then she don't say nothing for about three blocks.

"We gotta go home after McDonald's, Grandma?" My fingers is crossed 'cause I want her to say no.

"No, you boys are going to stay with me and your grandpa for a little while."

Me and Ricky give each other high fives again. But then I wanna know how long is a while so I ask. "How long is a while, Grandma?"

"It depends. It could be a week or a month or maybe even longer, I don't know right now."

I wanna know why we staying at her house for a while, so I ask, "Why we staying at your house for a while, Grandma?"

She don't say nothing at first, like she trying to come up with a good lie or something, like me and Ricky do when our mama ask us do we like her orange macaroni and cheese or what happened to those dollar bills in her purse. Before she get a chance to tell us the truth since we don't think Grandma would really lie to us, we pulling up to the drive-up window, but it's a long line and we at the back of it.

"Is her dead?" Ricky asks, like he's hoping he guessed right. "Did her OD like NoNo's mama did?"

"No, but she needs some time to do some things that will make her feel better."

"Drugs make her feel better," Ricky says.

"No they don't!" I say. "They just make her high and she act crazy and say mean stuff."

"She wants to stop," Grandma says. "What do you boys want?"

"McNuggets," Ricky says. "Please," he say, 'cause he just remembered we always supposed to say please and thank you when a grown-up asks you if you want something or if they give you something.

For some reason now I don't want no McNuggets. "I would

please just like a cheeseburger and fries, Grandma. Thank you. And our mama don't want to stop using drugs," I say.

"How do you know that?"

"Twinkle's brother told us. His name is Wally. He live on the first floor. One day he stopped me and Ricky by the elevator and he said, "Yo Mama gon' end up dead at the rate she going 'cause she don't know how to say no to them drugs."

"Does Twinkle have a job?"

"Yes!" Ricky says before I get a chance to say, "No she don't!"

"Her sell pussy. On Crenshaw."

"Shut up, Ricky!" I say.

"Please don't let me hear you say that word again, Ricky."

"You mean *pussy*?"

"Yes."

"Okay, but her do. I ain't lying. Mama said hers is better than Twinkle's 'cause Twinkle only get twenty dollars for her p-o-s-e and Mama said she get fifty for hers."

"That's enough," Grandma says.

I elbow Ricky to shut up. Sometime he say the first thing that come outta his mouth, which is one reason why he get in trouble so much in first grade. He live in time-outs.

When we finally get to the drive-up window, Grandma orders our stuff and a Filet-O-Fish and french fries for herself since me and Ricky know it ain't for Grandpa. He only eat fried chicken, tuna fish sandwiches, potato salad, beets, boiled eggs, bread sticks, Twizzlers, applesauce, oatmeal, and strawberry yogurt. And that's it. We know everything that go in his mouth, 'cause one time when our mama went to the drug hospital we spent all that time at they house and me and Ricky was big boys and helped Grandma out. Grandpa ate sitting up at the dining room table then and he knew who me and Ricky was. But since I got out of first grade, our mama said, "Pops is out to lunch," but that ain't the real name for what he got. Grandma told us but I can't remember how to say it. It's something some old people get when they can't remember. He can't even take medicine for it. Right now I'm smarter than he is and now he don't know who me and Ricky is. We done told him our names over fifty times. But we don't laugh at him. 'Cause it ain't funny not being able to remember a lot of stuff and when I get old and forget who my grandkids is I don't want nobody laughing at me. Plus, it just ain't nice to make fun of people.

And then I get a rainstorm! "Grandma, since you the biggest mama over our mama, when she come back to pick us up this time, why don't you 'Just say no'?!"

"Yeah! I mean, yes!" Ricky just have to say louder than me.

"Because I can't just decide to keep you boys. You belong with your mother. She loves you. And I love you too."

She don't know what she talking about. I seen love on TV and it ain't never happen like that in our apartment. But I'm little so I just keep my mouth shut so I don't be disrespected my grandma.

She hand us our food and we wanna wait to eat it when we get home. Grandma usually always talk to us when she driving but right now she just driving so it probably mean she got a lot on her mind. That's what our mama always say when we be saying something to her or ask her a question and she don't answer. "I got a lot on my mind, some stuff I need to figure out, so please don't bother me right now." And we didn't. I wanna take away some of the stuff running around inside my grandma's mind so she smile, so I say, "Guess what, Grandma?"

And she say, "Yes, Luther?"

"Today it was my turn to ask Mrs. Wilkerson any question I wanted, 'cause she told us, 'There are no stupid questions,' so you wanna know what I asked?"

"Well, of course I do," she says.

"Not me," Ricky say.

I pop him upside the head.

"Yes, I do. Yes, I do!"

"I asked her, 'Why fish don't have feet?'"

"Well, that was a good question. And what did she say?"

"She said because they don't walk. They swim and they use fins to swim through the water."

"That was a good answer."

"I know. But I got sixty-three other questions I wrote on a piece of paper I wanna ask her before second grade is over."

"That's just wonderful, Luther. You can also ask your grandma some, and if I don't have the answer, we can find it."

"But you don't got no computer," Ricky says.

"I don't have a computer," Grandma says

"Can we get one?" I ask. "Please, Grandma, please?"

"And can we get a puppy?" Ricky asks.

"We only staying awhile, Ricky. Puppies turn into dogs and they bite."

"Grandma needs a little time to think about just what we can and can't do right now, until we get everything figured out. Do you understand what that means?"

"I do," I say.

"I don't," Ricky says.

"Don't worry about Ricky, Grandma. I'll explain it to him."

When we get to Grandma's, Nurse Kim is telling her something about Grandpa. I sit on the couch. Ricky go back to his room to play. Grandma just nod her head up and down. Nurse Kim is fine. Even I know that. And she got nice round breasts I would like to touch, and I don't even know why. She always wear red lipstick and her hair is black and hang down past her shoulders. Our mama said, "That ain't her real hair. It's a weave. I don't know who she think she fooling." I think our mama only say that 'cause almost every lady in our building got a weave, and sometimes our mama sew or glue 'em in as long as they bring they own hair. I don't care if her hair is a weave. It's pretty. I don't think our mama like Nurse Kim 'cause she prettier than her even though I seen pictures of our mama when she was prettier than Nurse Kim is right now. Our mama told us, "She ain't no real nurse. So don't go getting sick around her, 'cause she won't know what to do." I was thinking about pretending to be sick just to see for myself. And so she would maybe touch me. I wanna know if her hands is warm or cold. Plus, she smell good. Like pears. And she always be very nice to me and Ricky. Our mama said, "She nice to you 'cause she get paid to be nice to everybody in Mama's house." That is not true. Grandma pay her to come over here and be with Grandpa so don't nothing happen to him. I think this is called a job.

"I wrote a story about a cat who can bark. You wanna read it, Nurse Kim?"

"If I didn't have to be at the nail shop I would love to read your story, Luther. Next time. I promise. You're such a smart little boy."

I didn't like her saying I was a smart little boy. I'll be a teenager in five years and a few months, I'm starting to wonder if Nurse Kim really like me or not. She is not friendly enough to me like I am to her. But I say bye and go play with Ricky. I sit down on the bed. He doing bicycles with his legs. I hear Nurse Kim say bye but I know she probably mean to Grandma. When the phone ring, I hear

Grandma say Miss Tammy's name. And then real loud she say, "She's having a what?" I know that probably only mean two things: somebody having a baby, or a surprise birthday party. Where we live, babies ain't never no surprise. I like Miss Tammy, but I thought when a lady get old like her she can't have no more kids. I think those eggs that make babies hatch expires (I learned that word today!), just like milk. Maybe some of her eggs is still fresh.

She is nice to us and let us swim in her pool all the time when we come over to Grandma's. She also gives us snacks and juice. No Pepsis! She the only white person we know. I think I like white people if they be like Miss Tammy. She funny. And Grandma say Miss Tammy is her best friend. Me and Ricky like the way she make tacos, too. Our mama don't like no white people. "All they want is your money," she say. But I always wonder why she be getting so mad at them, 'cause she ain't never got no money. I lay my head down on Ricky's pillow and take a nap, I guess, 'cause when I wake up it's almost dark.

I go out to the living room and Ricky already out there, coloring. Grandma is reading a lot of pieces of paper that somebody wrote on in cursive. She don't look like she like what she reading.

"What you reading, Grandma?"

"It's a letter from your uncle Dexter."

"That's the one I don't know 'cause I was not born yet when he moved, right?"

"Right."

"Where he live at again?"

"He *lives* in a place called a prison. Somewhere you never want to see the inside of."

"What he got to say?" I ask. I know I probably didn't say it right and I hope she don't make me fix it 'cause sometime I don't know how to fix it and sometime I just wanna say it any way it come out.

"I don't know yet. But I want you and Ricky to know this. If you ever answer the phone and they say, 'Collect call from Dexter, will you accept the charges?' I want you to say 'No,' and then hang up. Do you understand me?"

I nod. So do Ricky. But neither one of us know what *collect* mean. And right now, we don't wanna know.

Dexter

April 3, 2001

Dearest Ma:

   Thank you so much for the monetary reinforcement! And the envelopes and stamps. As you can see, six of them are on this letter but the reason it has taken me so long to write is because we've been on lockdown. Which means nothing moves until the white man says it can. It's also the reason why this letter is written in pencil. Somebody got stabbed with a ballpoint so . . . but the good news is we were just made aware that in the next 3–6 months, many changes are being made here, so please make note of them: 1) as inmates we will no longer be able to accept any property (none) from our families. It will all be done like a depository bank, so to speak. You will be able to deposit funds directly into my account (I'll send you the account information as soon as it's assigned) from which I will be able to purchase all of my necessities; 2) we're finally getting computers which come with printers so no more problems trying to decipher my handwriting or anything that's unclear, although I will have to sign up to reserve them; and 3) I will be coming up for parole again in three months. (I speak more about this later in this letter.)

Guess what? My feet grew! So if at all humanly possible, could you please send me another pair of <u>all white</u> sneakers (size 12) in the next couple of weeks because I'm renting another dude's size 12s for $3 a week—$3 I cannot afford right now, but otherwise I'd be walking around in flip-flops. I sold those 11s to a Mexican who wore a size 9 ½ but he didn't care. I took his money anyway which is how I'm paying for my sneaker rental and it was like Christmas because it afforded me additional trips to the snack machine (I'm addicted to bubble gum), and I was able to stock up on soap, lotion, deodorant, and toothpaste which I sorely needed. I was also able to buy five new (used, of course) paperbacks too. I finished reading "Dianetics" and "The 7 Spiritual Laws To Success." They're both in tune with most of what's been missing in my life. I am learning a lot more about why some of the things that led me here happened the way they did—for instance: going to prison for a crime somebody else committed and making me the fall guy by simply being in the wrong place at the wrong time. I admit I have anger issues, which is why I'm still taking Anger Management classes. However, I know, too, that all I can do is be grateful for the present, prepare as best I can for the future, and forgive and forget the past. Have you ever heard of Iyanla Vanzant? You should check her out, Ma, she has her hand on the pulse of the black man's problems. Although she deals with a lot of issues that plague people in general. There's quite a few white dudes in here who like her too, but not a single Aryan (ha ha). Before I forget, would you be able to send me a cheap watch (under $40 and please remember to attach the receipt and don't take it out of the box) because someone stole mine and we get tickets (fined $2) around here for not being on time for work and our classes. My so-called (now ex-) girlfriend—Skittles—(I'm not sure if you remember meeting her but don't even try) sent me a stopwatch by mistake. I had to cut her loose. Not only was she missing a few links, but I found out through a reliable source that she just had a baby by some other dude. Talk about loyalty.

Question: Have you been reading my letters? I'm not accusing, but sometimes you don't answer my questions, questions that I think deserve an answer, but it's all good. Anyway, if you recall, a few months back I sent you a copy of the District Judge's opinion regarding my civil case wherein the Judge described the conduct of the CDC officials as unconstitutional. I will say this, though, the U.S. District Court failed to review a State Prisoner's pro se civil rights action, filed under 43 U.S.C. 1984, in accordance with Fenton v. Gomez, 404 U.S. 520, 521 (1993), in which they violated a prisoner's right to access the Appeals Courts. I won't rehash all of the details again, Ma, however I just want to say that I'm still litigating this case because I feel I have rights to due process and equal protection of the law. As you know, I've spent the past five (5) years learning how to become an attorney, answering motions, and conducting discovery by mail. As I write this I'm waiting for a District Judge's ruling on my motion for Summary Judgment I prepared on behalf of another inmate. Some of my motions have been quite effective in that a few charges have been overturned.

I forgot to ask: How are you? And what about Daddy?
I know he's not going to get any better and hopefully I'll
be out of here before he leaves this tangible world and enters
that celestial one. I tried calling Quentin but he's blocked
all collect calls, which basically means he doesn't want to
speak to me because with his lifestyle who else could he
possibly know that would be calling him collect? I write him,
but of course he never writes me back. Did I miss another
wedding? Last time I checked he was on Wife #3. I think he's
confused about his manhood. I also think it's rude to block
collect calls because what if there was an emergency?
I haven't spoken to or heard from Aunt Arlene in almost two
(2) years and Uncle Rodney forced Aunt Venetia to stop
accepting my calls, against her faith, I might add. He has
never been fond of me, and the feeling is mutual. He seems
untrustworthy, as if he's always had another agenda.
Anyway, sorry for going off on a tangent. As you can tell,
I try not to call you and Daddy every week. I know you're on
a tight budget so I have tried to cut you more slack than
anybody. Anyway, Trinetta's home phone was disconnected
the last time I tried to call and I found out the hard way that
you can't call a cell phone collect. How is she, by the way?
When you see her next, tell her if she's wondering where
Luther's daddy's been hiding, he's in here. He just got
transferred from Folsom. Armed robbery. He's a giant, at
least 6'4" so he shouldn't have any problems in here. He was
always ridiculously stupid. It's a shame, but there are at
least four dudes in here I used to go to high school with. Do
you remember Scotty Blanchard, who lived six doors down?
We used to play together until they moved to the Jungle. He's

in here for Murder One. I don't know what's happening out there in the real world but black men are swelling up these prison walls.

Which brings me to the other reason for this letter (I mentioned earlier), which I'm trying to keep short, but some things I just have to say because you can only say so much in a 15-minute phone call. It's about my parole hearing. I know we've been through this process a number of times already, but I have to keep trying and it's my responsibility to remind you of the formalities just in case. So here goes. When I go before the board in three months, I'm going to have to be able to demonstrate (prove) that I have family and/ or community support in order to get paroled. I need to have in writing that I will have someplace to stay, that I may have a job waiting for me (I'll need your help on this one), I'll have a few funds available to me in a bank account, as well as transportation home. It would help a great deal for me to get as many letters of support as possible from family members, friends, and acquaintances, people who knew me before I found myself in here, e.g., like Miss Tammy across the street. (She didn't write one last time I went before the board, but I always thought she liked me. Would you ask her for me before I bother sending another letter?) I don't have very many legitimate people I can ask and even though I know Aunt Venetia and Aunt Arlene have issues with me, as Christians, I hope they are at least willing to forgive me for my sins and show some faith in me when I write them again. Please put in a few good words about my progress. Quentin pretends like I'm not even his brother, which is unfortunate, but blood is blood. One day he'll realize that. Anyway, I'm enclosing a sample copy of various things they can say about the positive aspects of my character and why they believe I'll not be a threat to society. I've added and embellished some things which are handwritten in the margins to help them. Please have photocopies made and distribute them and once they're returned to me I will deliver them to my Case Manager and he will then provide them to the Parole Committee. Time is of the essence, but you know the drill. I've read my complete file (except for the things they black out) and this time my psychological evaluations are up to par and my counselor's reports are stellar because I haven't had any run-ins with anybody. I have stayed out of trouble and done nothing except read law books, the thesaurus, encyclopedias, and books that inspire me and stimulate my mind—again, like the ones I mentioned at the beginning of this letter. If all goes well, and they accept my plan, I could be out of here in three to six months.

I hope you will let me live with you and Daddy until I get on my feet (it has to be a minimum of 180 days), because I don't have anywhere else to go. I'm going to have to find a job, which is often one of the hardest things to do when you're a felon, but my parole officer might be able to help me. They don't trust us around money, that's for sure, and we can't be bonded. But please keep in mind, Ma, that I feel like I am rehabilitated. This institution hasn't contributed to it one drop. I have had to fill in the missing parts from every source available to me. The thing that seems to hold a lot of people back in here is they spend more time debating about the wackiest stuff when none of them know what they're talking about because they didn't do the research and so they can't prove their point. I know I said that first time I was in here, but this time is different. I was young and cocky and thought I was invincible. I felt like I was entitled to things I wanted just because I wanted them. Prison has given me a Ph.D. in correcting my false sense of what I think is owed me. Nothing. I value my life more now. I've got two kids I don't even know and who may not even want to know me. I'm just glad I didn't kill anybody. I don't suffer from that kind of anger. Rage is closer to it. Anyway, I hope you haven't forgotten that I can build anything and fix anything.

I also want you to know that I get A's in all of my online law classes and I would really like to be in a position to help a lot of men like myself who got a raw deal because of our racist justice system. The problem I'm having right now is this: I need two textbooks for my law class but they cost $200, and of course I don't have that kind of money. I was wondering if you would be willing to <u>loan</u> me the money until after I become gainfully employed upon my release at which time I would be more than happy to repay you with interest? The sooner you can let me know, the better, because I can't register for the classes if I can't afford the books.

Did you read my letter where I told you some dudes jumped on me? For absolutely no reason I can ascertain. I had to get four stitches on my chin. I can't begin to tell you the violence you see in prison. I have to take a shower with my shoes on just to be prepared to run should something go down and we have to move fast. Of course, the one time I was washing them, some dude got stabbed, which is how I got athlete's foot. Things could be worse.

When I do leave these prison walls behind me, I'm still going to bring a lawsuit against the Attorney General of the State of California for violating my constitutional rights. (I've enclosed all of the documents I'm going to file just so you can see that I know what I'm talking about. It makes a good case if you take the time to read through them.)

I would like to assure you that I've learned that experience is the best teacher but it gives you the test first, and the lesson last. For nine years I've had people telling me when to wake up, when to sleep, how to sleep, how to walk, talk, and dress. They even tell me when I can study the law.

Please send me some photos and give Daddy a hug. Until next time.

Your loving son,
Dexter

P.S. I tried calling you three times last week but somebody just kept hanging up on me. Was that Daddy?

August 15, 2001

Dear Dexter: I just got a new computer and I can't believe how it corrects your spelling and grammar (which I certainly could use help on) but this letter will not be brief and will take as long as it takes to make my points. First of all, I am not sending you $200 for any law books. I want to know how you think you can save other black men when you have yet to save yourself? It seems like all you guys either become black militants or Muslims when you're in prison for a while and then it seems okay to blame all your problems on the white man and the racist justice system. This is probably why you haven't passed your parole board tests or whatever they call it the last three or four times you've gone before them. It amazes me how you still haven't taken any responsibility for what you've done. I'll be glad when you stop blaming it on Buddy, but it's not going to get you out of there. You have convinced yourself that you're innocent after all these years, even after being caught. Don't you think those parole folks can hear and see that based on your attitude you aren't the least bit sorry for what you've done but more sorry that you got caught? I've told you this for years, Dexter. Your daddy and me did not raise you to mistreat anybody and that's what you did. I am also sick and tired of hearing about your innocence. I also know there are a lot of men in there who aren't guilty, and they fight long and hard to get their wrongful convictions overturned. I see them on CNN a lot. But you seem to suffer a little bit from amnesia, because you were breaking the law long before you got where you are now, so I wish you would stop playing the victim. Have you ever thought about that woman? If she has nightmares about being carjacked every time she parks her car in a big lot? How scared she was, not knowing if she was going to die or not? You may have ruined her life and yet all you can think about is your future.

Do I read your letters? Yes and no. Some of them are too long and they're boring because all you talk about is Dexter. I don't want to be a lawyer and I don't understand all those legal documents you keep sending me when I've asked you not to. Do you remember Miss Lillian on the other side of the street where Scotty used to live? Well, two of her boys are locked up too. One's in San Quentin, and the other one not far from here. We used to talk about how proud we were of you boys and were sure the three of you would end up in college. Now we compare what you all write about in your letters from prison, and guess what? Their letters sound just like yours. Your world is the one that stopped, not folks out here, but you act like we don't have anything better to do than read your six- and ten-page letters where you just go on and on talking about your problems and how bad life is in prison as if anybody can do something to change it. I can't. I'm not apologizing for what I'm saying and I'm not going to lie. You are my son. You are thirty-four years old and you have spent eleven of them behind bars. And here we go again making promises about how you plan on cleaning up your act when you get out. I want to believe you but it is hard to believe something until you see it.

So I'll ask you again. Please stop filling up these letters describing all your fantasies of learning a new language and buying stock and all your business ideas and where you might like to live one day since the United States is not a good place for black men to make it. If this were true, Dexter, why don't you tell me in your next letter why there are millions of successful black men in America. Did somebody just hand them a college degree? Did somebody make them eat some anti-prison food or something? And I want to know how you think you can practice law if you've been a convicted felon? And how in the world am I supposed to help you find a job? And especially while you're still in prison? I'm not an employment agency, Dexter, and even if I were to ask someone, the first thing they're going to want to know is something about your background, your education, what kind of skills do you have, but more important than anything is if you're presently employed. This doesn't mean I won't keep my eye out for something.

I've got a lot on my plate, too, Dexter. Your sister has abandoned her kids, so Luther and Ricky are staying here until she resurfaces, but she's going to have to be clean in order to get them back. I'll go to court if I have to. Right now, Luther sleeps in your old room, and if the boys end up staying here, I don't know where you would sleep. To tell you the truth, I can't handle any more drama around here. I thought you had a choice about going to one of those halfway houses when you got out, which is where I really think you should go.

If you aren't getting rehabilitated in there, maybe by the time you get in front of that parole board, if you were to finally show some remorse, maybe they would see that you did just exercise bad judgment, that you're not a heartless black man, and if you can prove to them that you realize how valuable life is, that you have learned something about common decency and that the world doesn't revolve around you, something me and your daddy tried to teach all three of you when you were growing up, maybe I'll get a chance to see you soon. I'll do what I can, when I can, but I can't make folks write letters of support for you if they don't believe you are ready to be honest and civilized when you get out of there. I'll pray that this time things work out, and if so, I'll be more than happy to drive there to pick you up, but until then, try writing your sister and see if you can talk some sense into her unless you're only interested in saving black men.

As you can see, there's no money order in this envelope because I spent it on those sneakers. They should be there next week. You might have to use that stopwatch for a while or just ask somebody what time it is because I cannot afford to send you another watch. These kids cost money, and nobody in this house is rich. I don't even think I'm middle-class if you want the truth. It was nice of you to remember to ask about your daddy in your long letter, and just to fill you in, I'm trying to do right by him but his physical and mental health continue to decline. Everybody thinks it's time to put him in one of those places but I'm not sure I

can do that yet. Add to worrying about him, now I've got
Trinetta's kids here and I don't have any idea how long they're
going to be here. These kids weren't in my budget, which is
another reason why my money is funny. If Trinetta doesn't clean
up her act I might have to go down to the county to ask for some
help. Something I'm not good at.

Anyway, I'll send what I can when I get my income tax return.
I haven't filed it yet, because I've been too busy to get over to
H&R Block. Take care.

Love, Mama

P.S. We haven't been taking any pictures, which is why I didn't put
any in this letter.

P.S.S. I didn't mean to write this much, but my computer helps me
say what I want to say a whole lot faster than a ballpoint.

Betty Jean

I t's only been six long weeks but it feels like a year. I live in the laundry room and kitchen. I have never been crazy about cooking, but these kids think I'm their personal chef.

"Grandma, can you make us macaroni and cheese with fried pork chops tonight?" "When you gonna make us another peach cobbler, Grandma?" And so on and so on. I am teaching them how to appreciate vegetables, and not the kind they're used to eating, which they told me always came from a can. Broccoli scared them at first because it was green. I steamed it. Of course they could eat corn on the cob every day if I let them. And rice. Plain white bread, which they roll up into little balls. I can't look when they do that.

I think they must stare at the soap, because it's still dry after they take their baths, right up there with the washcloths. And toilet paper? I have had to show them how to count off no more than five sheets at a time and if there's a lot going on, flush, and then repeat it. They now know how to use a plunger, which they don't like, especially since they're not strong. I've bought them a whole new wardrobe at Sears. That zero balance is a thing of the past now, but they're worth it.

They also want my undivided attention, especially when I'm

reading or trying to watch *Access Hollywood*, CNN, or *Touched by an Angel*. I have never heard "Grandma" so many times in a single hour, but the thing I love most is it's because they're curious. They want to know everything about everything. A lot of this stuff I'm clueless about, because the world changes when you're not looking, which is why I didn't exactly tell Dexter the whole truth about buying a computer. I bought two. I didn't even know Sears sold computers but Lucinda from my job told me I would be making a big mistake sharing one with kids, because they lose their mind clicking those keys and the next thing you know the screen will go black, which means it's a virus and all of your important stuff will be gone. Forever. Right now all my important stuff is in a plastic case I got from Target, but I took her advice. The boys have shown me how to Yahoo. This means Tammy and me can sell those encyclopedias at our next earthquake or tremor or regular weekend yard sale even though I'm running out of stuff to sell.

Speaking of Tammy, she's been having her share of tremors across the street and up there in Montana. I swear family seems to cause you more problems than total strangers. Why is it the only thing people seem to fight over is money? And why is it that some folks want what they're not entitled to? We haven't had time to share her fears and misgivings, because she's over there wishing on a star, hoping Montana knows what she's doing and that Trevor, the Academy Award winner of 2025, will get a real job and the two of them will move out and live happily ever after. I've got ten dollars that Tammy'll be turning Max's room into a nursery in six months.

Although me and the kids have gotten somewhat of a routine down to a science, in the back of my mind I'm still hoping this setup is just temporary, which is why as soon as the boys finish their breakfast and Nurse Kim gets here, after I drop them off at school, I'm going over to Trinetta's apartment to see for myself what the hell is going on.

It takes me a couple of weeks before I'm able to pull into the parking lot of Trinetta's building because of all that occurred last month on September 11. It has been hard to accept how the world changed in a single day. I don't know what it all means but I know this kind of tragedy doesn't happen in America. But it did. And I've had nightmares of those people jumping out of those tower windows ever since. I am praying this never happens again. I am praying for all the people who died. I am praying that they catch those terrorists who planned this.

Since I don't see Trinetta's Taurus I suppose this means that Dante or whatever his name is must still have it, so I pull into her space. My heart is starting to pick up pace as I head toward the doorway. I used to have a key but they've changed the locks to this front door so many times, I just press the buzzer and wait.

The building is a bluish gray and not really all that bad, considering. There's grass and trees and even a little playground for the kids. But this neighborhood is still rough. Bullets fly through the air around here, sometimes in broad daylight. I don't know how Trinetta let these kids walk home from school, I don't care if it is only two blocks. To a child, it could feel more like two miles.

No answer. I press it again. No answer. I wish I knew that Twinkle girl's real name. Or at least her last name. What I do know is she's on the same floor and just down the hall. When I see two hip-hop-looking guys with baseball hats on turned backwards charging down the stairs, they open the door, hold it for me, and then one says, "Hello, ma'am," and the other one says, "How are you, ma'am?" I'm both shocked and surprised.

"I'm fine. Thank you for asking, young men."

I look at the stairs. Then at the elevator. Trinetta lives on the second floor. I take the elevator. The way these kids have been running me ragged, I cannot afford to aggravate my knee. I'm fighting surgery as it is. I press "2" and am pleased at how clean it is. These stainless waffled walls are free of everything except shine. Some folks take pride in what little they do have.

When the doors open I walk straight to Trinetta's apartment and stand there, trying to prepare myself for her bullshit. If she's in there, I'm not going to say a single solitary word and I'm not going to give her a chance to say anything either. I'm tired of excuses and apologies. I'm just going to turn around and leave.

Right before I knock I realize I hear kids running around and laughing on the other side of this door. So I tap. When it opens, a civilized-looking black man is standing in front of me. "May I help you with something?" he asks.

He does not look like Trinetta's type. He doesn't look like a drug addict. He looks like he has a job. Whoever he is, if she let this son of a bitch bring his kids up in here when I'm taking care of hers, I'm going to slap her into next year as soon as she steps in front of me. "Is Trinetta in there?"

"She doesn't live here anymore."

"Since when?"

"We moved in a little over a week ago. That's all I know. Is there a problem?"

"No. There's no problem. I'm sorry for disturbing you."

"You're not the first and I'm sure not the last person who's been here looking for her. But you look like kinfolk. And a worried one."

"I'm her mother. And don't know where she is. But thank you again."

"Good luck finding her, and I hope she's okay."

After he closes the door I walk down the hallway and just start knocking on one door after another until a woman I know who has to be Twinkle opens hers. "Hello," I say, "I'm sorry to bother you, but I'm Trinetta's mother. Are you a friend of hers?"

"Come on in, Miss Betty Jean! I'm Twinkle. I've heard so much about you but never had the pleasure of meeting you. Come on in!" She opens the door for me and I am shocked at how nicely decorated this place is. I'd swap this place for mine in a heartbeat. This doesn't look anything like Trinetta's apartment. It's calm in here. She also doesn't look like a drug addict, or a ho, if there is such a look. She has on a white T-shirt with jeans and sneakers. This is why you can't believe everything that comes out of a child's mouth.

"Have a seat. Can I get you a cup of coffee?"

She also doesn't sound like a ho or like she's from the streets, and if this is what a ho's den looks like maybe I'm in the wrong field. I sit down on her leather sofa. It's teal, a color I have always loved. She's got a rug to match. Everything else is beige and olive green. "No, but thank you, Twinkle. I'm wondering if you have any idea where Trinetta is."

"Indeed, I do. You mean she didn't tell you her and Dante were moving to Atlanta?"

"Atlanta?"

"Yes, indeedy. She told me you were keeping the kids over

there until she cleaned up her act—if you get my drift—and Dante's rapping career jumps off."

"Oh, did she now? Would you happen to know Dante's last name?"

"Of course. It's the same as Trinetta's: Luckett. You don't know your own daughter's married name?"

Married?

"I didn't know she took his name."

"How are the boys doing?"

"They're fine."

"Ricky is taking his meds, I hope?"

"Yes, but I'm going to get them rechecked soon."

"That's a good idea. Tell him and Luther that Auntie Twinkle sends her love. And bring them over anytime you need a break. My kids are about the same age."

"How many do you have?"

"Three. All girls. But they go to Catholic school. Their daddy pays for it. You sure you don't want a cup of coffee? It's Starbucks Verona!"

She looks at me like she could use some company but I shake my head no and stand up. "Have you heard from her since she left?"

"Not a peep. She said she'd be in touch once they got there."

"Well, if you happen to hear from her, would you please let her know I stopped by?"

"I will. That's kind of low for her not to tell you she was bailing and especially not to even say goodbye to her own damn kids. My bad. Sorry for swearing, Miss Betty. But Trinetta's been playing hard a long time and it's about time for her to get her act together. The state was going to take my girls, which is when I decided to stop spending so much time on the street, if you hear where I'm coming from, but Trinetta seems to be having a much harder time. Dante'll help her get it together. Even though he's got other issues I don't want to speak on right this minute."

I have no idea what she means, but right now the fact that my daughter is somewhere on an interstate highway with a man I don't know who's supposed to be her husband is enough to hold me for a while.

Trinetta

Get off at this exit coming up, Dante. I gotta pee."

"Can't you hold it till we get to the next gas station or rest stop?"

"I been holding it for the past twenty-six miles."

"Then why didn't you say something when we passed that rest stop?"

After he asks that he passes the damn exit and I just cross my arms. Sometimes, I don't know why I married his ass. He's stubborn as all hell and everything has to be his way or no way. I love him but it's hard for me trying to figure out how you can love somebody who gets on your damn nerves. He got his good traits but right now I can't think of none. Oh yeah. He got skills. He can sing pretty good. And his beats be serious. Some of 'em explode. He's almost handsome but there ain't no way in hell I'd have no baby by him. I'm through having kids. Three is plenty and I'm lucky I ain't got no stretch marks. Luther and Ricky is better off with my mama for the time being, until I get my act together. Noxema was a mistake, so it's good that she with her daddy. Don't nobody but Dexter know who Luther's daddy is and Ricky's daddy OD'd before he was born. Me and him was deep into it when I found out I was two months pregnant and it took me a month to taper off, which is why Ricky had to be put on medication. I feel bad about that but one of the nurses told me he was fortunate. He didn't have to go through no withdrawals, thank God. I wasn't doing nothing when I was carrying Luther, 'cause that's when I was still in my right mind. I was going to Los Angeles City College. Then I got stupid. Started running with the wrong folks. Then here come Ricky. I was clean during the whole nine months I carried Noxema. And they was the longest nine months of my life.

I am a terrible mother and I know it. They deserve more love than I'm able to give them right now. I believe in my heart that if it wasn't for them, I probably woulda been dead a long time ago. Kids give you a reason to live. But you gotta have something to give them. I ain't exactly no role model. Although I would like to be. One day.

"Where your phone at?" I ask Dante.

"Who you need to call?"

"Twinkle. I ain't talked to her since we left and I wanna say hi and see how she holding up without my company and plus I wanna know if she registered for cosmetology school like she said she was. She don't never do half the shit she say she gon' do."

"You should talk," he says, and hands me his little tacky Nokia. I been trying to get him to break down and buy one of those Palms but he too cheap. Which is probably one reason why he got a few dollars in the bank. He ain't no dummy. I picked that up when I first met him in rehab a couple of years ago. That's where we fell in love, and I guess I married him when we got out and both of us relapsed. To this day I don't remember marrying him. But he said we did. So I guess we did. I still ain't got no ring.

It's hard to stop using drugs just 'cause you want to. And last year me and Dante started dipping and dabbing again. But when he got busted with a little too much on him and was sentenced to nine months, somebody was looking out for him, 'cause it got thrown out of court. That's when he told me he was done. I wasn't. So he bailed. This made his second trip back to his parents' house, and I promised him I wanted to stop for real this time and I wanted to go back to school and see if it wasn't too late to finish that dental tech program even though I ain't that interested in teeth no more, or maybe I could find another trade that might be a little fun, 'cause I for real want to see what it feel like to be straight for more than a month and pay my bills and do right by my kids, and he gave me this one last ultimatum. So I took it.

I take the phone and dial Twinkle. "Bitch, why come you didn't tell your mama you was fleeing and abandoning your damn kids?"

"And I miss you, too. Ho."

"Come on, Trinetta. This is pretty fucked up. How could you just up and leave your kids with your mama?"

"You just asked the same question twice."

"And you ain't gave me no answer. Where in the hell you and Dante at?"

"I don't know. We only been on the road three days, 'cause he had to help his mama move and he was working on the car."

"You mean y'all driving that raggedy-ass Taurus all the way to Atlanta?"

"Dante put a new engine in it. He know how to fix anything and we ain't had no problems."

"When you gon' be in Atlanta?"

"When we gon' get to Atlanta, Dante?"

"A day or two. Tell Twinkle I said hey."

"Dante said hey, and he said we'll be there in a day or two. Guess what? We stopped and saw some crocodiles yesterday."

"Fuck you and a crocodile. You did hear about that 9/11 shit, didn't you?"

"Of course I did, Twinkle. It's like the shit you see in sci-fi movies. I just hope no terrorists come to Atlanta."

"You simple as hell, Trinetta. Anyway, your mama came over here worried as hell and you need to call her to let her know your stupid ass is still alive."

"I will."

"When?"

"Today."

"When, today?"

"Right after I hang up."

"Who you guys staying with in Atlanta?"

"Dante got a cousin down here who got connections in the whole rap scene."

"Yeah, right."

"I ain't gotta lie. Just stay tuned."

"And how long you planning on being in Atlanta?"

"Until Dante's rapping jumps off into full swing."

"You high?"

"No, I ain't high. I told you before I left. I'm chilling on that front."

"Call your mama."

"Wait. Did you sign up for school?"

"Yes I did. I'm too old to be on the streets and I told you I was tired of it. Plus my kids' future means a lot to me. They done seen too much and I don't like what they've seen. Anyway, call your mama. And don't be taking no shortcuts. Them rednecks will chop you and Dante into little pieces with the ax they keep in the back of their pickup and nobody'll ever hear from y'all black asses again."

And she hung up.

"Dante, this time I mean it. Get off at the next rest stop or gas station. I don't care which. Now, I gotta do more than pee."

He pulls into a Chevron. "I'm gon' run over to that Jack in the Box. You want a taco and some curly fries or something?"

"I'll take a cheeseburger and curly fries."

"Just one burger? We not stopping again until we see that sign that say WELCOME TO GEORGIA."

"Then make it two. I'll stock up on drinks."

As soon as I get out the car I walk over to the building where the bathroom's at and pray nobody's in the ladies' room, but when I get closer I see that both red dials say OCCUPIED, and I stand there for a few minutes and then a few minutes more and finally when a dude comes out of the men's bathroom I run in there and lock the door. I go into a stall and sit down on the toilet and get my stem out of my purse and put it between my legs, then I get my stash and lighter out of the zipper part and try to hang my purse handle over the lock but it keep falling on the damn floor. I don't bother to pick it up, 'cause it ain't nasty in here like it is in the ladies' room plus this won't take but a few minutes. I put a small rock inside the tip and light it. I roll the stem around until it start melting and then I lean back so the liquid won't drip out and burn me and tip it back and I inhale the clouds until they disappear and I hold it until I'm where I belong, which is right here inside heaven. I could run to the moon right now if I wanted to. But I know Dante might be looking for me and I swear to God I love that man and I can't wait for us to get to Atlanta and get our life in fifth gear. I wrap my stuff up and put it back in my purse and wash my hands and run out of here.

I can hear Dante rapping before I even get close to the car. He got one of the CDs on he burned. He got a lot of CDs of him rapping. Some of 'em weak. In all honesty, I think only a few of 'em is really worth listening to. And Dante like to rap loud, more like he screaming, like he trying to make sure you hear every word he saying. But sometime he ain't saying shit, and sometime some of the shit he be rapping about don't make no damn sense. I pretend like I like it just to build up his confidence. It's a lot of people out there who think they deep but only be hitting topsoil. Don't put no dent in nothing. I think Dante is more impressed with hisself than anybody. He sing much better than he rap and he sound kinda like that dude Mama and Mr. Butler used to listen to when I was little, the one that got caught with another dude in his car back when it wasn't cool and he ended up cripple, but I can't think of his name right now. If Babyface and L.A. Reid is still producing new singers and if Dante's cousin got the hookup with them, Dante might have a better shot making it as a singer.

I really don't want to do drugs and wish I could stop and feel just as good. But it don't work that way. If I had to chose between sex and crack, shit, ain't no comparison. Crack is way better. But it's probably 'cause I ain't doing nothing constructive with my life that gets me high. It's millions of people out here who don't even smoke cigarettes and they can deal. There's people who don't drink. Don't smoke weed. Or, like they said in rehab, some people like experiencing life with a clear head. It just seems like no matter what I do, I always make bad decisions and shit gets all fucked up and then my moms likes to cuss me out, and I don't think it was her that called CPS on me but if she did, I'd understand it. I know my kids is safe with her and I hope they don't end up being too much of a burden. Dante don't know I bailed on the kids. He think it was my mom's idea. I know she over there struggling, with Mr. Butler being out of it and everything. I call him that because he ain't my real father.

That's a book right there. I ain't supposed to let on I know but of course my Big Mouth Aunt Arlene was the one who told me when I was around thirteen.

"Trinetta, come sit on the couch next to me, baby. I've got something interesting to tell you and I think you're old enough to handle it."

She made me promise not to tell Mama and I told her I promised not to tell if she gave me fifty dollars. Which she did. I tried the whole blackmail thing again after seeing it on TV, but it didn't work on Aunt Arlene.

"Go on and tell her," she told me. By then I was about sixteen and had stopped giving a shit. I told her I wouldn't dare hurt my mama like that, throwing some bullshit in her face that may not even be true. And that's how we left it.

"Where the drinks at?" Dante asks when I get in the car.

"Oh shit, I forgot to get 'em 'cause there was a long-ass line."

"Do I look like I'm fucking stuck on stupid, Trinetta?"

"No."

"Look at your eyes. All dilated. And why you sweating? It ain't even hot. Let me see you eat that cheeseburger."

"I ain't hungry right this minute."

"You can't be doing this shit when we get to my cousin's house. He go to church and everything. You understand me?"

"I do. And plus I ain't got much left anyway."

He just rolled his eyes at me. "I'm going to get some water and Pepsis, plus I could use a Snickers. While the tank is filling up, if it ain't too much trouble, could you clean off the windows while I'm gone?"

"Can I use your phone again?"

"Who you gotta call now?"

"My mama."

"Why don't you wait till you come down?"

"Because I can say what I really feel like this."

He hands me his phone and I get out of the car and pop the

blades out and then dip the squeegee in the water and dial her number.

"Ma, it's me, Trinetta."

"And where might you be?"

"Ma, look. Please don't be mad at me but I just felt like I had to get outta L.A. before something bad happened to me and I didn't want the kids to be messed up and me and Dante just decided leaving would be a smart thing to do and even though you may not believe it he don't do drugs and he trying to make sure I stay clean and that's what I'm working on and I just want you to know that I love my kids and if you could give me six months or a year at most I should have my act together and then I can come back and get 'em."

I stand there, waiting for her to blast me, but I don't hear nothing. "Ma? You there?"

I still don't hear nothing. Did she just hang up on me? Hell, I don't much blame her. So I just finish cleaning the windows and when I hear the nozzle snap 'cause the tank is full, I put it back in the slot, get back in the car, and try my damnedest to eat at least one of those curly fries.

Lee David

Shit!"

"What're you shitting about now?" this ugly fat woman who is lying next to me just asked.

She puts her arms back around me and squeezes me, then kisses me on my forehead.

I want to say, "I don't know." But for some reason, I can't.

Shit.

Venetia

How are you holding up over there with those little ones, BB? Before you even answer, I was thinking, I haven't seen you or the boys in months and of course I've been so busy getting tutors lined up for the SATs coming up and of course Rodney's in Hong Kong and we had to put Pepper down so it's been too quiet around here during the day and I was wondering if you and the boys would like to come out for an early dinner on Saturday? I want to try a new recipe I saw Paula Deen make on the Food Network unless you're lactose intolerant because it's full of cream and cheese and butter and if I remember correctly I think Arlene told me you're trying to watch your weight and if this is the case I totally understand and I could make something lighter but something even the boys might enjoy."

"Slow down, Vennie? My goodness. You just said a mouthful and I don't know why you have to give me so much information at once. First of all, I'm sorry to hear about Pepper."

"Thank you, BB. Fourteen years."

"Are you okay? You sound a little frustrated."

"I'm fine. Just a lot going on." If I were to be honest I would tell her the truth. That I'm bored and lonely and I think my husband is cheating on me and all of a sudden it's starting to hit me that my kids are going to be leaving home soon and I don't know what in the world I'm going to do with myself. My world has revolved around them and Rodney, and the years go by so fast, you think things will just stay the same. But they don't.

"I have to find out if Tammy can look after Lee David. And for your and Arlene's information, I am not on a diet even though I'm very aware that I could stand to lose twenty pounds but that would also put all three of us in the same boat if we were to be honest and Paula Deen's meals are like eating a heart attack on a plate and I like my fat in small doses. Anyway, I'll call you back."

After I hang up, I realize that I feel sorry for BB in a lot of ways. She has too many burdens. First Lee David and then one by one her children disappear for all the wrong reasons. My sister doesn't deserve the weight of the things she's carried, and now she's got her grandkids to care for. I know she doesn't make much working at that hotel and I just wish she'd gone to college like the rest of us. Her life probably wouldn't have been such a struggle. But she doesn't complain, which is what I love about her. Even still, one person can only do so much, and I don't think BB recognizes that just because her own children have disappointed her, she might look at this as getting another chance to do a better job with her grandchildren. She was a darn good mother, considering she had to work. I think living in the ghetto is harmful to children. They see too much. Learn too many of the wrong things. And now that she's getting up in age, I don't know if BB remembers how much time and energy it takes to raise youngsters and how she's going to manage by herself. If Rodney didn't have the accountant monitor our spending, I'd be happy to help her out. But as things go, I'll just do as much as I can without having to answer for it. Those boys deserve as many opportunities and advantages as possible. After all, we're family.

I have to say that I do not for one minute think Lauren and Zach are picture-perfect. But I've done my best to be a good mom and it was my choice not to work. Well, it was actually Rodney's. That was one of the many terms and conditions of our getting married. This was the one I didn't mind. Of course, I'm proud of them and not the least bit worried about their futures. They are both honor students and participate in and do all the things they're supposed to that will ensure they get into top colleges. It's one of the reasons why, when the SUV hits sixty thousand miles, Rodney leases a new one. All I do is drive. I think we're on the eighth or ninth, I forget.

It may sound elitist, but it has been proven that the quality of your life improves with a college degree. I admit I never put my MBA to good use, but I don't regret getting it. And who knows, after the kids are gone, I might consider entering the workforce, since I'll have nothing else to do. This may be selfish, but I'm crossing my fingers the kids stay local. USC or Pepperdine or UCLA would be perfect and I would even be willing to drive all the way out to Irvine if it became necessary, or if push came to shove, UC Berkeley, and Lord knows I would be one proud mama should one of them get into Stanford.

I am forever jumping ahead of myself when what I need to be doing right this minute is getting the kids' dirty clothes and damp towels out of their hampers before they start to mildew. Or heaven forbid if the dye from one should soak into something that can't be bleached out. That's right up there with scraping my fingernail on a chalkboard. When the phone rings I scamper into the laundry room, drop the bundle on the floor, and grab the portable. It's BB. "Are we good to go?"

"I wish we could, Vennie, but Tammy can't watch Lee David on Saturday, because she's going to see Shania Twain."

"Well, that sounds like fun. Oh well, I was also going to invite Arlene and Omar over, too."

"I am not in the mood to spend more than five minutes with her right now, so this is a blessing."

"I know she can get on your nerves. But she means well. She's just so outspoken and doesn't seem to know that her opinions aren't always right or important and that we don't always need to hear them because she does not seem to exercise good judgment or tact when it's important and I don't think she's ever going to change which is why I just choose to love her the way she is."

"It would be a different story if she turned that camera on herself. I mean, come on. She walks around like her life is so perfect. It's like she's watching TV without cable."

"What?"

"Never mind."

"Did she tell you about Omar?"

"No, did something happen to him?"

"He's getting that Lap Band."

"What he needs is a lap dance. What exactly is a Lap Band, again?"

"It's when they go in and cut out part of your intestines so you eat like a mouse and get full and you lose like ten pounds or more in a week's time but Lord only knows what happens to all that flab and you and I both know that Omar could stand to lose an easy hundred pounds but the funny thing is that he hasn't even told Arlene but she was snooping around in his room like she always does and they say you can't see for looking and anyway she not only found all kinds of evidence but has since even heard him talking on the phone to some girl about it."

"I know Omar isn't talking to a real girl?"

"You know Arlene can't let on she knows what he's up to but I think it's exciting and what she needs because can you imagine what her life will be like if Omar were ever to move out and get married?"

"No, I can't. Anyway . . ."

"Wait. Talk to me. You are always so quick to get off the phone and I wanted to ask you a couple of things about the boys."

"Like what?"

"Well, for one, school's almost out and I was wondering how they were going to be spending the summer."

"I'm working on that."

"Well, BB, I just wanted you to know that if they're interested in going to one of those sleepover summer camps for a week or two where my kids always cried when I picked them up I'd be more than happy to pay for it and if there are day camps they can attend while you're at work I'd be more than happy to cover that and pick them up and take them."

"Are you serious?"

"Of course I am."

"Why in the world would you be willing to do all this, Vennie?"

"Because I want to and because I care and because I can and those kids deserve to do things they may not have the chance to do because it costs money and I have a lot of it and I know you don't and it would make me feel good. Plus, my kids have complained about not being able to drive since they've had their licenses, and without telling me, Rodney bought them both cars so my services have already started to diminish."

"Well, it's time, don't you think?"

"Time passes too fast. Anyway, that's one thing."

"What else?"

"Those boys need to go to church. At least a couple of times a month. I don't think I need to explain the obvious, but I would be more than happy to take them with me and the kids."

"This is very thoughtful of you, Vennie. And let me say this: I agree with you about church and it's been bothering me every night they say their prayers, but I can't afford to have someone watch Lee David on Sundays. So thank you. I'll go to Sears to get them a few nice things to wear."

"They don't have to wear suits, you know."

"Good. And as far as camp goes, I know the boys would love it. I admit I was just starting to worry about what I was going to do about them this summer. Ricky just asked me the other day if he could go to swim camp, too."

"Great. So take this off your worry chart. Before you go, how's Lee David hanging in there these days?"

"He's not doing any better but not doing any worse either, although I had to get him a wheelchair."

"Poor fella. I give you credit for not putting him in one of those dreadful places and it's a good thing you have Nurse Kim there. I'm sure she's a big help."

"Yes, she is."

"It also helps to put a little more faith in the Lord."

"Don't start, Vennie. We were doing fine."

"Just one more question. Do you have any idea where Trinetta might be or if and when she's planning on coming back to get the boys?"

"No to both of your questions."

"That child has been lost too long. She definitely needs Jesus in her life."

"Maybe one day she'll let him in. Anyway, before I say good-bye, how's everybody in your house doing?"

"Everybody's doing just fine."

"And Rodney?"

"He's good. He's been in Thailand for two weeks, and might not make it home for Lauren's performance which I'm sure you know nothing about but she's singing in a school play that I cannot remember the name of right this second."

"I thought you said he was in Hong Kong?"

"Did I?"

"Yes, you did, Vennie. Is something going on you don't want to talk about?"

"Not really. Well, maybe. Rodney and I have been going through a rough patch and I believe it's because he's never at home and I feel more like a single parent than anything and when he is home he doesn't seem to appreciate how much work it takes to make our home run as smoothly as a successful business but he seems to take it for granted and he doesn't seem to take prayer all that seriously anymore and were I to check his cell phone I am worried that I might find out information that could threaten our marriage so I prefer not to look at all. I will be honest with you, BB, and say this: I'm worried I might end up in this big house alone by the time the kids graduate, and because I never planned for nor anticipated a future without my husband in it, I don't know what I would do by myself."

"Vennie?"

"Yes," I say, because it's obvious she can hear these tears rolling down my face, and I'm a little upset because I usually do such a great job of pretending like everything is just perfect around here and inside me. I only do it because I don't want BB or Arlene to worry about me and I truly believe in my heart that God will do His will and fix this or show me a new path. "I apologize for being overly dramatic, BB, and worrying about something that hasn't even happened yet."

"Are you sure you're okay, though, Vennie? I haven't heard you sound like this before."

"I'm fine. The kids are hanging out with their friends and I think since I've missed four periods that I'm just getting super-emotional and overly sensitive. But please don't say a thing about this to Arlene, okay?"

"I won't."

"Promise."

"I promise."

"Wait! You know what, BB? I'm curious about something that you may not think is urgent, which it isn't, but I was just wondering since you don't go to church anymore, do you ever read your Bible?"

"No, I don't."

"Why not?"

"Because I already know the whole story."

"Do you hear what you're saying, BB?"

"All I'm saying is I don't believe a lot of the stuff in the Bible because too many people have altered it and put their spin on it, and of course I believe in God, but I prefer reading novels since I don't know how they end."

"But what about Jesus?"

"What about Him?"

"He died for our sins."

"And I'll always be grateful for it, which is why I try not to commit any. That's my other line and it looks like the boys' school. I'll call you back in a few days."

And she hangs up.

Principal Daniels

Is that you, Betty Jean?"

It doesn't look like I'm registering in her memory bank, so I decide to go ahead and let her off the hook.

"Warren Daniels? I was your sons' seventh grade science teacher. I also doubled as a basketball coach, which is why we never won any games."

It's probably this bald spot and gray hair and perhaps a little bit of a belly that might be throwing her off.

"It's nice to see you after all these years, Mr. Daniels. I'm here to find out why I was called and asked to come in to see you."

"Well, first of all, we tried phoning their mother but the phone was disconnected and you were listed to call in case of an emergency."

"Is there an emergency? Did something happen to one of my grandsons?"

"No. Nothing has *happened* to either one of them. But Ms. Jenkins has been complaining about Ricky's behavior. He's being disruptive and rude, making it difficult for her to conduct her class. Is everything all right in their home?"

"No, it isn't."

"Is their mother having the same type of problems she's had in the past?"

"That would be a yes."

"So, does this mean the boys are in your care?"

"They are."

"How long have they been living with you?"

"A few months."

I push my chair away from the desk and shake my foot a little because it's fallen asleep. This is how it usually starts. The grandparents are put in a position where they are often forced, mostly out of concern for the well-being of their grandchildren, into substitute parenting, and it's usually because the parent has fallen prey to the lure of drugs. It's sad to watch grandparents, who should be preparing for retirement, take on this burden, which is exactly what it is, but they do it so that their grandchildren don't have to be raised by strangers.

"Well," I say, pushing my chair back, "Luther, as you probably know, is an excellent student and he doesn't appear to be displaying any negative behavior. Ricky, on the other hand, has been quite a handful and our counselor, Mrs. Barlow, has done her best to work with him but to no avail. Which is why she asked that I reach out to you."

"Exactly how is he being disruptive?"

"Well, when Ms. Jenkins calls on another student, Ricky interrupts and yells out the answer. He likes to clown. Do things to get attention. He's also not being very polite. He told Ms. Jenkins to kiss his you-know-what."

"He said *what*?"

"I wouldn't make this up. He seems to be having a hard time sitting still. We see this kind of behavior all the time in children whose parents were drug users. Have you been able to maintain his medication regimen?"

"Well, Luther has been handling it since it appeared that this was just one of his responsibilities. But I'm not sure if he's run out. He hasn't said anything."

"Although Luther is a very bright little boy, Betty Jean— forgive me, may I call you Betty Jean?"

"Well, it's my name." She chuckles a little bit, which helps make this easier.

"Good. As I was saying, Luther is only in second grade, and notwithstanding how bright he is, this is still quite a lot of responsibility for a child his age."

"I agree. I'll start giving it to him myself. I did refill the prescription."

"Then perhaps Ricky's dosage might need to be reevaluated. After all, he is a growing boy. Our school psychologist thinks it would be in his and everyone's best interest if he were retested."

"Okay."

"Do you have temporary custody of your grandchildren?"

"You mean have I been to court or something?"

"Yes."

"No."

"So, are you aware what this means?"

"It means I'm taking care of my grandchildren until I can figure out what else to do."

"Have you been in touch with anyone from the Department of Social Services?"

"No. I've been thinking about it. But I wanted to wait until I had a better idea when my daughter might be coming back."

"Do you have any idea when that might happen?"

"No."

"Well, let me tell you a few things you might want to do, but this is strictly outside of my professional role, do you understand what I'm saying here?"

"I think so."

"Let me close my door first."

"I'll close it," she says, and gets up and does just that. She may be thicker but she's still a good-looking woman, and a good woman to take on this burden like too many women her age are being forced to do. She sits back down and moves her chair closer to the edge of my desk. I wish it were more impressive. Like oak or mahogany, something besides this maple veneer that's peeling at the corners.

"For starters, as the grandparent, without temporary custody, you have no legal right to make decisions for your grandsons. Were they to get sick, you don't have legal authority to take them to the doctor or a hospital. You can't register them for school, though of course you are authorized to pick them up and drop them off, but until you go through the expense and the legal maze of getting temporary custody, you're in for a bumpy ride."

"So what exactly are you saying?"

"Let me put it to you this way, Betty Jean. You have to learn how to play a game with the folks who work in these state agencies, especially those who are supposed to be there to help you. They can often feel like your worst enemy. And don't be fooled just because they're black. Which is why . . ."

Betty Jean is looking at me like we're on a game show and I'm about to give her the answer.

"First, let me ask you this. Are you a God-fearing woman?"

"Well, I'm a Christian if that's what you're asking."

"Would you be willing to exaggerate or stretch the truth or lie if that's what it would take in order to get some kind of help for your grandsons?"

"I suppose I would."

"Well, for starters, I'm going to get the nurse to give you the form that will allow us to have Ricky retested, as long as you make sure his mother's signature is on it, do you understand me?"

"I don't see that as being a problem."

"Good," I say, and stand up to shake her hand. I notice there's no ring on her left finger and I don't like being too forward or presumptuous, so I simply ask, "Are you a widow or divorced?"

"Neither," she says. "He's got Alzheimer's. Not doing so well now."

"I'm so sorry to hear that. You might not want to let those folks down at SS know this. Do you work?"

"I do. I was considering taking a short leave but I need the money more than ever. I'll figure things out. I don't have the same level of energy and patience I used to have, and Lord knows they need attention, and right now I'll do whatever I have to do to prevent them from going into foster care."

"I understand. It's like starting all over. Some grandparents don't have it in them."

"I don't have a choice. They didn't ask for this life."

"Ain't that the truth? I mean, well, just keep us apprised of how things go, when your status changes, and we'll do our best to help Ricky."

"Thank you, Mr. Daniels."

"It's Warren," I say, and stand up and walk around the desk to open the door for her. "Your sons should be in their midthirties if memory serves me right?"

"It's serving you right, Warren."

"How are they doing?"

"They're both doing just fine. And thank you for asking."

"You're quite welcome. And it's so nice to see you after all these years. You look wonderful. Time is definitely on your side. Now, don't be shy about calling should you have any problems or questions about any of this. Here's my card. I'm here to help."

Social Worker

S orry to have kept you waiting so long. It's a madhouse around here as you can see. Go ahead and have a seat while I review your preliminary chart, Mrs. Butler."

"You can call me Betty Jean."

"I prefer Mrs. Butler, if you don't mind."

She nods. *Why is it just because I'm black and female they think they can act like we're automatically connected? We are not friends. This is my job. I work for the State of California, and I don't want to be their friend. I can't wait to hear this one's story. After twenty-three years working in Child Services, I've heard it all. I glance up at Betty Jean. She's dressed like she could have a credit card at a department store. Her daughter's most likely a drug addict. Either crack or heroin. I'll bet myself a chocolate chip cookie with walnuts it's crack. She's nowhere to be found. Or maybe comes and goes. Regardless, she's probably out there on the streets, giving blow-jobs to pay for her disgusting habit and Grandma here probably got tired of watching everybody she loves be destroyed and took the kids or her daughter abandoned them. From the looks of this one, I'll bet a latte the daughter bailed. Betty here doesn't look like a happy camper, but she also doesn't look like she's ready for what we call our "second shift."*

"So, how long have the children been in your care?"

"Four months."

This woman is lying through her teeth. Almost all of them do. I wouldn't be surprised if it's only been a weekend.

"And what took you so long to come to Social Services?"

"Because I wasn't sure how long I'd have them."

Yeah, right. I'll bet the daughter's living in a Section 8 apartment with her boyfriend who's also a drug addict and they're collecting checks and getting food stamps, which they also sell. It's a B movie.

"Are you sure now how long they'll be living with you?"

"No, I'm not."

This just means she needs another source of income for as long as she can. She probably needs a new car. Maybe behind in a few of her bills. Something. The grandmothers are usually just as bad as their trifling-ass daughters, but will they accept any responsibility for it? No, they don't. Most of them are uneducated and just as ghetto as their grown children. Which is where they got it.

"So your daughter has a substance abuse problem."

She nods a yes.

"And what might her drug of choice be?"

"Crack cocaine is all I know about."

Cookie!

"It says here that your daughter's whereabouts are unknown?"

"No, I know where she is."

She's lying.

"And where might that be?"

"In the streets."

"And what about the children's father?"

"What about them?"

"Oh, so there are two?" *Surprise, surprise.*

"That's how it looks."

"Do you know either of them?"

"No, I do not."

"Do you know their whereabouts?"

"If I don't know them, how would I know where they are?"

Who in the hell does she think she's talking to? I'm the one who determines if I'm going to get her any help at all, so she needs to chill.

"I have to ask these questions."

"Un-hun."

"Excuse me?"

"I didn't say anything. I just want to know how long it might take for me to get some kind of help for my grandsons."

"It's the reason we're going over your information now. To determine if that's even going to be possible."

"I'm having a hard time including their expenses into our budget is all."

"It says here that you own your own home."

"Yes."

"Which means you could borrow against it if you needed to."

"We already have a second."

"Don't we all? So your husband's retired?"

"Yes."

"He was much older when you married, I see."

"What's that got to do with anything?"

"No need to get defensive, Mrs. Butler."

"I'm not. But out of all the things on my application I just find it inappropriate for you to say that."

"My apologies. I also didn't mean to imply that there was anything wrong with marrying someone with such a huge age difference."

"I agree. Which is why I married him."

Bitch.

"How long has he been retired?"

"Two years."

"And how's his health?"

"Excellent."

"And yours?"

"Excellent, also."

"So, this means he gets Social Security?"

"Yes."

"As well as a pension?"

"Yes. A small one."

She is trying too hard to impress me with this woe-is-me hard-luck story.

"I see you've worked in the hotel industry for quite some time."

"Yes."

"In what capacity?"

"I work out of our in-room-dining department."

"So you deliver food to the guests, then?"

"Yes."

"Which means you should do okay on tips."

"It depends on the season."

"Based on your salary, it doesn't look as if you report those tips. Or am I being too presumptuous?"

"I report them."

She must think I just look like a damn fool. I worked as a waitress during college and wouldn't dream of reporting a penny in tips. But whatever.

"And how many years before you retire?"

"I was considering taking early retirement in two or three years, but that may not be possible now. If I become legal guardian of my grandchildren, I'll probably need to wait."

"Well, that's sort of putting the chicken before the egg, wouldn't you say?"

"It's the reason I'm here. To find out if you can tell me which comes first."

I can tell I'm getting on her nerves. But part of my job is to make sure this isn't some kind of scam. That maybe she's just trying to get her grandkids so she can get a few extra dollars into the household. Plus, sometimes the parents don't even need our help. Betty here doesn't exactly look destitute.

"I thought as an employee of the state you worked in this department to help in the care of children, especially if it would prevent them from being put in foster care, which costs the state a lot more. Correct me if I'm wrong."

I try not to roll my eyes at her and keep reading.

"What shift do you work?"

"Morning."

"Then how will the children get to and from school?"

"I'll have to make some adjustments."

"Wasn't this the same problem their biological mother had?"

"What exactly do you mean by that?"

"Her adjustments didn't include the children and her arrangements weren't very carefully thought out or consistent, and had they been, these children would not be in your care, would they not?"

"And your point?"

"You could answer my question."

"Do you have children?"

"Yes."

"And it looks like you work every day."

"This isn't about me. I don't need financial help from the state."

"All I'm saying is that in order to survive in this day and age, to make a decent living, both parents usually work and there are many ways to get them to and from school, including after-school care. Does that answer your question, Mrs. Hunter?"

"No. But moving on."

"Let me say this. I'll do whatever it takes to make them feel safe and secure. It wasn't as if I planned this."

"I believe you, but it doesn't matter if I believe you or not."

"I'm not trying to convince you of anything. I'm just telling you why I'm here."

"Has your daughter ever disappeared like this before?"

"Yes."

"What's the longest she's been absent?"

"A week. Maybe two."

"What would you do if she suddenly reappeared and wanted her children back?"

"It depends on her situation."

"Well, I can tell you from experience, once they abandon their children, they usually appear out of nowhere and swear they're going to clean up their act, but it rarely lasts. Until your daughter gets treatment for her addiction, and can prove that she's been drug-free for at least ninety days, I suggest you file a petition with Family Court about getting temporary custody, at which time you come back to see us and we'll determine what we can do to help you at that time."

"So, you mean you can't help me even with food stamps?"

"Did I not make myself clear?"

"Very."

She gets up in a huff without so much as a thank-you for giving her a clue as to what steps she needs to take. She should be glad she has a source of income. Some of the grandparents that come in here are living on Social Security and food stamps. We are not a charitable organization. But they think just because they have trifling kids who didn't need to become parents in the first place, that it's our respon-sibility to pick up the slack. Everybody's got a sob story. I'm burned out listening to them. Burned out watching them act like beggars. I am tired of this job. Tired of being depressed all day long. Tired of not being able to fix everybody's lives. Tired of not breaking the rules and people hating me for it. Which is why I'm putting in for a transfer to a different department—any department—where no one is asking for money.

Quentin

Well, hello there, Mother. I'm calling just to see how you and Dad are doing."

"I'd have to say fair to middling."

"Is something wrong? Is it Dad?"

"No, it's not your dad."

"Then it must be you. Are you having health issues?"

"No, I'm fine."

"Then what is it, Mother? You don't sound like yourself at all."

"It's your sister. About four months ago she dropped the boys off for a weekend and decided to move to Atlanta with a fellow she's supposed to be married to and I haven't heard from her since."

"Then she's still using drugs, I take it?"

"What's it sound like, Quentin?"

"So that means you're taking care of them?"

"No, Quentin. I dropped them off at a group home."

"Is there anything I can do?"

"I could sure use some financial help."

"How much help?"

"I don't know for sure, Quentin, but three or four hundred dollars a month would be much appreciated."

"A month?"

"Well, you asked."

"You should be able to get help from Social Services in a situation like this."

"I've tried. They're not as helpful as you think. A lot of legal stuff, and lawyers are not cheap, and too many hoops you have to jump through. And then you just play a waiting game while they decide how you should or will be able to take care of your own grandchildren."

"I'm really sorry to hear this. Karen's mother went through this with one of her other daughter's kids. It was a grueling process, and finally, she just gave up."

"I do remember your telling me about that."

"So it sounds like you didn't fare any better."

"That social worker made me feel like I was responsible for the whole situation. As if I'm the one who made Trinetta become a drug addict. They make you feel low. And they make you feel like a beggar. But I'm not begging anybody for anything."

"And you shouldn't have to."

We are both quiet. I know I haven't given her a definitive answer as to how much financial assistance I can offer, but since I wasn't prepared for such a request, and because my circumstances are also changing, I need to be realistic and give this a little more thought.

I look out of our condo window. I can see three of our ten bridges. Portland is such a beautiful city. Crisp. Cold. Wet. Green. Hot. Clean. And water everywhere. Full of smart people. Of which I would like to think I am one.

"So, I hope you and Mindy are doing well."

"We are."

"So, what's the reason for this call?"

I snap out of my daze of gazing at the Steel Bridge, which is also my favorite. One of the reasons I don't call home as often as I should, and as often as I would like to, is because there's almost always some form of turmoil going on. More often than not, it's about my two siblings, both of whom have made some bad choices, the consequences of which I cannot undo nor remedy. Over the years, my impatience has turned into indifference, which is unfortunate because they are family. But their lives are like bad movies. You walk out before they end.

"Can't I call just to say hello?"

"Well, you don't usually call just to say hello, Quentin. So, go ahead, tell me your good news."

"Mindy and I are going to have a baby."

I don't hear anything for a few seconds and because I'm on my cell phone, I walk over to the window and sit in my burgundy leather chair. An airplane flies overhead. Perhaps this is the reason I lost my mother. I end the call and hit redial. "Quentin, are you there?"

"Yes, Mother, I'm here."

"Congratulations, to you and Mindy."

She doesn't sound excited at all. Which is understandable. Considering her circumstances. But I have no children and it would seem as if she could—considering how rarely she gets good news from my siblings—muster up some semblance of happiness. "Thank you, Mother. Mindy's a super gal, and I'm pretty sure she's a keeper."

"I certainly hope so. But you say the same thing about all of them until you divorce them, Quentin."

"That is so not true."

"Can you hold on a minute? I hear your daddy coughing and I want to make sure he's okay."

She drops the phone without waiting for me to answer. Over

the years, Mother has tried to make me out to be fickle when it comes to women. There may be a smidgen of truth to it because I admit to having made a number of bad choices, although I believe it's because I'm somewhat of a romantic. I can't help it if quite a few of the women I fell in love with, and the five I married, turned out to have flaws they artfully concealed that became intolerable. I'm getting smarter, and Mindy is proof of this. Mother also thinks I don't like black women, which is so not true. Can I help it if I happen to be attracted to white women? Is that a crime? She has gone so far as to question whether or not I wished I were white. Which is ridiculous. She thinks this simply because I tend to live in predominantly white neighborhoods (which I choose because they're safer), because I don't *sound* black when speaking, and because she doesn't think I have very many black friends, when in fact I have at least three. I am proud of my blackness. Very proud.

"Quentin, you still there?"

"I am, Mother, and let me say this. The best I can do for now is two or three hundred. Would that help?"

"A month?"

"No. Total."

"I'm grateful for whatever you can send, Quentin. I didn't mean to put you on the spot. But it's been hard."

"I can only imagine. Anyway, the other good news I want to share with you is you're going to get a chance to meet Mindy very soon."

"I know you're not coming to the hood for a visit?"

"Why would you say that?"

"Because you avoid coming down here except for weddings and funerals. At least that's the way it looks."

She's right. I don't like the ghetto. And never have. It's

dangerous and scary and it's the reason why I chose a college as far away from it as possible. I do not understand why Mother and Daddy still live in that pinched neighborhood on that ugly street in that same run-down house we grew up in.

"That's not true, Mother."

"When was the last time you were here?"

I'm thinking. I can't remember. I do know there was no funeral or wedding, whenever it was.

"Well, I'll try to be better, especially now that we're moving back to California!"

"Well, that's good news."

"Now that Mindy's pregnant, she really wants to be closer to her family, and they live outside of San Francisco, right across the Golden Gate Bridge in Marin County, so we're going to be moving back to California in the next three to four months. I've already joined a new practice, and of course Mindy's going to stay home with little Margaret. I hope you can take some pleasure in all of this, Mother."

"Nothing would make me happier."

And she hangs up.

Betty Jean

I n-room dining!" I yell after ringing the buzzer. I'm hoping there's no answer, because I'm just here to pick up their breakfast tray. I delivered it two hours ago. Walked in on something I do not understand. There were two women in the bed all snuggled up but it was a man who came to the door in his terry-cloth robe. Like always, I pretended not to see what I saw. I learned a long time ago not to judge but there are some things I just find hard to accept. There are a lot of freaks that stay in hotel rooms. And a whole lot of cheating goes on, too. I'm just glad I'm not in housekeeping, because people with money sure know how to trash a hotel room. And some of them are just downright nasty. It's hard to imagine how they live at home. On the other hand, most of the guests who stay here don't seem to have much respect for people who clean or deliver their food. Sometimes when I walk in I say, "Good morning," or "How's your day going so far?" If they're on their computer or talking to each other or just watching TV they act like they don't hear me or point to where they want their tray and just sign when I hand them the leather folder with the bill inside and then they hand it back, sometimes without even looking at me.

"In-room dining!" I say a little louder this time and press the buzzer again. The rule is, if there's no Do Not Disturb sign hanging on the door handle, we wait until we hear movement or they yell out, "Come back later!"

"In-room dining!" I say for the last time, only because Lorinda warned me before I brought up their breakfast that these folks were Russian and maybe even a part of the Russian mafia, so I should be extra nice to them. After I enter, I stop, lean forward a little, and say, "Good morning?" When I don't get a response, I walk into the large room and look at the king-size bed with the fake headboard that's nailed to the wall. The duvet, top sheet, and bath towels are piled up like a white mountain on the floor. That tray is sitting where I left it: on the big wooden table in front of the brown velveteen sofa. These folks use the furniture for things it wasn't meant for. There are grooves and scratches that will never come out until the hotel is renovated, which they've been promising they're going to do for the past four years. Sometimes I count cigarette burns on the carpet in nonsmoking rooms and dread lifting up the tray when it's next to the bed on the floor.

For some reason, I sit down on the couch and my left foot pushes the tray over to make room for my other foot. I look around. I have never stayed in a hotel. I don't know what it feels like to be waited on. I wonder what it feels like to call room service. I wonder what it feels like to come back and your room is clean. Bed made. Fresh towels in the bathroom. I don't really know why I pick up the remote control and press the red ON button. I click the channel button and stop when the screen is full of thousands of tropical fish swimming in what the announcer says is the Great Barrier Reef. I know this is Australia. I watch, for how long I don't even know, and when the fish become a blur of moving colors it's because of the tears that have suddenly started to run down my cheeks.

Even though I haven't told anybody, I'm scared. What if I can't handle all this responsibility? What if I've forgotten how to be a parent? It takes so much energy. What if I don't have enough to last? What if my daughter comes back next week or next year and wants them back? What if I die? What if I give them the wrong stuff like I did my kids? I don't want them to turn out like mine did. I want them to be proud, honest, dignified, civil, kind, and loving. I want them to be strangers to trouble.

And then there's Mister. I don't know how close he might be to going home. I know everybody wants me to just ship him off to one of those places, but I don't think I can. He's my husband. And I'm tired of folks telling me what they think I should do with him, like he's a pet that needs to be put down or something. He's my husband. I know I'm going to have to get used to him not being anywhere one day, but until that day comes, it won't kill me to be there for him.

I unroll the linen napkin and wipe my eyes on it. When I get up, I feel better even though I didn't know I was feeling bad. I just don't like to worry. It can wear you out and it doesn't fix whatever it is you're worrying about. This isn't even about me. It's about my grandkids. And they need me to take care of them and that's what I'm going to do. I hit OFF on the remote, pick up the tray, and leave. I take the service elevator down to the kitchen, where another order is waiting for me.

"Hi, Grandma!" Ricky says after jumping into the backseat and slamming the door like I've asked him a hundred times not to do.

"Hi, Grandma!" Luther says after doing the same, except he leans forward and kisses me on my ear first. He is such a sweet boy.

"Hi there, boys. And how was your day?"

"I was good, Grandma! I even got a Sharpie! See!" Ricky says,

and holds up a green one. I suppose the medication must be working, though I'm praying for the day when he can get off it.

"Principal Daniels wrote you a letter for me to give you 'cause
he don't have your address and it's in a white envelope in my backpack, Grandma. My teacher wrote one, too. I didn't do nothing—
I mean anything—bad or anything like that. I might get to skip
third grade and go to fourth."

"How would you know that?"

"I read both of the letters and they say the same thing. They
think I'm smart. And I am. Second grade is way too easy and it's
boring."

"Well, we'll talk more about this later after I have a chance to
read the letters, okay?"

"Okay."

"And you should never open mail that is not addressed to you,
Luther."

"But what about if it's about me?"

"It needs to have your name on the envelope."

"Well, that's silly."

"It is silly," Ricky says, then closes his eyes and drifts off. This
is what I don't like about this new medication he's on.

"Can we go to Disneyland for my birthday, Grandma? Please
please pretty please with bubble gum on top?" Luther asks me for
the third time in two days.

"Yes," I say, matter-of-factly.

"For real?"

"First I need to find out if Nurse Kim can go with us because
Grandma can't do all that walking and I want to be able to take
Grandpa with us, too."

"Goodie! Goodie! I hope Nurse Kim can go! Can I push
Grandpa in his wheelchair some of the time, too?"

"Yes, you can," I say.

As soon as we walk in the door, Nurse Kim jumps up from the recliner, where it is obvious she's been snoozing, and tries to act perky when she stretches out her arms for her boyfriend, Luther, to run inside them for his much-needed hug fix. Ricky is not aroused by Nurse Kim at all and just waves to her.

"Grandma said you want to go to Disneyland with us for my birthday and we can take Grandpa, right?"

Nurse Kim tries to act surprised. "You mean I'm invited?"

"Yep!"

"Maybe I can bring my new boyfriend."

"What new boyfriend?" Luther asks.

"Yeah, what new boyfriend?" Ricky asks.

"His name is Wendell."

"I don't like that name," Luther says.

"I don't like that name, too," Ricky says.

"Well, he's a very nice guy, but there might not be enough room for him anyway. We'll see."

"I just hope he don't—I mean doesn't—want to be your husband," Luther says, and then, "Because I want to marry you when I grow up. I will make a good husband and you will love me way more than him."

And he walks off to the back bedroom and Ricky follows him.

Nurse Kim just winks at me and tells me that Mister actually had a good day.

On Saturday morning, after washing and folding four loads of clothes, I carry the last basket down the hallway into the living room and can't believe I'm walking in water. When I look out toward the sunporch, there is Ricky watering the plastic flowers and plants from an empty Miracle Whip jar. "Ricky, what are you doing, baby?" I ask, trying to be very careful not to sound too worked up, which messes him up and then he gets wound up even more than me.

"I'm watering the plants, Grandma!"

"Well, I appreciate your help, but have you ever seen Grandma water them?"

"Nope, and that's why I'm doing it. We planted beans in a cup at school and Ms. Jenkins said all plants have to be watered or they won't grow. My bean is growing already. And I want to help your plants grow, too."

"Grandma really appreciates your help, Ricky, but these plants don't need water, because they're not real."

"They look real. How come they not real?"

That was a good question and I didn't have a good answer, so I just said, "Now that I know you're a good gardener, we can buy some real ones. How does that sound?"

"It sounds good. I can do a lot of things, you know."

"I know, Ricky. You make Grandma so proud I just want to hug you." And I do. And then I take that Miracle Whip jar back to the kitchen and put it back in the recycle bin. Ricky follows me, walking right over the wet floor without a care in the world.

"Ricky, are you good at mopping up water?"

"Yep," he says, and flies past me out to the back porch to get the mop. As I hold the door open for him, I hear the phone ringing.

"I'll answer it," Luther yells from my bedroom, where he's been curled on the bed watching cartoons all morning with his grandpa. When Ricky and I come back I ask Luther who it was that called.

"It was one of those collect calls from Uncle Dexter, so I hung up like we always do."

The phone rings again.

"I'll get it!" I say and reach for it. It's Dexter calling back. Which means it's important. I accept the call. "Hi, Dexter. Is something wrong?"

"Not at all, Ma. I've got great news. I'm finally going to be paroled!"

"Well, that is good news."

"Yes, it is!"

"How soon do you get released?"

"Well, that's the tricky part. Maybe two weeks but it can take up to another month. My parole plan is being sent to my parole officer, who has to look it over and approve it. He'll probably be calling you soon."

"Why would your parole officer be calling me?"

"Because he's going to have to review all of the rules you have to abide by having a parolee living with you."

"Who told him you were going to be living with me?"

"I did. Just for the first hundred and eighty days after I get out, find a job, and am able to get back on my feet. I thought you said I could, don't you remember?"

"No, I don't."

"Don't worry, Ma. You won't even know I'm there. I promise."

Nurse Kim

I do not like Disneyland. I didn't like it when I was little either. I do not like the giant Mickey and Minnie Mouse or Donald Duck and the rest of those suckers that scare little kids half to death when they walk up to 'em and hold out their thick rubber hands. And I can't stand the way Disneyland smells. Like hot syrup. Almost everything they have here to eat is sweet. And everywhere you turn there's nothing but little kids and enough strollers to fill a car dealership. And that music. Oh my God. Nothing but bells and organs and those damn accordions. Everything is a jingle. And that high-pitched singing never stops. What they could really use out here are a few good bars.

I just agreed to come so Miss Betty could spend some quality time with her grandsons and so they could escape the ghetto for a few hours and spend some time in a fantasy. I'm more than happy to push Mr. Lee around in his wheelchair, because he needs to inhale fresh air whenever possible. I'm not even going to charge Miss Betty overtime, because I know she's having a hard time manipulating her finances since these kids got here. She ain't mentioned nothing about when that trifling daughter of hers may be coming back, and even though I still ain't found no roommate and my rent is late and I might have to either quit this job or move back in with my granny, which Lord knows I do not want to do since she live way out there in Palmdale and I cannot deal with that traffic on the 14 but especially the 405 and plus she be all up in my business—even though I wouldn't have no business if I was to be living under her roof—it would be low of me to leave Miss Betty like this, so I think I might go on and put an ad on craigslist and pray I don't get another psycho.

I'm sitting on a bench under a little shade tree hoping to finish the last ninety pages of this Harry Potter book, which I cannot even believe I bought, 'cause it's pretty thick. But I love reading anything that could never happen so I figured what the hell, and Mr. Lee is dozing so I'm just turning those pages when Miss Betty walks over, limping, and says, "Kim, my knee is killing me. Would you mind if I sit here and you take the kids on a few more rides and then we can leave?"

"Not at all, Miss Betty." I fold the corner of the page I was on and drop the book in my purse. I take Luther's hand, which I dread, and that little Ricky needs a leash. I end up going through Space Mountain, Splash Mountain, and those spinning teacups I didn't think would ever fucking stop. Almost threw up floating through It's a Small World but I admit I did get a kick out of Pirates of the Caribbean after I downed one of my little bottles of tequila I keep in my purse just for times like this when I wish I was somewhere else but can't just up and leave.

After we get back to Miss Betty's house, I push Luther's dead head off my shoulder, since him and Ricky slept all the way, and then we lift Mr. Lee up the steps. He was out like a light, too. Once everybody gets settled in, Miss Betty comes out to the living room and collapses on the sofa. She pats the empty cushion next to her, so I sit. I know she's getting ready to tell me something heavy.

"It looks like my son Dexter is going to be living here for a few months," she says.

I don't say a word. But I'm thinking: Where the fuck is he gon' sleep?

"I do not know where he thinks he's supposed to sleep, but maybe he can fix up that room above the garage. He's handy, you know."

"No, I didn't know."

We just sit there a few more minutes and I know she wants to say something else.

"I wish he had somewhere else to go."

"I know. It's usually one hundred eighty days, unless they changed it."

"Oh, so you know."

I just look at her.

"Six months is a long time, and I just hope he doesn't cause me any problems or bring any mess to this house."

"Sometimes, when they get out, they either straighten up and fly right or do something stupid that violates their parole and back they go to the house with bars. At least Dexter didn't kill anybody."

"I suppose that makes me lucky, huh? Anyway, Kim, thanks for helping me out with the kids and Lee David today. Did you have fun?"

"I had a ball," I say. "I always loved Disneyland."

When I get home, I get my mail and toss it on the kitchen counter, since Cruella De Vil took her table. Ain't much left in here except my bedroom furniture, my burgundy velour sofa bed, which hurts your back if you sit on it too long, a twenty-five-inch

TV/VCR that I need my glasses to see unless I sit on the floor right in front of it. Cruella also had the cable disconnected, and since you have to be home for 'em to reconnect it, and I work during the day, and I ain't in no position to be taking any time off since I don't get paid if I don't work, I only watch old videos. Thank God I can read. And I got a fat fake-leather chair my granny gave me that's perfect.

After I microwave some Stouffer's lasagna and then take my shower I'm shocked shitless when the doorbell rings. Don't nobody visit me unless they call first. I make sure my robe is tied and peep through the peephole but you can't never recognize who the person is looking through these damn things, so I ask, "Who is it?"

"It's Ellory."

"I don't know nobody by that name. You must have the wrong apartment."

"Kim. I was Tierra's friend. Remember now?"

"What are you doing here? You should know she moved out."

"I'm very much aware of that. I just took a chance that you might still be living here."

"What is it you want?"

"I just wanted to see if we might have a cup of coffee or a drink one day and, since I didn't have your number, I just took a chance stopping by."

"What happened between you and Tierra?"

"She had issues I didn't exactly find attractive."

"Well, that makes two of us. Look, Ellis, I don't know you well enough to open this door, and I find this a little suspicious if you want to know the truth."

"It's Ellory, not Ellis, and I can understand your feeling this way. Let me say this: I enjoyed talking to you that day I was waiting for Tierra and I thought you were intelligent and beautiful and I was wondering if anything ever came out of that traveling nurse thing you were looking into?"

I crack the door open but do not remove the chain. I peek through the space and realize he's handsome and all but I am not about to let him in here just because he's wearing a suit. "You've got a good memory. Anyway, I applied and am just waiting to hear. Give me your number."

He hands me a business card. I glance down at it and I recognize that BMW logo but I'm still not about to let that influence my good judgment so I say, "I'll call you one day, but please don't ever come by my house again unless you're invited, okay?"

"I promise. It is not my style. Hope to hear from you soon. You have a good evening."

I push the door shut, walk over to the counter, put the mail inside my robe pocket, grab a nectarine out of the fruit bowl and a bottle of water from the fridge, and then drop his card in the trash under the sink because anybody stupid enough to sleep with Tierra can't come this way like I'm some sloppy seconds.

I pull my Harry Potter book out of my purse and put it in my lap after I sit in my granny's chair. Before I even open it, I decide I might as well get the depressing shit over with, so I get up and start flipping through all the envelopes I know are bills and just toss them on a pile. But then I come to one I know is no bill and I see that traveling nurse's organization logo on the top left corner, and I open it so fast I get a paper cut. When I read the first sentence, my eyes get big as plates.

Tammy

My brothers were still not happy with the settlement offer, which is why Jackson took it upon himself to get
on a plane and come to Los Angeles, I suppose to confront me. He had the nerve to call me from the airport an hour
ago to come pick him up. Which is where I'm headed now. I have
no idea what I'm going to say to him or what he's going to say to
me but what I'm really wondering is where in the hell he got the
money to get on an airplane that's not at an amusement park.

I didn't bother telling Montana her uncle was going to be a
temporary houseguest and I'm thinking that maybe I should've.
It might help her and Trevor speed up the move-out process since
they've pretty much worn out their welcome. Trevor is not going
to be anybody's movie star. Some people just refuse to admit that
they don't have what it takes. That their dreams may not come
true. But it's not the dream's fault. I can bear witness, but then
again, it takes some of us longer for the truth to click. Court reporting has turned out to be more enlightening than I believe
dancing ever would have, and I should win Academy Awards almost on a daily basis just for keeping a square face when what I
really feel like doing is grimacing or closing my eyes or screaming

at some of the gruesome shit I hear. And when they show pictures I pretend not to see them and just press those plastic keys a little harder.

When I pull up to baggage claim I see what looks like the shell of my brother. He's smoking a cigarette. He's also shrunk. Those jeans look like they once belonged to somebody else. He's like a blast from the past, as my son, Max, would say because he's wearing Reebok Pumps but the white leather is cracked and wrinkled at the toe. And even though it's dusk and the concrete overhead is casting even more of a shadow, his skin looks like a russet potato. What's left of his hair is thin and straggly, like some old hippie. I don't see any luggage but he's wearing a backpack that looks too heavy because it's hanging low on his back when he raises his hand up and waves. I was hoping to hate him, for all that he and Clay have tried to do to me to make me feel like Sister Dearest, but when I roll the window down and say, "Hi, bro," and he smiles at me as if I just rescued him from harm, my heart becomes a warm cushion.

He takes a long, final drag from his cigarette and then flicks it to the curb and doesn't notice how disgusting this is to the folks standing next to him. He's got too many bad habits. "Thanks for picking me up on such short notice," he says, and tosses his backpack on the backseat after he gets in. He acts like he wants to kiss me but isn't real sure if he should or not. So I bend over and give him a peck on the cheek, then squeeze his meatless shoulder. "So, this is my very first visit to the City of Angels."

"Welcome" is pretty much all I can think of to say. All I'm wondering is if I really just picked my brother up from LAX after not seeing him or Clay since Ma died a year after Daddy, which is going on five years. That's a long time not to see a sibling, but they didn't want to see me and threatened to disappear if I were to show up unannounced. I have never been one to go where I'm not welcome.

"I hope you're not upset because of my coming here this spontaneous and all, Tammy, but I needed to get away from Billings."

"Why's that?"

"I got myself in a little trouble."

"Can you be a little more specific, Jackson?"

He seems to suddenly start hyperventilating or something and then he calms himself down and while looking out the window says, "Would you mind if I smoked?"

"Yes, I would mind. You can't smoke anywhere near me the short time you're going to be here." This of course is better than a hint.

He does that "church is the steeple and this is all the people" thing with his fingers, which is giving me the heebie-jeebies, but I just wait to hear the latest episode of the ongoing saga that happens to be his life. You would think he would have changed the channel by now. "I owe some people and I don't have it and they're looking for me and I had nowhere else to go."

"So, you decided to come see your little sister for emotional support?"

He nods his head in slow motion. "Sort of."

"Are you some kind of drug dealer, Jackson?"

"No."

"I don't know if I believe you."

"Then don't."

"You are already trying my patience, Jackson. I mean, after years of trying to sue me and make my life miserable even though I gave you and Clay more than Ma and Daddy even left you now you call me out of fucking nowhere and ask me to pick you up at

the airport when you have never so much as picked up the goddamn phone to say, 'Hi, Tammy, we miss you' or 'How you doing?'
or 'Would you send us some pictures of your kids and are you still
married to that nigger?' No, you call me from the fucking airport
and ask me to stop doing whatever I was doing to come pick you
up and here I am and you sound and look like a drug dealer who's
fallen on hard times."

"I can't help how I look."

"Well, how is Clay doing these days?"

"Not so good."

"What is that supposed to mean, Jackson?"

"There was a fire in our house, Tammy."

"And what's that supposed to mean? Did Clay get hurt or
something?"

"He set it."

"What are you talking about?"

"He's been depressed a long while and he didn't try to get out."

"Didn't try? Or didn't get out?"

"The fire department got him."

"Are you sitting here telling me that our brother is dead?"

He nods again.

I say nothing. I am trying not to picture the house we grew up
in up in flames and my—our—brother inside it. I roll the window
down so I can breathe. And then start pounding my palms on the
steering wheel so hard it hurts. When I stop, I hear myself say,
"When did all this happen?"

"Four days ago."

"And you're just now telling me?"

"It was too hard to say over the phone, Tammy. I had to leave
before those folks got hold of me. Which is why I'm here."

He starts crying. Hard.

This feels like somebody else's nightmare I've been dragged into. A couple of hours ago I was planning on having a nice family sit-down with my daughter, who's six months pregnant, and the love of her life to tell them they have become a financial burden and are going to need to start thinking about making other living arrangements if at all humanly possible before that little girl arrives, because they have violated the terms of our agreement and I feel like they are taking advantage of me, and I don't appreciate it. But now, all I'm thinking is life is like a baseball game, and sometimes you can't see a curveball let alone trying to hit it.

"Where is he?"

"In my backpack."

"In your . . ." I turn to glance at that grungy backpack leaning sideways against the door and I turn away, unable to imagine my brother, Clay, six feet tall since he was sixteen, inside it. I don't realize I'm wailing at the top of my lungs until I feel Jackson's hand rubbing my right shoulder.

"I feel bad telling you this way. I feel bad that our brother did this to himself."

"Who made the decision to have him cremated?"

"Me, I guess. I didn't have much choice, Tammy."

"He could've been buried, Jackson. There are always remains."

"Nobody woulda showed up to Clay's funeral, Tammy, and I didn't have that kind of money and it was for the best."

"The best."

I put the car in drive, then slam on the brakes.

"How in the hell do you know who would or wouldn't show up to his funeral?"

"Because he didn't have any friends. And you know we don't have any relatives left in Billings."

"Where in the hell were you when the house was burning, tell me that?"

"At a bar. Word got to me pretty fast."

I pull out of the parking space and probably accelerate too much, because Jackson grasps the armrest. I feel like slamming on the brakes but I don't. "Why did you come here, of all places?"

"Because you're all I've got left."

"I'm really sorry to hear about your brother," BJ says.

"Me, too."

We are getting a manicure and pedicure and not because we need them, but because we both needed to get out of the house. BJ took the day off, something she hardly ever does, because the boys just left for overnight camp. They'll be gone a week. I personally think two would've been much better since Venetia offered to pay. But BJ wasn't sure how they would handle being away from home for that long. You never know until you try was my attitude but I didn't say it. Since the boys have been there, BJ hardly ever gets ten minutes to herself, except when they're asleep. I'm starting to know exactly how that feels.

"So how long is he going to be staying?" BJ asks, considering he's already been here two whole weeks.

"I don't know. He doesn't have anywhere else to go."

"He seems nice enough," she says, and takes a sip of her iced coffee.

"It feels like I'm grieving more for him than my dead brother, who just evaporated. Jackson is a loser. And he knows it. I can't even pretend I know how to save him and I don't know how to tell him, BJ."

"Does he have any skills?"

"None that I know of. But that's beside the point."

We both lean our heads back in the pedicure chairs that are massaging us and doze off.

"All finished!" the Vietnamese girl says after tapping me on my leg. I look over at BJ, who just opened her eyes and looks like she has no idea where she is. She needed this.

We put our feet in the paper slippers they give us and walk over to the manicure stations.

"We need to do this more often," she says after picking out her color. She chooses tangerine. I choose light pink. I don't know why, because I don't like pink.

"So, you want to hear the latest?" I ask her.

"Yep. And then you have to hear mine."

"Wait. It's not bad news, I hope?"

"It depends on how you look at it. I'm listening."

"Tanna has asked if she and Trevor can stay until after baby Clementine is born and—"

"Hold on. I know they're not really going to name that baby any Clementine."

"It's already a done deal, BJ. I personally don't like it because it reminds me of a cartoon I can't remember the name of for the life of me, and of course this is due to my disappearing hormones, which you know something about, but anyway back to the point: Trevor has gotten a real job with no future but a guaranteed weekly salary and he is studying to take the real estate exam like every other human being in Los Angeles who has no legitimate plans for their life, but at any rate, they have agreed to pay me a pittance while they save up and so they have bought four more months, I guess, but I don't know what it's going to be like having a screaming baby in the house or what I'm going to do with my chain-smoking, ale-drinking brother."

"This is like *As The World Turns*, isn't it?"

"One more pop-up and it's going to be more like *General Hospital*."

"Does your brother want to go back to Montana?"

"He has nothing to go back to. That's the problem."

"How old is he again?"

"I'm forty-six, so he has to be forty-eight or forty-nine."

"Well, Dexter's coming home soon and I can't lie, Tammy, I am not looking forward to seeing him. I know that's sad to say."

"No, it's not. It's not like he's been on vacation all these years, BJ, and you've already got a house full of people you're taking care of. The last thing you need is another dependent."

"You don't have to tell me. Plus, I don't know him."

"I don't know Jackson either. But what I do know is I'm being forced to embrace him like a family member since he is a family member but I almost feel like his aunt and not his sister."

"So what are you going to do about him, Tammy?"

"I don't know."

"Well, guess what's going on across the street from you? I'll answer that. Nurse Kim is leaving. She got accepted into that traveling nurse program."

"Shit."

"It'll be all right."

"How soon?"

"Seven or eight weeks."

"Wow. Where's she going?"

"She has no idea. And I don't think she really cares. She's still young enough to take chances, and if I was in her shoes, I'd be on a plane right now."

Arlene

You mean now that he's finally getting out you're going to let him live with you and those kids for the next six months?"

"He's my son and he doesn't have anywhere else to go."

"What happened to halfway houses?"

"They cost money."

"Oh, so you have to feed him, too?"

"First of all, Arlene, can you honestly sit here and tell me you wouldn't do the same for Omar?"

"Omar would not do anything that would land him in prison, so I can't even entertain the thought. I'm also standing, not sitting."

"The only reason I agreed to meet you for these nasty tacos is because you said you had something you wanted to tell me. I don't know why you couldn't tell me over the phone."

"Because ever since you've had those kids, we never seem to spend any time together anymore. Besides, some things are better said face-to-face."

"Like what, Arlene?"

"Can we finish our tacos first?"

"Let me say this, since it's been bothering me. You haven't

seen the kids in months and when you call you don't even ask how they're doing."

"How are they doing?"

"They're doing just fine, since you asked. Luther might get to skip third grade. He's bright. And Ricky is doing much better all around. He can draw anything."

"Is he still taking that medication?"

"Yes, he is. But he might grow out of it. Okay, Arlene, you've managed to show some interest in my grandkids, so tell me what you have to tell me."

"Wait a minute, would you? See how impatient you are? Who's watching them right now?"

"What?"

"Who's watching them while you're here with me?"

"Why?"

"I'm just curious."

"Montana. Tammy's daughter."

"Do you pay her?"

"That is none of your business. Why are you so nosy?"

"I'm not being nosy. It's called curious. No harm done. Anyway, have you heard from Trinetta or am I getting too personal?"

"No."

"Have you managed to get any help from the county yet?"

"No."

"Why not?"

"Because it's too complicated and they make you fill out form after form and still make you wait."

"So wait."

"Wait a minute. Let's back up. Who told you Dexter got paroled, Arlene?"

"He did."

"I know damn well you didn't write a letter for him?"

"Yes I did, Betty Jean."

I can tell she's shocked. I take a sip of my Pepsi. The only reason I did it was because Dexter had been in that place so long and he had written letter after letter begging and pleading me as his auntie to write to the parole board on top of telling me how no one believed in him, that he had no family support, that he's not young and stupid anymore, that people do change and he didn't want to have to spend another year behind bars for a crime he didn't commit. So I agreed to do it and lied to the parole board about how remorseful he is and how eager he is to rejoin us in the outside world and make a contribution to society, and that, in fact, he is ready to reinvent himself. I was somewhat impressed by his vocabulary and his knowledge of the law, but other than this, I didn't have a clue about what he was really capable of doing once he got out, and I still don't know. My hope was that he might be able to help Betty Jean with those kids until Trinetta brings her stupid ass back home and finishes raising them. Dexter failed to mention that he was planning on moving back in.

"You never told me you were in touch with Dexter, Arlene. Why didn't you ever bother mentioning it?"

"Because Dexter asked me not to. Just in case things didn't work out again."

"But you never liked him."

"I never said I didn't like Dexter. I said I didn't like some of the things he'd done. But people do stupid things when they're young. And they can change. He sounds like he's paid in years lost for a crime he still swears he didn't do. It was no big deal, really. I just wish he didn't have to live with you."

"You and me both. But thank you, Arlene."

"You're welcome. So, Omar has made some dramatic changes."

"Don't tell me he's finally moving out?"

"No. But he's lost about forty pounds. And counting."

"So he did get that Lap Band?"

"Who told you he was getting it?"

"I thought you did. Didn't you?"

"No, I did not. It had to be Venetia with her big mouth."

"Was it supposed to be a secret or something?"

"No. When I told Venetia, I didn't know he was actually going to do it. But he did."

"Isn't that expensive?"

"Insurance covered it."

"Well, good for Omar. He's a good-looking young man. This should do wonders for his self-esteem."

"What makes you think he doesn't have any self-esteem?"

"I didn't say he didn't have any. I just meant that with a few less pounds he'd probably feel better about himself. You knew what I meant, Arlene. Damn. Is this what you wanted to tell me?"

"That's one thing."

"What's the other one?"

"Have you talked to Venetia lately?"

"Not in a week or so, why?"

"Rodney's gone."

"Gone where?"

"Where do you think, Betty Jean?"

"Hell, I don't know. He's always gone. Wait. You mean to tell me this time he's not coming back?"

She reaches in her purse for her cell phone but I press my hand down hard on her forearm to stop her from bringing it up to her ear.

"Why didn't she tell me when she told you?"

"Well, she didn't exactly tell me herself."

"Then who the hell did? Not Rodney."

"Lauren called to tell me Venetia was having a hard time and the reason why."

"Why didn't she call me, too?"

"I don't know!"

"When the hell did all this happen?"

"Almost two weeks ago."

"Whose bright idea was it to keep me in the dark all this time?"

"Mine."

"This was not your damn call, Arlene. Why do you always have to play Oprah?"

"First of all, knowing that Dexter was coming home and all the mess that's been going on in your house, I thought it would be best to wait until Venetia felt like she wanted to tell you herself."

"She's our sister, Arlene, and this is not the way we were brought up—to just let folks fend for themselves, suffer on our own, you know that! I'm driving out to her house as soon as I leave here."

"I knew I shouldn't have told you."

I'm out here in Woodland Hills sitting in my car waiting for potential buyers to show up. The house is more than six thousand square feet and is really a souped-up tract house disguised as a custom home but some people don't know the difference. As long as it's big, has high ceilings, granite and marble, and a chandelier greeting them when they open the front door, they're impressed.

When my cell phone rings, I see it's Venetia, but I don't have the heart to answer it right now. So I let it go to voice mail. When it rings again, it's the buyers, telling me they're stuck in traffic on the 405 and could they possibly reschedule for tomorrow. I agree.

I get on the 405 and can't help but notice that there is no traffic on the other side. I don't understand what this means. If they found another house with another broker, then they should just have come right out and said so. I dial my voice mail and Venetia has left me a message: "Arlene, I just wanted you to know that I wish you had let me be the one to share my personal information with our sister, since you don't fully understand what's going on, and it would also have been better if you had called me to get the real truth instead of relying on a sixteen-year-old's interpretation of it. Thanks for caring so much about me."

After Betty Jean's lashing, I certainly don't feel like defending myself so I don't call her back. I decide to call Omar, who's at home since he gave up his last job to have this elective surgery. His phone goes to voice mail, so I call the house line and it goes to voice mail, too. Where in the world could he be? I'm suddenly worried that maybe something is wrong. So I step on it until the traffic begins to slow up and I'm forced to a crawl like usual.

When my cell rings and it's Omar, I pick it up immediately. "Are you okay? Where are you?"

"Take it easy, Ma," he says. "I was out looking at apartments."

"For who?"

"Me."

"Why?"

"'Cause it's time."

"But you don't have a job, Omar."

"I know that, which is why I wanted to ask if you'd be willing to cosign for me until I get on my feet."

"When did you make all these plans, Omar? First it was the Lap Band and now you want to move out?"

"Ma, I'm twenty-eight years old and have never lived on my own. Every time I've tried telling you I was thinking about it, you always came up with reasons why I shouldn't."

"That is not true."

"It is, Ma."

"Well, if you need my help, how do you call that living on your own?"

"Never mind."

And he hangs up.

When I call him back, it goes to voice mail again. And when I pull into the driveway, his BMW isn't in the garage, and it won't be for quite some time.

Venetia

Who's there?" I ask when I hear my doorbell chime. It's not a solicitor, since this is a gated community and I wasn't expecting any deliveries, which means it has to be someone on the approved list. But I can't imagine who it would be this time of day. I press my ear to the door, which is silly, but since I don't have my glasses on I can't see through the peephole.

"It's your sister."

"Which one?" I ask.

Sometimes I can't tell their voices apart but I open it anyway and am relieved it's BB and not Arlene. As I open the door I take a deep breath and quietly pray that there is nothing wrong that can't be remedied. "BB, what in God's name are you doing here this time of day and what made you drive all the way out here without giving me a heads-up?"

"Arlene just told me about Rodney."

"What about Rodney?"

"That he left you."

"He did not *leave* me. We're just taking a break from each other."

I step away from the door and she walks right past me. I love that plaid suit she's wearing, even if it is a little tight. "Come on back to the kitchen. I'm pretty sure this is Arlene's doing, isn't it? Don't even answer that, BB. She is notorious for spreading misinformation even though I know she means no harm, but she needs to learn how to verify stuff first and since I'm the person who was supposed to have been left why hasn't she bothered to call me?"

"She made it sound like she was trying to give you time to sort out your feelings."

"How in the world did she find out?"

"She said Lauren called her."

"Lauren?"

"That's what she told me."

"That is absolutely not true!"

"Who gives a shit—excuse me—no, I meant it, who gives a shit what Arlene thinks? She has no idea what being married is like and at the rate she's going she's never going to. Anyway, are you okay? Talk to me?"

"Sometimes I like it when you swear, BB. It means you're feeling passionate, and I'm glad it's about me this time. You want something cool to drink?"

"No. Tell me what in the world is going on?"

"Rodney is seeing someone and has been for quite some time. He feels conflicted about it but doesn't want a divorce. So he asked me if I would give him a little time to sort out his feelings."

"I know you didn't agree to that?"

"I did. I married him for better or for worse."

"But this isn't the first worse, is it?"

"I don't know what you're talking about, BB."

"Arlene told me about a few other times and you took him back then, too."

"Men don't always know how to say no to temptation."

"You sound like a damn fool, Venetia. What do you think would happen if *you* didn't say no to temptation, huh? You think Rodney would be so forgiving and keep giving you more chances?"

"I don't know. Would you like a smoothie?"

"What kind of smoothie?"

"Mango, strawberry, and banana."

"Okay. But just a small glass."

I slide the blender out away from the cabinet.

"Wait a minute. You mean you have to make it?"

"It'll only take a minute."

"Never mind. I don't want one. So how are the kids handling this?"

"Lauren refuses to speak to him when he calls."

"Good for her."

"He's still her father, BB."

"And Zachary?"

"He left him quite a disrespectful and scary message and called him something I can't repeat."

"Repeat it. You won't go to hell, since they're not your words."

I shake my head. I don't like using profanity even though sometimes I don't mind hearing it. Sometimes it's melodic and is not offensive, depending on the tone. I pour myself a glass of Arnold Palmer and BB watches me.

"Is that an Arnold Palmer?"

I nod.

"Then why didn't you ask me if I wanted a glass of that? Anyway—"

"Because you said you didn't want anything!"

"I still want to know what Zachary said to Rodney."

"And I just told you I wouldn't feel comfortable repeating it."

"Pretend you're an actress auditioning for a great role and you have to say these lines or you'll miss the opportunity of a lifetime."

"He said, 'You are one sneaky, lying, cheating, poor excuse for a husband. This isn't the first time you've hurt our mom but it's going to be the last, and I hope whoever the gold-digging bitch is, that she knows you're nothing but a selfish bastard who can't be trusted and the only person you really care about is yourself.'"

"Wow. He said all *that*?"

"Every word of it. So that should constitute an Academy Award. And I'm ashamed to admit it, but it felt kind of good saying that."

"And you're not on fire."

I hand her a glass and sit down at the end of the island. The black granite is so shiny I can see both of our reflections in it. I cleaned it this morning. Like I do every morning. "I just don't feel like destroying my children's lives right now, since they're so close to graduating."

"Kids? They're almost in college, Venetia. Do you see some of the stuff they watch on TV? They are hip to all of this mess. Which is why Zach could cuss out his daddy and not think twice about it. And he was being honest. Something you might want to try."

"What's that supposed to mean?"

"I mean, aren't you tired of making excuses for him? Aren't you tired of being lonely, which you have to be, since he's never here?"

"I am tired. But the Lord gives me strength to just hang in here until this passes."

"Are you fucking kidding me, Venetia?"

"If you have to keep using this kind of language talking to me,

BB, I might have to ask you to leave. I'm not kidding. I've heard enough ugly words from you today and I'm not going to be talked down to by Arlene and even the kids have accused me of being a doormat, but I don't need this right now. I really don't. God is the only one who doesn't judge me."

She gets up.

"Are you leaving?"

"I am. I drove out here just to make sure you were doing okay and I see that you're obviously in good hands since God is your best friend and, I hope, in the process of offering you a little common sense, so maybe you don't need a sister's input at all."

"You're starting to sound a lot like Arlene."

She cuts her eyes at me and takes her now empty glass over to the sink. I'm tempted to wash it but I will myself to not notice how much empty space surrounds it.

"Let me just ask you this. Do you still love Rodney?"

"That's a very good question. I don't know. What I do know is I don't like who he's become."

"And what is that?"

"Dishonest."

"You think that's something a person becomes and not who they always were because sometimes love can blind you so it makes it hard to see?"

"I don't think that rule applies to me. Rodney used to be a good husband and father."

"You just said 'used to' like he's going to get back to being that way again, as soon as he gets over this little bout of cheating, is that it?"

"You know what, BB, if your goal was to come out here to make me feel better, you have failed to do that."

"Well, I'm sorry. But tell me this, sis. What will you do if he says he wants a divorce?"

"What choice would I have?"

"You didn't answer my question."

She gives me a kiss on the cheek and lets herself out. As soon as she leaves I call Arlene and leave a long message giving her a piece of my mind. I don't care if she gets mad at me for not telling her about Rodney and me, and the reason I didn't is because I did not want to hear her criticize me for the way I'm handling all of it, which she would most certainly do, and now BB is reacting the same way. I don't need their advice and I didn't ask for it. And until my marriage issues are resolved, and my husband finds his way back home, I don't think talking to either one of them will be such a good idea.

Dexter

H i," I say to my nephews and Miss Tammy as soon as I walk up the front steps. They're peeking out from behind her. "Welcome home, Dexter," she says without much enthusiasm. She used to like me, but I can tell I'm on her shit list now.

"Lee David is fine and the boys have been on their very best behavior, so I'll see you later, BJ."

Ma thanks her and holds the screen door open and she heads across the street. I can't believe she's still living in this neighborhood after all these years. But from what Ma has told me, a lot of the original folks haven't left either. The boys run away and go sit down on the sofa. Then they both stare at me with a look of disdain, if I'm reading them right.

"Say hi to your uncle Dexter," Ma says.

The oldest one lifts his hand up like it weighs a hundred pounds and, without looking at me, waves. The other one mimics his brother. I'm wondering what Ma might have told them. Maybe they're scared of me. I hope not, so I say, "What grade are you fellas in?"

"I'm going into fourth even though I'm only supposed to be going into third," Luther says.

"I'm almost in second," Ricky says.

"Why you have to take my bed?" Luther asks, throwing me off guard.

"It might only be for a few weeks."

"Then you leaving, I hope," he says.

"Don't talk like that to your uncle, Luther. And it's not *your* bed," Ma says. "It was Dexter's bed when he was a little boy."

"He not little now."

"I can sleep on the couch," I say.

"No, you won't. We've already talked about this, haven't we?" They both nod.

"So let's try to be more respectful. Your uncle's been away for a long time and now he's going to live in the little apartment over the garage, but he has to fix it up first. I told you this."

"I wanna live on top of the garage," Ricky says. "You can have my whole room, Uncle Dexter."

"Thanks for the offer, Ricky, but it's okay."

"Why don't you have no wife to go live with now that you home from jail?" This is Luther. He's pissed because I am messing up his entire setup. I get it.

"Well, I made a big mistake a long time ago and I went to prison, and while I was in there, the lady I wanted to marry didn't want to wait for me to get out, so that's why I'm here."

"Why can't you go find her?"

"I think she married somebody else."

"So, you a criminal, then," Luther says, not asks.

"I was accused of committing a crime, so I guess that would be a yes."

"Boys," Ma says, 'cause I guess she can see how much I'm perspiring and looking like I might want to run and hide but I can't. "Be nice to Uncle Dexter. I've already told you both that a lot of people make mistakes and then they get another chance to do right. Just like when I have to put you both in time-outs. Ring a bell?"

"Yeah, but good thing time-out don't last as long as being in prison, huh, Grandma?" Ricky asks.

"Your uncle Dexter is going to be fixing up the space over the garage. How long do you think it might take you, Dexter?"

"It depends."

"Nobody's been up there in years, since your uncle Monroe spent a month up there after his wife chased him out of Shreveport—remember that?"

I shake my head no.

"That was about twelve or thirteen years ago, before your daddy started getting sick, and for a while we tried to keep it clean but then we just started using it for storage. We had it insulated but it might have a few leaks in the roof, and the floor might need to be secured, and you know there's no air-conditioning or heat up there. We did put in a tiny bathroom, but when you want to eat you have to come down here. It's livable."

"I'll go up there in the morning and check it out."

"I know how to measure," Luther says. "I can help you."

"I can hammer," Ricky says. "And I know how to carry stuff."

"Thank you, boys," I say. "I'm sure I can use your help."

"Go peek in at your daddy," Ma says, and I do.

He doesn't recognize me, and I don't recognize him either. He's shriveled up. Sunk inside that pillow. He looks like he's in a casket, and I don't like seeing him like this so I know I'm going to avoid coming in here. "How long can he live like this?"

"Like what?"

I just point.

"As long as he can breathe," she says.

"I mean, how long can he live like this at home?"

"I have an attendant who cares for him when I'm at work. Nurse Kim. Be nice to her and don't even think about trying to hit on her because she's pretty."

"She's fine!" Luther yells from the living room. "And she's mine!" he says.

I crack up. Nothing like your first crush. It feels good to laugh out loud. I can't even remember the last time I did. I pick up my small suitcase and take it to my old room. It's still light blue, and the paint is chipped in some spots, showing a different shade of blue underneath. The twin bed is still in here, and it almost looks like the same bedspread, too. I don't care. Pictures of me swinging a bat when I was seven on up to about eleven fill one whole wall. I feel weird being here, in the house I grew up in. It's much smaller. And I don't know how five people lived here for so many years. I'm not complaining. It's just striking how physical space stays the same and your perspective changes. I'll take this room and the one above the garage over a prison cell any day.

As I walk back out—and nobody has to use a key, so I can—I feel small and now the house feels like a mansion. "Everything looks the same," I say to Ma.

"That's the problem," she says. "Let's eat."

After we eat her famous spaghetti and meatballs and a real salad with real sourdough rolls, she surprises me with her famous peach cobbler. She has always gone overboard to make us happy, and I can see that hasn't changed, and now she's doing the same thing for these boys. After they're in bed, we go into the living room. Ma sits in her chair and I sit on the couch.

"So," she says. "Welcome home."

I know she's waiting for me to say something about how good it feels to be out of prison after nine years and how I'm going to do right by the law and by her and how I will not disappoint her and she doesn't have to worry about me bringing any riff-raff anywhere near this house, but it'll probably just sound like somebody who just got out of prison, who is grateful to be out and who has all kinds of big plans that I exaggerated to the parole board, but the truth is I don't really have any concrete plans because I don't have a clue about what I want to do because I don't know what I can do. I don't have any dreams about my future. I only know how to live from one day to the next. I don't want my mother to know any of this, because I don't want to scare her. So what I do say is this: "Thank you for letting me stay here, Ma. And I promise not to disappoint you."

"It's fine, Dexter. You should be feeling a little overwhelmed right now, so don't feel like you need to sit here making me all kinds of promises you don't know if you can even keep. Plus, you'll be here for a while. We have plenty of time to talk. Get some rest."

"Thank you, Ma." I walk over and kiss her on the cheek. She squeezes my hand and kisses it.

"Good night, Dexter," she says, and then picks up a book.

The first few nights, it's hard to get to sleep. When I roll over I'm not up against a concrete wall. I'm not on the top bunk. Nobody is farting or snoring. I don't hear anybody pissing, whispering, jerking off, or having sex. I'm not scared to walk down the hall to the bathroom. Nobody wakes me up. I get to stand in the kitchen and choose what I want to eat for breakfast. When I walk out onto the screened-in sunporch, I feel comfortable, like it's a shield that's protecting me from whatever is on the other side. I look out at the shrubs and trees and flowers and grass, even the sidewalks, and realize I can just open that aluminum door and walk outside, down the sidewalk in any direction I want to. But I don't know which direction to go. I don't know where I want to go. I don't have anywhere to go. Nobody to see. I don't know what to do with so much freedom.

I go see my parole officer and tell him I'm going to start looking for work the next day. He warns me not to be picky. He repeats what I was told before I was released. That with my record it's going to be hard to find a decent job. Be patient. Don't give up. Be glad I have family who's putting a roof over my head. He makes his visit to Ma's house and goes over all of the rules, which she understands, and he approves. I have to report to him once a month.

I wish I could say it takes me only a few days of pounding the pavement to find a job, but that is not the case. I am not allowed to drive and have taken at least sixty-three buses and gotten seventy-six "No"s after background checks or just being asked, "Have you ever been arrested? In prison?" And when I said yes to both, they didn't care for what or for how long; they just shook their heads.

My parole officer misses our next meeting but he calls, and when I tell him how frustrating my job search has been he finally suggests I try the Salvation Army or Goodwill because they both hire felons. I start tomorrow at the Salvation Army. I don't know what I'm going to be doing or how much I'm going to be making but it doesn't really matter at this point. I'm employed.

It only took a few weeks to get what I call my apartment fixed up. The boys did their best to help. They were funny and great company. For the time being, I have to run an extension cord to have light up there, but it's cool. It's free and there are no bars on the windows or door. Ma doesn't seem to mind my being here and I'm grateful for that. I try not to ask her for money but when I do, it's mostly for bus fare. I gave up smoking since they cost a damn fortune. I haven't asked Ma about Trinetta because it's obvious things aren't too cool or her kids wouldn't still be here. I would pay good money to have that Nurse Kim resuscitate me. She's even finer than I thought she would be but she treats me like an ex-con—with some amount of respect or maybe it's just tolerance. She makes me think about sex, and since I don't have any prospects or even old hookups, it's a good thing she's leaving. I know Luther is going to be heartbroken. And I'm definitely going to miss the way she makes this house smell, not to mention looking at her beautiful round ass.

Luther

What do a traveling nurse do, Nurse Kim?"
She looks up from this thick book she been reading seem like every day for like two weeks. It got a picture of some little white boy wearing corny glasses riding a broom on the cover. I thought Nurse Kim was smart enough to read grown-up books. But: my bad. I still love her. And I'm glad I got sick with a cold and when my grandma heard me coughing and sneezing this morning and she felt my head and said it was too warm she took my temperature and gave me some medicine and asked Nurse Kim if she would mind watching me today, and when Nurse Kim said she did not mind, I was thinking, shit, if I woulda knew all I had to do was to cough loud and be sneezing, two of the easiest things to pretend, I coulda been out here on this couch under the covers watching Nurse Kim read in Grandma's reading chair that go back way before my birthday and I coulda been looking at her legs crossed like I am right now and all I would have to do is cough and she would jump up and put her hand on my forehead to make sure I wasn't burning up and probably say, "I'ma make you some hot tea and soup, would you like that, Luther?" And I would nod my head just a little bit so when she came back with it and pushed the pillows up behind me a little bit she would dip the spoon in the bowl

and feed me, all 'cause I would act like I couldn't pick it up by myself.

"A traveling nurse travels, Luther."

"Then you already a traveling nurse. Don't you gotta, I mean have to, travel to get over here?"

"I drive."

"Ain't that—I mean—isn't that traveling?"

"You go much farther than California."

"Give me some examples."

"Don't know yet. Maybe Florida."

"That's way on the other side of the United States next to the Atlantic Ocean."

Her eyes get big like she just saw a spider.

"How do you know that?"

"'Cause I learned it. I'm almost in third grade, you know. But I might get to skip it and go right into fourth."

"You are one smart little boy."

"Why you reading a book that look like it's for little kids, Nurse Kim?"

"If it was for little kids you think I'd be reading it?"

"Well, it's got what look like a cartoon of a little white boy on the front of it and not no old man."

"It's about wizards and magic and witchcraft, but when you get right down to it it's about a little boy whose parents get killed and he gets stuck living with his evil-ass relatives and then ends up going to a special school sorta like a college for kids to learn how to use their magical powers, which Harry didn't even know he had, and at first he meets two friends who real cool but then he meets all kinds of fucked-up kids who bully him and are just jealous 'cause Harry come from good stock and they can't stand his ass, and while they try to fuck little Harry up some of Harry's friends try to help him out especially when the bullies try to steal this magical rock they ain't got no business having. That's where I am now. So, don't bother me unless you can't breathe, 'cause I'm almost finished and please don't tell your grandma I said those bad words."

"Can I read it when you done?"

"Yep. But it might be a little hard for you."

"I'm smarter than you think, Nurse Kim. I get A's in reading and I just told you I might get to skip third grade."

"Prove it," she say, and get up out the chair and stand over me, and when she hand me the book the soft part of her breasts squeeze together. I pretend I don't see neither one of them.

"What you want me to read?"

"Two sentences. Anywhere on this page."

"Why, you don't believe me?"

"I do, but I ain't never heard no second grader read something even I struggle with."

"Harry couldn't sleep, but the truth was that Harry kept being woken by his old nightmare, except that it was now worse than ever because there was a hooded figure dripping blood in it." I want to keep reading 'cause I want to know who that hooded figure is dripping with blood, but Nurse Kim grabs the book outta my hands like she think I'm gon' try to keep it or something.

"Damn. You wasn't lying. Who taught you how to read so good?"

"At school, and my grandma was always reading to me and Ricky at night but then sometimes she be tired so I started reading to her and Ricky."

"Good for you, Luther. Good for you."

"My grandma say anything you do a lot you get better at it."

"Not everything," she say.

"Name one thing," I say.

"Never mind. Let me ask you something. When is your mama coming back?"

"I don't know."

"How does it make you feel knowing she just dropped you and your brother off and . . . Wait, have you talked to her?"

I shake my head no.

"Why not? You ain't got her number or she haven't even called?"

I shake my head no twice.

"I don't like your mama, no offense. She trifling as hell, and see what them drugs do to your mind? Make you put your goddamn kids last or kick 'em to the curb. When you grow up, promise me you will say no to all drugs, not just some, 'cause they will fuck you up every time and make you do a lot of stupid shit and you won't get nowhere in life except maybe prison, like your stupid-ass uncle Dexter, no offense. Anyway, you and your little brother better always listen to your grandma and show her respect and don't get on her damn nerves, since she already old and this ain't no time in her life to be raising no little kids no damn way. And let me just say this one last thing. These streets out here is rough and they can rob you of common damn sense so you and your brother better not fall for the okey-doke and get in no trouble, 'cause if you do, y'all little asses could end up in foster care, and believe me, you don't want to live in no group home or with some fucked-up family who only doing it for the money, you understand what I'm saying, little dude?"

I nod my head and then correct her. "I ain't . . . I mean I am not little." I lift the quilt up to show her how long my legs is (are). "See how fast I'm growing?"

She just cover her mouth and laugh like she trying not to laugh at me, but I know it's 'cause I'm not a man yet.

"I wish you didn't have to be no . . . a traveling nurse, Nurse Kim, but I know it's 'cause you need to expand your horizons and get more opportunities."

Her eyes light up like she shocked, 'cause I know she didn't know I pay attention when my teacher and Grandma talk to us and plus Grandma sometimes make me and Ricky watch *Oprah* with her and we put on our listening ears and I remember what I think might be useful in the future.

"Who in the world taught you to memorize that?"

"I didn't memorize it."

"So you laying there telling me you know what you just said to me means?"

"I just said it, didn't I?"

"That you did."

"Nurse Kim, I want you to find your horizons and everything, but who's gon', I mean going to take care of my grandpa when you leave?"

"I'm sure your grandma won't have a problem finding somebody as nice as me to take good care of him."

"I miss you already," I say.

"That's sweet. But don't worry, I'll come back and visit whenever I come home."

"You promise?"

"I promise."

Me and Ricky or Ricky and I laying on top of the covers next to Grandpa eating nachos, watching *Who Wants to Be a Millionaire*. This is his favoritest thing to watch on TV. He don't like *Dora the Explorer* or cowboys no more. Even though Ricky and me don't understand the questions, sometimes we just guess and whoever guess right get a extra big nacho. Grandpa got his thick glasses on and the TV is up loud. He kinda act like me and Ricky ain't (aren't) even there until we get ready to get up and that's when he usually grab my leg and smile, so we put our head back on the pillows.

According to a proverb about hope, "There's always a light at the end of" what? (A) the journey, (B) the day, (C) the tunnel, (D) E.T.'s finger.

I yell out, "E.T.'s finger!"

Grandpa say, "The tunnel."

Me and Ricky wait and we look at each other when the man says, *"C! The tunnel!"*

Ricky pick up Grandpa's hand and turn it so we both give him a high five and a nacho, and he smile.

Which of these gambling games requires a pair of dice? (A) craps, (B) roulette, (C) poker, (D) blackjack.

"Craps!" me and Ricky yell out at the same time. Grandpa don't (doesn't) look too happy 'cause we got it right.

A person who "takes a backseat" to someone else is said to be play-ing what? (A) by the rules, (B) second fiddle, (C) dead, (D) hard to get.

"C. Dead!" I yell out.

"D. Hard to get!" Ricky yells louder.

"B," Grandpa says, and it's the right answer, and then he take his glasses off, which is how we know he's going to sleep.

Grandpa know a lot of the answers on *Who Wants to Be a Mil-lionaire*, and I don't know why everybody think he can't remem-ber stuff. Me and Ricky like watching this show with him 'cause it's making us smarter. And we both want to be smarter. And like our grandma always saying, "You can't be too smart."

While Ricky and me was taking our bath I remembered I had forgot to tell him what Nurse Kim told me to tell him and while we was putting on our pajamas he just said, "I ain't going to no prison when I grow up." After we clean out the tub and hang up our towels, Grandma go straight in to take her shower. "You boys did a nice job cleaning up after yourselves," she says, and then give us a pat on the head. We about to read. And then Grandma will say our prayers with us.

Ricky sit on the couch and I sit in the big chair when the phone ring. I answer it. "Hello," I say, like Grandma made me start saying instead of "Hi," 'cause she said it was not polite.

"Hi, Luther." I hear a lady's voice that sound like my mama's but I know it can't be her.

My heart seem like it start beating really fast and the phone slide right out my hand on the carpet but I bend over and pick it back up real fast. "Who may I ask is calling?" I say, like Grandma told me to even though I know it's our mama, but I just wanna hear her say it.

"It's Trinetta. Your *mother*."

"Who you want to speak to?"

"Why you acting like you don't know who this is?"

"'Cause I thought you died."

"Why in the hell would you think something stupid like that? Did anybody call and tell you I was dead?"

"No. But you have not called us."

"When you start talking all proper?"

"All the time. Grandma won't let us talk ghetto anymore."

"Ghetto?"

"Who you want to speak to?"

"What?"

"I said, who you want to speak to?"

"This ain't funny and please don't get cute."

"I'm not trying to be funny and—"

"Just tell me how you and Ricky been doing?"

"Fine."

"Where's Mama?"

"She's taking her shower."

"Well, how's Mr. Butler?"

"Who?"

"Your grandpa?"

"He can answer a lot of questions."

"No shit?"

"No shit. Where you calling us from?"

"I'm still in Atlanta. And watch your mouth, Luther. You ain't grown."

"You mean the capital of Georgia?"

"Well, well, well. You are smart for almost being in third grade."

"Fourth grade. I get to skip third. What do you want?"

"You need to watch your mouth, Luther. That ain't no way to talk to your own mama."

"What do you want me to tell Grandma?"

"Tell her I just want to talk to her about something."

"You ain't . . . you aren't coming back to get us, I hope?"

"What if I said I was?"

"Me and Ricky ain't . . . are not going nowhere with you."

"Oh yes you would, if I came back there."

"We don't want you to come back."

"Where's Ricky?"

"He doesn't want to talk to you."

"How you know that?"

"'Cause he won't get up to come over here to the phone."

"Well, guess what?"

"I don't feel like guessing."

"You might have a little sister or brother sometime next year."

That's when I press the button on the phone that make it hang up, and then I pull that long rubber cord out the wall like Grandma showed me and Ricky how to do when Uncle Dexter used to call and she didn't feel like hearing the phone ring.

When she comes out the bathroom with that pink towel piled up around her head like cotton candy, she say, "Who was that calling, baby?"

And I just say, "Nobody."

Trinetta

I don't know if I should even call back. Here I been out here trying to get my life together knowing my kids was safe with Ma and Luther old enough to know I've had a problem, and so just when I get my courage up to reach out 'cause I been missing seeing him and Ricky and hearing their voices, see what happened?

Luther wasn't too thrilled hearing my voice. But who can blame him? Sometimes you make bad decisions and you just gotta live with 'em. I hope him and Ricky don't hate me and I hope they don't give up on me. Yet. I still ain't got nothing to bring to the table, and can't really teach 'em much of nothing. Yet. I ain't even close to being no role model, but at least I'm trying. I shoulda learned a lot from Ma, 'cause she was a good mother to us. She put up with a lot of our bullshit but she never gave up on us. She rammed right and wrong down our throats and we didn't listen. She was a good example of what being a good example is, but we just chose not to hear her or Mr. Butler when they had our best interest at heart. And now look at what being deaf on purpose done added up to. The only person I blame is myself. I'm the one who been fucking up and my kids been suffering. I hope I get the chance to correct some of my wrongs.

I also ain't thrilled about being pregnant. When me and Dante hooked up, I told him I didn't want no more kids, but since I been almost totally clean for almost four months he musta slipped up and didn't put his condom on and shit happened, and since he ain't got no kids of his own he begged me to keep it.

"I ain't even taking care of the three I got."

"What you mean, three?"

"I told you about Noxema when we was in rehab, but I guess you don't remember. Her daddy went to court and he got custody."

"And how old is she?" he asked.

"She should be almost five."

"Well, I can tell you right now, you gon' take care of this one. And you need to be trying to figure out how you gon' get them boys back. Think about bringing them out here. This the South. It's a good place to bring up kids."

"What they supposed to eat? Air?"

"It wouldn't kill you to find a trade, Trinetta. It's a lot of things you can learn how to do real quick."

"Like what?"

I remember crossing my arms and they squeezing my breasts, which was already starting to get sore, but I was waiting for Mr. Donald Trump to tell me how to start a career, since his ain't exactly off to no running start yet either. Turns out his cousin ain't got no connections and don't nobody know how to get in touch with L.A. and Babyface 'cause word on the street is they breaking up. And on top of everything Dante's cousin is so deep in the church we had to get outta there 'cause they had Bible study twice a week in the living room, during *Monday Night Football* and on the night I watch *Law & Order*. They tried to get Dante to join the choir. I told 'em I can't even hum on key so don't look at me. Plus, it's a Pentecostal church and even though I ain't got nothing against folks getting the Holy Ghost and what have you, I just don't like being preached to about heaven and hell when I don't know nobody that's ever been to either one and lived to tell it. Hell can't be no hotter than Atlanta. So Dante got us a room with a kitchenette in it, which I ain't crazy about, and I've seen these giant-ass cockroaches like I ain't never seen in L.A. strolling across the floor and parking on the damn walls. They dare you to try to kill 'em, and I don't even try 'cause spiders and bugs and insects make me itch. I told Dante we can't stay here too long, 'cause I'm tired of scratching.

In all honesty, I'm bored to death. And when I get bored I have a tendency to get high. But I promised Dante I wouldn't do nothing to hurt this baby like I maybe did when I was carrying Ricky, but I only dipped and dabbed, and from what I saw, he just a little hyper and good thing I hadn't hit that pipe until after Luther was born. Anyway, I don't care what they say about how the South has changed, it's still the South, and I don't like living down here. It's a lotta white people that let you know they don't like black people. I guess black people down here must be used to it, 'cause they don't seem to pay 'em no mind. But coming from California, where everybody seem to like everybody, it kinda feel like going back in time. It's pretty and modern and got a whole lotta serious houses and everything is green and the shopping is good, if you got money to shop, and I really dig the rain and the loud thunderstorms and even the lightning—a nice change from every-day-is-the-same L.A.—but I'm thinking we should go somewhere like Oakland or Vallejo or where the seasons almost change. They got lots of rappers up in the Bay Area and I think it even snow sometimes. Plus they got bridges and water everywhere and they ain't got no smog or no humidity. I'ma run this by Dante tonight. As soon as he get back from choir practice.

I only got eighteen minutes left on this phone and since Dante got the car I can't go to the store to buy some more, but then again, maybe I could call collect. Which is what I decide to go ahead and do. My heart is beating fast 'cause I'm hoping one of the kids don't answer this time and if Ma does, that she will accept the charges. When a man's voice answers, I know it's my brother Dexter. Of course he accepts the charges.

"Bro, when you get out?"

"A few months back. How are you these days? You're calling collect so I'm hoping you're not behind bars. Talk to me."

"Not even close. I don't do jail. Just a little low on funds right now and almost out of minutes on my phone, and . . ."

"What area code is this?"

"I don't really know, to tell you the truth. It's one of those throwaways."

"You still in Atlanta?"

"Yeah."

"What you doing down there?"

"Trying to get my life together."

"Yeah, well, how's that working out?"

"So-so."

"You still hitting that pipe?"

"Hell to the no. Anyway, glad you finally got paroled."

"That makes two of us."

"So, what's it like?"

"What do you mean by that?"

"First off, I know you not staying at Ma's?"

"I am, but it's just temporary. It's one of my parole require-ments. I fixed up the spot above the garage."

"What's my boys like?"

"They're smart. And well behaved. Luther looks just like his daddy."

"So, you saw him in there?"

"He's not going anywhere anytime soon."

"You seen your kids since you been out?"

"I would if I knew how to find their mothers."

"So, how's it feel to be able to come and go as you please and not having nobody telling you when to go to bed and when to wake up and shit, just being able to walk down the street when you want to?"

"I'm not even going to answer that, Trinetta. So, I suppose you want to speak to the boys?"

I don't know how to tell him they don't want to talk to me, so I just play it off. "First let me say hi to Ma, if she's there."

"She's here. But hold up a minute. When are you coming back to get your kids?"

"Why is this any of your business, Dexter?"

"Because this is hard as hell on Ma. She goes to work five days a week and then comes home to care for them, and she's not a spring chicken and these are growing boys and they cost money, something she doesn't have a lot of, you know that, and you haven't exactly been helping and you need to figure out a way to take care of your own damn kids and cut Ma some slack."

"How much rent you paying?"

"That's really none of your business, now, is it?"

"So that means none. You got a job?"

"I work at the Salvation Army."

"At the what?"

"You heard me."

"Doing what?"

"Whatever they need me to do. It's work and I'm grateful for it."

"What happen to your woman? Skittles? She still in the picture?"

"No. So what exactly are you doing down there in Atlanta?"

"I'm staying clean and going to school."

"What kind of school? To do what?"

This catches me off guard, so I just tell another lie and say, "Hair."

"You still got those dreadlocks?"

"No, I cut 'em off 'cause it was too hot down here."

"What's your boyfriend's name?"

"Husband. And his name is Dante."

"Husband? And he let you run off and leave your kids?"

"He thinks Ma asked if she could keep 'em until I cleaned up my act, so when you meet him please don't treat him like he ain't shit."

"When will you be finished with school?"

"Next year."

"A whole year? Let me get Ma. Hold on. Oh, and by the way, your sons are at a sleepover. So you missed them anyway. See you when I see you."

I hear him call Ma. I hear her ask who it is.

"It's your daughter!"

I hear him put the phone down. I'm scared what she's gonna say to me. I'm not sure if I can handle a lecture right now, but what the fuck.

"What rock did you crawl from under?"

"A lot of them."

I have to change my tone and language when I talk to Ma, 'cause she gets pissed when I talk "ghetto," as Luther would say.

"And? The boys aren't here if you want to talk to them."

"Dexter told me they're at a sleepover, but I talked to Luther a few days ago. Didn't he tell you I called?"

"No, he didn't."

"What?"

"I said he didn't tell me you called or that he spoke to you. Why, what did you say to him?"

"I just wanted him and Ricky to know that I miss 'em, that I'm trying to figure out how to come back there correct so me and Dante can take care of 'em."

"Oh, did you really, now?"

"Go ahead and yell at me, Ma. I know how I did this was all wrong but I was doing that stuff and needed to get myself together and Dante threatened to leave me if I didn't."

"Doesn't he do them, too?"

"No. He's been clean almost two years. He's in the church."

"Well, this makes me feel warm and fuzzy inside. I feel really grateful that you finally took the time out of your busy schedule after I don't even know how many months to call and say what?"

"That I miss them."

"That's sweet."

"Look, Ma. It's taken me a while to get my head on straight, and now that I'm in school, after I complete the program, I just want you to know me and Dante will be coming back to get them."

"What did you just say?"

"You heard me."

"Well, let me say this. If you for one damn minute think you and Donkey Kong or whatever his damn name is can just come back here and get these kids like you're picking them up from camp, think again. I'm not going to let you put them through any more of your bullshit. If you want to come visit them, that's fine, but if you act like you want to take them, I'll go to court because this is their address and they're staying right here with me and your daddy."

"He is not my daddy."

"Since when? I thought you said you weren't doing drugs."

"Aunt Arlene told me he wasn't my daddy."

"Your aunt Arlene doesn't know what the hell she's talking about. You are serious, aren't you?"

"Dead serious. Anyway, I'll say this with no disrespect intended, Ma. Those are my kids, and if I come back to Los Angeles next week or next year, I can take them. So please don't get it twisted."

I wait for her to say something to that but she don't say another word. I don't even hear her breathing. I don't hear nothing. I'm beginning to think that this shit must be in our genes.

Betty Jean

Luther, why didn't you tell me your mama called?"

"I forgot."

"I know you're not lying to your grandma, are you?"

He drops his head. Stirs his spoon around in his oatmeal. Ricky is pretending he's deaf.

"Did she say something that upset you, baby?"

"She said she having a baby."

"She's having a what?"

"A baby."

"The kind that drinks milk out a bottle and cries till you pick it up," Ricky says.

Why am I not shocked that Trinetta didn't bother mentioning it? "Well, how do you two feel about that?"

Luther hunches his shoulders. Ricky does the same.

"Do you miss her?" I haven't bothered to ask them this the whole time they've been here, because it never seemed like it made a lot of sense to ask them something as stupid as that, but now it feels right.

"I don't," Luther says.

"Me neither."

"Why not?" I ask.

"Because. When you a mother you supposed to take care of your own kids and not leave 'em at their grandma's house for a weekend and then don't come back to pick 'em up and then don't call until after you turn eight when you was . . . I mean, were seven when you left."

Ricky just nods in agreement.

I really don't know what to say to that, so I just say, "Look. Sometimes, as mothers, we make mistakes. And sometimes we hurt our children when we make some mistakes even though we didn't mean to hurt them. Do you two understand that?"

"No. I don't. Because when you got kids you supposed to be more careful about the mistakes you make."

"Who told you that, Luther?"

"Nurse Kim."

"And how would she know? She doesn't even have kids."

"I think she musta read it in her Harry Potter book."

"You mean that book you're reading?"

He nods.

"Is it about mothers who leave their kids?"

"No," Luther says. "Harry's parents get killed so he gotta go live with his mean relatives and then he goes to the Hogwarts School and—"

"It's got wizards in it, Grandma," Ricky says.

"What was Nurse Kim doing reading a book like this?"

"'Cause grown-ups like magic, too," Luther says.

"What exactly is a wizard?" I ask, just to see what he says.

"They can fly and do magic!" Ricky yells.

"I miss Nurse Kim more than I miss my mama," Luther says out of nowhere. This makes me feel terrible even though I do understand what would make him say it.

"Nurse Kim hasn't been gone a week, Luther."

He just looks at me. "And I don't like the way Mrs. Nurse Hattie smells."

"What does she smell like?"

"A skunk."

"That is not nice," I say.

"I'm not saying it to sound mean, Grandma. Plus she is old and fat."

"Well, so am I."

Ricky shakes his head back and forth like he's possessed. "Uh-un. You is not old as Mrs. Nurse Hattie, Grandma, but me and Luther want you to go on a diet."

Luther elbows him.

"Aunt Venetia told us you would just be able to walk better and your knee probably would not hurt you so much if you was . . . I mean, were to lose like twenty pounds."

"Her said, 'But thirty would be better,'" Ricky says.

"I'll think about which one would make me more attractive. Okay, so do you boys know what you want to be for Halloween?"

"I want to be Batman," Luther says.

"I wanna be a wizard," says Ricky.

It's raining like crazy when Tammy bangs on the front door.

"I'll get it!" Ricky says while running toward it, then stops dead in his tracks. I'm so glad he remembered. "You do not open the door without first asking who it is," I've told him a million times. He takes his little brown hand off the doorknob and asks, "Who is it?"

"It's Tammy, Ricky! Open the door, hurry! I've got good news! I'm a grandma!"

He opens it a little, just to be on the safe side, but Tammy barges in anyway. "Clementine weighed in at seven pounds, three ounces!"

"Who's Clementine?" Luther asks, looking up from his new Harry Potter book. Something about a chamber full of secrets.

"Well, welcome to the Grandmothers' Club," I say. I walk over and give her a big squeeze. Tammy looks different. Tired. Older. We haven't seen all that much of each other since her brother got here and since she's been redecorating the room that used to be her sewing room and turned it into a nursery. I call it the cupcake room, because everything in it looks like frosting. I've just gone along with it, since every time she bought something new she would drag me over there to see if I approved, not like it made a difference. I was of the mind that Montana and Trevor were going to be moving out sooner rather than later, but it looks to me like Tammy forgot all about those plans. I have kept my thoughts to myself.

"You boys go see if your grandpa is okay," I say.

"He okay," Ricky says.

"I can take a hint, Grandma. Come on, Ricky. This is what grown folks say when they don't want you to hear what they say."

I wink at him.

"What's going on, BJ?"

"Trinetta called."

"Oh, so she's come back from the dead? Wait. That's not funny. Sorry."

"She's still in Atlanta with what's-his-name. And she's pregnant."

"You have got to be shittin' me."

"And she claims she might be coming back to get the boys."

"What did you say to that?"

"I told her if she even thought about it, I'd see her in court."

"Good for you. Good for you. Who in the hell does she think she is just calling out of nowhere like she's been on vacation and now she's coming home to pick up where she left off and I guess she's saying thank you for babysitting?"

"But I don't know if I'd really do that, Tammy. I mean, they're her kids. Not mine."

"But look at what she's exposed them to, BJ. This is about what's in their best interest. They're innocent. Trinetta is not. I'm sorry to have to say it like that."

"This is just a mess. I mean, you know I would love nothing better than for my daughter to get her life on the straight and narrow, Tammy, but my grandsons don't need any more instability in their lives than they've already had. Do they?"

"No, they do not."

"I'm not sure what would happen if she was just to show up. Plus, they don't want to live with her."

"And they shouldn't have to."

She gives me a big hug, pushes the screen door with her hip, and opens her umbrella. "Clementine'll be home tomorrow. Come see her. And bring the boys. On second thought, let's wait on that one."

I decide to use my Sears card to buy a present for Clementine and a few more clothes for church for the boys, hoping I'm not up to my limit since I bought those computers and that air conditioner for the kitchen window.

"What you buying us in here this time, Grandma?" Ricky asks.

"Don't be so greedy, Ricky. Money don't grow on trees, you know. Right, Grandma?"

"No, it *doesn't*, but he's just being curious, Luther."

"I'm always curious," he says, and Lord knows he's right about that.

"I have to get a baby gift for Montana and a few shirts and pants for church."

"I don't like church," Ricky says.

"I don't like Aunt Venetia's church," Luther says.

Even though I can understand why, I want to hear them say it, but more than anything, I don't want them to say they don't like church. "Why not?" I ask both of them.

"Because we the only black people in the whole church and it's way too big and I don't like the way those people behind the minister be singing. I mean sing. I mean, there ain't . . . isn't no beat and all the songs sound the same."

Ricky just nods.

"Well, Aunt Venetia is just trying to be nice by taking you boys since I have to stay with your grandpa, but you know we already talked about why it's important for you to attend church sometimes, didn't we?"

"To get to know God," Ricky says.

"And to find out how to be thankful and learn how to care about somebody besides yourself, right, Grandma?"

"That's good enough. Don't you boys sit with Lauren and Zachary?"

"They don't hardly be there," Ricky says.

"They pretend like they got . . . like they have too much homework, but I know the real deal, Grandma."

"And what is the *real deal*?"

"They don't like going to church either, 'cause they both told me. Lauren said that Aunt Venetia dragged them there every single Sunday for their whole life and now that she got us to drag, it let her and Zach off the hook. She even said thank you to me and Ricky, huh, Ricky?"

"Yep."

"What I do like though, Grandma, is she take us to eat but she call it brunch and we get to go to a restaurant with chairs and the table have a flower on it and everything. We get to pick anything we want off the menu. The best part about going to church is when it's over, huh, Ricky?"

"Yep."

"Well, just make sure you thank Aunt Venetia for taking you to church and to brunch, because she doesn't do it because she has to. She does it because she cares about you boys. Understand?"

They both nod.

I'm just grateful when my card is accepted.

The baby is cute. But it's rare you see an ugly baby these days. I know I shouldn't be thinking anything like this but I can't help it. Doesn't look to me like Montana and Trevor are going anywhere anytime soon. The whole house looks like the baby department at Target. Jackson is nice enough, putting on a pound or two, and it looks like Tammy has found another use for the money she got from selling off a few more acres: She's paying for Jackson to go to truck-driving school. I wish Dexter could go, too, but there are a lot of jobs you can't get if you're a convicted felon, doesn't matter how many years you've been out of prison. Dexter works long hours at the Salvation Army and I hardly ever see him. I leave a plate out for him, which is always clean and in the dish rack when I wake up. Sometimes it feels like he's still in prison.

Arlene asked me to stop by on my way home because she made a big pot of chili and wanted me to take some home for the boys and freeze some for later. I don't know why I opened my big mouth and told her about Trinetta. Arlene has a way of making you feel small inside. Like whatever choices you make aren't the right ones. Like she's so much smarter than everybody else. Like she can do a better job figuring out your life than you can. She says whatever she's thinking and doesn't seem to care if it hurts your feelings. It's been this way since we were kids. And she hasn't changed. What's funny is when you can see what's wrong with everybody else's life but you can't see what's wrong with yours. But when you need to tell somebody what you're going through, some-times family is the closest to you.

"I say let her have them back. They're her kids and regardless of if she's fit or not, she has a right to come and get them and take them home with her, wherever home might be."

"Did I ask you what you thought, Arlene?"

"I'm just voicing my opinion. For what it's worth. Even when you get sick it's always good to get a second opinion. Sometimes three."

"How is Omar doing these days?"

She gets the weirdest look on her face, like I struck a nerve or something.

"Omar is fine. Why wouldn't he be?"

"Did I give you the impression that I was thinking something might not be?"

"No, but I'm just telling you."

"Is he still losing weight?"

"Yes."

"How much is he going to lose?"

"Your guess is as good as mine."

"Well, tell him I said hi and he can stop by every now and then to say hi. He told me he would like to take the boys to a movie one day. So I'm hoping that invitation still stands. Would you ask him for me?"

"When I see him."

At first I was going to confront her about what Trinetta said she told her about Lee David not being Trinetta's daddy, and even though it's true she didn't have any damn right telling her. This was an accident that happened when Lee David and I were thinking about getting a divorce and then decided not to. I told Lee David after we got back together, and he said he knew Trinetta wasn't his blood, but she was now his daughter. I knew I shouldn't have told Arlene. She's got a big-ass mouth, and I'm still trying to figure out what I did to her years ago that would've possessed her to tell Trinetta something as hurtful as this in the first place.

It can wait.

Ricky

"Grandma?"

"Yes, baby."

"I've been thinking."

"About what, baby?"

"I wanna be on the swim team."

"Well, we can certainly look into that."

"I swim fast, you know."

"I know you do, baby. You swim like a shark."

"You wanna know something else, Grandma?"

"I'm all ears."

"I ain't taking no more of these pills. And that's my final answer."

Dante

been parked out in front of Trinetta's parents' house for going on two hours. A old lady who must be the one taking care of her daddy came to the door right after I first got here.

"Can I help you, son?"

I just shook my head.

"Who might you be looking for?"

"Mrs. Butler."

"Well, she won't be home for at least another hour or so. After she picks the boys up from school, they usually stop by the pool and the library. What day is it?"

"Last time I checked, it was still Tuesday, ma'am."

"Yes, this is Tuesday's schedule. And who might you be, son?"

"I'm Dante."

"Are you family?"

"You could say that."

"Well, you're welcome to come in and sit on the sunporch, where it's nice and cool."

"I'm fine out here, ma'am."

"Well, just knock if you need something."

"I will," I say.

I never met Trinetta's family and this ain't exactly the way I wanted to. I couldn't call on the phone. That wouldn't be right. Plus, I know they probably gon' think I'm the one responsible for what happened. But I tried to get her to straighten up and fly right. I was the one who talked her into going to Atlanta and tried to get her into the church after I joined and found out how good it felt to be saved. But even carrying our child she couldn't see her way on the path to Jesus and fell down into that deep hell she was living in back in L.A. When you love drugs more than you love yourself and even your unborn baby, God is about the only thing that can save you. But Trinetta hid from God. She hid from goodness. She even hid from love. I loved her 'cause I saw the goodness inside her. Something she didn't even know was there.

When I hear somebody knocking on the window, I look out and it's a middle-aged white woman. I'm trying to figure out what she doing in this neighborhood and what would possess her to even think about approaching me. I roll the window down.

"Hello, young man. I'm Tammy. I live in that house right across the street and since I can't help but notice you're sitting in a car in front of my best friend's house with your engine running, I'm wondering if there's something I might be able to do to help you if you're lost?"

"I'm not lost, ma'am. I'm waiting on Mrs. Butler."

She looks at me strange like. Like she suddenly know who I am and what I'm doing here. Then she get this look of terror on her face and cover up her mouth with both her hands and start walking backwards away from the car. "You must be that Dante."

"That Dante?"

"I'm sorry. Where is Trinetta?"

I don't know this woman and I don't think it would be right for me to tell her where Trinetta is, I don't care if she do live right across the street from her mama. So I don't say nothing.

"Is she in California?"

I shake my head no.

"Can she talk?"

"Not to us," I say before catching myself. And that's when I let my head drop and it hits the steering wheel and I grab hold of it and then put the car in drive but have to slam on the brakes when I almost run into Mrs. Butler, who is coming around me and about to pull into the driveway. I see Ricky and Luther in the backseat. They wave to me in slow motion. When Mrs. Butler stops the car and gets out, she stands in the driveway with her hands on her hips, as if she waiting for me to say something, and then she lets them drop.

"Go on inside, boys," she says, and they do exactly what she tell 'em to do.

"Where is she, Dante?"

"At the morgue."

"Here or in Georgia?"

"Georgia."

I look into Mrs. Butler's eyes and she look into mine, and somehow she can see that this was not my doing. "I'm sorry," I say, and walk over to hug her.

"I know," she says. And hugs me back. "I know."

Betty Jean

The boys didn't cry until they saw me cry.

"We didn't want our mama to die, did we, Ricky?"

Ricky shakes his head in slow motion.

"I feel very sad," Luther says.

"I wanted her to maybe come live with us here with you, Grandma. So we could help her with the new baby."

I want to say something, but sitting on this couch with the two of them and listening to what's pouring out of their little hearts is breaking mine. I don't know how I can find the words to comfort them when I'm aching all over. I regret hanging up on her. I regret not helping her try to get off drugs, no matter how many times it took. I regret abandoning her, knowing she had become a stranger to herself. I regret not telling her how much faith I still had in her. How much I still hoped for her. I thought my anger and impatience and disappointment was telling her just how much I loved her because I was watching the smart, sweet daughter I raised disappear. I regret not cheering for her more. I regret trying to be her conscience, her common sense. I regret that I didn't have the power to save her. It is clear to me right this minute that regret is just a wasted emotion.

I look at both of my beautiful grandsons, kiss them on top of the head, then put my arms around them and hold them close. I realize I am now responsible for their future. I don't know how you can tell how much of what you give children will determine how they turn out. But all I can do is try to give them the best of what I have to offer. I hope it's enough.

After I tuck them in, I hear Dexter come in. I walk out to the kitchen and there he is, hunched over the counter. He has heard. "I'm sorry, Ma."

He stands up and attempts to hug me, but for some reason I find myself backing away and pointing my finger at him. "I just want to say this. Parents are supposed to die before their children, Dexter. So I'm begging you right now, please don't make me have to go through this again. Please."

"I won't, Ma. I promise you."

Quentin couldn't—or didn't—make it to Trinetta's service, claiming little Margaret was too young to travel. Why he felt the need to bring her is beyond me. Dexter brought his old—and I suppose now his new—girlfriend, Skittles (whose real name is Karen), who tried her best not to look like a stripper but came up short. She cooked something that nobody touched, not even the boys, who eat anything yellow. And to everybody's surprise, Omar didn't sit next to Arlene, but way in the back of the church with his cousins Lauren and Zachary. Since he's lost all that weight, he looks just like his father. Venetia sat next to me and squeezed my hand so hard I thought the bones in all of my fingers would break. Twinkle sent flowers and left me a message saying she had been praying this wouldn't happen to Trinetta, which is why she moved her daughters back to Memphis, where she grew up. She said she couldn't afford a plane ticket but wanted me to know she's finishing cosmetology training. I don't know how Nurse Kim heard about Trinetta's passing but she sent a very nice card. It was postmarked from Alaska.

From one week to the next, and as these weeks turn into months, I'm still having a hard time accepting that my daughter is not coming back. I'm hoping she calls and tells me this has just been a big misunderstanding. But she doesn't call. I go to work under a cloud. I am surprised when I put a meal on the table and don't remember cooking it. Sometimes, cars honk at me to move when the light changes. I have lost weight but would take it back if it could reverse what has happened. I wish I knew how long grief lasts, because it is so heavy on your heart and doesn't seem to make room to let in any kind of joy. Children seem to recover much faster from loss and disappointment than adults. I wish I could steal some of that energy. I don't want to pretend like I didn't lose my daughter, I just want to be able to remember her and smile.

Venetia and I made up. I apologized for being insensitive at a time when she just needed someone to listen to how she was feeling, not why. Of course, Rodney is still pretending to be a bachelor and Venetia's still pretending like he's just on a working vacation. Whatever works for them works for me. I just want my sister to be happy, and knowing that she's not is what makes me sad sometimes. Arlene, on the other hand, still has the same attitude but bit her lip and broke down and told Venetia that she just didn't like the way her husband had been taking advantage of her all these years, that she was angry for Venetia and wished Venetia would realize that adultery is a sin and go ahead and divorce Rodney's cheating ass so she can sell that house, which she told Venetia she could get a good price for, and Arlene said she would be more than happy to find her a more contemporary condo, since Venetia was only one child away from being free now that Zach was away at college. She meant well.

When Arlene calls me and even mentions Venetia's name, I change the subject or pretend I'm busy and ask if I can call her back. Most of the time I don't, and I think she's starting to take the hint. Yesterday, she just left me a message, which to my surprise had nothing to do with Venetia. "Betty Jean, I was just wondering if you've been down to Social Services yet and filed those papers, since you're entitled to monthly assistance for those boys, and if you're having a hard time over there, please don't be too proud to say so, because I would be more than happy to give, not lend, you whatever you might need to help you get through this difficult time. Call me when it's convenient."

I had to replay this at least two or three times because, first of all, Arlene's voice was pleasant, I'd even say warm, and I was thinking maybe she might be drunk or something, but by the third listen, I realized she was just being nice. I was so moved, I called and told her how much I appreciated her offer and for caring, and should things get to that point, I would certainly take her up on it.

It takes me six months to finally find the energy to come back to Social Services to ask for their help. My credit cards are up to their limit and my car, which is going on seventeen years old, is starting to need attention, and that attention also costs money. According to Dexter and Luther, I really need a new one. I am not in a position to add any more monthly payments to the ones I'm already making. I'll worry about it when it breaks down.

Ricky is nickel-and-diming me, being on the swim team. Twice a week I sit by that pool and watch him torpedo his way through that water and try not to think about all the hidden costs that I was not prepared for. For seven years old he's outswimming some of the nine-year-olds in freestyle, and he's learning the breaststroke even though his little chest barely pops above those waves. I am so proud of him. And it is becoming obvious that his attention in class has improved since being weaned off that medication. Not all pills work, and there are too many kids out here on medication for one thing, when it seems to cause something else.

I'm grateful Luther doesn't have expensive hobbies, but the boy is growing like Jack and the Beanstalk. Every time I look around I have to buy him new shirts, pants, and sneakers. He's still a bookworm and reads anything and everything.

When I hear my name being called, I cannot believe I get the same bitch that didn't help me before. When I sit down and she starts looking over my chart, she acts like this is the first time she's ever laid eyes on me. She is wearing that same boring gray suit and still looks like she has never had sex and doesn't care. I don't know who told her red lipstick looks good on her. It doesn't. Especially on her top two teeth. But I'm not about to say a word.

"So, what brings you back," she asks, looking over my form, and then looks back up and says, "Mrs. Butler?"

I can tell she still doesn't like me, or anybody else that comes in here, for that matter. I don't know why some people work in public jobs if they don't like the public. "My situation has changed."

"Did your daughter come back?"

"Yes, she did."

"Sometimes they do. So what brings you here today?"

I hand her the death certificate. She gives me an evil eye.

"What happened to her?"

"What difference does it make?"

She sucks her teeth and that lipstick just smudges.

"I need to put the cause of death in the file."

"She OD'd in the backseat of a car. How's that?"

"I'm sorry for your loss."

I want to say, "Once more with feeling, bitch!" but of course all I want to know is how long it will take to get some aid and how much they will be able to help me.

"Thank you."

"I see it's been six months since she passed on. What took you so long to apply for assistance?"

"I've been a little overwhelmed."

"I'm sure you have. Has your financial situation changed since you were last here?"

"Yes, it has."

"In what way?"

"It's worse."

"Are you still working?"

"Yes, but I don't know for how much longer."

"Why is that?"

"Because my grandsons require a lot of time and attention and they participate in after-school activities and my husband is terminally ill and . . ."

"You didn't say anything about your husband being sick last time."

"Well, he is. Do you want me to get the diagnosis from his doctor to prove it?"

"It might help. And again, I'm sorry. It's obvious you've got a lot on your plate."

"Probably no more than most of the folks who come in here."

"Well, I'll do my best to expedite your application but I can authorize some emergency food stamps for you today, if that would help?"

"Anything would help."

"Now, it still might take a few weeks because this is just part of a bureaucratic process, but here's my card should you have any unforeseen problems."

She stands up, walks me to the door, and rubs my shoulder.

"Thank you for your help," I say, and turn back around and move my index finger back and forth in front of my mouth. "Wipe your teeth. You've got lipstick on them."

She does it and then smiles. "Thank you," she says.

Quentin

Mother refuses to answer the phone when I call. She also refuses to call back. She did send a card and a twenty-dollar gift card from Target congratulating us on little Margaret's birth but she has not said a word about the photos we've sent. I know she's probably angry with me for not attending my sister's funeral, but I didn't want to go so I didn't. It would have been too depressing seeing all those relatives I've been estranged from for years, and in some cases, not being able to even recognize many of them. Of course I loved Trinetta, at least I used to, but after she stopped loving herself and her children, I lost all respect for her. Besides, she didn't like that I married outside our race and she made sure to remind me of it. I always knew drugs were going to be the cause of her demise, and my attending her funeral would only have confirmed it and it wouldn't bring her back. I in no way could offer Mother any comfort, and I was also worried about my own daughter. She was born with some immune-system issues and I couldn't imagine leaving her here with Mindy to care for alone even though Mindy's parents live less than a half hour's drive away, but they both work, and heaven forbid, should there be an emergency, the thought of being hours away from little Margaret caused me too much strife.

I did, however, send three hundred dollars in lieu of flowers, with the hope that it would help mitigate the cost of the service, which I know was not covered by any insurance, and since my felonious brother, Dexter, is now living above the garage in a makeshift apartment he now calls home, I doubted that he would be of much, if any, help to Mother under the circumstances.

I'm in Los Angeles for a three-day chiropractic conference and have decided to pay Mother a visit with the hope that she won't embarrass me in front of my wife. I've already warned Mindy that we are going to be visiting the ghetto and not to be shocked by what she sees. She is prepared and has agreed to not let anyone touch little Margaret without first washing their hands.

I haven't seen my dad in a couple of years, and although I doubt he'll even recognize me, it'll still be good to see him. His funeral I will attend because he has been a good father. It was he who encouraged me to fulfill my dreams of becoming a chiropractor. "What's a few more years of college?" he said. He'd never been to college at all, and that meant a lot to me. Mother simply liked the fact that I was going to be some kind of doctor, and I believe she put money on my being a success after she saw the highway Dexter was traveling down, and Trinetta meandering down avenues and boulevards with busted-out streetlights. They were always in danger of self-destructing, and what was sad was how easily they managed to accomplish nothing of merit when both of our parents, especially Mother, did the best they could pointing us in the right direction. Her love sustained me, and Dad's confidence more than compensated for my insecurities.

I decided to phone first, just for the heck of it, knowing what time she'd be in, since her schedule at that dreadful hotel hasn't changed. It has lost a star, from what I gather, and I for one will be glad when she finally retires. Although now that she's taken on a second shift at parenting, I am at a loss as to how she's going to manage it. Children require a certain set of skills that, over time, would seem to diminish because they have not been necessary or have been used up. Since grandparenting requires a different kind of love, I wonder if it's even possible to raise grandchildren to achieve the requisite confidence and ambition as well as acquire the myriad skills and facilities one needs to be a success in this technologically driven age. I mean, what are those boys going to be exposed to, being educated in inferior schools where they most likely won't be able to pass standardized tests?

If my practice grows in the Bay Area at the rate it did in Portland, I would be more than willing to help aid in these boys getting a quality education. I don't know if I have the power, or if there'll still be time, to preempt the pull of the streets.

"Hello," a boy's voice says.

"Hello," I say. "And to whom am I speaking?"

"You are speaking with Luther. And who may I ask is calling?"

I am impressed not only by his tone but his diction, and he is not mocking me. "Well, Luther, this is your uncle Quentin calling and I was hoping to speak with your grandmother, who also happens to be my mother, if she's available."

"My grandma's here. Hold on a minute, please."

He drops the phone. I like Luther already. He sounds about eight or nine, but you never know. I wait. I'm at a five-star hotel on Wilshire Boulevard and Mindy's breastfeeding little Margaret, who is being fussy, which is why I chose to come out into the living room.

"What is it you want?" she asks in a mean-spirited voice.

"I know you're undoubtedly still angry with me, Mother, and I do understand, but I also wish you would have understood that my newly arrived daughter was suffering from a health condition we

216

weren't sure about at the time Trinetta passed, and I am deeply sorry that I wasn't able to attend and I am hoping that you can find it in your heart to forgive me since Mindy and little Margaret and I are here in Los Angeles for a couple of days and wondered if we could possibly drop by to say hello and spend an hour or so?"

"You use far too many words to say so little, but I forgive you. Come on over. I'm making dinner, if you can stomach the food we eat in the hood."

"We'll see you in about forty-five minutes, depending on traffic. Is there anything I can bring?"

"Don't ask," she says, and hangs up.

"Don't apologize," Mindy says when we turn onto my old street. "You aren't the first black man to grow up in this kind of environment, Quentin, and it's nothing to be ashamed of. I'm going to see to it that as Margaret grows up she gets to see where both of her families come from."

"You don't have to say this to make me feel better."

"Oh, stop playing the victim, Quentin. It's not always about you. Your mother has been forced to raise her grandsons with little or no support, and all you're worrying about is how things look? Do you not ever watch BET?"

"No, I don't."

"You give new meaning to being black and proud, and I'm not going to let you pass it on to our daughter."

I can't respond to that. I pull into the driveway, behind my mother's 1986 beige La Sabre. I say nothing but help Mindy get all of the baby gear and then maneuver little Margaret out of the backseat. There are so many hooks to keep them strapped in, I sometimes wonder how you would get a child out were you to be unfortunate enough to have an accident. She whimpers but then gurgles.

"One hour, tops, Mindy. And if you are uncomfortable before then, just give me a wink and I'll come up with a reason why we must be going."

"Quentin, sometimes you really get on my nerves."

I see the porch light come on even though it's just approaching dusk. My mother opens the screen and stands guard behind two handsome young boys, one of whom comes up to her shoulders already. I assume that must be Luther. They wave and then run down the three steps toward us and hold out their hands to shake mine.

"Pleased to meet you, Uncle Quentin. I'm Luther, and this is Ricky."

"The pleasure is all mine," I say, and shake both of their hands.

"Hello, son," Mother says, and walks right past me toward my wife. "It's so nice to finally meet you and Miss Margaret, Mindy," and she wraps her arms around Mindy to give her a hug and bends down and kisses little Margaret on the nose. Mindy doesn't so much as flinch. "What a cutie. She looks just like you, Mindy. Lucky for her. Come on in, and watch the bottom step. Dexter has been promising to fix it but he works day and night."

"Is he here?" I ask, hoping he's not.

"No, he's working."

When we walk in I can hear the floor panels under the carpet creak, as if the house is lopsided, which it probably is. Mindy sits down on the sofa I grew up sitting on and places little Margaret's carrier on the floor by her foot.

"Can I hold the baby?" Ricky asks as he plops down next to Mindy.

"Sure, you can. Do you know how to hold a little baby?"

"Yep. I mean, yes. I mean, no, maybe if you showed me."

"I know how," Luther says.

"Would you two mind washing your hands first?" I ask.

"Grandma made us wash them right before you got here 'cause she knew you were gonna have a real live baby and she wanted to make sure we were clean, right, Grandma?"

"That's right."

Mindy just gives me a look to not press this, and places little Margaret in Ricky's arms. He looks down at her, breathing on her, and I do my best not to blow a gasket.

"So, it's nice to finally meet you, Mrs. Butler," Mindy says. "And you, too, boys."

"The feeling is mutual. You can drop the 'Mrs. Butler' and just call me 'Mom' or 'BJ'—short for Betty Jean."

"I like 'Mom.'"

"Well, Mindy, I've got a soulful dinner here for you to enjoy unless you're one of those vegans or a vegetarian or worried about your cholesterol."

"I'll eat whatever you put on my plate."

"Quentin, your father's asleep, but if you'd like to take a peek at him, that would be nice."

"I will in a sec, Mom. Just want to make sure the boys handle little Margaret with kid gloves."

"Her mother is sitting right next to them, Quentin, and I'm standing in front of them. What are you worried about?"

"Please repeat that, Mom," Mindy says.

"Oh, never mind. I can't help it if I'm an overprotective dad. She's my first."

I walk back to Mother and Dad's room, and I'm almost afraid to turn on the light but I do, since it's the only way I can see what's left of him. He is small and he looks unfamiliar. His eyes are closed and he doesn't move. I go over to touch him just to make sure he's warm, and am relieved that he is. I remember when Dexter and I used to jump on this bed like it was a trampoline and Dad wouldn't tell Mother how the slats broke after we'd gotten too big. When I hear little Margaret begin to cry I dash out to where everyone is now sitting, and Mother is holding her and giving my daughter a bottle.

"Is she okay? I can take her."

"Babies usually cry when they're hungry or need to be changed, Quentin."

"I know that, Mother."

"Why do you keep calling her 'little' Margaret?" Ricky asks.

"Because she's little."

"Will you call her 'big' Margaret when she grows up?"

"I don't think so," I say. "Mother, although we appreciate your going to all this trouble to make dinner for us, we really can't stay."

"Yes, we can, Mom," Mindy says.

"I was already frying pork chops when you called, Quentin. So I didn't go out of my way."

I try to smile but I am finding it difficult to understand why Mindy has contradicted me from the time we got here and doesn't seem the least bit concerned about our daughter's health.

"I'm dying for a pork chop," Mindy says. "And what else is it that smells so good?"

"Macaroni and cheese, candied yams, and steamed broccoli," Mother says.

"One day I hope you'll show me how to make all of it!" Mindy says. "Unless you have an objection to it, Quentin."

Everybody looks at me. Including little Margaret. I grab a plate and begin to fill it up with all the things I no longer eat.

After dinner I pull Mother aside while Mindy and the boys play with little Margaret. I can't believe Mindy didn't ask them to wash their hands again; after all, I could see chocolate frosting on Ricky's knuckles.

"I like this one," Mother says before I have a chance to ask. "She's got your number, so I'd calm down if I were you."

"She loves me."

"Anyway, although you're still on my shit list, I'm being civil because I don't feel like getting ugly in front of your lovely wife or the boys, and as much as I do love you, you have a way of getting on my last nerve because of how you do things without any regard for others. Most of us are not perfect like you seem to think you are, and mark my words, if you don't learn how to accept anybody who falls short of your standards, you're going to end up a lonely old man. Thanks for stopping by."

Tammy

I can't live here," Jackson says to me.

"Oh, really," is all I can say to that.

"L.A. is too big and spread out, it's ugly, smoggy, full of freaks, it's way too crowded, and there's too many goddamn cars on the freeway. It takes too long to go nowhere and I think it's one overrated city and I prefer to watch stuff that goes down here on TV, because that's where it seems a whole lot more real. I also don't like how hard everybody here tries to be beautiful. Even men. As if it's really worth the price they put on it."

"Is that about it?" I ask. We're having breakfast at Denny's, Jackson's favorite haunt. He doesn't even know he's white trash, and what I love about him is he doesn't give a shit what I or anybody else thinks about him. I have to give him credit, though, for cutting back on ale, learning how to drive a big rig, and owning up to how many years of his life he wasted doing nothing.

"I'm better off out in the plains and prairie. I'm better off where there's horses and elk. Where you can actually see the mountains. Where you can drink the water right out of a stream or river and not worry about what's in it that might kill you. I'm better off where everybody isn't a stranger."

"So, what are you saying, Jackson? You come here in bad shape

222

and bring me bad news and I do my best to help you get on your feet, get used to having you around, and now you're ready to bail on me?"

"Can I smoke in here?"

"You see that No Smoking sign over there?"

He turns to look. "That's another thing. You can still smoke in restaurants in Montana. And in Wyoming, which is where I believe I'm headed."

"What's for you in Wyoming?"

"Everything I just described. Plus I've got some friends there. One of whom is a female."

"I thought you were asexual, brother."

"I'm not a homosexual. You should know better than that."

"I said 'asexual,' which means you could live without it."

"It seems to me that's more befitting of you, sister, since I haven't exactly seen you ruffling anybody's feathers since I've been here and you still look like you could benefit from a date every now and then."

"I've been busy."

"You've been playing Mama when you ain't a mama, just like Betty Jean across the street, but at least she's got a good reason. What's your excuse? Montana is an adult."

"I'm just helping my daughter get on her feet."

"I think she's pretty close to Rollerblading by the looks of things. You appear to be more like a built-in babysitter who doesn't get paid. Forgive me if I'm out of line, sis, but since I'm about to vamoose, I figured I might as well get a few things off my chest."

"Well, don't let me stop you, Dr. Phil."

"Who's Dr. Phil?"

"Never mind. I'm all ears. More coffee?"

"No, thank you. Anyway, that Trevor fella is cheating on your daughter, you know."

"How would you know that?"

"There are obvious signs."

"Like what?"

"Notice how nice he looks when he goes for auditions he never gets?"

"He also has a full-time job."

"Does he pay rent?"

"Some."

"But not enough. Because any man with a kid wouldn't want to be mooching off his wife's parents, and in this case, her mother, and notice how Montana only smiles at the baby when he's in the same room?"

"So?"

"When a woman is getting laid, she smiles at the man that's giving it to her right."

What I'm thinking right this minute is how long it's been since I smiled at a man.

"How many teeth does Clementine have now?"

"What? Six. Almost eight. Why?"

"Weren't they supposed to have moved out before she started teething?"

"It's expensive to live here."

"Is Montana crippled?"

"What do you mean by that?"

"Didn't she get a college degree in something that would make her employable?"

"Yes. Maybe. No."

"Why do parents always make excuses for their kids when they don't live up to their expectations?"

"You should talk, Jackson."

"My point exactly. I know me and Clay were fuck-ups and we

were major disappointments to Ma and Paps, but unlike you modern parents, they didn't apologize for us. They were pissed off at how we turned out and let us know it."

"I'm not apologizing for Montana. She's just young. And trying to find her way."

"Why couldn't she have found it before she had a baby? And how hard was she looking?"

I just look at him.

"Well, I've heard her sing. And she sounds like you wouldn't turn the channel on the radio if you were to hear her."

"A lot of people can sing in L.A."

"He doesn't love her anymore."

"How in the hell do you know that?"

"Because he told me."

"He told *you*?"

"I wouldn't lie."

"Since when did you two get so chummy?"

"Since he met somebody else."

I kick him under the table. "And you couldn't fucking say anything?"

"I'm saying it now. Look. He's not a bad guy, he's just not that bright. I don't know why Montana couldn't see past his good looks, but women see what they want to see in a man, which is why they end up lonely."

"You need your own talk show, Jackson, since you've got it all figured out."

"I didn't say that, now did I? I'm trying to run into instead of away from myself, for which I thank you dearly because had you not opened your heart and your front door to me, I'd probably be dead, too."

"You're my brother, for Christ's sake."

"Yeah, and so what? But this Trevor is bad news for your daughter and my niece, and he doesn't know jack shit about being a father and is not interested in being a husband."

"He couldn't possibly have told you all this. Was he drunk or on something?"

"No. Sometimes people need to talk to whoever's willing to listen. And that's all I did."

"And what makes you so insightful?"

"Because I used to be just like him."

"So when is it you plan on abandoning me and your niece and maybe her ex-boyfriend?"

"As soon as I get my next paycheck, which should be in two weeks. I'll have something for you, too."

"Oh, buy yourself a calf," I say. "And by the way, looks like I've got an offer on the rest of the property."

"I wish you all the best."

"You can have half of what I get."

"I don't want half of what you get."

"Why not?"

He slides his chair away from the table and pulls out his cigarettes.

"Buy yourself a condo. And move as far away as possible from all these niggers."

"Ricky won another trophy," BJ tells me as we sit in my backyard with our feet in the pool. "I'm getting sick of pools," she says, and stands up. "I also don't know where I'm going to put all these doggone trophies. My living room is swimming in them. Get it? Anyway, I don't know how much longer I can do this swim team."

"I hate to say it, but I'm getting a little sick of Ms. Clementine and her mother and her baby daddy, too."

"I would like to think so. That little girl will be in kindergarten before you know it."

"Yeah, and I'm worried that Mr. Movie Star's love appears to have strayed, but he is in no position to leave just yet."

"Why do you think that?"

"I'm just assuming. I hear them upstairs arguing low-like and they don't smile at each other like they did before Clementine got here. I'm just tired of running a nursery and a free hotel."

"Then tell them to leave."

I just look at her.

"Come on, Tammy, you're letting them take advantage of you and you need to put your foot down and speak up. I don't know why you're so scared to say something."

"Maybe I will."

"What about your brother? I haven't seen him in weeks."

"He decided to move away from 'freaks, smog, and niggers,' unquote."

"And he couldn't say bye?"

I just look at her.

"Turns out some stereotypes are true. I had given him the benefit of the doubt. But some folks just aren't ready for prime time. Anyway, how are you? I hardly ever see you these days. You look tired as all hell."

"I don't even know where to start, Tammy."

I'm sitting on the second-to-last stair that leads upstairs when I hear Trevor's car pull into the driveway. I've had two glasses of wine, I won't lie, because I needed a little assistance to say what I've been wanting to say.

"Hi there, Tammy," says Mr. Movie Star, surprised, of course, to see me relaxing on the stairway looking like I was waiting for somebody. He's wearing some kind of denim getup you see in music videos. His hair looks wet even though it's dry. He whitens his teeth about once a month, which is why I can see them glistening from over here. He has a membership to one of those tanning booths. I know because he dropped it on the front porch one day and I hid it. Now, all of a sudden, he's got muscles galore but does not belong to any gym to my knowledge.

"How are you today, Trevor?"

"I'm okay, I guess. Is everything all right?"

"You tell me."

"I'm not sure what you mean. Should I sit down for this?"

"Suit yourself."

"Did I do something wrong?"

I try hard not to cut my eyes at him but I'm not so sure I succeed. "You know I don't like you, don't you?"

He walks over and sits down at the far end of the white sofa, which his daughter has smeared with orange yogurt.

"No, I didn't know you didn't like me. I know you've had issues with me, but that's different, isn't it?"

"What did you tell my brother?"

"I'm not sure what you mean."

"Didn't you tell him you didn't love Montana?"

"Are you serious?"

"And you've met somebody else?"

"You are serious. First of all, Tammy, I love Montana and she knows it. I never had a conversation with your brother about anything except our daughter. And if this were true, why on earth would I tell him?"

"I do not have an answer for that."

"I feel like a loser, if you want to know the truth, because I have brought a child into the world and can't afford to take care of her. I didn't plan this."

"So, are you saying that Montana did?"

"No. But she knew why I came to Los Angeles, to pursue my acting career. She said she was going to the Peace Corps in a year. We fell in love and the next thing I knew she's pregnant and she said she wanted to keep it. And here we are."

"And here we are."

"What do you want me to do, Tammy?"

"What can you do, Trevor? Tell me that, would you?"

"Keep working at my craft with the hope that it'll pay off soon and Montana and Clementine and me can move into our own place."

"You guys did this all ass-backwards, you know that? I was not this dumb when I was your and Montana's age. You don't bring a kid into the world and then move in with your parents until you get your shit together. You move out of your parents' house and get your shit together on your own."

"I agree."

I stand up because I'm tired of talking to him. I wish I had the nerve to tell him to get out of my house and take my daughter and that granddaughter of mine with him. But I can't. They're just young. And stupid. And who knows, maybe one day they'll thank me for the hospitality.

Omar

My mother is too honest as well as dishonest. She has lied to me about a lot of things, the most important one being who my father was. It's also taken me twenty-eight years to understand how much she's done to make me dependent on her. How she used food to make me love her and she used food to cripple me. I know it wasn't on purpose, but now that I'm on to her, there is no tactful way for me to tell her, which is why I didn't tell her I was getting the Lap Band and why I chose to leave the way I did. If I'd told her, she would've done everything possible to try to talk me out of doing both.

I was tired of being fat. Tired of not saying no to myself even when I wanted to. Tired of her asking me every time I walked out the door where I was going and what time I was coming back. I was tired of jerking off every day, too. Tired of not knowing what it felt like to be inside a girl, or hell, a woman. She made me afraid of them. Her list of requirements was so high no girl could've fulfilled them. Which is why I had to learn how to fuck by watching porn. It has taken me probably two hundred jars of Vaseline to finally realize it was time to touch a woman, but first I was going to have to learn how not to be afraid to talk to one. I did not want to do it weighing three hundred pounds.

My mother has a good heart but she's a control freak and I can't do anything about that. I just need a break from her. I want to know what it's like not to have to hear her opinion about every- thing. And I mean everything. I want to not have to hear her criti- cize everything and everybody. I want her to stop making excuses for me, about why I still haven't managed to find my place in the world or why I haven't managed to get an AA degree from a junior college. I wasn't born to be a failure even though I've failed at a lot of things. I don't know what I'm good at because I haven't been given the chance to find out. "Try this," she'd say. "It'll look good on paper." But I don't want to just look good on paper. I want to feel excited about something—hell, anything. My mother has tried to find a career for me, which is why I don't have one. Deep down inside, I have wanted to please her, but I also wanted to disappoint her. I didn't want her to take credit for anything I did that would make me succeed.

When I left her that message a few months ago telling her I was leaving in an attempt to do some serious soul-searching, I meant it.

It wasn't hard finding out who my father was. I've known who the motherfucker was for years. All I did was go through her papers, which she kept in a trunk at the foot of her bed. I didn't need the key, since one of my homeboys from shop class taught me how to pick a lock—and trunks don't even count. I don't know if or when I'm going to tell her that I found two different birth certificates in that trunk. One had "Unknown" next to "Father" (which was the one she used when I went to camp), and the other one said "Samuel Nelson" (which is the one she used to get my passport when we went to Mexico). I didn't feel like telling her I knew who he was after years of her telling me he was dead. What a rotten thing to do. But when I really thought about why she did this, I figured she must have had a good reason. I could find him if I really wanted to, but at this point in my life, I honestly don't know what difference it would make. I've got enough identity issues right now without adding him into the mix. Who knows, if my curiosity ever gets the best of me, I'll find him.

Right now I'm driving along the Pacific Coast Highway in my new used Honda because I sold that stupid 325i I never wanted in the first place and rented a large studio apartment. I'm not going anywhere in particular when my cell phone rings. It's Luther. My little second cousin I think of more as a nephew and who thinks he's a cool cucumber 'cause he can read damn near anything. For not even being ten, I see a future in his future. Him and Ricky need some kind of a big brother or uncle figure, and since Uncle Dexter doesn't seem to be bringing anything to the table, I told Aunt Betty I would always be available to take them to the movies, Disneyland, the Tar Pits, the beach—hell, anywhere they want to go—just to give her a break. I told her this way before Trinetta died. I saw this coming a long time ago. One thing I am grateful for is never having any interest in drugs. As quiet as is kept, if Trinetta were here, I'd like to kick her ass. I know it's not cool to speak ill of the dead, but she could've found a better way to get off, one that wouldn't rob her soul and put her kids' well-being on the bottom of the totem pole. But who am I to talk? A lot of folks thought I had the same kind of love affair with food, that I was on the verge of eating myself straight toward a heart attack, and I probably was.

"What's up, little smurf," I say to Luther.

"This is Luther, Omar."

"I can see the phone number on my cell phone, son. How many times do I have to tell you that?"

"Whatcha doing?"

"Driving."

"Where are you driving to?"

"Nowhere. Just driving."

"That's kinda dumb to be driving nowhere, Omar. Then how are you supposed to know when you get there?"

"You ask too many questions. What can I do for you?"

"Nothing."

"Then why'd you call me?"

"Just to say hi."

"Where's your grandma?"

"I don't know."

"What do you mean you don't know?"

"She didn't come home from work yet."

"Is Nurse Hattie still there?"

"Yep."

"Who picked you and Ricky up from school?"

"Miss Tammy."

"Why?"

"She said Grandma was not feeling good and had to stop at the hospital but she would be home for dinner. But it's already dinner and she ain't . . . she isn't here yet."

"Did you try her cell phone?"

"Yep. She didn't answer. Wait. Hold on a minute."

I'm already off the highway and heading toward Pico. I don't know if I should be afraid or not, but this doesn't sound right. A few seconds later, Luther comes back on the line.

"She said to tell you she's fine and will be home in fifteen or twenty minutes. She had to get a shot in her knee at the emergency room. She asks me to ask you to stop on by if you could."

"Tell her I'm on my way. But do not call my mother."

"Why not?"

"That is none of your business. Would you please just tell her what I said?"

"Okay. Ricky said hey."

Aunt Betty is my favorite aunt. I like Aunt Venetia too, but being around her is like being in church. Everything with her is a sermon. I like Aunt Betty's spunk and especially when she slips and swears. When I pull in front of the house Aunt Betty is parked in the driveway, the engine off, just sitting in her car. This is not cool. I walk over to the driver's side. She's crying. I knock on the window and she lets it roll down.

"Aunt Betty, what's wrong?"

"I'm too old for all of this," she says.

"Too old for all of what?"

She flings her hand up so high it hits the roof of the car. "Everything," she says. "I don't know what made me think I could take care of two growing boys, no matter how much I love 'em. I've got a dying husband inside that house I can't do anything for. I can't afford to retire but my knee is finally starting to give out and I'm on my feet for almost eight hours, five days a week. I've got arthritis in the right one and these shots only last so long. I so need a vacation, baby. Just someplace to go and sit back and be waited on."

"I know, Auntie."

She looks up at me.

"You have grown into a fine young man, you know that, don't you, Omar?"

"I don't know all about that, Aunt Betty."

"Look, your mama is enough to get on anybody's nerves, but I see you took the reins of your life and lost all that weight, and I heard you're dating and everything."

"I'm not dating anybody."

"That's what your mama told me. Why would she lie?"

"Why wouldn't she? I'm sorry. I didn't mean to say that."

"Luther said you didn't want me to tell her you were coming over here. Why not?"

"You didn't tell her, did you?"

"No. I don't talk to your mama on a daily basis. Sometimes once a week is too much."

"Thank you. I'm just taking a little time away from my mom to figure out what kind of man I can be."

"I say hallelujah to that. Your secret is safe with me."

"Thank you, Aunt Betty. Now, is there anything I can do for you and the boys right now? Buy them dinner?"

"See how thoughtful you are? I stopped and got them Burger King, which of course I'm not eating, but anyway, I'm sorry for making a spectacle of myself, Omar. I just needed to calm down before I walked into the house. I don't want the boys to have to deal with any more sadness. They've had enough of it. I was just having a moment."

She goes to open the door and I hear the front door swing open and both of the boys run out to the car. They jump up and down like they haven't seen her in years. She hugs them the exact same way.

Principal Daniels

As much as I admit to looking forward to seeing Betty Jean again, I dread the circumstances. Unfortunately, I've had a lot of them over the years. Sometimes I have felt like throwing in the towel, taking my twenty-six-footer and just cruising around until I reach the end of the world. When I retire, I have promised myself to spend every summer traveling to a place I've always wanted to see. Why not? In the winter, which I love, I'm going to spend a month in the snow. Lake Tahoe. Or maybe even Colorado.

I have spent so many years worrying about the welfare of children that I suppose I might be what is commonly known as being burned out. I am tired of tragedy. Tired of not being able to save these children from the streets and, in too many cases, from their own parents. Teachers cannot parent. They are paid to do one job and that is to teach. Sometimes I fear for their safety in some of the classrooms and have come to understand why charter schools are becoming so popular. No child left behind is an understatement.

I knew it was a matter of time before these boys' mother would succumb to what has become a pandemic in our community. I have learned that it has nothing to do with how much or how little they love their child or children. Crack seems to be more of

236

a mental aphrodisiac than physical. I'm grateful that my biggest weakness is olives. Any kind of olive. There is not a day goes by that I don't devour—at minimum—a dozen of them. Perhaps if I still had a wife, I wouldn't lust over them, but after thirty years of marriage, she came out as a lesbian and left me for a woman and I haven't met anyone to take her place. Of course I was hurt, but she made it clear that I was not to blame. That she would always love me. And I her. She is so much happier now, for sure. And although our children are all adults, I was the one who had to persuade them that their mother was and would always be their mother and they should continue to love and respect her. If I could, surely it shouldn't be that hard for them.

I also must admit that I had a crush on Betty Jean back in the day but I would not let on that she impressed me save for being a very hands-on mother, which I admired. Her sons had promise, especially Quentin, but Dexter was always somewhat of a hothead and not a very good sport. In fact, he once got in a fight with one of his own team members and I was forced to make him sit out the rest of the season.

I straighten my tie and suck my teeth to make sure there's no evidence of the spaghetti I had for lunch and lotion my hands because they look dull. When I hear a light knock, I walk over and open the door. I still find her beautiful but rid myself of the thought or it could be too obvious.

"Thanks for coming on such short notice, Betty."

"I've been meaning to bring you the information about getting custody of Ricky and Luther but you beat me to it."

"Can I get you a cup of coffee? Water? Anything?"

She shakes her head.

I slide the chair out for her, giving her room to cross her legs, which she doesn't do. I walk around my desk and sit. It feels too formal, so I push the chair back, cross my legs, then fold my hands on my lap. She makes me nervous. "I'm very sorry to hear about your daughter."

"I know. I know."

"So, I'm sure you're curious about why I asked you to come in to see me."

"I am. Is it Ricky?"

"Yes and no. Let me say this. He's a bright youngster who has a few issues that for a while seemed under control, but I'm not sure whether since his mother passed this isn't having an emotional effect on him that you may not be aware of."

"Is he misbehaving in class?"

"Just the opposite. He's been rather quiet."

"That's understandable, though, wouldn't you say?"

"Yes, but then Luther, on the other hand, has been getting bullied. Hasn't he told you about it?"

"No, this is the first I'm hearing anything about this. In what way?"

"Well, you know he's tall for his age, and as a result he seems to pose more of a threat to his classmates than he really is."

She looks at me as if she wants me to hurry up and get to the point. I wish she could spend the day.

"You know we have kids here who have siblings who are gang-affiliated, right?"

"I would imagine."

"Well, one youngster has been picking on Ricky, and Luther got wind of it and took matters into his own hands and—"

"Wait a minute. What are you trying to say?"

"Luther beat up another youngster, who told his brother, who happens to be a seventh grader, and he's threatened to hurt Luther, for lack of a better way of putting it."

"Are you fucking serious?" she says, and jumps to a standing position. "I'm sorry for swearing. I apologize. Where's Luther? And when did this happen? And how did you find out about this? And what's being done to protect my grandsons?"

She drops back into the chair. Her shoulders drop, too. I know this is not what she needs to hear, and it is one of the things that break my heart when grandparents take on the burden—which is precisely what it is—of raising their grandchildren.

"No apology needed, Betty. Luther is in class. He's fine. We had both boys come in and speak to security and explain what happened. They both lied, of course, but what has become apparent is that the other youngster has put the word out that Luther is a threat. This kind of information spreads quickly, and it's the reason I asked to see you today."

"Can I get a glass of water, please, Mr. Daniels?"

"Of course. Remember, it's Warren."

"Thank you, Warren. But what am I supposed to do about this?"

"Just a second."

I press the intercom and ask if a bottle of Sparkletts can be brought in. I push my chair up to my desk and lean against the metal. "Let me ask you a few things, first, just so I'm clear. Did you ever file for assistance through Social Services?"

"I did. First, before Trinetta passed, and they were of no help, and then a couple of months ago, I brought in all the documentation they needed, including her certificate of . . . well, you know . . . and I was given two hundred dollars' worth of food stamps but haven't heard anything from them since."

"You have to hound them."

"I don't have time to hound anybody, Mr. Daniels. Warren."

"Even if it's just phone call after phone call, do it until you get on their nerves. Didn't you get a card from a social worker?"

239

"I did. And she seemed so sincere about trying to help and get it all pushed through quickly."

"They lie with sincerity. Call. Harass her. Find out who her supervisor is if you have to. That works."

A student aide brings in a bottle of water. She must be eleven. She's a lucky one. Just got a scholarship to attend Perrotta Charter School in the Valley, but it'll be worth the drive. I smile and thank her.

"I don't have a nice way of putting this to you, but I'm just going to ask: Do you have any friends or family who live in an area that has a good reputation for its school district?"

"I have two sisters who live in nice areas. One is way out in the Valley and the other one lives in Baldwin Hills Estates."

"Are you on good terms with one or both of them?"

"What would make you ask that?"

"Well, let's face it. Family is family. Need I say more?"

"We get along okay. So, tell me what it is you're suggesting."

"Of course, I'm not supposed to *suggest* anything like this to you, but if there was any way your sister would allow you to use her address, and if there was any possible way that you could get the boys to and from the elementary school—and I'm very familiar with both the elementary and the middle school up there—then you would be doing your grandsons a huge 'solid,' as these youngsters say."

She looks like she's going over it in her head. But she doesn't seem so sure.

"Let me think about how I'd propose something like this to her, because she can be a real stickler when it comes to doing everything by the book."

"People do this all the time. It's what's in the best interest of the children. Does she have any of her own?"

240

"One, but he's an adult."

"And I'm sure he attended good schools, am I right?"

She nods.

"And she has seen for herself what a difference it can make in a child's future, right?"

"Well, it sure helps," she says.

"So, if she's at all concerned about the children's well-being and safety, being ever conscious that you're trying to do what's best for them, I would like to think this would be an easy decision for her to make."

"I'd like to think so, too."

"Then why don't you discuss the situation with her as soon as possible, and in the meantime please know that the boys are being watched closely by our security guards and I can assure you that they're safe inside school grounds."

She stands up and holds out her hand to shake mine. Instead, I give her a supportive hug. Perhaps I was being too forward, because she steps back, then pats my arm as her way of thanking me.

"How's your husband doing, by the way?"

She just shakes her head.

Arlene

I wouldn't want to be Betty Jean for all the money in the world. Now she's having some kind of problems with them at their school she needs to talk to me about. I can only imagine. So, once again, I agreed to meet her in another public setting, this time, however, at a restaurant that has a menu that's not laminated.

Here she comes now. Looking distraught and forlorn. I am not in the mood for bad news. Omar left me a message and said he wants to pick up his computer and a few other personal items. I wonder if this means he really is moving out, or has he moved out and I just haven't been willing to accept it? I was just happy to hear his voice. In fact, I played the message about four times. If he has moved out, I'm thinking about taking a vacation. If he hasn't, I might ask him if he'd like to go on one with me.

"I don't want any coffee and I don't want to eat anything," she says before she even sits down. She whips out a bottle of water from her purse and sets it on the table. She's wearing a new wig. At least this one is modern and could almost be mistaken as her hair, which I suppose is the point. I don't know what her thing is about her real hair. But then again, I haven't seen it in years.

242

"I'm just having decaf. Anyway, I like your new hair," I say, just to break the ice. I'm nervous and not sure what this little meeting is going to be about that required we see each other face-to-face. But I'm ready for whatever it is. "So, how've you been holding up down there? I never see you anymore."

"I'm busy, Arlene. But you already know this, so don't act like you don't. Wait. I'm sorry. I didn't mean to say that or say it like that or use that tone. I've just got a lot of things on my mind."

"Well, I can't begin to imagine what it's like juggling all that you are, and if there's anything I can do to help, just let me know."

"Can I use your address so the kids can go to school in your neighborhood because a gang member has threatened Luther at his school?"

"You're not serious, Betty Jean?"

"Very."

"Is *this* what you wanted to talk to me about?"

She nods yes.

"I can't do that. It's illegal, and what would happen if I were to get caught?"

"People do it all the time, Arlene. It's not such a big deal."

"I can't. This is way outside of my comfort zone."

"You don't have to do anything."

"What if the gang members find out where I live?"

"How in the hell would they figure that out?"

"They're hoodlums but they're smart hoodlums."

"And what would be the point? Luther is ten. He's not on some hit list. The principal just thinks that because he and Ricky have already been exposed to so much this past year, and because Luther's such a good student and Ricky's improving, he asked if I had a family member or friend that lived in a good school

243

district who would let me use their address because it would be better for the boys. That's all."

"You mean the principal suggested this?"

She nods again.

"Did you ask Venetia?"

"She lives too far."

"You have to forgive me, Betty Jean. I mean, I do care about the welfare of your grandsons, but this is asking a lot. I have a reputation in my community, in my homeowners' association, not to mention professionally, and what if I got caught doing something like this?"

"Well, we wouldn't want you to get thrown into homeowners' prison, now would we? Never mind, Arlene."

"Don't you have any friends at your job that live in nice neighborhoods who might not have as much to lose you could ask?"

"No, everybody I work with is poor, Arlene. I said, never mind. Remind me never to ask you for a favor. I've gotta get back to work."

"Don't be mad at me, please?"

"I'm not mad. I should've known better."

"What's that supposed to mean?"

"Nothing. By the way, Arlene, how's Omar doing these days?"

"He's fine. Why would you ask?"

"I haven't seen him in ages. Tell him I said hello and the boys are waiting for him to take them to Knott's Berry Farm."

"I'll tell him when I see him, but we've been missing each other since he started back to school."

"Then maybe I'll have the boys call him. He gave them his cell phone number, you know."

"No. I didn't know. But I'll let him know tonight."

"They'll appreciate that. Nothing like family."

She grabs her bottle of water and leaves. She has been in the ghetto far too long. Far too long.

When I pull into the driveway, Omar isn't there. I postponed the closing until tomorrow. Told the buyers the loan docs weren't finished. I don't like to lie but sometimes you have to. I wanted to make sure I was here when Omar showed up. I'm nervous for the second time today, but this is different. This is my son. And his well-being is of utmost importance to me. I will try not to badger him about where he's been and why he's doing this to me and why we couldn't talk about whatever it was that was bothering him. I want him to get his own apartment and I think it's a brave thing for him to live on his own, but I just wasn't expecting him to tell me in the manner that he did. It threw me completely off guard. He could've had the common courtesy of giving me, as his mother, some kind of advance notice that he wasn't happy living at home anymore.

The door leading to the kitchen isn't locked, which means Omar has probably already been here. I push it open and rush up the stairs to his room. That door is wide open. His computer and printer are gone, and most of his sneakers. His closet is full of big-and-tall clothes that don't fit him anymore. On his bed is what looks like a printed-out letter. I pick it up. It's one page. This now makes three times today I've been nervous, but now I feel like I'm about to have a heart attack because why is it that my son of twenty-eight years suddenly finds it hard to talk to his own mother? I'm already crying but decide they might be wasted tears, so I dry my eyes and read:

Dear Mom: This may seem cowardly to you, and I may very well be doing this all wrong, and it is not my intention to hurt you even though I probably have already. When I decided to lose weight it was the beginning of my taking responsibility for myself as a man. The only problem is that it has been hard if not impossible to do living under the same roof with you all these years. I know you mean well, and I am grateful for all that you have done for me. But it's time for me to venture out on my own, make my own mistakes, my own decisions, and not feel the need to get your approval. Please understand that I am not "divorcing" you, I just feel I need some time and space to be alone. I sold my car and got an old Honda. I just moved into a studio apartment and am looking into working on a cruise ship. There are many job opportunities and a chance to see some of the world, for free! I have recently met someone from my past who has embraced me, which I won't get into now. Please know that I love you and as soon as something good happens to me, you will be the first to know. Take good care of yourself, and I hope you finally begin to live your life for yourself, and not for me. I'll be in touch. Please don't worry about me. I'm fine. Love you, Omar.

At first, I'm numb. But by the time I read it three or four more times, I'm pissed off and hurt by what my son is doing to me and I don't know why he chose to just up and disappear out of my life and leave me here all by myself to do nothing but worry about whether or not he's okay, if he's happy and safe, and I don't know what would make him decide to get a job on a damn cruise ship. I wonder who put this idea in his head?

When I left Louisiana, I told my parents far enough in advance so as not to cause them any long-term grief. Plus, I think they were glad to see me go. They were country folk and didn't rely on books to tell them how to raise their kids, but they certainly could've used a few educated tips.

I thought I was doing a good job raising Omar. I tried to make sure he got all the love a child needed. I may have gone overboard, but I never thought there was such a thing as too much love. Is there? Spoiled is one thing. And I did spoil him, but most onlies are spoiled, since they don't have to share until they get to preschool. *Sesame Street* helped. Or so I thought. I have now come to believe that maybe Omar is one of those privileged children who never wanted for anything and now it's backfiring. He's throwing it in my face, maybe not knowingly, but it's how it feels.

As a parent, how in the world are you supposed to know if the way you're raising your kids is sufficient until they grow up and you just watch to see what they absorbed or what you may have forgotten to give them? I don't think this is covered in Dr. Spock.

I suppose I shouldn't have lied to him about who his father was, or wasn't. But I figured knowing wouldn't do him much good, since Sam was married, and admittedly, I knew that when I met him. But I didn't care. Back in those days, I was pretty and had a good body and I knew what to wear. It was a game I played, and I played it too well. What I was more interested in was seeing how much it would take to attract them and then to fall in love. I was also pretty good in bed. Somewhat of a freak, as the saying goes. I let Sam, and a few others, do things to me I wouldn't even consider tolerating in later years. My tactics didn't work, but quite a lot of them had their share of fun inside and outside of my body. Sex was just sex to them. I learned this the hard way. I kept thinking that being educated would help me win at least one of their hearts, but it never happened. I admit I also never bothered to think about the wives. I don't know what this says about me, but it wasn't good. Especially for someone who majored in psychology. In all honesty, I believe it was pure ego. I wanted to know my own power and what it could get me. As it turned out, not much, with one exception, and his name is Omar.

Betty Jean

Mrs. Butler, I'm afraid Mr. Butler is having problems I can't manage," Mrs. Nurse Hattie says to me.

"What's happening?" I ask.

"Well, for starters, I've mentioned how he wishes I were Nurse Kim, whom he affectionately refers to as 'Kimmie,' and I've told him about a hundred times that I am not Nurse Kim, which usually upsets him, but today, when I sat him up to give him his meds, he pushed the dispenser aside, making the pills go all over the bed and floor, and he grabbed my breasts and tried to pull me down on top of him. So I slapped him."

I can't help but laugh. And it's finally good to have a reason to.

"I didn't hurt him, Mrs. Butler. It was my reflexes that made me do what I did to stop him, but I'm used to this kind of behavior with men who're suffering from dementia."

Now this is even funnier. Mrs. Nurse Hattie doesn't realize this is a case of mistaken identity because, dementia or not, she is not exactly a turn-on. Like Luther said, she is old and fat and, even though she doesn't smell like a skunk, she could stand to use stronger deodorant. I have not figured out a polite way to tell her she carries an odor, but I don't have to be around her all day and Mister obviously couldn't care less, so I just try to stay out of range.

"Mrs. Butler, this is not the problem I can't manage."

"Then what is it?"

"It's psoriasis."

"Mister's got psoriasis? Where?"

"Lots of areas I am not comfortable touching."

"Really? Did he just break out?"

"Well, since he is rather dark-skinned and often ashy no matter how much lotion I put on him, at first I started noticing dry patches on his elbows and then the backs of his arms but now they're turning red and scaly, and when I gave him his sponge bath this morning, I saw that they're now in an area I consider off limits under the circumstances."

"You mean the rash is on his penis?"

"Not exactly, Mrs. Butler, but in the general vicinity. You want me to show you some of them?"

"No. I'll take your word for it. I'll call his doctor first thing in the morning. Is he itching?"

"I would think so."

"Don't we have any ointment to rub on those areas?"

"I'll look."

"And maybe turn on that vitamin D light. He doesn't get enough sunlight."

"If he'd let me take him outside, it would help. But getting him to the bathroom takes all the strength I have. Oh, by the way, Mr. Jones told me to thank you for your years of kindness and fried chicken but today was officially his last day delivering mail."

Finally is all I can think. Except I sure hope I'm next.

I don't stay in the examination room with Mister but when the doctor comes out, he tells me something I wasn't expecting to hear.

"The psoriasis is treatable, Mrs. Butler, but it's his prostate I'm a little concerned about."

"His prostate? He doesn't have cancer, does he?"

"I'm not sure, but has he complained about not being able to urinate?"

"No. He doesn't complain about much of anything. But he doesn't seem to have to go very often."

"Since I've only been treating him for dementia, I don't see anything in his chart from his previous doctor that shows when he had a prostate exam. Do you recall when he last had one?"

"I don't know."

"Well, because of his age and since he may not be able to express his discomfort, I'd like to do a simple test to check his prostate while he's here."

"Please, do."

"Have a seat in the waiting area. It won't take long at all."

After he closes the door, a few minutes later, I hear Lee David behind it making squealing sounds as if someone is choking him. Two nurses walk past me and into the examination room, I'm sure to hold him down, and I pick up a *People* magazine and pretend not to hear him and pretend to read it. I pray he doesn't have cancer. He doesn't need another disease. Especially one I can't do anything for. He is a good man and shouldn't have to suffer any more than he has already. He's been robbed of real joy the past ten years, and it wouldn't seem fair for him to have anything else to endure.

When the door opens, he sits in his wheelchair, not sure where he is or what he's doing here, and I realize this is what's left of the man I married, a man who used to come up to the door frame and now can barely reach out to turn the doorknob. I remember when we used to go dancing and he would twirl me around until I was giddy. When he wore Polo cologne and white shirts open at the collar. When we stayed up after the kids were asleep and ate popcorn and watched scary movies and he would wrap his arms around me and kiss me right before I screamed. I remember how hard he laughed at the kids' corny jokes. And when he climbed that tall ladder and fixed the roof with no help, I made him drink my lemonade so he would stay cool.

When I see the look on the doctor's face, I feel a sense of relief.

"Well, the good news is I detected just a small lump and I'm going to recommend he be tested again in six months, just to be on the safe side. If, however, you notice any changes in his urinary stream, and this can include frequency, and if it seems painful for him, please let us know immediately."

"I will."

"And here's a few prescriptions for the psoriasis. Two are topical and one is medication to help boost his immune response."

"Thank you so much, doctor."

"If at all possible, it would be good if you could invest in a vitamin D light for Mr. Butler. They help tremendously."

When we get home, I catch Dexter in the kitchen, scouring through the fridge.

"Looking for something to eat?"

"Just something to snack on."

"Would it occur to you to offer to pay for anything, Dexter?"

"Ma, you know how much I earn working at the SA?"

"Enough to party on the weekend with Skittles, and I notice you don't seem to be low on funds when it comes to spending it at Frederick's or Target, now do you?"

"Have you been snooping around my room?"

"Snooping? I beg your pardon."

"Well, have you? Otherwise, how would you know what I spend my money on?"

"First of all, you can watch the tone of your voice talking to me, and second, since you're too busy to take the trash out but not too busy to fill it up, I happened to see the bags and some of the receipts by accident. You seem to be spending a lot more money than you make. How's that work?"

"I work on commission."

"At the Salvation Army? What color does stupid come in, Dexter, would you tell me that?"

"There's a place down the street from them that sells all kinds of auto parts and stuff and they let me take a cut of everything I sell, and if I help drum up business for them."

"Oh, really."

"I'm being straight with you, Ma."

"Then let me ask you this, son. With your extra cash would it occur to you to ask me if I might need any help with anything? Say, for instance, like food or gas money or maybe you might want to look under my hood and see if there's anything you can do to help save me a few dollars since you know I don't have what's called disposal income?"

"You've never asked me for any help."

"Then this means you didn't read my letters."

"I did. But from what I see, you seem to be doing okay."

"I feel like slapping your ass across the street, you know that?"

"Oh, is Miss Tammy home or maybe her racist brother? Oh, my bad, I heard he left the hood and beelined it back to Montana, where no black folks live."

I just look at him. This is not my son. He wouldn't talk to me this way. "Dexter, please don't tell me you're using drugs?"

"What would make you twist your mouth to ask me something as ridiculous as that, Ma?"

"I know how Trinetta acted, and this feels too familiar."

"What is? I'm not even doing anything!"

"What's making you talk to me this way?"

"What way?"

"Never mind. But I'm curious about something else, Dexter."

"I'm all ears, Ma."

"Remember when you were in prison and how you were always reading law books and the big plans you made to help some of the other black prisoners when you got out?"

"Of course I remember."

"What happened to those plans, Dexter?"

"I had to find a job, and you and I both know how long that took, and look at what kind of work I'm doing."

"And is this my fault?"

"Does it sound like I'm blaming you, Ma? I blame society for discriminating against us once we do our time and try to rejoin society."

"But you didn't do all of your time. You're on probation."

"I did enough time for a crime I didn't commit."

"Let's not go there, again, Dexter, please. I was just wondering whatever happened to those plans, because you seemed to care about some of those men who'd been wrongly accused."

"I still care. But first things first. And right now I'm just trying to make it from one day to the next."

"Well, since you're obviously earning a few extra dollars, I would appreciate it if you would start giving me at least fifty to seventy-five a week."

"A week?"

"You can't stay in a cheap hotel or eat at Denny's for that

much, and not only that but you use my water to bathe and to wash your nasty work clothes and you eat up my food and you don't do a goddamn thing around here to help me. So yes."

"Starting when?"

"How about right now?"

He reaches in his back pocket and pulls out a wad of bills. He hands me five twenties. "Will this help?"

I just look at him. Something different is in his eyes. He looks wound up. Tight. I haven't seen him like this before. Or maybe because of us passing in the night, I just haven't noticed.

"Everything helps," I say.

"Good. Is there anything you need me to do?"

"When was the last time you checked in on your daddy?"

"A couple of days ago. All he does is sleep or hide under the covers, and lately he seems to be scratching. What's up with that?"

"He's got psoriasis."

"Well, at least that's curable."

"Where does Skittles live?"

"Why are you asking me this out of the blue?"

"Because if you don't change your attitude, you might have to ask her if she has any room for you."

Venetia

just got served," I tell Betty Jean.

"What do you mean, 'just'?"

"This morning."

"Where are you?"

"At church."

"Get up off your knees, Venetia. Right now. I mean it."

"I'm in the parking lot."

"Then back that damn car up and meet me at my hotel. I'm booking our best suite for you and don't say no and don't stop by your house to pick up anything, just drive. I'm not leaving until you get here."

Click.

And she hangs up.

I make a big mistake and call Arlene.

"Fuck Rodney," she says. "Where are you? And please don't say church."

"I'm on my way to BB's hotel. She's booked me a suite."

"I'll meet you there."

Click.

I don't know why they always have to swear to make their point. I understand they do it for emphasis but they should know

256

it's not necessary. On the other hand, I have to admit that since Rodney's been away I have found myself saying s-h-i-t and occasionally the "F" word to myself, and what is odd is how I'm finding swearing to be a new way of releasing stress, like this morning, for instance, when my doorbell rang. Right after I opened the door, I already knew what it was, when the well-dressed but homely blonde handed me an envelope and smiled while she did it, like she was an old friend here to get reacquainted. Years ago she would've been the Avon lady. Our mother used to sell Avon and the house always had a confusing smell of talcum powder and flowery perfume, but I've watched enough people getting served on television to know, and I know they would never have let her through the front gate if she wasn't legal. All I said was "Thank you. And tell my husband I said, 'Fuck you, you lying, cheating son of a bitch, and I hope you enjoy your young whore but be very clear that I'm not moving and do remember how much Yale and Stanford cost because you'll be paying for the next five years!'" And I slammed the door. Ephesians 4:29 tells us, "Do not let any unwholesome talk come out of your mouths, but only what is helpful for building others up according to their needs, that it may benefit those who listen." I really believe that is exactly what I was doing.

As I pull out of the parking space, Brother Armstrong holds his hand up to stop me. Not only is he one of the few Caucasian men I have found attractive, but whenever I find myself in his presence he always seems to cause me quite a bit of female unrest. I don't know if it's because he's tall and reminds me of Cary Grant when he was young, although Brother Armstrong must be in his mid- to late forties and has been suffering the loss of his wife, who died of breast cancer a few years ago, but he always seems to love it when I take his hand and squeeze it, and, unless it's all in my head, he doesn't seem too keen on letting go until I do.

"Well, hello, Mrs. Parsons," he says. "What a pleasant surprise."

"Hello, Brother Armstrong."

"Please, call me Patrick."

"Hello, Patrick. And you can call me Venetia."

"Are you okay? You look a little flustered, and I've never seen you here except on Sunday."

"I'm fine. I was thinking about going in but changed my mind. What brings you here?"

"I was thinking about going in but changed my mind when I saw you."

I am starting to feel warm and the steering wheel is feeling rather sticky so I turn up the air and say, "I was going to pray for my soon-to-be ex-husband. What about you?"

His face lights up at my bad news.

"I would love to say I'm sorry for your loss but that would be dishonest. I can count how many times he accompanied you to church on any given Sunday, and a family that prays together, for lack of a better cliché, usually stays together."

I don't know what to say to that.

"Would you like to get a cool drink, maybe an Arnold Palmer at that diner over there?"

"Why not?" I say, without thinking that I may be committing adultery, but then I realize I am not doing anything immoral and no one—not a man who was not my husband (and even he has not invited me to do anything except have sex on occasion in twenty-two years)—has invited me for an Arnold Palmer, so I'm going to order the biggest size they have.

"We can walk, if you don't mind walking," Brother . . . Patrick says.

I pull back into the parking space and turn the engine off and get out. I look at myself in the mirror, hoping I might be attractive and embarrassed for even thinking this on the day I find out my husband wants to divorce me even though I've known it for years, and had I not worried about what I would do without him, I probably would've ended this marriage a long time ago. I stayed because of our children. I hate the idea of broken homes and did not want to be a statistic. I used the church as the reason for staying even though I know my sisters saw it as an excuse. I don't know why their approval is so important to me, but maybe it's more about acceptance.

Since there's always traffic, I won't bother to call until I'm near the hotel. Besides, how long does it take to drink an Arnold Palmer anyway?

Two hours.

"That must have been some bad accident," Arlene says right after I enter this amazing suite BB got for me. I hope she's getting a good employee discount and I don't know what I'm going to do in here and how long I'm supposed to stay but I decide to take it one minute at a time. I also can't remember the last time I stayed in a hotel. Oh, yes I do. It was when Rodney took the kids and me to Disney World in Florida. It wasn't exactly romantic and since I have vertigo I didn't go on any rides and we had to stay on the third floor. We're on the tenth floor here, but no way will I be walking anywhere near those windows.

"I didn't really see it," I say. "Where's BB?"

"Finishing up. She was here an hour ago and had to run and pick up the kids and then make sure her white-trash neighbor could watch them until she got home."

"You know what, Arlene. I sincerely believe that with your attitude you might be headed straight to hell."

"I was just being facetious."

"No, you weren't. You sound like a racist. And it's an ugly way to feel about people who aren't black, Arlene. In fact, I think sometimes you're racist toward black people, too."

"You are obviously grieving the loss of your husband, because I can't even believe you're talking like this, Venetia."

"I've been wanting to say this a long time, Arlene, and for your information, I'm glad Rodney's getting out of my life, since he hasn't been in it for years anyway."

BB walks in just in time to hear me say this and looks stunned. She rushes over and hugs me. She loves me. And genuinely cares about me. I'm sure Arlene does, too. She just has an unusual way of showing it.

"I know this is hard to accept, and you don't have to try to sound so brave in front of us especially since it's probably not how you're really feeling."

"Yes it is, BB."

"But I thought you said you didn't want a divorce."

"People do come to their senses sometimes, Betty Jean. My goodness. He was a dog. You deserve better, Venetia."

"How would you know, Arlene? When was the last time you were even in a relationship?"

BB is riled, and although I love both of my sisters, I know they think I have a tendency to be wishy-washy and exercise bad judgment or give too much power to the Lord, but I am grateful that BB doesn't attack my integrity and in some cases, like this one, comes to my defense.

"What in the hell does that have to do with anything?"

"Everything," BB says. "You have never been married, which means you have no idea what it feels like to get a divorce, so just shut the hell up."

"Whoa, what is going on here?" I ask. "Have I missed something?"

"No," BB says, and sits down at the dining room table.

"She's mad at me because I told her I didn't think I could let her use my address so her grandsons could go to school in my district."

"Why can't you?" I ask. "I mean, what is the big deal? Everybody in L.A. does it to get their kids into good schools. I've done it for quite a few people who go to my church."

I look at Arlene. Then at BB. Then back at Arlene.

"Well, to be honest, I've had some time to give it more thought and it doesn't seem as if it would be much of an inconvenience, and those boys really do deserve to get a quality education, since their home life isn't as good as it could be."

"You know what, Arlene, would it just kill you to be nice?"

"I'm being nice. I'm nice a lot. You're just not around me enough to see it."

BB holds her head down.

"You're right," I say. "Maybe something is going on in your life that's making you a little short-circuited? Is Omar okay?"

"Omar is just fine, thank you. Look, we came here to console you so, why don't we take a stab at it?"

"So, should I be saying thank you, Arlene? Because I'm still not clear if you've actually agreed to do this or not," BB asks.

"Can't you tell when somebody's had a change of heart?" Arlene asks as she pours one of those little bottles of whiskey into a glass from the minibar.

"I can," I say.

"Thank you, Arlene. Me and the boys appreciate it."

"Now, can we order room service, Betty Jean? I'm starving," Arlene says. "Is anybody else hungry?"

"I'm not," I say. "In fact, as much as I love that you've gotten this beautiful hotel room for me, BB, I can't sleep here. I want to go home and sleep in my own bed by myself, which I'm used to doing anyway, and figure out what the next step in my life is going to be."

"Dang," BB says to me. "What's happened that has made you have such a change of heart? Did God send you a certified SOS or something? Did you pray on this today?"

"I pray every day for everybody. But mostly I pray for patience and guidance, and I know I've been very patient but now I'm not too proud to admit that I'm tired of being treated like I'm undesirable, when I am. I'm tired of being treated like I don't matter, when I do. And more than anything, I'm tired of being taken for granted by my kids and my husband. I'm just tired of being tired and it feels good to finally fucking admit it."

Arlene and BB look at each other as if these words couldn't possibly have come out of my mouth, but I can't believe I just said them either.

II

HOW YOU CARRY IT

Betty Jean

Mister's been gone now for almost three years. As much as I always made myself believe I didn't love him, it turns out I did. It wasn't that Hollywood kind of love: full of flames, hurricanes, or ten-foot waves. It was smooth and steady, the kind that makes you want to stay with a person because they don't take anything from you. It's not until they're gone that you realize how much they added to your life. I didn't worry about half the things I worry about now. Even at the end, it wasn't hard making all the arrangements, because he had already made them. Our insurance premiums were always paid up, which is how, after I took care of everything having to do with his burial, I had a little money left to pay down my credit cards and finally trade in that junker for a brand-new one. I bought myself another Buick—since I love me some Buicks—because it was in my price range and I can afford the payments. Of course, the boys wanted me to get one of those SUV things, but with my driving knee begging for surgery, I couldn't chance trying to lift myself up that high to get in and out of it. They're happy with the smell of newness. Luther pleaded with me to get black, but since the garage is full of junk I have yet to get rid of, he and Ricky decided that white was just as cool and they seem to love washing it. I'm pretty sure Mister would like it, too.

I hope the next funeral I go to is mine. I'm sick of death, and tired of losing people. We lost relatives we didn't know we had during Katrina, and some we did, but we didn't and couldn't get down there. Of course, our parents lived so far outside New Orleans they weren't physically affected by it, but mentally is a whole different story. I don't know how some people survive after experiencing this kind of tragedy. I really don't. I felt the same way after 9/11. It is one of the reasons why my problems seem small, because they're at least predictable and manageable.

I'm also glad I don't live in this house by myself. I don't know what it would've been like without my grandsons being here to help me through the loss of my husband of over forty years. My own sons were no help. Dexter violated his parole, went back to jail, and now has to wear one of those ankle things for a year or else he's going back to prison. Quentin made an appearance but left right after the service. Of course my sisters were sad to see Mister leave this way, but they also had enough going on in their lives that limited the amount of grieving they could do. In all honesty, Tammy took it harder than my sisters did. She pretends like she's still trying to figure out how to get Montana and Clementine out of her house. I don't know why she just doesn't come out and admit that she likes having them there and stop complaining. Trevor moved out, and what a sour note that turned out to be. Montana changed her mind (again) about teaching and is now turning her attention to beauty. She'll be thirty before you know it and she seems to be even more confused about what to do with her life now than when she was all set to go to the Peace Corps. I feel sorry for her in a way. And Tammy is not helping.

"Grandma! Thank you thank you thank you so much for frying us chicken!" Luther says, running back to the kitchen and bending down to hug me. Ricky is right behind him. It's been hard for me to fry chicken for them since Mister's been gone, and I don't fry anything that often anymore. My cholesterol went up, plus I know it's not healthy to eat fried food all the time. Omar, who it turns out is becoming a chef, has been showing me how to broil, bake, sear, and stir-fry. These boys will eat anything you put in front of them, as long as it smells good.

"You're quite welcome. And how was school today?"

"Boring," Ricky says, as usual. "But I did manage to get a C-plus on my Spanish test if that impresses you, Grandma."

"I'm impressed."

"I just found out I'm going to be in advanced biology when I enter ninth grade, but you didn't hear it from me, now did you, Grandma?"

"I believe I did."

I give him a high five. The way he and Ricky give them, with their hands high and palms hitting.

"Is there anything you need us to do first?" Ricky asks.

"Don't ask a stupid question, Ricky."

"I was wondering, Grandma," Ricky says. "Is a puppy still out of the question?"

"A what?"

"A puppy. You know: *woof woof!*" Luther says.

"Who's going to feed it?"

"We will!" they say at the same time.

"Who's going to walk it?"

"We will!" they say at the same time.

"If it doesn't end up weighing more than thirty pounds, and don't even think about a pit bull or a Rottweiler. It has to be the kind of dog that doesn't bite, doesn't bark loud, and enjoys being in the backyard."

"Are you kidding me?" Ricky says, jumping in the air like he's pedaling a bicycle.

"We need to have a conference about this after dinner," Luther says to Ricky. "And thank you for considering our request, Grandma, even if it took you almost five years!"

"That's a supersized thank-you, Grandma."

"We will hose down the driveway, trim all the dead leaves off the bushes in the front yard, paint, scrub, wash clothes, do the dishes, windows, vacuum—whatever you want us to do until we leave for college—we will do," Luther says, and he elbows Ricky.

"Speak for yourself, dude. I'm staying right here with you, Grandma. You need somebody to protect you."

College?

After we eat, I hear the boys outside playing with the hose. They have been more than helpful since Dexter left. What they don't know how to do, they ask the son of the man who still lives next to Tammy, or they Google it. Luther is very resourceful and has taught me how to Google. I feel sorry for the encyclopedia companies. It's terrible when something you always thought would be useful becomes obsolete.

Which is how I'm starting to feel. I had to go on and have that knee surgery and was on disability for two months and just went back to work. My doctor told me that losing a few more pounds and keeping them off would speed up my recovery process, but I wouldn't know. I've been trying to learn how to say no to chocolate chip cookies, sour cream potato chips, and sorbet, which I have become too fond of, thanks to Tammy bringing me a pint to sample from Whole Foods. Now I'm addicted to that blood orange and passion fruit and have learned how much tastier they are when I eat them together. Tammy does yoga and wants me to try it now that I'm healed. But I do enough bending and stretching at work. If I had any sense, I'd retire today. But what would I do sitting around the house? It's something I should seriously be thinking about, because if I blink too long, these boys are going to be gone.

It's hard to believe that Luther is headed to high school and Ricky's going into seventh grade. Sometimes it feels like they just got here. Luther has never been off the honor roll, and if he keeps it up, he could end up with a scholarship. He's about to start playing football even though everybody swore up and down he was meant to dunk. He's almost fourteen and six foot two. I think he's still growing. He wears a size thirteen shoe. And even though Social Services did come through, the aid is not enough to take care of two growing boys in this day and age. I can't get away with buying cheap anything anymore. Ricky isn't short but he's not going to be tall like his brother, and he doesn't care. He's not as interested in swimming competitively like he used to be, but he still loves being in the water. We did have to put him back on a low dose of that medication a while back but he's doing pretty well in most of the courses except math and English, which is why I just got him a tutor. Luther helps him, too.

Luther comes in first and washes his hands. We were supposed to watch a movie called *Wedding Crashers*, which the boys promised I'd find laugh-out-loud funny. Why anybody would want to see a movie twice I do not know.

"Where's Ricky?" I ask.

"He told me he was going to finish putting the rakes and stuff away and he'll be in in a few minutes."

"Do you smell a skunk?" I ask.

Luther gets the weirdest look on his face, takes a few whiffs, and says, "No, I don't smell anything except that fried chicken, and I think I'll have another piece before we watch the movie, if you don't mind, Grandma."

"Knock yourself out," I say. "But tell Ricky to hurry up, because I know I won't make it to the end."

"Betty Jean," Lorinda tells me through the walkie-talkie we use at work, "you've got a phone call. It's your grandkids' school calling."

"Tell them I'll be right there."

I know it's most likely got something to do with Ricky but I'm just hoping it's nothing serious. I have caught him in so many little lies it's starting to bother me that he sometimes doesn't seem to know he's lying, even after I catch him in one. They're usually things that can be proven, like: Did you finish your homework? Did you rinse out the shower? Change your sheets? A lie is still a lie, and I've just been hoping and praying it's something he'll grow out of.

When I get down to the kitchen I go into the office and close the door. The blinking light makes my heart flutter. "Hello, this is Betty Jean Butler."

"Hello, Mrs. Butler, this is Vice Principal Brooks and I'm calling to advise you that Ricky's science teacher caught him cheating on a test today, which is a violation of Education Code 316.82 and is grounds for a one-day suspension. We are calling to see if you can make arrangements to pick him up."

Without thinking, I hear myself say, "I'm at work and can't leave right now."

"Well, if you authorize us to allow him to take the bus home, since he's told us this is how he gets to school, we can put your verbal release in his file."

"It's okay if he takes the bus," I say, and then hang up. I sit there for a few minutes, grinding my teeth, catching myself and then trying not to, but I'm mad. Ricky must have a short memory. But I will refresh it for him as soon as I get home.

Luther

'm trying to watch *Monday Night Football* but I can't hear because Grandma is lighting into Ricky for getting suspended. I'm hoping she whops him for being so sneaky. Ricky has never been a straight-A student but he's not dumb either. He does a lot of dumb shit, really dumb shit, and I've tried to tell him that if he keeps it up, he's going to get in real trouble, but did he listen to me? No, he did not.

I hear the bedroom door open and turn to look at them both. Grandma looks pissed. Ricky looks like he took a punch or two.

"Luther, can you order a pizza for you two, because I don't have the energy to cook. Just get my Visa card out of my wallet, please."

"Okay, Grandma," I say, and do it.

As soon as she heads for the bathroom to take her shower, I roll my eyes at Ricky.

"Okay, so I didn't study. Was that a crime?"

"Cheating is. And so is getting suspended, even if it's only for one day, Ricky. Why didn't you study?"

"I fell asleep."

"You seem to be falling asleep a lot. Are you taking your meds?"

"Off and on. Anyway, I've already been lectured enough, please don't you start."

"Just tell me some of what she said."

"She asked me if I remembered our talk after our mama died, and I told her I did."

"You mean about staying out of trouble and what could happen?"

He just nods.

"Then make sure this is as bad as it gets, you hear me?"

"I hear you. Damn, Luther. You sound just like a grown-up."

"I'm your older brother and I just want to remind you that Grandma is getting up in age and can't handle a lot of stress or this kind of bullshit, and if this is the beginning of more to come, this is how kids end up in foster care."

He nods like he gets it.

"Personally, I'm not worried," I say.

"Me either," he says. "Can we order the pizza now?"

Grandma is driving us to the bus stop. It doesn't take us long but since she has to take a different freeway to get to work, this is faster. Plus, we're old enough to catch a bus and we've got monthly passes and now we even go to a charter school, which is also pretty cool, but starting in September I'm going to be going to Dorsey High and I can't wait to start summer football training. A lot of famous NFL players went to Dorsey, and I hope I'm going to be added to that list one day. I love football. Everybody thought because I'm tall I was going to play basketball, but basketball isn't as much fun to me because you don't get to run anywhere. Grandma let me go to football camp last summer, and I'm going again this summer just to get stronger and make sure I can get on the junior varsity squad.

"Are you boys coming straight home after school?"

"I have track practice," I say.

"I do, too," Ricky says, lying through his teeth.

"I have physical therapy today, so you can warm up that lasagna and make a salad if you want to."

"We'll save you some," I say, and give her a kiss on the cheek when we get to the bus stop. Ricky leans over from the backseat and does the same.

"Be careful," she says after we get out of the car. "And give everything you do everything you've got today."

"We always do," I say, and close the door. She says this every morning and I like it. She said it's called a mantra. Sort of like praying. If you say something over and over and over it has the power to come true. I don't think Ricky really says it, though.

We see the bus about five or six stops away and there's a lot of traffic but Ricky and I stand with a group of other kids around the bus stop pole so that some older people can sit down since it's starting to rain.

"You better check yourself, Ricky," I say to him. Most of them can't hear what I'm saying to him, because almost all of them are listening to music on their iPods. Grandma said maybe we might be able to get one for Christmas, but I really don't care. Looks like Ricky won't be needing one, because I saw one on his bed this morning. I just didn't feel like saying anything.

"I don't know what you're talking about, Luther," he says as he reaches into his backpack and whips out that iPod and puts those little headphones in his ears.

I snatch them out.

"What the fuck are you doing?" he asks.

"Where'd you get these?"

"That's none of your business," he says, and snatches them back. Some of the kids are starting to look at us even though most of them know we're brothers so they know this isn't going to lead to any action.

"I smelled that shit and Grandma did, too, and wherever you're getting it and however you're getting it, you better not bring it anywhere near Grandma's house or I'm going to kick your ass myself. You got that?"

"I don't know what you're talking about, Luther." He plugs his earphones back in and gets in line ahead of me when the bus pulls up.

When I get on, he's already sitting next to a Mexican kid, and I walk right past him like I don't know him and sit next to a black girl, who happens to be pretty but I pretend like I don't notice. Most of the kids on this bus are black, Mexican, and Korean, and now a lot are Armenian, even though I don't know why.

"Hey," I say to the girl.

"Hey," she says back.

And that's that.

I look out the window, wishing I had that little umbrella Grandma has told Ricky and me to keep in our backpacks because "you never know when it's going to rain and you can't go by what that weather girl says." Today, like most days, Grandma's right, and now it's starting to pour down. I really like the rain a lot and I don't know why. Maybe because nothing ever falls from the sky here in Los Angeles and rain makes it feel like a different season. I know one thing for sure: I want to go to college somewhere where it gets cold, and maybe even snows. I like snow, even though I've never touched it before. It's pretty and looks clean and soft, and I would love to throw a snowball or make a giant angel like

I've seen on TV. Plus, it seems like it makes more sense to have four seasons instead of just one.

"Noxema, did you finish your book report?" I hear the girl behind me say to the girl sitting next to me.

"Of course I did. You know my mom would kill me if I didn't."

That girl did just call her Noxema, didn't she? I had a little sister with this same name and I'm just wondering how many of them could there be in this neighborhood? I don't want to stare, since she's sitting right next to me, but she did just say that her *mom* would kill her so maybe she isn't who I'm thinking she could or might be.

"What grade are you in?" I ask her without thinking about it.

"Why?"

"Just curious."

"Sixth. Are you in high school?"

"Almost. I've never seen you on this bus before."

"We just moved."

"Who is we?"

"Why are you so nosy?"

"I'm just curious because a long time ago I had a little sister with your same name."

"And what happened to her?"

"I don't know. Her father took her from our mother when she was a baby."

"Really," she says, like she's not that impressed. "Who is 'us'?"

"That boy up there with the fat neck wearing earplugs."

"Oh, that's Ricky. He's bad news. Sorry to tell you."

"I thought you said you just moved here?"

"I just moved to this neighborhood but I didn't have to change schools and my parents just started letting me take the bus."

"Why is Ricky bad news?"

"I don't know if it's cool for me to be telling you stuff about your own brother."

"Tell me."

"He's been hanging around people we don't like to hang around."

"You don't mean like a gang or something, do you?"

"I don't know. But he's in my science class and he sleeps through most of it and sometimes at lunch he's selling joints."

"And you know this for a fact?"

She turns around to look at her friend, who is nodding her head up and down.

"Okay. Well, thanks for the heads-up."

"So let's get back to the whole parent thing, or do you smoke the stuff, too?"

"Are you kidding me? College is in my future."

"Anyway, I was adopted when I was two because my father was raising me all by himself, but he got killed in a head-on collision and I ended up in foster care and my parents adopted me, so I could be your sister. Wouldn't that be something?"

And she starts laughing. Like cracking up. I don't think this shit is one bit funny. I mean, what if I'm really sitting next to my half-sister?

"What's so funny?"

"You believed me."

"What if you are our sister?"

"That's impossible because I live with my real parents. I just made that shit up. I make a lot of shit up just to see if I can make people believe me. And you did. I want to be an actress."

"What about what you said about my brother?"

"Oh, Ricky? That shit is true. So pay attention before he ends up in juvie."

When the bus comes to a stop, all the kids jump up and rush off. Ricky ignores me. I'll be so glad when I don't have to take this bus and so glad when I don't have to look at Ricky's face in the cafeteria or in the hallway, because he is starting to not only get on my nerves but I would really like to kick his ass because of some of the shit he's doing that he knows he shouldn't be doing. That girl Noxema waves to me, and for some weird reason I don't believe what she said to me. I'll bet she is our sister. She's just too scared to admit it. But then again maybe she doesn't know. And maybe I shouldn't care.

Tammy

I absolutely love my new breasts! Sometimes I just stand in front of the mirror and stare at them. They're beautiful. They didn't look anywhere near this good before I had the twins. It's amazing what money can buy. Now, if only I had someone to touch them and appreciate them as much as I do, I will have turned a major corner.

I admit I've become partial to low-cut tops except at work. It is not appropriate to show so much as an ounce of cleavage in a courtroom, especially if the criminal is male. They love to find a focal point when they're on the witness stand and even more so when they're lying. I do not want my breasts to help them make shit up. I believe even Montana may be jealous of them!

My daughter has let Trevor back into her life and occasionally into my house, but at least he has made his mark in television. He has managed to become a roll of toilet paper and a bumblebee (for Bumble Bee tuna); he got to prove how effective an insect repellent can be when you're in the woods; and I think in the last one he drove a carpet-cleaning van. In not one of them did he get to open his mouth to utter a syllable, so he's still not in the SAG union.

Jackson, I'm pleased to say, has been living in Jackson Hole, Wyoming, for the past two and a half years and had the nerve to make a baby with what has to be senior citizen sperm. He also has his own big rig. He has sent pictures of him and his homely wife and that little girl who already looks like she's old enough to order a drink. Sometimes, if they're lucky, children grow up and don't favor their parents, or if they're real lucky, pull just the right amount of genes from both to pass as attractive. I will pray for that little girl, whose name escapes me right now. Oh, yes, I forgot to remember, Dick. It's Jane. It's obvious they put a whole lot of thought into it.

Anyway, I've been trying to fix up the room Jackson slept in when he was here, because Max is coming home from Paris in three weeks for a week or two and is bringing a young lady he said he's going to marry. (It's amazing how young folks just spring life-changing events on you without any advance notice and you don't have one minute to even digest it and sometimes you don't even know if it's worth swallowing.) She is Senegalese and her skin looks like brown satin. Sometimes I wish I were black. Her name is Awa. I wanted to know what it meant so I Googled it. It means she is seen as enthusiastic and passionate about anything and everything, that she is one who lives in the moment and takes pleasure in the small things. Maybe I should've put more thought into naming Montana. Awa is beautiful and tall and has perfect white teeth, the kind movie stars pay big money for here, but I know those are hers. She graduated from the Sorbonne (which I had to Google just to make sure I pronounced it right) in art history. I don't know if that makes her employable over there, but she'd be shit out of luck here in L.A.

Since my cooking skills are minimal I have asked my soul sister who lives across the street and who I just realized is also my BFF (Best Friend Forever) to help her white sistah-girl out in the kitchen with a few basic meals that reflect blackness so I can impress my future daughter-in-law that I'm down on many levels. On second thought, I've been around black folks so long, who knows, maybe I am black and just look white? LOL. (I just learned this new acronym, too.)

So BJ is on her way over here in a few minutes. She has not said one word about my breasts. It's been well over a month since the surgery. Although the boys are old enough to care for themselves most of the time, me and BJ work different hours these days, and I only see her a couple of days a week, especially since Lee David's been gone. She doesn't talk to me about a lot of what's going on over there anymore. I know Dexter moved out and is still living with that stripper, and I wish to hell my daughter would do the same (move out, not strip) but I have not figured out how to put my flesh and blood out of my house without getting eaten up alive by guilt. Preschool costs almost as much as college these days. As it turns out, Montana has turned to her father for help without telling me. Over the last few years, Howard kept his word and reimbursed me for his half of the kids' college fees, which is why I was surprised when he called one day to ask me if Montana still needed his help with her tuition. What tuition? I couldn't answer that question. He is also disappointed in our daughter but basically said he didn't want her to feel bad, because he remembered what it was like to be young and in love. I had to stop him right there.

So, Montana is back in school. This time she's hoping to become an esthetician. If she manages to finish this program, she'll definitely be able to finally make some money, since people in L.A. will spend their rent money on anything to make them think they look beautiful. Including men, since so many of them are now what they call metrosexual these days, which in my opinion is another word for gay. I don't have anything against gays. From what I gather, when Montana worked at Bed Bath & Beyond over the Christmas holiday, their credit cards always got approved.

"Open this door, Martha!"

BJ knows I have watched Martha Stewart's show over the years, but most of that shit takes too long to prepare and costs too much and I could never find half the ingredients anywhere near this neighborhood and then a lot of the stuff I did make had a peculiar taste and then you didn't know what to eat it with that didn't compete with the one dish that seemed to take all damn day to make. She sure makes it look easy on TV. BJ told me about some little girl named Rachael Ray on the Food Network that makes meals in thirty minutes. But now I really don't give a damn because I don't spend that much time in the kitchen except for holidays and when I have houseguests, like now.

"It's open!" I yell, and make sure my apron is hanging on the hook near my little pantry. I'm wearing a yellow V-neck T-shirt that highlights my new additions, and which I will not cover up until BJ says something about them. Even if I have to put her on the spot. As soon as I know she's in the kitchen I turn around and lean against the sink. "Did you bring some recipes?"

She stops dead in her tracks. "I see them, Tammy. Everybody on the block sees them when you water the grass. When you go to the mailbox. They're big and round and they look fake as hell but as long as you're happy, I'm happy. What I wanna know is what did you do with all your old bras?"

"You think they're too big?"

"Honestly?"

"Honestly, even though I can't return them and if you don't

like them I really don't give a shit, because I love them. But what do you think?"

"I think they'd make good headlights if they light up. So, what is it you want to learn how to make today?"

"Where are the recipes?"

"I'm black, Tammy. In case you haven't noticed. We don't use recipes."

"Then how in the hell are you supposed to know how much of anything to put into whatever it is you're making?"

"You taste-test as you go along."

"Give me an example. Say, mac and cheese."

"I don't eat macaroni and cheese, because I'm lactose intolerant, but I make it for the kids. Didn't you say this young lady is African?"

"Yes, but she was raised in France."

"So why are you trippin', as the boys would say? She wouldn't know soul food if you threw it at her. Make the same boring meals you've been making and call it a day."

"I know how to bake a ham and fry chicken, but it's not half as good as yours. Maybe she's never had fried chicken. Just tell me how to make it taste like yours."

"You got a chicken handy?"

"No, but I can get one. When is your next free day off?"

"Two days from now, Thursday."

"Okay, then just tell me this. Can you show me how to make a sweet potato pie, collard greens, homemade cornbread, and your lasagna I like so much?"

"You know what might be even better?"

"I'm listening."

"Has she ever been to the States before?"

"Nope."

"Then refuse any help in the kitchen and make sure to send them out sightseeing, and how about I'll make most of this and you can just pretend like you did?"

"But that's just wrong, BJ, and I want to learn how to make some of this stuff."

"Then why in the hell did you wait twenty years to ask me?"

"That's a good question. Are you all right? You seem a little testy."

"What would make you say that?"

"I don't know. It's been a while since we just sat down and chatted."

"I don't feel like chatting."

"See, that's what I'm talking about. Who is it you know you can always talk to without being judged?"

She points to me.

"And who is it that will listen to you when I need to be judged?"

She points to me.

"Where are the boys?"

"Luther went to run the bleachers at the Rose Bowl with two boys that'll be on Dorsey's football team."

"How'd they get out there?"

"One of the boys' dads takes them."

"What about Ricky? What's he up to?"

"I think no good."

"Can you be more specific?"

"His grades are going down and the tutor says he doesn't seem all that interested in trying to improve."

"He's probably smoking pot. Max went through this around his age. It'll pass."

"I wonder if I should just come out and ask him?"

"Are you kidding me? You think he's going to say, 'Sure, Grandma, I'm smoking pot. You got a problem with that?'"

"I'll ask Luther to ask him."

"If he is, believe me, Luther knows it."

"Luther's a good boy."

"That he is, but they also don't blab on each other."

"I can't handle any trouble from these kids, Tammy. I'm not up to it."

"Don't worry. Seriously. You've been doing a good job with the two of them and they know right from wrong."

"What about you? Besides your new breasts, how are things going with Montana and Trevor?"

"I don't even know how to answer that question."

"You let him move back in here, didn't you?"

"No. He does spend the night sometimes."

"You want my opinion?"

"I already know what you're going to say."

"And what might that be?"

"Threaten to keep Clementine and just kick Montana out!"

BJ starts cracking up.

"But I don't want her little ass here either! I'm beginning to wonder how I ever had the patience for them."

"Them?"

"Kids."

"I don't know, Tammy. I'm beginning to think family takes us for granted because they're family."

"I think I spoiled Montana and she's just lazy."

"Hell, you work in a courtroom all day and you know what happens when there's consequences for what you do."

"And when there are none for what you don't."

I know there's more to this than she's letting on, so to lighten up I just come right on out and ask her. "Is there any way we can make something today? Like an apple pie or anything? I've got Pillsbury pie crust in the fridge and a bag of those green Granny apples just sitting over there on the counter waiting for Martha to tell me how to bake them with no soul, and then there's you."

She stands up. "Where's an apron?"

I hold up two that are hanging on a hook in the pantry. One you tie at the waist. The other one slips over your head. She looks at my chest. Then down at hers. Leaves me holding the short one.

Quentin

Mindy has left me, Mother."

"I'm sorry to hear that, Quentin."

"And my practice isn't doing so well up here. I think race might have something to do with it."

"I'm sorry to hear that, too."

"It's all too much to handle simultaneously."

"Did something happen that made her leave, Quentin?"

"No."

"I find that hard to believe."

"Well, we've been fighting over money."

"That's it?"

"And there's my office manager."

"And what's her name?"

"Caroline."

"So, you cheated on Mindy?"

"No! Contrary to popular belief, Mother, I have never cheated on any of my wives. Mindy just thinks it because Caroline appears to have developed a small crush on me."

"Is she blonde?"

"What's that got to do with anything?"

"Nothing, Quentin."

"I'm a mess, Mother. And I miss my daughter."

"When did they move out?"

"A few months ago."

"What took you so long to tell me?"

"I was hoping it was just temporary."

"Has she said anything about filing for divorce?"

"Not to me. Not yet."

"Do you want a divorce, Quentin?"

"Absolutely not! Why would you ask me that at a time like this? Can't you hear the desperation in my voice?"

"Well, this would be a first."

"I'm lonely being in this house all alone. It's too quiet in here."

"Well, where'd they move to?"

"She's renting a condo in Sausalito, a really expensive condo."

"Where is Sausalito?"

"About fifteen minutes from here. It's a ritzy, touristy town right on the water. The harbor is filled with sailboats and yachts. Great shops, art galleries, and the best restaurants. You can take a ferry to San Francisco that goes right past the Golden Gate Bridge."

"I thought you said once you all got settled you were going to invite me and the boys up there for a visit? Ricky loves the water. I love bridges and have never been to San Francisco."

"Could we possibly have this conversation another day?"

"You're right. And I'm sorry."

"I love Mindy."

"Do you know how many times I've heard you say this, Quentin?"

"As a matter of fact I do. But Mindy's different."

"I've heard this one, too. But I have to admit that Mindy's got more personality and spunk than the rest of them and she was the only one who seemed to have your number."

"And what number would that be, Mother?"

"Why don't you think about that one?"

"I would much rather you come on out and say it, so that I might learn something I obviously don't know about myself."

"Your intolerance."

"Could you be more specific, please?"

"Why don't you give it some thought during this alone time?"

"Anything else I'm missing?"

"I didn't say you were *missing* anything, but you might have what some call tunnel vision."

"That is so not true. I consider myself to be quite open-minded."

"Well, look, Quentin. I'm your mother, not your wife, so you don't have to worry about pleasing me anymore."

"I couldn't disagree with you more."

"Well, you've got a funny way of showing it, but let's not go there today."

"No, let's not."

"Is there anything I can do to help? I really liked Mindy and I was hoping to get to know my granddaughter."

"Would you call her?"

"Call her and say what?"

"I don't know. Tell her that I love her and promise to be a better person, a better man, a better husband."

"Why didn't you tell her that?"

"She didn't believe me."

"Then why should I? Never mind. What's her number?"

"So, you're really willing to do this for me, Mother?"

"I just said I would, didn't I?"

I give her Mindy's cell phone number.

"She absolutely adores you, in case you didn't know it."

"I do know it. How's Miss Margaret handling all of this?"

"To her, it's an adventure. Will you call me back after you've spoken with her?"

"Absolutely."

"I love you, Mother."

"Then wish me a happy sixtieth birthday," she says, and hangs up.

With so much on my mind, it's hard to remember even the most important things. I order a hundred-dollar exotic floral arrangement that I hope will make up for my forgetfulness.

After I haven't heard from her in six long hours, Mother finally calls back. "Did you talk to her?"

"Talk to who?" a young male with a changing voice says. I know this must be Luther.

"Luther?"

"Yes, it is."

"Where's Mother?"

"Well, my grandma is taking a nap because we had a surprise birthday party for her at her favorite Mexican restaurant."

"Who is we?"

"Ricky, Auntie Venetia, Auntie Arlene, Miss Tammy and her daughter and son, Max, who brought his fine Senegalese girl-friend from Paris. Uncle Dexter came with Miss Skittles, and Ms. Lorinda from her job."

"That was nice."

"Yes, it was."

"So, are you calling just to tell me that Mother's napping?"

"Oh, no, Uncle Quentin. It's a lot deeper than that."

"Is something going on I should know about?"

"That's why I'm calling you instead of her."

"I'm listening."

"And please don't cut me off, because I have to say this. Since you haven't shown your mother and our grand*mother* any respect since we've been here, I wanted to personally call and tell you what a fucked-up son you are for not being of any use or any help to your own mother and for being such an Uncle Tom. You aren't the first black man to make it in America that came from the hood, but you act like you're too good to come back. In case you forgot, this is where you were born and this is where your family lives. I am also sick and tired of you missing our grandma's birthday and sending her these weak-ass flowers. She doesn't need flowers, she needs gas money and some new furniture and a vacation because of all she's done for my brother and me. Every time you call her she gets depressed after she hangs up. All you seem to think about is yourself, Uncle Quentin. And from what Grandma said, Mindy is smart, which is why she's leaving, and I just wanted to call and let you know that she called Grandma back and said she does not think she can take you back because you're a cheater and a liar and if she'd known you were going to pretend like you were white and not show your own parents any genuine love and respect she never would've married you. So all this is to say that the next time you call *our* house, you better have nothing but good news, because I'm telling you right now, when I graduate from college and regardless if I get drafted into the NFL or not, Grandma's not going to have to rely on you for anything, because my brother and I will take care of her, just like she's been doing us."

Click.

I am at a loss for words. And I have no idea where he gets his information. But it is wrong. It is so wrong. Talk about disrespect? He's a teenager and shouldn't speak to any adult in this manner. Perhaps it might be in everyone's best interest if I backed off for a while. Give them all a chance to come to their senses. I just hope Mother liked the flowers.

Omar

I didn't like having sex with women. I tried, I swear to God I did, but something was missing, and to this day I don't quite know what it was. I mean, it was warm and cushiony and I appreciated the suction and the pushing and pulling and all, and I was able to come but the women didn't have much to do with it. I found breasts to be more of a distraction than anything and I maneuvered them in much the same way I did when I learned how to knead dough at culinary school. I was always glad when it was over, and didn't know what to do afterward except pretend to feel something I didn't, which was passion and a closeness I was hoping would magically occur but never did. It wasn't until I was at sea that I discovered who I really was.

It doesn't matter what his name was. I'm just grateful to have met him. To have been able to talk to him, man to man, and as a result, not feel ashamed to admit how much more at ease I felt being with him, and then later, realizing what being with a man really felt like. It wasn't just sex, it was more of a kinship, a closeness, a sense of honesty I'd never felt with anybody before. I didn't have to put on an act, didn't have to feel embarrassed about my body. I didn't have to apologize for anything. It was liberating, to say the least, and after two years of going from port to port, I literally got seasick, or, I should say, sick of the sea. I started out working in the kitchen as a dishwasher, and then was allowed to help with all the chopping and slicing and dicing, and after watching the artistry and beauty that went into preparing so many types of meals, I finally understood that this is what excites me. And this is why after my contract was up, I came home and enrolled in a really good culinary arts program in Pasadena, which is also where I live.

I've been trying to figure out when and how to tell my mom who I am and what I've been doing and what I'm doing with my life now, but I don't know if I've found the courage yet. Even though it may have been the cowardly thing to do, it took a lot of courage for me to be a coward. I'm afraid of my mom, though. Afraid she won't understand. Afraid she won't think of me as her son because I don't fit the image she may have had of me in her mind. She has never hassled me about getting married or having grandkids because deep down inside I think she wanted to keep me all to herself. It's also one thing to hear how open-minded people are toward homosexuals but it's a little different when they find out their child is one.

It has taken me thirty-two years to realize I was living in a walk-in closet, and now that I've walked out of it, I'm not going to pretend this was an accident or a mistake.

I promised Luther I would take him to the Rose Bowl to practice driving in the parking lot, but I know this is really just another stall tactic. How do you pick the right time or day to tell your mother you're gay? Chances are I'll do it when I force myself to stop coming up with excuses.

Of course, Ricky insisted on coming. Not that I mind. From what Luther's told me, Ricky's going through something and probably needs to do something constructive. I don't know how you stop kids from getting into trouble or from going down the wrong path. My aunt Betty has done the best she could to give her grandkids all those values on a plate but if the boys choose not to let them become part of their diet, that's on them. So many parents put so much effort and energy into parenting, I'm sure it's heartbreaking when their kids appear to be lost. I might be a good example of taking much longer than most to find my way. But better late than never.

I think of Luther and Ricky as the little brothers I wish I'd had. The boys haven't had a man in their life to look up to, and although I'm certain that not having a father had absolutely no bearing on my sexuality, it would've been nice to know what it felt like to have someone to look up to. Someone to teach me how to be a man, show me how to do things. My cousins Quentin and Dexter don't even register on the Richter for obvious reasons. They're not that much older than me but my mom saw to it that we never got close. Quentin has serious issues with women I can't put my finger on, but he can't keep one, that's for damn sure. On the other hand, I don't think he really values them, because he treats them like they're disposable and easily replaceable. From what I've seen, he treats Aunt Betty the same way. And what more can be said about Dexter?

The parking lot is too crowded today.

"Earth to Omar!" Luther says.

"You trying to kill us?" Ricky asks.

"I'm sorry, fellas. I've got a lot on my mind today."

"Like what?" Ricky asks.

"You wouldn't understand."

"You don't know what I can understand," he says.

"I'll bet I can guess," Luther says.

I shake my head. "You couldn't possibly."

"You're gay and you're scared to tell Auntie Arlene."

I know I didn't just hear him say that. I couldn't possibly have heard him say what he just said. "What would make you say something like that?"

"Because you try to pretend like you're not," Luther says.

"Yeah, and it's not a big deal," Ricky says. "If I was gay I think I'd let everybody know it. And I wouldn't really give a flying fuck what anybody thought."

"Aren't you just going into seventh grade?"

"And?"

"First of all, watch your mouth, dude."

"My bad."

"Anyway, how in the world can you even be thinking like this at your age?"

"You know how many kids in our school are gay?"

Luther nods in agreement.

"Times have changed, cuz. We're cool with it. So did I guess right or what?"

"I'm afraid to tell her."

"Aren't you like kind of old to be coming out?" Luther asks.

"I'm thirty-two."

"That's old," Ricky says.

I don't believe these kids are saying this stuff to me. Times have obviously changed since I was in middle and high school. I can't imagine what my life would've been like if things were like this. I can't believe they aren't tripping or freaking out or making fun of me.

"Why haven't you guys ever said anything to me if you thought you knew this about me?"

"What were we supposed to say?" Luther asks.

Ricky nods. "Grandma knows, too."

"What?"

"Nurse Kim told her a long time ago," Luther says.

"But how would she know?"

"Because her brother is gay, too. And she said she could just tell. Anyway, this was right after you took us to see *Batman*, and after you left I was sitting outside on the steps and Nurse Kim was saying something to Grandma and I put my ear up to the door, hoping Nurse Kim would say something nice about me, which she didn't, but this is what she said and I am not making any of this up. 'Miss Betty, since I'm leaving and I been on my best behavior and tried to watch my mouth, I just wanna tell you that your nephew Omar is gay.' And then Grandma said, 'Why would you say that, Nurse Kim?' And that's when Nurse Kim told Grandma that her brother was gay and she knew how to tell. She called you a young man and said you were suffering inside."

I am shocked that all this was going on behind my back all this time and I didn't have a clue. I never liked Nurse Kim until now.

"Just tell her," Luther says. "If she can't handle it, let it be her problem."

"Yeah, right," Ricky says. "But everything pisses Auntie Arlene off anyway and . . . Can I just swear today, please?

"Go ahead. But just today."

"You're a grown-ass man, Cousin Omar, so act like one. What can she do? Beat your ass? I don't think so."

"I agree with Ricky. For once," Luther says.

I really wish it were that easy.

Ricky leans over from the backseat again. "Now that we got all this settled, all I wanna know is when are you gonna let me get behind the wheel, dude?"

Aunt Betty comes out to the car when I'm dropping the boys off. They called her on the way to give her a heads-up, on more than one level.

"Get out of that car," she says to me, and I do. And she gives me the same kind of hug she gave those boys years ago.

Arlene

'm a nervous wreck.

Omar left me a message at the office and said he wanted to talk to me. At my convenience. That it's important. I returned his call but got his voice mail. I asked him where would he like to meet and what time would work for him. He left me another message when I was out showing a property and said that six o'clock would work for him. That he would prefer somewhere quiet. I called him back and suggested a restaurant we used to love. He sent me an e-mail this time and said, "See you there."

I don't know why he didn't just want to come to the house, since whatever it is he wants to talk about could easily be said without anyone hearing it, unless it's going to be something that could qualify as turbulent, although I can't imagine what that could be. If he's married or something, I can live with that, though I would have wanted to be invited to the wedding.

Wait! It could be that he did meet his father and has had a relationship with him all this time, and is about to express his resentment to me for keeping it from him all these years.

Who the hell knows?

All of this feels surreal, especially how Omar has pretty much removed himself from my life. Sure, he's sent me birthday cards, flowers for Mother's Day, and gift cards from Nordstrom's at Christmas. But I have missed my son. I have no one to talk to when I get home except my sisters, and I know I get on their nerves but not half as much as they get on mine. I can't remember the last time I had close friends. In fact, were it not for selling houses and even making some improvements on ours to prepare it for the market, I don't know what I'd have done all this time.

Anyway, I'm trying not to talk myself into anything negative as I pull up to valet parking at Shutters Hotel. It's in Santa Monica. A lot of famous people stay here. I have never had a reason to sleep here, since I live less than thirty-five minutes away depending on traffic. Plus, it's a hotel made for lovers. Not old ladies who haven't had sex in more than twenty years and haven't even thought about it until now. Something is wrong with this picture and I'm beginning to wonder if something might be wrong with me.

I see my son as soon as I walk inside the restaurant. He looks so different. Like his dad, thirty years ago. He's wearing a plaid button-down shirt, and when he stands up I can't believe how nice and slim he is. He must have lost at least a hundred pounds. I don't know. He smiles at me and his teeth are nice and white, too. I walk into his arms like he's my long-lost son and squeeze him so hard I can feel his rib cage.

"I am so glad to see you, Omar," I say, not realizing I'm crying.

"It's good to see you, too, Mom."

He steps back.

"Please don't cry, Mom."

"These are happy tears."

He doesn't look like he's buying it, and it's only partially true. I'm crying because I can't believe I just hugged my son after more than two years and because he feels more like a distant relative. Where'd my original son disappear to? And who exactly is this one? He slides the chair out for me and I sit down. This is already too formal. I look at him again as he sits. I think I liked him better fat.

"What would you like to drink?" he asks.

"What I always have, Omar."

"You could have developed a taste for something new," he says.

"I like the same things I always liked. Don't you?"

"Look at me, Mom," he says, and flings both arms up.

"Okay, I get it. I'll have a gin and tonic. What about you?"

"I've already had a club soda, but I think I'll have another one."

When the waiter comes he orders for us both.

"So, how've you been?" I ask him. I can't believe I'm talking to my son like he's someone I used to know.

"I've been good."

"Are you mad at me for something?" I blurt out.

"Not at all. What would make you ask that?"

I just give him a *look.* Then, "After thirty-two years, Omar, you decide to do something drastic to lose weight without so much as conferring with me about it and then out of nowhere you decide to move out and then get a job on a cruise ship, and now out of the blue you decide you want to talk to me about something that's so important you have to meet me in a public place to tell me. What is it?"

"I'm gay."

I don't think I heard him right.

"Say it again because I don't think I heard you right."

"I said I'm gay, Mom."

I look him dead in the eye and realize that he really means this. "Why?"

"Why what?"

"Why are you gay?"

301

"I don't know. Because I just am."

"Since when did you become gay? It was on that cruise ship, wasn't it?"

"No, it wasn't on the cruise ship, Mom."

"Then when did you decide to become gay?"

"It wasn't a decision."

"Well, you weren't gay for thirty years, why now?"

"I probably always was."

"No, you weren't."

"You don't know me better than I do, Mom."

"I think I do."

"That's always been the problem, you know."

"Oh, so are you blaming me for making you gay? Is that what this little meet-and-greet is for?"

"No."

"I thought you were going to tell me you were married or you'd met your goddamn father after all these years and you were going to lay it on me for keeping it from you."

"I did meet him."

"You what?"

"I met him."

I almost feel like I'm about to have a heart attack. I can't handle so much bad news at one time.

"When did this happen?"

"Two years ago."

"And you're just telling me now?"

"I haven't seen you, Mom."

"How'd you meet him?"

"I don't feel much like getting all into this. It's not the reason I asked you here."

"Oh, so you want to get back to the whole gay topic, then, is that it?"

"Let me say this. I met the man. I didn't like him, and I don't think he cared much for me. We tried to pretend like we were going to make up for lost time, but that's impossible. I lost his number. And that's the end of it."

"So what am I supposed to do? Be excited and happy for you or something?"

"It would be nice if you would just accept me."

"I do accept you. As my son. Just not as my gay son."

And I get up and walk out.

By the time my car is brought around, I'm so pissed off I'm ready to drive right into that fucking ocean. Gay? Just the thought of him kissing another man and Lord only knows what else they do is enough to make me want to throw up. Omar should be ashamed of himself. And he should've kept this new disgusting habit of his to himself. I wonder if it's because I spoiled him rotten. Turned him into a sissy. But he never acted like a sissy. I should've slapped him. That's what I should've done. He's got some nerve.

Without even realizing it I pick up my cell phone and call Betty Jean. "You will never in a million years guess what my son just fucking told me."

"That he's gay."

I pull the phone away from my ear and just look at it because what she just said was not a good guess; it was more or less a declarative statement.

Betty Jean

You are such an evil bitch," I said to Arlene, right after she said, "I'm on my way over there and you better open that goddamn door and tell me what you meant by what you just said because if you've known this about my son and didn't tell me, you've got some explaining to do!"

I turn the porch light on and, even though it's getting cold, I sit on the steps and just wait for her to turn the corner. Tammy steps outside her front door. Puts her hands on her hips. "BJ, what in the hell are you doing out there? I can see your horns from here. Is this going to be on the eleven o'clock news or what?"

"It's Arlene. Omar just told her he's gay and she's freaking out and coming over here to give me a piece of her mind because she now realizes I already knew. I'm ready for her ass."

"Just don't let it to come to blows, because you know you've been storing up a lot of shit to say to her. Try to stay on topic, BJ, because you know we don't need the po-po on our block since we've cleaned it up."

She laughs.

"Anyway, how are Max and Okra enjoying themselves?"

"It's Awa. And they're fine. Loved your meal and my pie!

304

They're leaving tomorrow to drive up the coast and then on to Napa to look for a place to live."

"Good thing some folks are looking, wouldn't you say?"

"It may come to blows over here in a minute."

"You talk a lot of shit, Tammy, you know that."

"I know. I'm just one long contradiction."

"Aren't we all?"

"Anyway, I'm glad Max has his head on his shoulders, and he is sure in love with that girl. I like her."

"That is so nice. She is so black and pretty and her skin looks like grapes. Max isn't doing too bad either. Looking more and more like his dad."

"Speaking of dads, you will not even believe this, BJ. You know Howard lives in Manhattan Beach? Don't answer that. Anyway, he invited all of us out there for dinner. It was nice. And guess what?"

"What what what? Get to the damn point before Arlene gets here."

"I felt something."

"What are you talking about?"

"When I saw Howard."

"Well, at least you know you're still alive."

"He asked me out."

"Are you serious, Tammy?"

"I am indeed."

"And?"

"I'm going."

"Well, nothing like a blast from the past, as the saying goes."

"He still looks good enough to take a bite out of and he's about to retire and . . . I think that's Arlene's Batmobile turning the corner! Yell if you need me to come pull you off of her. Or vice versa!"

She disappears and slams the door shut. I love that woman.

Arlene pulls into the driveway and gets out of the car. I just look at her. For someone who has money, she doesn't dress like it. She is wearing a navy blue pinstripe pantsuit that draws more attention to the stripes than the space between them. The blouse is red. She puts her hands on her hips. "Now, what is it you think you knew about my son that I didn't know?"

"What difference does it make, Arlene?"

"I want to know how in the world you knew my son was a faggot before I did."

"He's not a faggot. He's gay, which means he's a homosexual, and don't use that word in front of me again."

"You didn't answer my question, Betty Jean."

"Nurse Kim told me."

"How in the hell would that ho know what my son was?"

"Because her brother is gay and she says she just knew."

"Oh, so what is it? You need some kind of special senses or something to automatically be able to tell?"

"I don't know."

"And you just took her word for it?"

"I never questioned Omar about it, if that's what you mean."

"But you just assumed it after that? Just because he never had a girlfriend?"

"No. But maybe it was because he didn't want one. You ever thought of that?"

"How in the hell was I supposed to know I was raising a damn faggot?"

"You need to watch your disgusting mouth! Right now! Before I slap you in it, Arlene!"

"I meant exactly what I said and I don't know who—"

That's when I haul off and smack her dead in her mouth. She is stunned and I give her an I-dare-you-to-act-like-you-want-to-hit-me-back look.

"It's no wonder you don't have any friends and you've never been able to find a man, let alone keep one! No, you always had to try to steal someone else's, not caring about anybody but your damn self, Arlene. I sometimes wonder if your heart is made out of rubber, because you don't seem to have an ounce of warmth in your entire body. Just look at what you're doing to your own son, for God's sake! Don't you know that people have feelings, Arlene? It's not always about you! I swear to God. Sometimes I wonder if we really came from the same family! I still love you and I do apologize for slapping you and swearing so much but you have really pissed me off."

"You can keep your love to yourself," she says, and storms over to her car, opens the door, and turns to look at me and says, "I have tolerated your weaknesses and your years of making one bad decision after another, which is why your kids are all so trifling and why you're stuck taking care of your goddamn grandkids, who I feel sorry for since you obviously did such a great job with your own. Maybe if your dumb ass had gotten a college education you might be more qualified to offer them more than a roof over their head, and oh, what a ghetto-ass roof it is! And let's be clear about something right now. I will never speak to you as long as I live. Have a good life." She gets in the car, backs it out slowly, and drives off.

"She doesn't mean that," Tammy says, walking across the street and sitting next to me on the steps.

"Oh, yes she does," I say. "Oh, yes she does."

Of course I'm sorry for slapping my sister but I can't take it back. I've called her but she won't answer when she sees my number, and over the past few weeks I've left quite a few messages apologizing for the mean things I said but I didn't take back any of it. I skipped over that part mostly because I meant it. Arlene said some pretty cruel things herself. Some of what she said was true but I'm not going to hold it against her for the rest of our lives. I just wish there was a way we could disagree without being so disagreeable. Maybe I need to learn how to keep some of my thoughts to myself and stop telling her so much of what goes on in my life. I might have to put Venetia on the same list because she tells Arlene everything I tell her and then they discuss and debate about my problems, as if they have the remedy for them. Which they don't. Just like I can't fix theirs.

I wave to my neighbor, the one who lives on the left of Tammy. His name is Eli Heaven. A weird last name for a black person if you ask me, but after all these years, he barely says two words to me, and none that I know of to Tammy.

"How are you?" he says, and almost gives me a heart attack.

"I'm fine. And you, Mr. Heaven?"

"Fair to middling. After a hundred years, I think it's okay if you call me Eli."

"Okay then, Eli. I haven't seen your son in quite some time. How's he doing?"

"Against my wishes, he joined the U.S. Marine Corps last year and is on his first tour in Iraq."

"I suppose it's okay for me to say I'm sorry to hear that and I'll pray that he stays safe from harm."

"I appreciate that. I was sorry to hear about your husband passing a while back. I put a card in your mailbox. Did you not get it?"

"Not that I remember, but thank you for your thoughtfulness, Eli. You know there was a lot of theft going on around that same time, remember?"

He nods. He's a giant of a man, and if it weren't for his soft voice he could scare you. I always understood why Tammy never complained about all those damn avocados, lemons, and olives that fell over the fence into her yard. There's only so much guacamole you can eat.

"How are your grandsons doing?"

"How do you know they're my grandsons?"

"Because it's obvious, Mrs. Butler."

"You can call me Betty Jean."

"Okay, Betty Jean. Are they good boys?"

"They are very good boys."

"That's good to hear. You know how much influence these streets can have over these youngsters, which is why I sent my son to private school."

"If I could've afforded it, I would have. But they take the bus up to Baldwin Hills."

"Good. So, what's going on with your house?"

I turn around to look at it. "What do you mean? I know it could stand to be painted and those front steps need to be redone and maybe new window frames, but other than that . . . Do you see something I don't?"

"I've noticed those things, too," he says with a little chuckle.

"But I was also curious about what's going on with the space over the garage."

"Oh, that. My son, Dexter, he moved out a while back, and I haven't been up there since."

"You interested in turning it into a real rental?"

"Well, of course I would, but I can't afford to do any improvements right now. Why do you ask?"

"Well," he says, and turns to look at his house, which is one of the best-looking homes on the whole block. "Since I'm retired, I've got a little extra time on my hands and wouldn't mind lending a helping hand. You've been a pleasant enough neighbor all these years."

I don't exactly know what to say. I'm wondering if maybe he's suddenly hitting the bottle or something. He has never been this friendly, and I can't wait to tell Tammy. No. Wait. Maybe I shouldn't. But she's nosy as hell, which means if there's a way Eli can do something to my house, Tammy will notice it and we may have another racial issue going on, and I don't know if I want to start anything after all these years.

"That's very kind of you to offer, Eli, but would you mind if I mulled this over a little while, because I've got so much going on and these boys are costing me a pretty penny?"

"Take your time. But please understand that I own a small construction company and I would be more than happy to do this at my expense. It's a small space. Anyway, you think on it. And have a nice day."

"You do the same, Eli."

I get the mail and walk back into the house in slow motion because it feels weird that my neighbor would make such a kind and generous offer after all these years. We've seen him doing things to improve the looks of his house over the years, but we didn't want to make comparisons. Personally, I was just glad to look at it. Tammy's house is an eyesore and she could stand to put a few more dollars into it provided she doesn't spend any more on plastic surgery.

The phone rings as I'm flipping through the mail, and when I see LOS ANGELES POLICE DEPARTMENT appear on the caller ID, my heart drops to the floor. It feels like I just got a phone call like this one a few weeks ago. But the police department is a long way from middle school. I'm just praying it's not something tragic. Or that no harm has been done to Ricky, or none caused by him. I know this is about Ricky because Luther doesn't give me any cause to worry. I went through this mess with their mama and with Dexter, and I told both of them a while ago that I was not going to tolerate bad behavior and I meant it. "Hello, this is Betty Jean Butler," I say like I work in an office or something.

"Hello, Mrs. Butler. This is Officer D'Agostino and I'm calling from the Los Angeles Police Department's downtown division to advise you that your grandson, Ricky Butler, was detained here for allegedly being in possession of a controlled substance."

"What kind of controlled substance?"

"An officer confiscated approximately six grams of marijuana from his backpack after witnessing your grandson accept ten dollars in exchange for a portion of the marijuana."

"You mean he was selling it?"

"The officer said that allegedly this is what appeared to be occurring. Look, ma'am, this call is to advise you that after processing your grandson, because we have no facilities here to house a minor, he is being transferred to Juvenile Hall, which is located around the corner from here. I can give you that number. He will be there soon."

And he does. And I call. And I speak to someone who tells me that he has been processed, has a court appearance before a judge two days from now, but since Ricky has no prior offenses, I am welcome to pick him up and take him home within seven hours. "What if I can't pick him up?"

"We can keep him here at our facility until his court appearance."

"I think that would be for the best," I say, and write down the time and place of his hearing.

Ricky

The backseat of a police car is much smaller than it looks on TV. I didn't like those handcuffs either. They're cold and heavy. But on that drive downtown to the police station that took what felt like hours, all I was thinking about was that my grandma was going to kill my ass when she found out I've been arrested for dealing weed. I just prayed my buzz would wear off before we got there, 'cause my heart was beating like it used to when I swam the 200, but there wasn't nothing I could do to slow it down.

As soon as we got there they took me into a glass room but they didn't take off those handcuffs. Police are everywhere. I feel like a real criminal. I sit in here for like ten minutes but it feels more like hours and then the police officer that arrested me comes back with some papers in his hand and tells me because I don't have a history of any prior arrests, they're going to call my parents.

"I don't live with my parents," I say.

"Well, what's your mother's number, son?"

"She's dead."

"Who do you live with?"

"My grandma."

"Does she have legal custody of you?"

"I think so."

I give him Grandma's number, and as I sit there and watch him press the buttons on that phone I start crying. He holds up a finger to let me know it's going to be all right, but I know it's not going to be all right. I fucked up. I should never have let those dudes talk me into selling this stuff. But they made it sound easy. And I liked having a little extra money in my pocket, since Grandma's cash flow is limited.

I listen to him explain to her what I've done and how I'm being transferred to a juvenile facility. He gives her a phone number and tells her the phone number and hangs up.

"What did she say?"

"You'll get a chance to call her once you're fingerprinted and processed at the other facility."

They put me back in the backseat of a different police car and drive me a few blocks to Juvenile Hall. When I get in there, all I see is a lot of teenagers, mostly black and Mexican, mostly boys, but quite a few girls, and quite a few of them wearing red and blue.

I'm glad I'm not in a gang. They say once you get in, you can never get out. This is why my grandma and Principal Daniels got me and Luther to go to a safer and nicer school near my aunt Arlene even though I don't like her.

I get fingerprinted again.

I can already tell I don't like being a criminal. And I don't like being treated like a criminal. I am not one and I don't plan on being one. This was just me being stupid, and it's what I get for lying and trying to be slick when I ain't slick. I was mostly just wanting to buy stuff kids need in this day and age. But I guess if I gotta sell weed to get it, maybe I don't need it all that bad. It ain't worth being up in here, that much I do know. Since we were little, Grandma was always saying, "Just because you want it doesn't mean you have to have it." All's I know is I don't wanna end up in jail or nobody's prison like my uncle Dexter. He's in jail right now, and this time they might take that monitor off his leg and send his stupid ass back to the pen. I'm wondering if this is how he started out. If this was his first stop before he ended up in prison. I ain't going to nobody's prison, that much I do know.

This feels like a good time to pray, and I promise God I won't sell no more weed and won't smoke none and I won't get in no more trouble if He'll just let me go home with my grandma when she comes to pick me up, but right before I say "Amen" I hear the door open and I open my eyes.

"Come with me, son," a different police officer says. He takes me by the arm and puts me into another room, but this time the glass is smaller and it's got black square lines going through it. I sit there and try to count them until an old black guy about forty comes in and sits down in a metal chair behind a long wooden table. He is not wearing a police uniform. Which means he's probably vice or something.

"How are you doing, Ricky?"

"Not so hot."

"Well, that's understandable. This won't take long. I just need to ask you a few questions so we can get your side of the events that transpired that led to your being brought here. Do you understand that?"

I just nod.

Then he reads me something he called my Miranda rights and says I had a right to an attorney, which I know means the same as a lawyer, and if I can't afford one the court will get me one, but I didn't know this was so serious that I would need a

315

lawyer, so when he asks me if I understand what he just said I say, "I guess so," but then he tells me I have to say yes or no, so I say, "Yes. But how am I supposed to know if I need an attorney?"

"Don't worry, when you go before the judge, the court—"

"You mean I have to go to court?"

"Yes, you do, son."

"But why?"

"Well, after reviewing all the circumstances surrounding your case, the judge will decide if you get to go home or if you'll be required to spend time in Juvenile Hall."

"I promise I won't do this again. I mean it, sir."

"I know. But I'm not the one you need to convince. At any rate, I need to tell you that the court will provide you with an attorney, and he or she is called a public defender."

"I've seen them on *Law and Order*," I say, even though they always lose their cases.

He smiles at me and I don't know why. Then he says, "Now that I have just read you your rights, do you wish to speak to me?"

"I've been speaking to you."

"You need to say yes or no."

"Yes."

"Do you have any suicidal thoughts?"

"You mean do I feel like killing myself?"

He nods.

"Hell no. I mean, no, sir."

"Have you used drugs in the last forty-eight hours?"

"Do I have to answer that one?"

"No."

But then he stands up and tells me I have to go see a nurse, and this time I stand up and say, "Yes, I had just smoked some weed right before the policeman picked me up."

I have to go see the nurse anyway, who is very nice, and afterward, I sit in a white plastic chair until that same plainclothes dude takes me back to the same room and he tells me that my court appearance is two days from now. And then he says that because I am not a threat and have not committed a violent crime, I can call my grandma to come and take me home. But I'm too scared. "Can you call her for me?"

He says okay.

I sit there and listen to him explain to my grandma who he is and he repeats what I did and by the time he asks if she can pick me up and bring me back to my hearing in two days, I hear him say, "I'll let him know," and he hangs up.

"How soon will she be here?" I ask.

"She's not coming," he says.

"Why not?"

"She said she couldn't make it."

"Can I take the bus home, then? Or maybe can a police officer give me a ride?"

"I'm afraid not, son. But you can stay in the dormitory we have here."

"Did she say what time she could pick me up tomorrow?"

He just shakes his head no.

I don't eat or sleep for the next two days.

There's a lot of teenage criminals in here. Some of them are scary as hell. I'm just glad they didn't put me in a dormitory with murderers or gangbangers or I might not have been able to put on this orange jumpsuit thing and be led into a courtroom where the first person I see sitting out there is my grandma. Tears start running down my eyes and I want to run out there and hug her but I can't, and I can see tears in her eyes, too, and I know she can see how ashamed I am but I can't turn away from her, and when they make me sit down next to my public defender I hear the judge say that the crime I have committed is severe enough that he could remove me from home and place me in this detention facility for three months or he could remove me from my grandma's house and put me into foster care, and when I hear him say *foster care* I turn to look at my grandma, and she is shaking her head back and forth like she's saying, "Not my grandson," and I shake my head back and forth, but then when I hear the judge say that he chooses not to do either one, that he is going to let me go home with my grandma today and my progress will be monitored for the next six months and I'm going to have to meet with a probation officer once a month and if I am so much as late for class, he will enforce one of these two conditions. He asks me if I have anything to say, and I just hear myself say, "I'm sorry for what I did and I promise I won't do it again, Your Honor," and then I hear him ask my grandma if she has anything to say, and I hear her say, "My grandson is a good boy who has made one mistake and I can assure you that he won't make it again," and she sits down.

The judge looks at me, like he feels sorry for me, like I could be his grandson or something, and he says, "Do you understand the terms of your probation, son?"

"Yes, I do, Your Honor."

Then he looks at my grandma.

"And do you, Mrs. Butler, understand the terms of your grandson's probation?"

"I do, Your Honor."

"Noted," he says, and takes that wooden hammer and pounds it on his wooden throne.

I look over at my grandma, who holds up a Target shopping

bag, which I know has new clothes in it. She walks over and hands it to me, and I go in the bathroom and change like they told me to. When I come out I hand that orange jumpsuit to the policeman standing there with his gun in a holster. I kiss my grandma on both of her cheeks and then give her a hug. She takes me by the hand and we walk out of this place knowing I will never give her or me any reason to come back.

Venetia

Did you really slap Arlene?" I ask BB.

"I pressed my hand against her face with a little force. But she deserved it."

I start laughing, even though it's not funny, as I pick out one beautiful bead after another from a long line of trays that are spread out all over this store. We're at a bead store. I'm forcing BB to take a necklace-making class with me just because she could use some relief from all that she's been going through with Ricky. There's a part of me that feels like some of the trouble he's gotten into isn't completely his fault. I mean, in all fairness to him he was born with various degrees of physical and psychological dis-advantages.

"She's still mad at you, you know."

"Tell me something I don't know, Venetia. Look, I've tried apologizing but she refuses to accept it, so to hell with her."

"She'll come around, BB. Anyway, is it true that Omar is gay?"

"You already know the answer to that, and if you start getting all evangelical on me about homosexuality being a sin I'm going to drop this tray of beads and walk out of here right now."

"I think he should be supported and not criticized, because he can't help it if he was born that way."

She actually sets her tray of beads down sideways, right on top of two bins full of my favorite desert sun and dichroic glass ones, and just looks at me like she can't believe I just said what I just said.

"I read *People* magazine and I watch Dr. Phil and CNN, just so you know."

"What in the world has gotten into you?" she asks. "You sound different. You look different. Have I missed out on something?"

"I can't tell you."

"Why not?"

"Because it's too early to talk about."

"What's too early to talk about?"

"Pick out some more beads, BB. You should stick with glass. They're easier to slide on the cord. You're a silver person, aren't you?"

"Hold on a minute. I know when I'm getting the big brush off and you're hiding something, and I want to know what it is, Venetia."

"It's nothing I'm ashamed of."

"Then why won't you share it?"

"Because I don't want to hear your reaction."

"Don't confuse me with Arlene."

"Rodney's back."

This time her tray falls out of her hands and the twenty or so cat's eye and bumpy beads hit the tile and roll everywhere. I wish I could learn to keep my big mouth shut. I wish I could keep a secret. I wish I didn't worry so much about what my sisters think about me, even though I know they think of me as the lightweight, and because I pray more than they do, because I put more faith in God than they seem to, that I'm passive, but I'm not. I'm patient. I believe we all make mistakes. I believe in the sanctity of marriage. I believe in second chances. And I believe in forgiveness.

"Back from where?" she asks as she bends down to start

picking up the beads, but the Korean lady who owns this store holds her hand up to stop her.

"What difference does it make?"

"Apparently none."

"I hear the sarcasm in your voice, BB, which is why I didn't want to say anything."

"Then this means you didn't mention it to Arlene."

"Of course not."

"So what exactly are you saying, Venetia?"

"I'm saying that Rodney has asked me to give him another chance."

"Just like that?"

"In a manner of speaking, yes."

"What if you had cheated on him all these years? Do you think he'd be as forgiving?"

"I don't know."

"What made him want to come back?"

"He said he still loves me."

"Oh, so it took him filing for a divorce, and getting it, in order to have a spiritual awakening, I guess is what they call this?"

"He didn't have a spiritual awakening. But he does have prostate cancer."

"Are you serious?"

"Stage One."

"Oh, so does this mean now that you've raised the kids and they're off to college and you finally get a few minutes where you can start stringing beads, now he wants to come running back to you to help him convalesce?"

"He'll recover."

"Let's just hope you do. I also don't feel like making a necklace, Venetia. In fact, I don't even wear necklaces, because they make me feel like I'm choking or that something is hanging around my neck, and I don't like either one of those feelings. And to be completely honest, I haven't had any hobbies in almost sixty-one years and I am not that crazy about starting a new one today. But thanks for offering. Make me something pretty for Christmas. How's that?"

"Are you mad at me?"

"Of course not. We all do what we think is in our own best interest. I just came downtown with you because I thought you needed some company."

"I thought you needed to take your mind off of your grandkids."

"I don't mind my mind being on them."

And she puts her empty tray down, gives me a kiss and a hug, and walks out the front door.

I pick up my tray and set it on the counter because I don't much feel like stringing any beads now.

"If you want to take your husband back, then do it. Who am I to get mad at you for not doing what I think you should do?"

"Are you serious, BB?"

I turn around and BB is standing there with her arms crossed.

"Very. If it works, I'll be happy for you. And if it doesn't, I'll be here for you."

I walk over and hug her.

"Now. Even though I don't like necklaces, I definitely love bracelets."

Luther

'm putting my books in my locker when I feel somebody tapping me on my shoulder. When I turn around, it's that girl, Noxema.

"What happened to our mother?"

After I hug her, I close my locker and slide down to the floor. She sits down next to me.

And I tell her.

Afterward, she reaches inside her backpack and pulls out some napkins she took from the cafeteria and we use them to wipe our eyes. Then she takes out a bag of Twizzlers and offers me some. I take three.

"So, what happened to your father?"

And she tells me.

"Grandma! Where are you? There's someone who wants to meet you!"

"And you will never in a million years guess who it is!" Ricky says.

I elbow him.

"I'm coming!" Grandma says, and we hear the bathroom door

open, and like always, she has a white towel wrapped around her head like those women in Africa wear and the flowered bathrobe Ricky and I gave her last Christmas. When she comes down the hallway, she stops dead in her tracks before she even gets to the living room. Then she covers her mouth with her hand.

Noxema is standing between Ricky and me.

"You look just like she did when she was your age," Grandma says. "Come here, baby."

And our sister walks over and stands in front of her and just says, "Hi, Grandma. So nice to meet you. I'm Noxema."

III

CLEAR THE WATER

Tammy

Mom, Clemmie and I are moving out," Montana says to me as soon as I walk in from work.

"I'll believe it when I see it," I say.

"Believe it. Trevor just landed the role of a lifetime!"

"And what, pray tell, would that be?"

"A major part in a sitcom. On a network. He's got a contract and everything! Isn't that great news?"

"Super. I always knew Trevor had what it took and he persevered, so I give him credit for believing in himself and following his dreams."

"Mom, who are you kidding? You thought he was a loser and not good enough for me."

"Busted."

"Check this out," she says, and holds out her left hand, which has a ring with a tiny diamond on it.

"Congratulations," I say with as much enthusiasm as I can muster.

"We did it in Vegas. But wait. I've got tons more good news."

"Please don't tell me you're pregnant again?"

She shakes her head back and forth.

"No no no. Trevor has leased us a lovely two-bedroom,

two-bath condo in Burbank. We have a view and a garage and access to a pool and everything."

"How long is the lease for?"

She gives me a shove and laughs at the same time. But I'm serious.

"How long?" I ask again.

"Two years."

She is swinging her body from side to side, like she's so happy she can't stand still, and I now feel like kicking myself in the ass for putting a damper on it.

"I know you won't believe this considering how much I've waffled these past four years, but I'm going to UCLA to get my teaching credentials."

"What happened to skin care?"

"I can still do that part time, but as you know firsthand, Mom, all of this has been a long, slow process, and Trevor and I are both so grateful to you for your patience. He wants you to like him."

"Okay. Tell him I like him."

"Seriously, Mom. He's a good guy."

"Okay. Enough about Trevor. I think you'll make a good teacher. But I always thought you'd be good at anything you put your mind to, sweetheart. You're a good mother. But can you do me a big favor?"

"And what's that, Mom?"

"Follow your own lesson plan for your life."

"I'm trying. Are you following yours?"

This throws me off. "I'm revising it. That's what you do when you make plans and sometimes things happen and you end up on a different path. Babies are a good example of this. But to answer your question, Tanna, all I know right now is I'm going to Billings next month to finally bury my brother's ashes next to our parents and I'm hoping while I'm flying through those clouds that my next move becomes crystal frigging clear."

Of course, hugs.

"BJ, look out the sunporch window! There's a moving truck in front of the Songs' house. Hallefuckinglujah!"

"Oh oh, Nana, you just said a very bad word!"

Shit fuck goddamnit! As much as I love my granddaughter, I will be glad when she finally waves bye-bye to me from her car seat and sleeps in her own bedroom three busy freeways away and I can finally stop tiptoeing in my own goddamn house and talking in that Elmo voice and praising all of the dumb shit she does and I won't have to watch or listen to all those ridiculous educational shows and cartoons every morning, noon, and night, especially that *Yo Gabba Gabba* and *The Backyardigans* (except for Uniqua, that's my girl), and I can get rid of all the miniature bowls, sippy cups, plates, and glasses, and maybe now my house won't look like Toys R Us and I can stop pretending to enjoy her company after about an hour and I can just get in my brand-new Porsche Carrera I bought from the interest I earned on that Apple stock that split, and Little Miss Clementine can hug and kiss her nana all she wants when I visit for birthdays and holidays, and maybe if and when her parents make enough money to actually take a vacation and can afford DirecTV, I would be more inclined to babysit, but on the other hand, if there was a way I could see Clementine when she's closer to puberty, we might be able to have a decent conversation and I wouldn't have to chase her all over the house or forget we're playing hide-'n'-go-seek when I start running my mouth with BJ like I'm about to do now right now.

"Nana was just kidding! I thought you were Snow White!"

"I am Snow White!" she says, and runs to get that Snow White dress I made the mistake of buying her, along with about five or six more. She thinks she's a princess and some days she gets pissed off at me if she puts one of them on and I get confused about what princess she is.

"Can you believe this, BJ?"

"I can believe almost anything. I have lived long enough to see our first black president get elected. I met my long-lost granddaughter. One of my sisters hasn't spoken to me in almost two years. My grandsons are in high school. Ricky has not been in any trouble and gets good-enough grades. And because of Luther being an honor student and the way he runs that football, he gets to pick and choose what college he wants to go to. I'm sad to say I couldn't tell you if my oldest son is single or on wife number six or if the other one is dead or alive. And last but not least, I'm still too stupid to retire. And my best friend is having an affair with her ex-husband. What day are you leaving again?"

"Next Friday. It's not an affair. We're having sex. And it's good. I don't know how I managed to live without it for as long as I have."

"Enjoy it and him for as long as you can. And tell Howard I said hi. So, are you excited about seeing your brother?"

"I'm looking forward to seeing him. Just not under these circumstances. Did I tell you he moved to Colorado?"

"I don't think you did."

"Yep. He's still with his ugly wife, and lucky for that little girl she's struggling to be attractive and maybe in a few more years she'll settle into some level of appealing."

"You can be such a bitch, Tammy."

"I know, and I'm so glad. Anyway, Jackson's meeting me in Billings. It's just going to be the two of us. But that's enough."

"I'll keep an eye out for you."

"I can't wait to see who moves into the Songs' house. Want to make a bet they're Armenian? They're taking over L.A., you know."

"I don't care what nationality or what color they are as long as they get a gardener."

Logan Airport in Billings is up-to-the-minute modern. I don't know why I'm surprised. It's not like Montana is hicksville. It just feels like it's a beautiful woman stranded out in the middle of nowhere surrounded by mountains and rivers. I'm grateful I grew up to experience open space and freezing sunshine, but I'm still glad I escaped.

"Hey, sis," Jackson says when he spots me. He has finally put on weight and looks like he's been eating his share of elk.

"You look healthy," I say.

"So do you. A little more endowed if you don't mind my saying it, but I can't help but notice."

"Nice you can buy what you've always coveted," I say, and pull on my hair. He doesn't get it.

"They're called extensions. Every movie star you see on those award shows swinging those luscious tresses has one. Don't be fooled by beauty. Anyway, after we get the rental car, you want to get something to eat before we check into the hotel?"

"I thought it was a motel."

I push him.

Both of us have carry-ons and I'm just glad to see that he's got a new burgundy North Face backpack.

"You drive," I say after we get the rental car, which is really some kind of miniature SUV since it's January.

Montana is definitely a giant postcard. The one thing these

developers can't buy and ruin is the mountains. Thank the Lord. But it looks to me like everything on the ground has sure changed. Before Jackson drives past our property, he warns me that it's got its own zip code now. It's called "Sacred Cow" and is what is commonly known as a subdivision that has given birth to hundreds of homes that cover the land where our horses and cows once roamed.

When I see a sign that says MONTANA REDNECKS 4 OBAMA I say, "Stop the car, Jackson."

And he does.

"What in the world is going on?"

"Well, in all honesty, sis, I could very well have one of these signs in front of my house except I'd swap Colorado for Montana."

I just look at him like he's not my brother.

"You can't be serious, Jackson."

"I voted for President Obama."

"Go ahead and tell me why."

"Because I trust him. Because he's smart and I like a lot of the things he's trying to do for us folks who are poor or don't have much. He's not trying to be the president just for black people, but for everybody. Now let's be clear. I still don't want to be BFFs with anybody black, but I sure as hell don't think I'm superior just because I'm white. I don't like being a racist, and out there on the road listening to some of the shit these truckers have to say about black people makes me angry enough to want to throw up. I don't have a right to hate black people, because they've never done anything to me. I think deep down I've always been afraid of them. But President Obama has changed that."

"Wow."

"I know it's a lot to take in, and I apologize for using that 'N' word. It's not in my vocabulary anymore."

"Well, damn, Jackson!"

"To be honest, sis, I also wanted to be a part of making history. Are you hungry?"

"I'm starving," I say, and squeeze his hand extra hard, more to give myself a reality check.

When we get into town, which is also very up-to-the-minute modern and even has buildings that could be considered small skyscrapers, I'm über-impressed. We eat at a cool Brewing Company with a menu that seems to have a million choices. We drink some good ale. I have fish and chips, and Jackson eats a sandwich called "Scarface," which has all things Italian on it. I've never noticed any Italians in Montana, but as we sit here I can't help but notice that I have not seen one black person or ethnic minority since I got off the airplane. But I don't feel like bringing this up, since it's obvious my brother has come a long way.

We bury our brother next to our parents and it is not ceremonial but we both feel better. We hug at the airport and before we head to different terminals, he squeezes my hand and says, "So, what do you see in your future, sis?"

This question catches me completely off guard. Out of all the parting words he could've said, I'm wondering why he chose to ask me this out of the blue. "I really don't know, Jackson," is the most honest answer I can give because I've been so busy living from one day to the next, being so preoccupied with my daughter's and granddaughter's futures, I haven't given all that much thought to mine.

When I drive down our street, I can't help but smile, since all twenty-two homes still have an Obama-Biden sign stuck in the front yard, including my Korean neighbors, who have a manicured lawn bursting with flowers. Everybody took pictures of our block before the election and we are just too proud to take them down. When I pull into my driveway, something looks different. I look around the yard and realize I can see the sky, which is when I notice large branches full of avocados and lemons falling into my yard. I also hear what is obviously one of those chain saw things in my neighbor's yard. Without going into the house, and without even thinking that he could possibly use that equipment on me, I walk along the sidewalk and stand in front of his house. He turns to look at me and turns off that saw.

"What are you doing?" I ask as politely as I possibly can.

"Getting rid of these trees. The olive trees are next. I know they've been a nuisance all these years, and I figured I might as well cut them down now."

"Have I ever complained about any of the trees?"

"No, but I didn't much blame you. I wasn't a very neighborly neighbor."

"Well, except for that one time my brother parked his big rig out front, we never had any problems with each other."

"Yeah, well, back then I didn't like the idea of you living in our neighborhood."

"I know that. But it was my neighborhood, too."

"True. There's something you don't know about the house you've been living in."

I turn to look at it. "I know it needs major work and I've been trying to decide if it's worth fixing up or if there's any chance in hell I could sell it, which is probably not possible considering what's going on."

"My great-grandparents owned that house. And this one. But I think it may be time for me to finally leave here, and I don't care what I get for mine."

"Has something bad happened? Wait. Don't tell me. It's your son, isn't it?"

He nods his head yes.

"In Iraq?"

He nods his head yes again.

"I'm so, so sorry, Mr. Heaven. Is there anything I can do to help?"

"Well, if you wouldn't mind, there's going to be a lot of folks stopping by tomorrow and I would appreciate it if you would let them park in front of your house and in your driveway for a couple of hours."

"Absolutely. I'm sure all of us can. Betty Jean for sure."

"She's already said yes. Thank you."

"Do you know my name?"

"It's Tammy Whitaker. And your children's names are Max and Montana. And they're good kids. And from what I saw of him over the years, your husband appeared to be a good man. Anyway, that's none of my business. So, a while back, I offered to help Mrs. Butler make a few improvements on her home and that unit above the garage, since I'm retired. I suffer from a little arthritis in my knees but I would be more than happy to help you, too, should you decide to stay."

"That's very nice of you, Mr. Heaven."

"It's Eli."

"But where would you move?"

"I haven't thought that far ahead yet."

"Don't go," I hear myself blurt out.

He looks up and down the block. I do the same. Some of the homes are old and run down, some even sagging, but all but one of the yards are well manicured and it is clear that folks still take pride in what little they do have.

337

"This is our *hood*," I say, "and we should make sure we keep it that way, don't you think?"

"I don't know right now."

"I don't think I'd want anybody nice moving in next to me," I say, and he chuckles.

"Well, let me take some time to think on it," he says.

"I understand this is hard. I can't even begin to imagine what it feels like losing a child. Betty Jean lost her daughter, you know."

"I know. And I don't know how she's managed to care for those boys."

"We do what we have to," I say.

He just nods.

"Do me a favor, Mr. Heaven. And forgive me—but I like your last name, and right now we could all use a little more of it down here."

He smiles for the second time in twenty years. "What kind of favor might that be?"

"Could you please not cut the olive trees down?"

He looks up at them. "I won't."

Dexter

January 20, 2009

Dear Ma:

    I'm sorry to have to write you from here. Again. This time I have no one to blame but myself. As you can see, I'm writing this by hand because the computer just felt too impersonal to say what I have to say.

    Of course I violated my parole for doing something stupid and now I'll have to do the balance of my time from the previous offense as well as two more years for getting caught with a few too many pills. I'll be forty-five when I get out but I'm sure you're not interested in hearing this now. Aunt Arlene has filled me in on a few happenings between you and her and about Omar being gay and how hard she took it. I'm hoping she'll come around. One day. But we all have to figure out how to accept each other for who we are and not who we want them to be.

    I have to admit something to you after all these years. It was me who told that woman to get out of her car, not Buddy. It was me who pushed a penlight flashlight against her ribs. It was me who took the sixty dollars in cash out of her wallet. It

339

was me who was behind the wheel when we got pulled over. The whole idea was mine. I was only thinking about how exciting it would be to speed off in a car and just drive fast and I knew it would be years before I would ever be able to afford one. I was not thinking about the fear and terror I was causing that woman. Daddy was right when he disavowed me for being so callous and insensitive by thinking this was just a temporary inconvenience for this woman but in reality I may very well have destroyed her life. She might always be afraid to get behind the wheel in a parking lot. I did that to her and I had no right to. I wrote her a letter through her then attorney and apologized for what I did to her. I have no idea if she ever received it, since I haven't heard from either her or the attorney. I feel better for owning up to what I did after all these years and for finally coming to terms with the pain my arrogance undoubtedly caused someone who didn't deserve it. It's probably why I found my way back here. There are still more lessons for me to learn and things I have to pay for.

I am ashamed of myself, Ma. What I have failed to do with my life especially since you and Daddy did all that you could to raise all three of us right. What has happened to me is my fault. Not yours. What happened to Trinetta just proved how much more power drugs can have over your heart and mind. Because what mother in her right mind would abandon her kids? And whatever is up with Quentin, his need for constant companionship is going to be on him until he can figure out what to do by himself.

I admit, I'm lost. I haven't been able to figure out what my purpose is. It wasn't law. I can't save anybody until I learn how to save myself from myself. Which has been very hard to do. I don't know where you find confidence, why it hides from you when it's what you need, and why hope lives with it. This letter was not meant to be a self-pity letter, but I'm just thinking out loud. You are probably through with me, I would think, by now, anyway, so it shouldn't matter what I think or feel about myself.

I just wish I had amounted to more, Ma. I wish I had done something to make you and Daddy proud of me. Not this. I also feel plenty bad that we now have an African-American president and I had to celebrate it behind bars. With thousands of other black men. I also have a four-year-old son, Kwame, who visits me here. I am torn between my own selfishness—not wanting him to not know who I am and not wanting someone else to raise him—but Skittles cleaned up her act, not that her act was ever raggedy—she did a little dancing back when, but it was me who encouraged her because it was fast money. She went to a trade school and now she's a dental technician (remember that's what Trinetta was going for?). Chances are Skittles is going to get tired of coming way up here to see me, just like you did back in the day, and I wouldn't much blame her. As I write this, I'm beginning to think that maybe Kwame will be better off not coming to this place of brick and mortar and steel. I don't want this place or me in it to be his frame of reference.

I've been here now more than a year. The only thing that's changed is technology. It has taken me a lot of courage to write you, but even that was selfish, because I'm sure you were wondering if I was dead or alive. I've got a pattern of doing things backwards, but one thing I did do was get my GED. I'm just going to work on being a better person while I'm here. They've got members from the Church of Latter-Day Saints here trying to spread the gospel, but they've also got

Muslims spreading theirs, too. I'll hear what everybody has to say, but I don't believe there is any specific doctrine we have to follow to be a good person. I want the rest of my life to add up to something. Because I'm tired of subtracting from it.

I love you, Ma. And please forgive me for all the pain I've caused you. I'm sorry.

Love love love,
Dexter

P.S. I don't expect to hear back from you anytime soon, and it's okay. I'm going to keep writing anyway.

January 23, 2009

Dear Dexter,

It was very nice to hear from you. Of course I'm sorry you're back in that place, but you sound like you may have learned something this time around. I'm glad you finally admitted what you did, even though your daddy and me always knew it. I believe in my heart that now God will forgive you, too.

Anyway, even though you didn't ask for any, I have put $200 into your account just for toiletries and things of that nature. I would also like to come visit you, so please send me the forms to fill out and let me know when it might be best to come. I finally retired, and now volunteer part-time at the senior center. I know that sounds funny, but I'm not old. I'm just retired. Some people really do need help, so why not?

Maybe you can ask Skittles if she can bring Kwame over to visit us sometime. I'm good with kids, you know. It would be nice to get to know all my grandchildren while I'm alive. Your nephews are doing well. Ricky has stayed out of trouble since that Juvenile Hall experience scared the heck out of him. (You may not even know about that.) He's working to keep his grades up. Swimming some but he really seems to love diving. He's not interested in going to the Olympics, but he's certified and might teach little kids in the neighborhood how to swim. He's in tenth grade now. Luther is still a straight-A honor student, and he's a senior. Getting letters from almost every college you can think of. He plays football and ran a little track. Did you know he's 6'5"? I guess his daddy was tall. Anyway, he's going on these college tour visits and he's got every color jersey you can think of but he hasn't made up his mind just yet. I'm so glad the streets didn't steal them from me. They deserve the best life has to offer and I've given them what I could.

I have decided that I am not going to write you any letters with negative things in them, because all it will do is make you feel bad and I know you already feel bad. All of us make mistakes. And some of us have to pay for them. And if we're lucky, some of us learn from them. You are not a bad person, Dexter. You still have a good heart and I'm still glad you are my son.

Let me know if there's anything you need. I'll do whatever I can.

Love,
Mom

P.S. Do you like the font I used?

P.P.S. I will send pictures of Luther's graduation.

Venetia

Rodney is paying for the thirty-year low-interest mortgage he had on my life. I don't know why I ever loved him. That is not true. I loved him because he took good care of me and took away my worries. But I know now that it's healthy to worry about some things, otherwise you take far too much for granted. Rodney was not good for me. He thought he had done me a favor being married to me all these years and my prize was our children and that mansion and being able to stay at home, and because I was hell-bent on impressing him, I went overboard, which is why I never bothered to find out what else I was good at or who I was. I never wanted to crunch numbers, but Rodney convinced me you could never go wrong with a business degree. I wanted to prove I was smart enough to achieve it, but I don't really think he was all that impressed. I have always found it hard to say no even when I really wanted to, but after years of saying yes to everybody but me, I'm discovering that it's just as scary to try something new as it is not to try anything at all.

I have prayed over it and have come to realize that God can't fix all of our problems, that He can't heal all of our wounds, that He can't tell us what to do or which way to go. It's up to us to pay attention, to slow down long enough to notice the signs, the hints

344

God gives us to look, to change our direction if we ever hope to be astonished. I'm already feeling lighter, even joyous, because I finally own my life.

I sold the house and moved into a nice condo out here in the Marina. I didn't bring any of that old fuddy-duddy furniture either. Since I don't have to worry about where my next meal is coming from I sold it all and donated every penny of it to charities that help feed children. I also didn't want to be reminded of what used to be, since my new mission is to discover what is still possible.

I have joined a new church, which I absolutely love. It's non-denominational and right here in my neighborhood. It looks like America inside, because it's a legitimate rainbow coalition and everybody is represented, including gays, lesbians, and even the transgenders. I am not afraid of the outside world as much as I used to be, and of course the unknown can be scary, but not so scary it's not worth taking a peek.

I have a view of the ocean and for some reason it makes me feel young. In much the same way as when I went off to college. I have invested in scented candles. I have refused to walk on stuffy carpet. No more funeral parlor drapes. I am not a queen and don't need marble to remind me of it. Everything doesn't have to shine. I think I am finally hip and have a purple wall to prove it. The kids love it here. They find excuses to visit. To stay over. Sometimes we sleep on the balcony and listen to the waves. Watch movies on our laptops. Eat chips and salsa. Chicken enchiladas. Rice and beans. We guzzle margaritas. Laugh at nothing and at everything.

"We love the new and improved version of you, Mom," Zach has said with his head in my lap.

"So nice to finally meet you again, Mom," Lauren said when she found out I had moved out of the house before it sold.

BB likes it mostly because it's closer to her and Ricky likes being anywhere near water. "I'm glad you figured out what was best for you, Venetia. I've been waiting a long time to see you happy and silly. You're actually fun, now."

Even with this housing crisis going on, Arlene would only do the deal if I promised not to talk about Omar or BB. Which is why I let someone else sell the house and help me find the condo. I don't know why people hold grudges for as long as they do. It's not solving anything. So one person is right but the other person might be right, too. Duh. I still find it hard to believe that my sisters have not spoken to each other after all this time. I think BB just stopped calling even though it's killing her inside. She loves Arlene and Arlene knows it.

I have eaten at the very chic restaurant Omar works at, and from what I understand he and his boyfriend might buy it. Omar made me the most unbelievable dish called Ravioli di Costine (I have the menu right here in front of me), which was fresh hand-made ravioli filled with shredded braised short ribs and topped with brunoise vegetables, orange zest, and port wine reduction at a cost of $15 but he gave it to me for free since Betty Jean told me where the place was and it was his birthday and he couldn't believe I remembered. Of course I remembered. We have the exact same birthday. He has kept the weight off, and I didn't want to bring up his mother and he didn't bring her up either but I invited him and Stephen to church and they said they'd love to come one Sunday.

I have prayed for all of us to come to our senses even though I know it's an ongoing process. We're not getting any younger and family is family. It is also the reason why I'm taking a Zumba class at a gym where they make you hot tea. I will try yoga in the future, but right now I am loving my jewelry-making classes and might consider selling some of my wares, since people are starting to ask where I bought them. I have started taking long drives, something I've always loved to do. I sometimes go five or eight miles over the speed limit and usually go very early along the Pacific Coast Highway. I roll my windows down so I can hear the birds and the wind and the tide. Sometimes I let the cool mist on my face be my latte.

Zach did work on President Obama's campaign. He knocked on doors to make sure people were registered to vote. For the first time in my life I volunteered. I made phone calls to folks in those battleground states asking if they were going to vote for Barack Obama. A lot of them hung up on me. Some swore. But quite a few of them said, "Absolutely!" I was Zach's date for the inauguration. Of course we didn't get to sit down and we almost froze to death but we didn't care. We were there along with two million other folks of every race, packed so closely we couldn't move, many of us crying loudly and unable to wipe the smiles off of our faces at the same time. We waved to him, gave him high fives in the air, chanted, "Obama! Obama!" As he was being sworn in, you could hear a pin drop as we listened to him tell us what he hoped to do for us as a people, and for this country over the next four years. We left knowing he had our backs, and we were there because we wanted him to know we had his.

I am also proud of my children. And, I like them. They know what they stand for and they make sure you know it. I am learning a lot from them, and I am getting such a kick watching them become whomever and whatever it is they're growing toward or into.

I have been on my own for a while now, and I have made and

am continuing to make changes in my day-to-day life. I finish what's important, not just what I start. It excites me to let the laundry pile up. I am no longer afraid of mildew. If I see dust balls forming, I either ignore them or blow on them so the housekeeper can destroy them. I iron nothing. There is a laundry and dry-cleaner downstairs. I rarely cook for myself, because I realize it's a waste of time, plus I'm not very good at it. It's also cheaper to eat out or order in, and now that I am no longer embarrassed for being divorced or single or even alone, I often sit in the window of a restaurant and smile at people who walk by, especially children, and sometimes even men. I'm not trying to pick up a stranger. I'm just trying to get used to not being one.

Quentin

I'm engaged.

    Mindy divorced me after a year of counseling that did more for me than it did her. I discovered how screwed up I really am. For starters, I am an Uncle Tom. But not because I want to be, and not because I reject blackness. Growing up, I wanted our neighborhood to be clean and safe and beautiful. But it wasn't. It felt hostile, which is why I chose to escape. This is when I started living a lie. I fabricated a faux world, one in which I insulated myself from anything and everybody that reminded me of where I came from. Unfortunately, this included my parents. I believe it was my way of punishing them because they seemed more concerned, preoccupied, and worried about Trinetta and Dexter than me. They were the fuckups. I take that back. They were fucking up. My sister and brother were just as smart if not smarter than me, and it angered me how easy it was for them to be seduced by the lure of the streets. They gave their power away and let the streets win. To me, it was cowardly, how they took the easy way out, which turned out to be a whole lot harder on them. I was angry at them for not following the example I was trying to set. As the oldest, I spent six years in college to become a medical practitioner because I wanted to make people feel better. I wanted my parents to be proud of me. I wanted them to express it with even half of the energy they showed in their concern for my sister and brother. Dad did. But Mother didn't. She seemed more critical of my personal choices and my accomplishments took a backseat. It hurt not to be celebrated for doing what they wanted for us: to get a college education and become a success. I wanted this for my sister and brother, too. I wanted us to be happy and proud. I didn't want us to disappoint our parents but especially ourselves.

Now that we have the first African-American president, I couldn't be prouder. I voted for him, and not because he is black, but because he represents what integrity looks like on us. He is living proof of the slogan "Yes We Can." I'm hopeful that youngsters growing up where I came from will understand that they have more power than they think. They can change the world. They can follow in his footsteps. They can renounce poverty and failure if they're willing to swim through all the muck until they reach clear water.

I've been trying to change things about myself that have alienated and hurt the people I care about most. My mother has been fed up with me forever. Sometimes I don't think she likes me. I'm sure she thinks I'm elitist, but that's not true. It has cost a lot for me to pretend others don't see my skin color when in fact they do. I don't blend in and I finally get it. I've been trying to prove my worth to strangers. My mother's acceptance is far more important to me, especially now that she's getting up in age and I'm all she has left. I want her to know that she can count on me.

And there's Mindy. Who could blame her for wanting out? I was controlling, but the most accurate term is *control freak*. I wore her out. After she divorced me, I was determined not to jump into a new relationship just to avoid being by myself. It has taken four years of living alone for me to realize I didn't know what to do with silence. It was uncomfortable spending so much time with myself. This is also when a number of things started becoming obvious to me very quickly. I was not that likable. Nor was I all that interesting. In fact, I often bored myself. Many of the things I'd always thought were important turned out to be quite superficial. I cared about how things looked on paper, including me. I believe I was fortunate to have been given this wake-up call but only because I knew it was time to wake up.

After dropping Margaret off months ago, Mindy told me how nice it was to see my goodness return, that I was warm again, and I felt much like the man she fell in love with. I don't know what possessed me to ask her to marry me again but I did and she shocked me and said yes. She said she had never stopped loving me. She had just stopped liking me.

She agreed to let me tell Margaret, who's now in second grade, so I decided to take her to Pier 39 at Fisherman's Wharf, one of her favorite places, to break the news, hoping she'll be happy that we're going to be a family again.

As we walk toward the sea lions, we lean against the wooden fence to watch them. "You know Dad still loves your mother, right?"

"If you say so, Dad," she says as she takes a big bite of the bright blue cotton candy.

Without notice, she turns to walk up toward the street, and I seem to be following her until she sits on a bench and begins to feed the pigeons from a bag. I don't feed them, because I think they're disgusting.

"How would you feel if I told you your mom and I are going to get married again?"

"Really? Can I come to the wedding? Please?"

"Of course you can, if we have a wedding."

"Please, Dad! I didn't get to go to the first one!"

"That's because you weren't born yet."

"Well, I'm born this time!"

"So does this make you happy?"

"Yes indeedy! I like having you for my dad. So are you going to live with us or do we have to go back to that other crib?"

Crib? "No."

"Can we move to the hood, Dad, please?"

The hood? What is going on here? "What do you know about the 'hood'?"

"I want to live with my homies."

"And who might they be?"

"People that look like me. It's why I don't like my school. There are no black people there."

"And that bothers you?"

"I just said so, Dad. Duh."

"Well, I found us a very cool home and it's up in the Berkeley Hills, where all different races of people live, and I'm pretty sure you'll have lots of homies in your new school. In fact, I'm sure of it."

She tosses the entire contents of the bag to the pigeons and gives me a hug and immediately stands up straight.

"Can we have a baby?"

"I don't know about that, Margaret."

"Please? I'm tired of pretending Baby Alive is real."

"I thought you liked playing with her?"

"She has gotten on my nerves. At first I was happy she could drink a bottle and pee and I could feed her and she would poop, but Baby Alive still doesn't have any teeth and it's because she's not ever going to grow up."

I am laughing. "Well, we can ask Mom how she feels about adding to our family, how's that?"

"That sounds good to me."

"So, let me ask you something silly. Where'd you learn the terms *hood* and *homies*?"

"From my cousins. Ricky and Luther."

"Do you talk to them on the phone?"

"Yes indeedy! They're my boys!"

"I'm not sure if I like this language."

"Oh, Dad, take a chill pill! They make me laugh. Last time when I was there Grandma BJ took us to Disneyland!"

"You mean you've been down there?"

"Yes indeedy! I'm going to spend a whole week with Grandma BJ this summer."

"But your mother never got my permission for you to do this."

"But you're not her dad, Dad."

"I know. And you're right. And it's fine."

"Now that you're getting married again, you can drive down with us! We're going to Palm Tree Springs because Cousin Luther is being released from high school with many honors. Mom said I can also celebrate my black roots while we're there."

"Your what?"

"My black roots. The part of me I don't know. But I'm going to find them in Los Angeles."

"Good for you, Margaret. Good for you."

"Mom said she hopes President Obama will help you find your black roots since your Uncle Tom is finally leaving. Who is he?"

"A stranger."

"Hello, Mom."

"Who is this?"

"It's me. Quentin."

"What did you just call me?"

"Mom."

"Why?"

"Because I know you've never liked me calling you 'Mother.'"

"I've gotten used to it."

"But what would you prefer that I call you?"

"What you've been calling me, Quentin."

"But you don't find it annoying anymore?"

"No, what would be annoying is if you suddenly started calling me 'Mom.'"

"So, is it true that Margaret's going to be spending a little time with you and the boys, then?"

"Yes, she is. She's a little pistol. We Skype, you know."

"No, I didn't know you Skype."

"Did you know she could sing?"

"No, I didn't."

"You might as well know now that this won't be the first time she's been down here."

"I've heard."

"Mindy's brought her down here quite a few times. She's not afraid of the ghetto like some people."

"I don't fear the ghetto, it has just always made me feel uncomfortable. But that's changing, Mother."

"Sure sure sure. Everybody understands this about you, Quentin, so don't even worry about it. Besides, the ghetto is doing just fine without you."

"Mindy and I are remarrying and moving to the Berkeley Hills, where I've bought a house with a three-bridge view. And ever since I moved my practice, business has been booming, so it wasn't race after all, and it should definitely thrive in the East Bay, so all this is to say that I'd like to invite you and the boys up for a long weekend once we get settled, and this time, I mean it. I'd also like to know if there's anything I can do for you, and for Luther's graduation?"

"Lord have mercy! I love good news. Before I congratulate you for getting lucky twice, I just want you to know that I don't need anything and you can call Luther and ask him what he might want for graduation. And thank you, son. Okay, now. Congratulations! I knew Miss Mindy truly loved you and she's been struggling over it for quite a while, but whatever you did to come around, keep doing it."

"I'm trying to learn how to be more open-minded."

"Why start now?"

"Because sometimes I feel cut off from my own family and I know it's my own doing."

"Well, I still love you, Quentin, even if your mind stays closed forever," she says with a chuckle.

"That's nice to know, Mother. And I love you, too."

Nurse Kim

Hello! Anybody home?"

"Your voice sure sounds familiar!"

"Well, yours sure doesn't!" I say to the Kobe Bryant clone standing behind the brand-new front door who must be Luther, the little boy who had a crush on me seven or eight years ago.

"Nurse Kim! You came back into my life," he says in a voice so deep it sounds like he's faking it. But of course he's not.

"Where's your grandma?"

"She went to get her oil changed."

"Why couldn't you do it for her?"

"Because she won't let me drive her car."

"Why not?"

"Because I wrecked it. Twice."

"Did you kill anybody?"

"No."

"Did she have insurance?"

"Yes."

"Then I don't know what the problem is, Evel Knievel. Can I come in or what?"

"Of course. My bad. I was not expecting to see you when I opened the door, Nurse Kim."

"You can drop the 'Nurse Kim,' sugar."

"You're not a nurse anymore?"

"In many ways, yes. But I've been a licensed physical therapist about four years now."

After I finally get inside, I am shocked at what I see. That 1960s beige shag carpet is gone and now it looks like I'm standing on oak or what looks like oak. And I know that can't be a real leather couch? As I get closer and sit down I realize it is not pleather and it's a pretty-ass navy blue. I didn't even know this couch came in navy blue when I saw it in Jennifer Convertibles. The cocktail table is cherry red. Even the rug underneath it is the kind you see in Macy's Home. I wonder who picked this out? Even the frames and glass on all those old family pictures on the wall are new, and hell, so is the wall! That is a real flat-screen TV, isn't it? And you mean to tell me Miss Betty finally broke down and got rid of that lazy-ass La-Z-Boy and got a modern recliner, and she had the nerve to get white leather! I'm thinking maybe she won one of those before-and-after rooms from HGTV, because Miss Betty did not have any decorating skills. Hey! I can see back into the kitchen and I know a new refrigerator when I see one, and that floor is cork, and it's not even necessary for me to walk back there to check to see if all the appliances been replaced. When you get rid of old shit and replace it with new shit, it means a whole lot of shit has happened. I'm wondering if maybe Miss Betty hit the lottery, but probably not, or she would've bought a whole new house in a different neighborhood, but whatever happened, God has done His magic in here.

"Hold on a minute. Who did the remodeling and decorating, if you don't mind my asking?"

"Well, it's a long story, but our neighbor across the street, the one who lives next to Ms. Tammy, Mr. Heaven, did all of the remodeling inside and outside the house and he even helped Grandma get the apartment over the garage turned into a legal dwelling, so she rents it out to a guitarist who should find another profession, but also, do you remember my uncle Quentin?"

"You mean the one who only married white women?"

"Yes, him."

"What number is he up to?"

"He's still on five. They say the second time's a charm."

"Get out! So he finally slowed his roll?"

"Well, he remarried his wife. Anyway, since he didn't have to pay any more child support or alimony, he gave Grandma a wad and—wal-la!"

"No shit? Guilt is a bitch, ain't it? Forgive me for swearing."

"It's fine. You're a full-fledged adult."

"Did he see the light or something?"

"What kind of light?"

"Never mind, sweetie."

"Anyway, he's been calling us a lot. Talking to Ricky and me about college and sports and cars, and he even invited us to come up to the Bay Area. He and Grandma were on the outs for a minute there, but seems like things are smoothing out."

"Listen at you. Something had to happen that made him start acting like a son and finally help his damn mama out."

He shrugs those wide shoulders. Damn, if I was twenty or thirty years younger. "What's your girlfriend's name?"

"I don't have a girlfriend."

"Why not? And I know you're not gay."

"Because my buddies and I made a pact in our junior year to write off girls so we could maintain our focus. We wanted to do well on the SATs, plus I've got so many AP classes I didn't want to get sidetracked."

"What's a 'AP' class?"

"Advanced Placement. It's an honors class."

I raise my hand up to get a high five and he gives me one. It hurts but I don't say anything.

"Well, you're still beautiful, Nurse Kim."

"What did I just tell you?"

"Miss Kim."

"Thank you. Anyway, what I do is put professional athletes back together again. I help them heal. And from what I understand, you might be headed the same way one day, too."

"Where'd you get that information?"

"Well, you know Derrick Graves, who jumped twenty-five feet in the long jump?"

"He's my boy. He's probably going to London in 2012."

"He's my nephew and he's been telling me what you've been doing out on that football field, and that you've also been nominated for valedictorian. Ask me why am I not surprised? No, don't."

"I'm one of eleven. We have to write an essay to be considered, and I don't know if it's that important to me."

"Write it."

"I've got time to decide."

"Did you pick a college yet?"

"Not yet."

"Do you know what a big deal it is to be able to *choose* what college you want to go to instead of praying they accept you?"

"My grandma's sure excited. She has a box she keeps of all the letters I get. When I get home from school, she plays the voice messages back for me and jumps up and down, even on her bad knee. She's funny."

"She's proud. And so am I. Damn, you musta took after your daddy, 'cause you sure in hell are tall, Luther."

"I wouldn't know. But it's no big deal. Anyway, Miss Kim, if you want to wait for me after I'm out of college I'll save myself for you, since I don't see a wedding ring."

He cracks up.

"If this is your way of asking if I ever got married, the answer is no. Did I ever have any kids? The answer is no. I did the traveling nurse thing quite a few years but missed home, and then my granny took sick and I came home until she passed, and now, here I am, pushing forty, and I have to admit, I like coming and going as I please and not having any responsibilities except for myself."

"You just haven't met the right guy."

"You watch too much television. In all honesty, you and Ricky are the only children I ever liked. How is he doing?"

"Good. He's a sophomore. Still swimming but mostly diving."

"Did he ever get off that horrible medication?"

He nods.

"Is he heading to college, too?"

"Not sure if he's cut out for it, but he's got lots of talents, so he's going to be fine. We talk."

"Good. And how's your grandma doing these days?"

"She's fine. Finally retired. She comes to all my games and is pretty active in our Neighborhood Watch, and now they have a beautification project she and Miss Tammy are operating. Those two keep it going around here."

"And what about Omar and your aunts Arlene and Venetia?"

"How much time do you have?"

"Does your grandma have a beer or some cheap wine in the fridge?"

"I believe there's something back there. What's in that box?"

"Take a wild guess, Harry."

"Get out!"

"It's a token gift for graduating with such class and for being our Harry Potter and such a good kid and for falling in love with me when you were a little tyke and making us all so very proud."

He laughs all the way to the kitchen, and by the time he fills me in on all the mess my favorite person of all time has caused, I finish my second glass of decent white wine and decide it's time to pay her ass a visit.

Of course I pass right by Miss Betty, so I honk and she hits those brakes like this is an emergency. I back up. We roll down our windows. "I thought that looked like you, Nurse Kim! Where you going? Turn that car back around and come and talk to me. How are you? Was Luther at home?"

"Hold on, Miss Thang! I just stopped by to drop off a graduation present for Luther since I couldn't call, because for one thing you don't have a land line and stupid me forgot to take my cell phone out of my jeans pocket when I washed them, but anyway, I did not expect Luther to answer the door. I can't believe how tall and handsome he is, and I know you're one proud granny. You look good, Miss Betty. You doing all right, then?"

"I'm doing fine. No complaints."

"Good. I want to take you to lunch or dinner. How's that sound?"

"You're still something else, Nurse Kim. Either one would be nice."

"Gotta run. Talk soon."

"I want to buy a house," I say to Arlene, who's trying to act like she doesn't remember me but I know she damn well does because she never liked me. She always thought I was a slutty nurse and she was right, but hey, I did my job and I couldn't help it if I was hot and sexy, and since then I've been all over the goddamn world, which is why I'm going to use my yes-I-work-for-the-NFL voice instead of my more comfortable ghetto one. Of course I'm not stupid, and if you got any damn sense you pay attention and watch what rich people do with their money, which is exactly what I did when I was caring for so many of 'em over the years, and I invested my money, too, which is why I've got enough for a down payment on something even though I didn't come in here to buy anything, and if I was interested I damn sure wouldn't come to Arlene.

"Did Betty Jean send you here to harass me?"

I look at her like she's crazy.

"Why on earth would she want to harass you and what would make you think she could get me to do it? How are you, Arlene?"

"I'm fine. Kim, isn't it?"

"That's right."

"What kind of house are you in the market for?"

"Not the kind you've built for yourself."

She gets up and closes her door so hard the blinds make noise. I cross my legs. I can tell she still hates me. All I can say is it's not my fault I'm still hot and sexy and I can't help it if time is not being nice to her. As my granny always said, "A nasty attitude can make you ugly."

"Why don't you tell me what you're really doing here so we can get this over with? I've got real buyers waiting for me to show them real homes."

"Who fucked you over when you were a child, Arlene? Would you tell me that?"

"What in the world are you talking about? You don't know me well enough to come strolling into my office talking about something you have no idea about."

"Somebody did something to make you so unlikable and so judgmental and so goddamn mean. Who was it?"

She doesn't say anything, which is a surprise to me.

"I mean, people aren't born bitches, Arlene. But you don't seem to be able to recognize your own symptoms, and I thought you got a degree in psychology or some shit like that."

"You don't know a damn thing about me."

"I know what abuse looks like. And I know a lot of women who act just like you. Don't like no-damn-body. You get your rocks off pointing out everybody else's flaws and weaknesses but you don't bother taking a few damn minutes to look at your own. That's why Omar was so fucked up."

"Omar was not fucked up."

"Oh, yes he was. You pulled some shit on him you only see on Dr. Phil. Feeding him to comfort yourself. And then when he was finally able to see through the shit, he bailed, and he tried to tell you who he really was and you turned against your own goddamn son for trying to be honest with his own goddamn mama."

"Where did you get your information?"

"The *L.A. Times*. What fucking difference do it, I mean, does it make? You done pushed your son away. Do you have any idea how hard it must have been for him to know this about hisself all these years and didn't have nobody to tell it to? And look at what happened when he told your cold insensitive ass."

"You don't have to call me names."

"I'm sorry, *Arlene*. And to find out you haven't spoken to your own sister because she knew your son was gay before you did and she didn't bother telling you. Can't you see why she didn't tell you?"

She just nods, and I might be hallucinating or something, because those look like tears rolling down her face.

"I don't like being this way."

"And what way is that? Can you put a name on it for me?"

"Mean and judgmental and impatient and intolerant."

"Then stop it, Arlene."

"I don't know how."

"You can start by twisting your mouth to say you're sorry, and then accepting that you aren't always right and that just because people can't be who you want them to be doesn't mean something is wrong with *them*."

"His name was Monroe."

"And who was he?"

"My first cousin."

"And what did he do to you?"

"Too many things."

"Have you ever told anybody?"

She shakes her head no.

"Well, you just told me. And you don't even like me."

"I do now."

"I'm glad. Now. Can you show me what you got in the four- to five-hundred-thousand-dollar range with a view?"

Arlene

'm wrong. And I've been wrong about a lot of things. I've said a lot of things I shouldn't have said about things that were none of my business. For some reason it has taken me fifty-some-odd years to own up to the fact that what others do is not my business. If someone like Kim didn't like me because she was able to see right through me, and she's not even that bright, then it must mean I am a full-fledged bitch.

Being mean has cost me my sister and my son. I have been lonely and it's been hard trying to pretend like I don't have a son or a sister. I have always been jealous of Betty Jean. When we were kids, she was the one who got straight A's, she was the one who knew all the dance moves, and on Saturday mornings when our parents had people over, she was the one who performed. She's the one who got applause. Venetia clapped, too. But I just couldn't. And it's the reason I cut her hair off. She had too much of everything and more than me, and I wanted her to know what it felt like to have less. I've dragged this attitude into our adulthood, except I'm the one who ended up with the college degrees and she didn't and for a while I was glad her life hadn't amounted to much (although I didn't want her to suffer). But she was happy for years, raising her kids, and Lee David was a decent enough fellow. He did the best he could, and I have never known what that felt like, to be loved by a man.

And now what I have done to my son is right up there with many of the other cruel things I've done. My son may be gay but he's still my son. And I don't not love him because he's gay. I think I just wasn't expecting him to be anything but Omar. But he's still Omar. Although I have tried hard not to think about it, not to own up to it, but now, everywhere I go and almost everything I do, I'm doing it with or around someone who is gay. I've been wondering where they've been hiding all these years because it feels like they all just came out overnight. I'm also starting to think that maybe God has made them the third gender. I watched *Will and Grace* for years and always liked the Jack character the best even though he wasn't the star but he was by far the funniest, and it dawned on me when I started recording it that I wasn't bothered by the fact that these guys were gay, and in fact, half the time I wasn't thinking about it because they were just funny. When I look back, I'm starting to realize that Omar is just a guy who likes guys, and is his being gay hurting me? No, it is not.

I don't know how Kim was able to decipher that someone must have done something cruel to me to make me behave the way I do. And even though it's true, I can't put all the blame for my adult behavior on him. Still, I hate him. I have hated him for a long time, and for someone with a master's degree in psychology it shouldn't have taken me this long to figure out why my tolerance for others is so low and why I don't hold myself accountable for much of anything I do or say.

I am ashamed of myself for what I've put Omar and Betty Jean through. But admitting I'm wrong is one of the hardest things I've ever had to learn, and because I haven't learned how to do it yet, I'm trying to work up to it.

I even miss those boys. I remember when they were little. I don't like a lot of young people but I like them. Venetia has kept me in the know. She told me that Ricky has stayed out of trouble and is doing substantially better in school. Luther (praise the Lord) is graduating with honors and has offers from more than twenty top universities.

I made my son my center and forgot that one day he was going to grow up and live his own life on his own terms. Just like I did. Our parents didn't like the idea of me traipsing off to California either. They thought us girls were abandoning them, which we were from their perspective, but from ours, we were trying to find out where we fit in the world, and inside our own skin.

This is as far as I've gotten.

I pull into the parking lot of the restaurant Omar works at and, from what Venetia has told me, that he might soon be co-owner of, with his partner. It has very high ratings. I Googled it and my heart skipped a beat with genuine delight when I saw all the nice things patrons had said.

I have no idea what I'm going to say, and of course I called in advance to make sure he was going to be in, but now that I'm here I don't know how to say I'm sorry to my son for what I've done to him all these years and what I didn't do for him.

When I walk inside, the lighting is dim but the décor looks clean, like I've seen in *Décor* magazine. Most of the tables are full and I'm not sure what to do, but then I hear Omar's voice.

"Welcome, Mom."

My handsome, slim son is standing in front of me with a smile on his face, but I must have walked through the glass door because I don't remember how I got in here. He bends down to hug me and I almost squeeze the life out of him. "I'm sorry," I whisper in his ear.

"It's okay," he says, and leads me to the open fire pit, where a handsome guy who looks Italian or Greek is standing.

"Hello," he says, and kisses my hand, then gives me a hug. "I'm Stephen," he says.

I hug him back.

When I walk into the senior center where I understand Betty Jean volunteers twice a week, the first person I see is Tammy, who is reading to a silver-haired black man and what looks to be his girlfriend, who is white-haired, and they're holding hands on a sofa and look fully engaged. As soon as she spots me, she smiles, which I know is phony because I know she never cared for me. I can't remember why I couldn't stand her. Oh yes, because she married a black man. Back then, that seemed like a good enough reason, but of course now it seems totally ridiculous.

"Happy birthday, Arlene!" she says, and walks over and gives me a big hug. Hell, I forgot it was my birthday. I guess I just turned sixty-five or sixty-six, I haven't kept track.

"Happy birthday, Arlene!" at least thirty other seniors bellow out.

"Why, thank you, Tammy, and everyone," I say, looking around to see if I can spot my sister, but I don't see her. "How'd you know it was my birthday? Never mind. Dumb question."

"Betty Jean told me. She should be here in a minute or two. She's just coming back from the park. How've you been, Arlene?"

"Fair to middling. And you?"

"Good. Just helping Betty Jean, since they're a little short of staff."

"You're too young to retire, aren't you?"

"You're absolutely right, but I did it anyway!"

"How's that work?"

"If you mean how can I afford it? It's called investments and property, something you know a little bit about, wouldn't you say?"

"I suppose."

If I'm not mistaken, I believe she just winked at me, and I think I feel a smile showing up on my face.

"Betty Jean will be so happy to see you," she says.

"How do you know that?"

"Because she misses you."

"What if she's still mad at me?"

"She was never mad at you."

"Well, I was the one who lashed out at her."

"I can bear witness that she did lash out first and got you good."

We both start laughing.

When I see a line of seniors marching through the door, all in exercise clothes, holding hands, and then I see my sister, whose hair is also graying, which means I hope she finally got rid of those disgusting wigs, and it looks like she's lost a few pounds and is probably a size fourteen, a size she hasn't been in centuries, and she looks good, damn good, I wave at her and she waves right back.

Ricky

"Grandma."

"Yes, baby?"

"After I graduate, I want to work underwater."

"You mean you want to be a scuba diver?"

"Nope."

"Can you get to the point, please, sweetheart, or I'm going to be late."

"Where you going, Grandma?"

"To a concert."

"Jay-Z or Snoop Dogg?"

"Maybe next time they're in town. Anyway, your aunt Venetia and I are going to see Gladys Knight and I don't want to get caught in traffic. So spit it out."

"It's called underwater welding. You have be a certified diver, which, thanks to you, I am, and then go to welding school."

"Well, what exactly would you be doing down there?"

"The possibilities are endless. Just kidding, Grandma. Okay, really quickly: I'd get to repair or do construction on ships, oil rigs, barges, bridges, and I'd get to be out in the sea and travel all over the world. I'll stop there."

"Well, it certainly sounds interesting. How long does it take to learn how to do this?"

"At least two years."

"Then do your research, baby."

"I already have. The school I want to go to is in Florida."

"Florida?"

"It's one of the best."

"They don't have any of these welding schools in L.A.?"

"Not as good as the one in Florida."

"I thought you said you wanted to stay close to home?"

"I won't be gone that long! And like you always said, 'You have to be willing to give up something to get something.'"

"Then you were paying attention. Anyway, baby, it sounds very interesting and you seem pretty excited about it."

"This is what I want to do with my life, Grandma."

"So, is this your final answer?"

I just wink at her.

Luther

I chose USC. Not just because they have a great football team, that's too obvious. But the coach promised that I'd still be able to play receiver, which is my first love, and I know I'll be getting a top-notch education, plus I want to stay close to my grandma. She's getting up in age, and even though Ricky will be here at least a couple more years, I just feel better knowing I can be at her house in fifteen minutes or less if she ever needs anything. I don't have any guarantee I'll one day be in the NFL, so I don't want to count my chickens before they hatch. Plus, as soon as I started getting all those recruiting letters, my grandma said, "You can throw that football, Luther. And you can run fast with those long legs. But I want to see you make touchdowns on and off the field. Which is why you need a backup plan." I know she's right. Grandma's always right. I want a career. Now that we have an African-American president, I will seriously give politics some thought. I hate that I was too young to vote, but I'll save it for when he gets reelected! Right now, I'm clueless about what I'm going to major in but luckily they give you time to figure out what you like to do and may want to do. But how are you supposed to know what you want to do for the rest of your life when you just turned eighteen? Too bad I can't major in reading.

The week before graduation, Uncle Quentin came down and said, "Will you take a ride with me, Luther?"

At first I was a little skeptical because, although he's been acting different, Ricky and I weren't sure what he might have up his sleeve, since I never apologized to him for cussing him out. "Can Ricky come with us?"

"Sure," he said, and of course Ricky was in the backseat of that 500 SEL before I could open the front door.

"How long will we be gone? I have a date," I lied.

"With who?" Ricky asked.

"None of your business."

"Just hold on, fellas," Uncle Quentin said.

And then he just drove and we were all quiet. I like his Benz but I wouldn't want one. It screams L.A. When Uncle Quentin pulled into the Toyota dealership, he stopped the car.

"What are we doing here?" I asked.

"So you won't have to take the bus on your date or when you come visit your grandma, my mother."

"Get the fuck outta here! My bad. I'm sorry for swearing, Uncle Quentin."

"I think it's warranted."

"So is this why you were always quizzing me about rides?"

"I'm good, huh?"

I chose a black Highlander to get plenty of legroom. I gave Uncle Quentin a high five and a hug and told him I was sorry for all the things I said to him way back when.

"You don't have any reason to be sorry" is all he said.

The graduation cards with hundred-dollar bills, checks, and gift cards have been rolling in. I don't even know half these people but I am not turning down free loot. It's really nice to know that people care about you when you didn't know they knew you even existed. Some of them are from people on our block. Some from people Grandma worked with at the hotel. Even Uncle Rodney! But there are two that threw me off. One was from a prison, and I didn't recognize the last name and all those numbers didn't mean anything, but when I opened it, there was a picture of a guy who looked just like me and the card said, "Congratulations! You Did It!" on the outside, and on the inside: "I wish I could have played a part in where you're headed. I'm just glad you're headed in the right direction. Love, Your Father, Luther Bridges." So now I know who he is and where he is and what my last name was supposed to be, but it's been Butler for eighteen years and it'll always be Butler. I don't know if I'm going to write him back or not.

The other card was from my elementary school principal, Principal Daniels. I couldn't believe he remembered me, not to mention how he knew when and where I was graduating from, but he put a twenty-five-dollar Visa gift card inside it and said, "I knew you were going to excel, Luther, and I just want you to know how proud I am to have known you as a youngster. Your grandmother has done a fine job with you and your brother. I've got season tickets to the Trojans' home games and I'll be rooting for you. Congratulations again! Warren Daniels. P.S. I have recently retired. Do give my best to your grandma."

Grandma got the weirdest smile on her face when I let her read that one. She didn't get that worked up over the one my biological sent me, except I heard her say, "Sometimes it is better never than late."

Grandma wasn't upset when I told her the reason I didn't want to write the letter about why I wanted to be valedictorian was because I didn't want to be valedictorian. I didn't want to have to stand up in front of an auditorium full of people explaining what my graduating class will mean to the world and the stuff we accomplished in four years, and I didn't really have anything inspirational to say to help them on their way. All I wanted to do was thank my grandma for everything she's done for me, and for Ricky, and how were it not for her I probably wouldn't be graduating with honors.

"It's okay, baby. I know you'll be marching with that special tassel hanging from your cap and there's going to be an asterisk beside your name in that program that tells everybody in that auditorium that my grandson, Luther Butler, is graduating with one of the highest grade-point averages, and everybody who knows me knows you're going to be a Trojan!"

And she hugged me so hard I was so glad I was towering over her, so she couldn't see me crying like a big baby, but then Tupac started barking and I said, "It's okay, dude. Now sit," and he sat right next to Grandma, his black tail just a-wagging.

But then I got a grip and backed away from her and stood in the middle of the living room, opened up a piece of very nice stationery I bought from Office Depot with one of my gift cards, and I said, "I want to read you something that I hope you keep forever, Grandma."

She didn't say a word, just listened.

"Dear Grandma. I want you to know how much I appreciate everything you've done for me and Ricky all these years. I know we were a burden even if you didn't think of us that way. You have gone out of your way all these years to teach us all the right things, from good manners to how to give everything our all. You helped me appreciate reading and how much you can learn from a book. You said our prayers with us when I knew you were tired coming in from work. You made sure we were clean and you cooked us the best dinners ever. If it wasn't for your love, Ricky and I would've been in foster care and we might never have had the chance to be around you. I hope you know that our mother loved you, too, because she always told us so when we were little. She was always saying how sorry she was that she couldn't do more for us and for you. Back then, I didn't believe her, but I do now. I see how hard it is taking care of kids. How much we cost. How much time we take. How much you sacrifice to try to keep us happy. I'm glad Ricky got straight, and this letter is for him, too. Anyway, I didn't mean to meander (one of the things my English teacher is always accusing me of) but we both owe you so much and we will do our very best to never disappoint you. Ever.

If I do make it to the NFL, I want you to know that I'll be one of those dudes waving and giving a shout out to his grandma, and if I don't make it to the NFL I'm still going to be giving you a shout-out.

Thank you for everything.

Love,
Luther

P.S. I owe you a vacation. When I get a real paycheck after I graduate from college, I promise to take you anywhere you want to go."

I fold the letter up, put it inside the envelope, and hand it to Grandma.

Betty Jean

I can't believe I'm going on a date. A real live date. I don't remember if I've ever even been on one. Mister never formally
asked me out and picked me up, we just agreed to meet at
different establishments, since back in the day he didn't have a
car. But this is an official date, and here I am a legitimate, full-
fledged senior citizen, and I am going to answer my front door
and there's going to be a man on the other side of it. It has taken
Warren almost ten years to ask me out. To be honest, I always
thought he leaned toward handsome and I felt some kind of mag-
netic pull toward him, but I pretended to ignore this energy field
because it seemed dangerous at the time. And I wasn't even all that
religious. Of course, I've always believed in God and the sanctity
of marriage, but as a woman, just letting my eyes meet another
man's was making a suggestion. So I always avoided Warren's, especially when Mister and I sat on the sidelines watching our sons
play basketball and he coached them. He would often smile at me
when there was a good play. I admit I was shocked and even more
thrilled when I learned he was my grandsons' principal. And had
Mister not been sick, I would've given myself permission to finally
look into his eyes when he sat across from me. And Lord, when
he gave me that hug. If he only knew I could've lived inside his

arms. I couldn't remember the last time my breasts touched a man's chest standing face-to-face, even if he was wearing a suit. I could still feel his heartbeat and I assumed he could feel mine, too, which is why I backed away as fast as I could. There has always been something warm about Warren's demeanor that I liked. He wasn't afraid to show how much he cared about others, and at the time, I just thought how lucky his wife must be.

I pushed those feelings inside a cabinet all these years and allowed myself to unlock it only when I was weary, tired, or angry. I would sit in my new recliner that Quentin bought me, lean all the way back, and put my iPod earplugs in and listen to Nina Simone singing "Feeling Good" over and over and over. Sometimes I'd wake up, wondering where the boys were. I would smile and remember that Luther's almost a junior at USC and lives in a house with four other football players. Ricky is in Florida, going to that welding school. Noxema's at UCLA. She wants to be an actress and swings by to keep me company from time to time.

I live alone. But I'm not lonely. There's Tupac, who is my protector since the boys have been gone. We never figured out what kind of dog he was, but when we went to the pound to pick one out, he sat in his little jail cell and cried when he saw us, and within seconds he was licking Ricky's and Luther's hands, and minutes later he was ours. Tupac was faking, because he can put on the very same act when he thinks he's being ignored. He was also afraid to sleep in the backyard, and lasted only an hour in that doghouse we ended up returning. He eats a whole lot less than my grandsons, though!

The good news is that I am finally at a point in my life where I can do almost anything I want to do whenever I want to do it. Within reason. I am not struggling anymore. Thanks to my husband, I have a few dollars in the bank and own this house free and clear. This is why I splurged. I am now driving a white Cadillac. People stare at me in this car, and I can't lie, I love the attention. All I have to pay for these days are my utilities, cable, credit cards (my Sears card is back down to zero), and my cell phone. I get a manicure and pedicure and my eyebrows waxed every two weeks, and once a month I go to my favorite natural hair salon that's only five blocks away and get a deep-conditioning, hot-oil treatment, and a rinse that makes my gray look metallic. I am always getting compliments on my hair, and I never got any when I wore wigs. I have felt like a hoarder because it took all these years for me to get up the courage to throw out all thirteen of them. I go to the movies once a week. Sometimes twice. I like those independent films that only play at some theaters, but I like the ones on Wilshire Boulevard because they have the best popcorn and some have those kosher hot dogs I love.

I still volunteer down at the senior center, but I also have a part-time job working as a receptionist and, I suppose, office manager at Mr. Heaven's construction company. He changed his mind about calling it quits. He said too many people were having a hard time holding on to their homes and the least he could do was help them make improvements if they were lucky enough to be able to sell. He is a generous man. I must say it doesn't feel or look like the old ghetto around here anymore. We have a homeowners' association. Our block is clean. Our street is now blacktopped. A few more yards have emerald green velvety grass, hedges trimmed in all kinds of shapes and patterns, and flowers of every color you can imagine. The palm trees seem to protect us. Thanks to Mr. Heaven, my house is now peach with white trim. Tammy's is still ugly, but it's her fault for choosing light cocoa with that dark brown trim. But she likes it. We are proud of our neighborhood. We are proud to be representing, as my grandsons would say.

Speaking of making improvements, I also now have hobbies. I started a book club and about nine of my neighbors are members. We rotate at each other's homes once a month. I went ahead and had that surgery on my other knee, and on top of losing about twenty-five pounds on Jenny Craig, neither one of them bothers me much anymore. I have learned how to walk farther than my mailbox.

I also didn't think it was possible to change the way you think after you reach a certain age, but I was wrong. Quentin is living proof of this. In fact, he is getting on my nerves. He calls so much I had Luther put a ringtone on my phone for him, so now when I hear Kanye West rapping I know not to break my neck to answer it. He also likes to visit. And since they've got that new baby boy, I just am not in the mood for so much noise and activity like I once was. Which is why I sometimes lie to him about my plans. Quentin thinks I've become quite the social butterfly. Almost. He now has two chiropractor offices, and sometimes I'll go to the mailbox and there's a check for five hundred dollars inside a card. I don't have a problem cashing them even though I've told him I don't need his help. On the other hand, because of my son's new attitudes, I'm going to spend New Year's in New York City so I can watch that ball drop from my hotel room. I have given up on making angels, but there are a lot of things I thought I wanted to do or see only to find out I'm doing just fine without them. Snow is one.

I have also begun to appreciate my sisters. We have walking dates. One way to get to know someone better and get closer to them is by walking miles next to them. We prefer the beach. I don't really know if it's the ocean air or the waves or the sand between our toes or the seagulls flying over us, but for some reason, it seems easier to be honest with both of my sisters and say what's on our minds and in our hearts out there. It's also so much

easier to listen when they talk. I have come to realize how different we are and yet how alike, too. After all these years, we have
finally acknowledged just how grateful we are to be in each other's
lives even if we get on each other's nerves sometimes. We are also
learning how not to get so worked up when we disagree and when
to keep our thoughts to ourselves. That we don't always need to
be heard, that we will never agree on everything, especially how
to live our lives.

I don't see Tammy as much as I used to, because she spends most
of her time between Manhattan Beach and taking Clementine to
every kiddie movie, everything on ice, and every circus that comes
to town. She is happy. And I believe that's the point of all this.

When my cell phone rings, something tells me it's Warren, and it
is. He just got back from Fiji. Since he retired he has become
quite the world traveler. I like that about him. He's still curious,
too. "Hello, Warren. Are we still on?"

"Of course we're still on, Betty Jean. I was wondering if you
wouldn't mind if we went to dinner in Laguna Beach instead of
L.A., since it's such a beautiful drive. Unless, of course, you have
a curfew!"

"Laguna Beach would be fine, Warren. And I can stay out as
late as I want to."

"Then this means I'll need to pick you up an hour earlier.
Does this give you enough time?"

I look at the clock. That's less than an hour from now.

"Plenty. I'll see you then."

OMG! As my grandsons would say. How in the world I am going to pull this all together in forty-eight minutes I do not know.
Something tells me he's going to be on time, and I don't want him

sitting out here in the living room waiting for me like we're going to the prom or I'm some senior diva or something.

"Wait!" I hear him say just as I'm about to hang up. "Bring a sweater. It can get pretty chilly out on the ocean. But if you forget, not to worry, I won't let you get cold."

OMG! All of a sudden I don't know what to wear. I'm not sure if I have anything worth wearing to Laguna Beach. I try on a yellow dress I got on sale at J.C. Penney, since they have gotten a little snazzier these past few years. I look at myself in the mirror. I look just like my mama forty years ago. It's almost scary to know how much time has passed and what has happened to me. But I'm not going to stand here thinking about what I wish I'd done differently. Regret seems like such a wasted emotion. And the past is where it should be. Right now, I'm looking at myself in the mirror with a smile on my face, but I do wish the boys were here to say, "Grandma, you are working that yellow!" Or, if I modeled it for Mister, he would probably just grunt and wink.

I hunt for the right pumps and wonder if I should wear panty hose, since they're kind of out of style. Wait a minute? Laguna Beach means sand, and I can't walk in sand with any heels on, so I run back to my closet and hunt for some flat sandals. I find a pleasant pair that have pink and yellow plastic flowers on them. I look for a sweater but then decide to forget it. I'm so glad I took my shower so I could fool around with my hair. This is when wigs come in handy, but I managed to pull out some of those kinky curls to form a soft halo over my head. If I learned how to put on makeup one day, I probably could not only be more attractive but also subtract a few years. Oy vey, as Tammy likes to say. I spray one of my favorite colognes on my wrists, behind my ears, and mist it over my hair because it's important to smell good in public.

What do you talk about on a date when most of your life is

over? The past, or the future? Hell, maybe just right now. What I do know is I'm still interested in being exposed to new things, because I'm still curious, too. Like Warren, I plan on doing a little traveling myself. Alone or maybe with a companion. I'm just glad there's not enough you can ever know. That you can take what you can use to live a better, richer life, and toss out the rest. This is why I'm so happy my grandsons are on the right path. I just hope I gave them enough of what they need to help them navigate their way on this journey. I apologize for what my kids didn't get, especially Trinetta. I did the best I could back then. Now it's my turn to do what I think works for Betty Jean. And I'm not going to worry about who doesn't like it. Sometimes you have to know when to trust your instincts about how you live your life and especially how you feel. We all have a right to make our own mistakes as long as we're willing to pay for them.

As I stand in the mirror, I turn from side to side, but I'm not real sure if I look as good in this dress as I think I do. Maybe this yellow is too loud. Maybe that rose-colored one might be better. I take a picture of myself in both of them with my new cell phone and send it to Arlene, Venetia, and Tammy to ask what they think. I just hope they hurry up. I don't have all day.

Acknowledgments

I want to thank the following people for being so supportive during the writing of this novel: Carole DeSanti, Christopher Russell, Molly Friedrich, Lucy Carson, Molly Schulman, Beena Kamlani, Bonnie Ross, Steve Levitt, and Roberta Ponder. I am also grateful to Derrick Fryson, Barbara McKay, and Kristi and Terrence Zenno for their expertise, as well as for being so generous with their time, and to Gail Jackson, for her gracious hospitality in providing me a month of solace at the Treehouse Resort in Negril, Jamaica.